Tangled Fates

Yasmin Lake

Published by Yasmin Lake, 2024.

This is a work of fiction. Similarities to real people, places, or events are entirely coincidental.

TANGLED FATES

First edition. November 10, 2024.

Copyright © 2024 Yasmin Lake.

ISBN: 979-8227966650

Written by Yasmin Lake.

Chapter 1: A Chance Meeting in the City of Light

The café was tucked away on a quiet street, its entrance a mere sliver of light between two grand buildings. I stepped inside, the warmth of it wrapping around me like a soft, familiar blanket. There was something in the air here, a particular scent of freshly ground coffee beans mingled with a hint of buttered croissants, the aroma of Paris itself. I hadn't planned on being here tonight, but somehow, I found myself lingering, savoring the moment. I didn't want to rush my first evening in Paris; I wanted to soak it all in—the murmur of French voices, the clink of silverware, the soft jazz music drifting from a corner speaker. The city had a rhythm, and I had no intention of disrupting it.

The warmth of the café made the chill of the Parisian streets feel like an old memory, one that seemed so far removed from this new chapter I was trying to write. I hadn't expected this trip to be anything other than a brief escape—an opportunity to recharge, to experience life through a different lens, to find something, or perhaps someone, that could anchor me in a way I didn't even realize I needed.

But then, as I glanced up from the menu, my eyes caught something—or rather, someone—that made my pulse quicken.

Jonah.

Of course, I hadn't expected to run into him. Why would I? We were just two strangers sharing a screen and a few whispered exchanges in the dead of night. A kind of digital friendship that had evolved without much thought. His voice had always been comforting, familiar, and undeniably soothing, like an old song that never quite left your head, but you never remembered when it had first played.

Tonight, though, his presence shook me.

He was sitting at a corner table, his back to the window. The way he was positioned, one elbow propped lazily on the table, fingers tracing the rim of his wine glass, felt entirely too intimate for someone I had only ever spoken to online. The shape of his profile caught my eye first—sharp jawline, the tousled hair I always assumed was a deliberate choice to add to his charm. But it was his eyes, the ones I had never seen in real life, that locked me into place. They were just as I remembered, the kind of gaze that could draw you in and make you feel like you were the only person in the room, even when there were dozens.

Jonah.

It was him, and yet, it wasn't.

My mind raced through the years, the late-night conversations, the laughter, the confessions. But somewhere, hidden deep in the back of my mind, I also remembered a memory I had tried so hard to bury: a goodbye that had never quite been final, a moment that had left me wondering what went wrong between us.

I should have walked away then. Should have turned on my heel and slipped back into the night, leaving whatever happened here behind me. But instead, my legs moved on their own accord, pulling me closer to his table. Each step felt like it was happening in slow motion, like I had entered a dream I couldn't escape from.

And then I was standing there, staring down at him, his face unreadable, his expression a mixture of surprise and something else—something darker, a flicker of recognition that made me wonder just how much he had remembered of that past between us.

"Jonah," I said his name softly, the word catching in my throat as if it were something I had swallowed long ago.

He didn't speak at first, just let the silence hang there, a heavy, unfamiliar weight between us. His fingers twitched slightly on the glass, his eyes narrowing just enough that I knew he was trying to place me. The familiarity of his gaze, the cool, collected way he regarded me, suddenly felt suffocating, like I had walked into the middle of a conversation I wasn't prepared for.

"Do I know you?" he asked, his voice low and controlled, a hint of something in his tone that made my heart skip.

I blinked, unsure whether I should laugh or apologize, unsure of anything really. Wasn't that the question I had been asking myself all these years? Did he remember me? Was I just a blip on his radar, a passing conversation that meant nothing in the grand scheme of things? Or had he carried the same weight of regret that I had?

"I think so," I said finally, my words a little too soft, a little too uncertain. "I—I'm the one who... well, I didn't expect to see you here."

His eyes searched mine, his expression unreadable. The years of messages we had exchanged seemed to vanish between us, swallowed up by the awkwardness of the moment. How could we bridge the gap that had formed between us? How could I explain the history we shared without sounding like a fool?

"I didn't expect to see you either," Jonah said, his voice tinged with something I couldn't place. "I wasn't sure it was really you."

And there it was, that hint of the past, the unspoken truth that lingered just beneath the surface of his words. We had once been so close, so familiar with each other's thoughts, our secrets slipping into the safe space between us. But now, in this small, dimly lit café, we were strangers once more.

I could feel the heat rising in my cheeks, the embarrassment of it all sweeping over me. Had he forgotten the goodbye we'd shared? The one where we both pretended we would be fine, even though we both knew we wouldn't be?

I hesitated for a long moment, unsure of whether to sit or leave, my mind spinning with all the unspoken things we had left behind in the past. Jonah was waiting, his expression shifting, softening just a little as though he were giving me permission to fill the silence with something, anything.

So, I did.

"Maybe we should talk," I said, my voice barely more than a whisper, but it was enough.

We sat at the small table by the window, a thin line of rain tapping lightly against the glass as though it too, was curious about the storm brewing between us. Jonah had taken a sip of his wine, eyes still on me, but there was a tension in his jaw that made it impossible for me to look away. Every part of him seemed carefully curated, from the deliberate rumple of his shirt to the way he shifted in his seat as though he were suddenly a stranger to his own body. The years of late-night confessions seemed to have folded neatly into the back of his mind, hidden behind a mask I didn't recognize.

I cleared my throat, a nervous little sound that barely made it past my lips. "So... Paris." The word hung there in the air, like it had somehow become the most banal thing in the world, and yet, here we were, two ghosts from a shared past, wandering into the same room.

His brow furrowed. "Yes. Paris." He paused, then looked down at the table, his fingers tapping once, then twice, on the edge of his glass. "Funny, isn't it?" he murmured, his voice soft but edged with something that made my pulse race. "That we'd meet here."

The weight of his words hit me like a punch to the gut. Of course, it was funny. It was funny that out of all the cities in the world, I would end up in the same place as him, the place where everything had changed—the place where our last conversation had ended. The one I hadn't been able to forget, despite my best efforts to bury it beneath new memories, new faces.

I leaned forward, unable to hide the tremor in my voice. "Do you... do you ever think about that night?" The words slipped out before I could stop them, and once they were out, there was no taking them back.

Jonah's lips pressed together, the silence between us stretching. For a moment, he said nothing, just stared at me with those unreadable eyes, as if trying to gauge how much he should reveal. The air was thick with unspoken things, and I could practically hear the wheels turning in his mind, weighing whether to speak, whether to let the truth spill from him like a confession or keep it locked in a place I had no access to.

"I think about it," he said finally, and the simple truth of his words made my heart ache. "But not in the way you think."

I blinked, thrown off balance by his bluntness. "Not in what way?"

His gaze softened for a fraction of a second before hardening again. "I think about it because I never understood why it happened the way it did. Why you didn't fight for us."

The words hit like a cold gust of wind, unexpected and sharp. I had always assumed that I was the one left in the dark, that I had been the one whose heart had cracked open that night. But hearing Jonah say it—that he had wondered, had felt the weight of that goodbye—turned everything inside me upside down. My mouth went dry, and I could feel the walls around me crumbling, revealing an ache I had forgotten existed.

"I didn't want to fight for something I wasn't sure you wanted," I said, my voice barely a whisper.

Jonah's eyes flickered to mine, and for the first time, I saw the ghost of something I recognized—the person I had once shared everything with, the person whose words used to fill the silence between us like a comforting rhythm. It was fleeting, just a split second, but it was there, a brief window into the past.

"I wanted you," he said, the words low and deliberate. "More than anything. But you... you shut me out. You built a wall around yourself that I couldn't break through. And I don't know why."

I swallowed hard, trying to find my voice again, trying to push past the vulnerability that clawed its way into my chest. "I didn't know how to let you in," I admitted, my words raw and unpolished. "I was terrified. I thought if I let myself care too much, if I let myself trust—really trust—then it would all fall apart. That's how I've always been, Jonah. I don't... I don't know how to be any other way."

There it was—the truth I had never allowed myself to speak. The raw, ugly fear that had dictated everything in my life. The fear that love would always be something I couldn't hold on to, that it would slip away like water between my fingers, leaving me grasping at air.

He was silent for a long time, and I thought, for a moment, that perhaps he was done with this conversation, done with me. But then he leaned forward, his eyes fixed on mine with an intensity that felt like it was pulling me in, like the pull of gravity. "And now? Are you still afraid of loving, of trusting?"

I shook my head before I could stop myself. "I don't know," I whispered. "But I don't think I can walk away from this again. From you." My heart hammered against my ribcage as I said the words. Could I really let myself feel this way again, after everything? Could I trust him to not break me, to not leave me the way he had before?

Jonah took a deep breath, as if my words had landed somewhere deep inside him, stirring things he hadn't expected to be stirred. "I don't want to walk away," he said softly, his voice uncharacteristically quiet. "But I'm not sure I can do this again, either. Not without knowing that we're both ready to let go of what happened before."

A shiver ran down my spine. There it was, the catch—the thing we had never been able to navigate before. The past, always standing between us like a wall we couldn't see over. Could we tear it down and rebuild, or were we doomed to stay stuck in its shadow forever?

I opened my mouth to respond, but before I could, Jonah stood abruptly, the chair scraping loudly against the floor. I froze, startled by the sudden movement, my pulse spiking.

"I think I need a walk," he said, his voice hoarse, a slight tremor there. "I need to clear my head."

Before I could say a word, he turned and walked out into the Parisian night, leaving me there, staring after him, unsure of whether I had just made a colossal mistake—or if I had somehow, just maybe, begun to piece together something beautiful.

I watched him go, feeling the weight of his absence in the space between us like a wall. He didn't look back, didn't hesitate, just walked out into the cool Parisian evening like it was any other night. I tried to breathe, tried to steady the frantic pace of my heart, but the sudden emptiness of the table left me grasping at nothing. My fingers curled around the stem of my wine glass, but the taste of it was bitter now, nothing like the smoothness it had been moments ago.

The night outside seemed to press in, the city now distant, as though Paris itself had somehow grown cold in the wake of Jonah's departure. I sat there for a long while, lost in the whirlwind of our words, trying to make sense of the mess I'd created, the connections I'd frayed without even knowing it. The idea of him walking away again—the idea of me walking away again—seemed impossible. But there was a truth in what he'd said, a bitter pill I hadn't swallowed before: we weren't ready. And maybe that was something neither of us could change.

As if on cue, the door swung open, and a rush of cold air followed by the hum of street noise flooded the room. A figure stepped inside, brushing the rain from their coat, their movements quick and purposeful. At first, I thought it was Jonah, returning—perhaps to explain, to undo what had just been left unsaid. But as the figure turned and their gaze met mine, I knew it wasn't him.

This person was tall, but their posture was different. Confident, almost brash. Their eyes, dark and sharp, locked onto mine with an intensity that reminded me of Jonah, but colder, somehow. I didn't know why, but I felt a shiver run down my spine, like a warning that had come too late.

I must have been staring, because they raised an eyebrow, a slight smirk tugging at the corner of their lips. "You're the one, aren't you?" Their voice was smooth, but there was something oddly challenging in it.

I blinked, momentarily thrown off balance by the sudden attention. "Excuse me?"

The stranger stepped closer, their presence undeniable, like a storm on the horizon. "You're the one Jonah's been avoiding." The words came without hesitation, as if they knew something I didn't, something that was far more complicated than just a chance meeting.

My heart skipped. "I don't know what you're talking about," I said, my voice coming out sharper than I intended. But the sudden unease in my chest had me on edge. Who was this person? What did they know?

The stranger just smiled, but it wasn't a friendly one. More of a knowing smile, like they'd caught me in something I hadn't even realized I was guilty of. "Oh, I think you do." They leaned in slightly, their voice dropping to a near whisper. "You've got more than a few things to answer for, don't you?"

I opened my mouth to respond, to ask who they were, why they thought they had any right to speak to me this way, but the words died on my tongue. My mind was still trying to catch up with what they had just said. Was Jonah—had he—been avoiding me?

Before I could ask any of the questions that swirled through my brain, the stranger took a step back, clearly enjoying the moment. "It's funny, isn't it?" They said, as if we were engaged in some kind of trivial conversation. "All these years of running into the past, trying to bury it, trying to outrun it. And then, here you are. Paris. The city of second chances. The city that never forgets."

I tried to steady myself, leaning back in my chair as if I had all the time in the world to figure out what was going on. But the tremor in my hands betrayed me. The stranger's words stuck with me—Jonah's been avoiding you. Why would he avoid me? We had barely exchanged more than a few awkward sentences just moments ago. Was it really possible that everything I had believed was wrong?

"I don't know who you are," I managed, forcing my voice to sound steady despite the sudden rush of panic building in my chest. "And frankly, I don't think I care."

The stranger chuckled, the sound dark and knowing, as though they had seen something in me I hadn't even realized. "No, I suppose you don't." They straightened, their smirk softening just a touch. "But you will. Eventually."

With that, they turned on their heel, their coat sweeping behind them like some strange, dramatic exit. I watched them disappear out the door, my mind spinning, my heart still racing. What the hell had just happened? And why did it feel like this was only the beginning?

I wanted to chase after them, demand answers, but something stopped me. Maybe it was fear—fear that I was unraveling something far deeper than I could handle. Fear that whatever Jonah and I had started was already too late to fix. The stranger's words echoed in my head: You've got more than a few things to answer for.

What had Jonah gotten himself into? What had I gotten myself into?

I reached for my purse, fingers trembling as I stood up from the table, determined to find him. But as I stepped toward the door, something caught my eye—a piece of paper, crumpled and half-hidden under my chair. I bent to pick it up, and as I unfolded it, my stomach dropped.

There, scrawled hastily in black ink, was a single sentence:

I know what you did.

I felt the room tilt, the walls pressing in as I stood frozen, the note trembling in my hand. Everything in me screamed to run, to leave this place behind. But my feet were rooted to the ground, as the weight of those words settled over me like a cold shroud.

And then, I heard the unmistakable sound of footsteps behind me, slow and deliberate.

"Leaving so soon?" The voice was too familiar, too close.

It was Jonah.

Chapter 2: Shadows of the Past

The night air in Montmartre held a chill, sharp enough to make me pull my coat tighter around my shoulders, but the lingering warmth of the past kept me close to him. The cobblestones beneath our feet, uneven and aged, seemed to stretch forever, as if the street itself was trying to remind us that time had a way of folding in on itself here. Jonah walked beside me, his profile sharp against the city lights, the way his jaw set hard, his hands jammed deep in his pockets. He wasn't looking at me, but I could feel the weight of his gaze—heavy, accusatory, like a stormcloud waiting to burst.

I had expected the tension, had prepared for the sharpness of his words and the coldness that hung between us like an unspoken sentence. But still, there was something undeniably magnetic about the way we moved together through the streets of Paris. It was as though the city itself refused to let go of its claim on us, drawing us back into its embrace despite everything that had happened.

Jonah's voice cut through the silence first, rough and strained, as though speaking to me was a chore, a necessity he would have preferred to avoid. "Paris," he said, his words dripping with something I couldn't quite place, "is a place where time doesn't just pass. It gets trapped, like flies in amber."

I couldn't suppress the flicker of a smile, despite myself. "Sounds like a horror story. Or a poem no one wants to hear."

He shot me a glance, his mouth twitching with something almost like a laugh, but his eyes stayed cold. "Maybe it is. You'd be the first to know."

The sharpness of his tone bit at my skin, but it didn't sting quite the way it used to. It was familiar now, the way he pushed me away and pulled me back, a dance we'd mastered long before we realized the music had stopped.

We turned a corner, and the labyrinth of Montmartre opened up before us, the narrow streets giving way to the broader expanse of Place du Tertre. The cafes and galleries that lined the square were empty for the night, the shutters drawn, the city feeling more like a painting than a living, breathing place. In the quiet, I could almost hear the ghosts of artists past whispering on the breeze—Picasso, Van Gogh, and all the others who had come to this corner of the world to find solace, inspiration, or maybe escape.

And that's when I felt it again—the pull. The ache that I hadn't quite understood when I first left. It had been months, years even, and yet here we were, standing on the edge of a history I couldn't shake.

Jonah stopped walking, and I did too, nearly colliding with him. He had that look on his face, the one that said he was about to say something important, or at least something that would make him feel better for saying it.

"Do you ever think about that night?" His voice was so low I almost missed it, and for a moment, I couldn't breathe. The question hung between us like the smoke of a thousand cigarettes, lingering long after the fire had gone out.

I swallowed, trying to steady my pulse. The memory of that night hit me with the force of a thousand fists—too real, too fresh. But I couldn't let him see that. Not now, not when he was already so determined to hate me for it.

I looked away, my eyes scanning the empty square, searching for something to anchor me. "I think about a lot of things," I said, my voice too casual, too practiced. "But that's in the past, Jonah."

He scoffed, the sound bitter on his tongue. "The past, right. The thing is, some things don't stay in the past, no matter how hard you try to bury them."

I could feel his words digging into me, just like they always had, and I hated that. I hated that he had the power to make me feel small, to make me want to apologize even though I knew I had nothing to apologize for.

I turned to face him then, my feet shifting on the cobblestones, the slight crunch beneath me the only sound that broke the silence. "I didn't leave because I wanted to," I said, my voice soft but firm, the words catching in my throat. "I had no choice, Jonah. You have to believe that."

For a long moment, he didn't speak. He just looked at me, his gaze sharp, dissecting, and I felt the weight of it settle over me like a blanket made of lead. The silence between us stretched, pulling taut like a wire, until I thought it might snap. And then, as if to break the tension, Jonah exhaled slowly, the sound barely audible.

"Do I believe that?" His voice was quieter now, almost thoughtful. "Maybe. But it doesn't change anything, does it?"

I shook my head, a small, wry smile tugging at my lips. "No," I said, my voice thick with the weight of everything unsaid, "it doesn't. But it doesn't mean I'm sorry either."

His lips parted as if he was about to respond, but before he could, a distant sound broke through the moment—footsteps, hurried and uneven, coming from behind us. Jonah glanced over his shoulder, and the moment between us shattered like glass.

I didn't even have to ask. I could see it in the way his body tensed, the way his shoulders squared in an instant. Something had changed in him, something darker, something that hadn't been there before.

"Keep walking," he said, his voice low but commanding. There was no hesitation now, just a warning buried beneath the words.

I didn't ask him what he meant. There was something in his tone, something in the air around us, that told me everything I needed to know.

The footsteps behind us grew louder, closer, the sound of heels clicking against the stone growing sharper with every passing second. It wasn't the usual shuffle of a late-night wanderer or the rhythmic march of a couple headed home after dinner. No, this was purposeful—someone on a mission, and by the way Jonah's spine stiffened, I could tell he knew exactly who it was.

"Keep walking," Jonah repeated, this time with a hint of urgency that cut through the calm of the night like a knife. The hairs on the back of my neck stood at attention, and I could feel the weight of the city pressing down on me, every corner, every shadow suddenly charged with meaning.

For a brief moment, I thought of ignoring him. Just spinning around to face whatever this was. But I knew that look in his eyes—the one that said there were things I wasn't meant to know, things better left buried in the past. So, I did as he asked, my feet moving, matching his stride as we threaded our way through the maze of cobbled streets, the lamplight casting long, flickering shadows along the walls.

The tension between us was palpable now, a thick cloud of it swirling in the crisp night air. We didn't speak as we walked—didn't need to. I knew exactly how he felt. The way his jaw clenched with each step, the way his shoulders were squared and ready for whatever confrontation loomed just out of sight. And I wasn't sure if it was his anger, his fear, or the memories of what we used to be that made my heart race faster.

Eventually, Jonah slowed his pace, a subtle shift, barely noticeable unless you were paying attention. He stopped just shy of a corner, turning his back to the street, his head tilting slightly as if listening for something beyond the ordinary. And I did what anyone with a heartbeat would do: I followed his lead, stepping into the shadows with him.

There was no sound for a moment. No footsteps, no breath—just the quiet of Montmartre at midnight, that heavy silence that seemed to press against my chest, squeezing until I couldn't breathe.

And then, the world exploded.

The figure appeared almost out of nowhere, a blur of movement before it solidified into a face I'd hoped never to see again. A tall man, wearing a leather jacket that seemed too stiff for someone who clearly wanted to blend in. He looked as though he'd just stepped out of a spy thriller—tough, mysterious, and with an air of danger that made me instinctively take a step back. He stood there for a moment, eyes locked on Jonah, before his lips curled into a grin. It was a smile that didn't reach his eyes, one that carried all the warmth of an ice pick.

Jonah's posture didn't shift an inch, but I could feel the air between them tense, coiling tightly like a spring ready to snap.

"Well, well," the man said, his voice low and drawling. "Didn't think I'd see you again, Jonah. Or maybe I just hoped I wouldn't."

I couldn't see Jonah's face, but I could hear the tightness in his voice when he spoke. "What do you want, Nico?"

The man, Nico, shrugged, his hands slipping into the pockets of his jacket. "Not much. Just came to see if the rumors were true. Thought I'd find you hiding out here, in the land of broken dreams."

I raised an eyebrow at that, my eyes flicking to Jonah, who had yet to make a move. Something was off—something about the way he stood so still, like a predator waiting for its prey to make the first move. But the truth was, I didn't know the rules of this game, and neither did Jonah. Not anymore.

Nico chuckled, the sound low and dark, like a storm brewing in the distance. "Still the same Jonah, huh? Always acting like you're above it all. But don't worry, I'm not here to ruin your little vacation." His gaze shifted to me, slow and deliberate. "Though I'm sure your company's... interesting."

I wasn't sure if he was talking about me as a distraction or if he genuinely found my presence a complication, but either way, I wasn't about to let him get the upper hand. "I don't suppose we could go back to pretending we don't know each other, could we?" I asked, my voice light, a slight edge to it. "Because I'm really not in the mood for old scores being settled."

Jonah's eyes flicked to me for a fraction of a second, and then his attention was back on Nico. "Not now, Nico," he said, his voice steady, controlled. "Not here."

But Nico wasn't listening. He was too busy assessing me, his gaze flicking over my face like I was the puzzle piece he couldn't quite fit into his picture. "What's your story, sweetheart?" he asked, his tone not quite mocking but full of a strange, unsettling curiosity. "Jonah's not exactly known for keeping company, and yet, here you are, walking through the ghost streets of Paris with him like it's just another Tuesday. What's the deal?"

I didn't flinch under his gaze. Instead, I gave him a smile—one that felt more like a weapon than a gesture of goodwill. "Let's just say I've got a thing for men who can keep a secret. And right now, it looks like you're the one with the most to hide, not me."

Nico's grin faltered for a second, and I could tell that struck a chord. But he recovered quickly, eyes narrowing, the playful menace replaced by something colder.

"You don't know what you're getting into, sweetheart," Nico said, stepping closer. His words were sharp, his breath warm against the cool night air. "Jonah's got a past you wouldn't understand. And trust me, you don't want to."

My heart was thumping now, louder than my breath. There was something dark in his tone, something familiar, and I couldn't shake the feeling that this wasn't about us. This was about something else—something bigger, something that Jonah wasn't telling me.

Jonah's hand moved, just a slight shift of his fingers, but it was enough to let me know that whatever Nico was implying, Jonah wasn't going to let him take this any further. Not here. Not now. Not with me watching.

The air shifted suddenly, and I felt a rush of cold that had nothing to do with the evening chill. Nico's presence was like a stone thrown into a pond, creating ripples that distorted everything around us. The tension between the three of us thickened, a pressure building in the space where words had stopped flowing. He wasn't just a reminder of Jonah's past—he was a piece of it, dark and sharp like a splinter of glass you couldn't remove without causing more damage.

I didn't know if I was more surprised by the fact that Nico had come looking for us or that Jonah hadn't been quick enough to stop him. There was something in the way he held himself now—tight, controlled, like a man on the verge of breaking—but he wasn't breaking for me. Not tonight. He was doing it for a different reason.

Nico didn't wait for Jonah to speak again. Instead, he took a step forward, his boots making an almost musical sound on the cobblestones. I didn't know if he was trying to intimidate me or just fill the empty space between us with something, anything that didn't feel so suffocating.

"Tell me, sweetheart," he said, his voice as smooth as oil, "what's your angle? I can see the way you look at him. Like he's a puzzle piece that doesn't quite fit, but you're determined to make it work anyway."

I tilted my head slightly, a half-smile curling at the edges of my lips. "You're right about one thing," I said, my tone light, "I don't have a clue what's going on here. But I'm not sure I need to."

Nico's expression faltered for just a second, the crack in his confidence barely noticeable. But Jonah—Jonah was already two steps ahead. Without warning, he stepped forward, breaking the tension with a move so swift it made Nico flinch.

"You really don't know when to quit, do you?" Jonah's voice was colder now, the mask of indifference slipping as something darker began to emerge. I could feel it, the shift, a change in the air that told me this wasn't about me anymore. This was a war Jonah had been fighting on his own, long before I ever showed up.

Nico didn't back down, not even an inch. "I'm not the one who's been hiding, Jonah. You think I don't know what you've been up to? You think I don't know what you've lost?" His words hit hard, but I could tell they weren't meant for me. They were meant for Jonah, and whatever secret he was holding onto was the thing that tethered him to the past like an anchor in the deep, dark sea.

I stepped in, partly to break the silence, partly because I wasn't sure how much more I could take of the two of them staring each other down like they were preparing for battle. "What is this, some kind of old grudge match?" I forced a laugh, trying to cut through the heavy air. "We're not in a noir film, Nico. There's no need for the dramatic standoff."

But Nico wasn't having any of it. His gaze shifted to me again, cold and calculating. "Maybe you're the one who doesn't belong here, sweetheart," he said, his words slow and deliberate, "because let me tell you something: Jonah's got a history—a bad one. And no matter how far he tries to run from it, no matter how many new faces he throws into the mix, that history always catches up."

Jonah moved then, his body tensing, his hand outstretched as though he meant to stop whatever Nico was going to say next. But it was too late. The words had already landed between us, and I could feel them like a weight pressing down on my chest. There were so many things Jonah had never told me—things I'd been content to leave buried, thinking that the past was best left forgotten. But Nico wasn't letting any of it go.

The wind shifted again, and with it, something more than just the chill of the evening crept in. Something old and painful. I could see it in Jonah's eyes—the flicker of a memory, a moment he'd been trying to outrun, and for the first time, I wondered if maybe he hadn't been running from me at all. Maybe he'd been running from this.

Nico wasn't done. "You're not the first person who's tried to change Jonah, sweetheart," he continued, his voice thick with mockery. "But trust me, it's a waste of time. He'll drag you down with him, and when the storm hits, you won't even know which way is up."

I turned to Jonah then, seeking something—anything—to help me understand the weight of Nico's words. Jonah's face was unreadable, his eyes locked on Nico, but for the first time, I saw the cracks, the subtle tremor of something he was trying desperately to keep under control.

"What's he talking about?" I asked, my voice quieter than I intended, a thread of doubt slipping into my tone.

Jonah's jaw tightened, but he didn't answer.

Nico, however, answered for him. "I guess you're about to find out," he said, the grin back on his face, cold and sharp. "But don't say I didn't warn you."

Before I could respond, before I could make sense of any of it, the sound of footsteps echoed once again from the street behind us. And this time, they weren't alone. Several sets of footsteps, too many to ignore, drawing closer with alarming speed.

Nico's expression darkened, his eyes darting toward the noise. For the first time, the smugness in his voice faltered, replaced by a brief flicker of unease. He turned to Jonah. "You didn't think this was over, did you?"

Jonah's lips parted, but whatever he was about to say was drowned out by the sound of the approaching footsteps. And then I saw them—shadows in the distance, moving fast, too fast.

Something told me this wasn't a coincidence. Something told me that what Nico had said wasn't just a threat—it was a warning.

And just as the first figure emerged from the shadows, a flash of silver gleaming in the dim light, I knew we were no longer standing on the edge of Jonah's past. We had just fallen headfirst into it.

Chapter 3: An Unlikely Proposal

Jonah's fingers felt warm against mine, a shock that startled me despite the seemingly mundane gesture. There was nothing romantic about the handshake—no lingering gaze or flirtatious smile, but the mere connection between us sent an electric pulse up my arm. I should have been used to the sensation by now, the way the past still whispered in the corners of my mind, stubbornly refusing to fade. But no, it still took me by surprise, the way Jonah could stir something in me with the slightest touch.

He straightened up, pulling his hand away with that faint smile of his—the one that always seemed half-formed, as though he were still trying to decide if he wanted to be amused by the world or frustrated with it. His eyes glinted, though, the same deep blue that had once made me lose my breath. They were almost too intense, as though they could see straight through the layers I'd spent years building around myself. The café was a dimly lit little nook on the edge of town, the sort of place where time could slip away unnoticed. It was the perfect place for secrets. Jonah's secret. And maybe mine, too.

"So, we're doing this?" I asked, my voice too casual, even for my own liking. I wanted to sound like I was in control, but I wasn't. Not by a long shot.

He shrugged, the casual gesture belying the intensity in his gaze. "We're doing this," he said, the words slow, deliberate. I could hear the weight in them, the kind of weight that carried an implication too heavy for a casual chat over coffee. He'd asked me, just hours before, to meet him here. He'd sounded almost desperate on the phone, the urgency in his voice compelling me to say yes. As much as I hated to admit it, I was curious.

"What do you mean by 'finish what we started'?" I asked, trying to force my voice into a nonchalant tone.

Jonah didn't answer immediately, choosing instead to stir his coffee, the quiet scrape of the spoon against the porcelain cup almost exaggerated in the silence that settled between us. He stared into his mug like it held some great mystery. I wasn't sure what had happened between us all those years ago, but the longer I stared at him, the more it felt like he was trying to avoid answering the question.

He sighed, almost imperceptibly, and finally looked up at me, his expression shifting, flickering between something I couldn't quite place and a resolve that felt almost unsettling. "I need to show you who I've become. You've been away too long, Sophie. There's... more to me than what you knew. And there's more to us than what we were."

I swallowed, feeling the sting of his words. We had been young when we first crossed paths, so full of hope and ambition and naive dreams. I had left, running from whatever it was we had back then. I hadn't been ready, and I'd convinced myself I wasn't the type of woman who could have what he wanted. He wanted stability, a future—things I had only dreamed about but couldn't hold onto. I had thought that if I could disappear far enough away, I wouldn't have to confront that mistake.

But now, years later, here I was, sitting across from him. And he was asking me to step back into a life I had carefully constructed a distance from. "And what's in it for me?" I asked, the words sharper than I intended.

He leaned forward then, his voice dropping low, drawing me in, making me feel like the only person in the room. "You get closure. You get to see what could have been. You get to decide if the life you walked away from is still worth anything."

I blinked, trying to understand the layers of meaning behind his words. Closure. He couldn't possibly think that what happened between us was something I could just revisit after so many years. Could he?

"But it's not real, right? This... act. It's just pretend?" I wanted to be clear.

Jonah met my gaze, his expression unreadable for a moment. Then he nodded slowly. "Just pretend. But I need you to make it believable." His voice softened. "I need to believe it, too."

The last part hung in the air, lingering like a weight I couldn't avoid. I could feel my heart picking up speed, a faint tremor beneath my calm exterior. What was I getting myself into?

"You're asking me to lie," I said, almost as an afterthought, more to myself than to him.

He chuckled, a sound so familiar it almost knocked the breath from my chest. It was the same laugh that had once made me feel like I was in on some private joke, a secret between us. "Maybe. Or maybe I'm asking you to remember what was real. For a little while."

I wasn't sure if I wanted to slap him or kiss him. The temptation to lash out at him was there, but the memory of our past was stronger. Jonah was a man who knew exactly how to make you question everything you thought you knew. He had always been like that, clever and frustrating in equal measure.

I shifted in my seat, my thoughts a tangled mess, each one more tangled than the last. There was no easy answer here. No neat, tidy conclusion. There was only the unknown. And the fear that maybe, just maybe, this thing between us had never really ended.

"Alright," I said, my voice a little unsteady. "We'll do it. But just so we're clear—this is only for you, Jonah. I'm not doing this for me. I don't need any of this. I've moved on."

He didn't look convinced, but there was a flicker of something in his eyes, something dangerous and enticing. And in that moment, I realized—maybe I hadn't moved on at all.

The days following our strange agreement passed with the sort of surreal unease that comes with knowing you've made a decision you'll soon regret. But I didn't regret it yet, not exactly. Jonah had this uncanny ability to make everything feel urgent, even when it was anything but. And so, I let myself believe that perhaps this little game—this charade we were about to launch ourselves into—was something I could control. I told myself it would be easy. I'd play along. I'd nod at all the right moments, laugh at the things he said, just as I had so many times before. But the reality of it wasn't nearly as simple as I had imagined.

The first few days of our arrangement were a mixture of awkward glances and forced smiles, neither of us quite sure how to step back into a role we had long since discarded. Jonah had booked a table at a restaurant that used to be our spot—one with soft, flickering candles and a menu that always felt like it belonged to another life, like something we had stolen from someone else's happily ever after. I caught myself hesitating when he opened the door for me, the old familiarity of the gesture stirring something inside me that I wasn't ready to face.

We sat across from each other, the same table, the same corner of the restaurant, but everything had changed. We weren't the people we once were, and yet, in that space, we couldn't help but try to recreate something that had never quite left us. Jonah had become someone else—someone quieter, more guarded. The laugh I remembered from years ago, the one that had once come so easily, now felt buried under layers of what I could only assume was regret. And as for me—well, I wasn't the same either. The woman across from him now was no longer the girl who had followed him into reckless nights and whispered dreams. That girl had long since been replaced by someone a little more cynical, a little less willing to believe in the magic of what had once been.

"So," Jonah said, setting down his glass of wine with more care than necessary, his eyes scanning the menu like it held the key to some cosmic riddle. "Do you ever wonder what would have happened if we'd—"

"No," I said, cutting him off before he could finish the sentence. "I don't. I think that's the whole point of us being here. We're pretending, remember?"

He arched an eyebrow, clearly amused by my abruptness. "Right. We're pretending."

I could feel the heat of his gaze, the way it seemed to linger just a moment too long, and I hated it. I hated how easy it was to fall back into that unspoken connection between us. But I wasn't going to let it get to me—not this time. I had made my decision, and I would stick to it.

"So, how's your life been?" I asked, leaning back in my chair, forcing an air of casual indifference that didn't match the tightness in my chest. "The big, successful Jonah I've heard so much about."

His lips twitched into a smile, the kind of smile that held a trace of something I couldn't quite place. It wasn't pride, but something more fragile, more elusive. "I've done alright. The company's good, the house is too big, and I'm... well, I'm fine. You?"

"Fine," I echoed, unable to suppress the sardonic note in my voice. "Just living the dream. You know how it is."

He studied me for a moment, like he was searching for something behind my words, something deeper, maybe even something I wasn't ready to admit. But I wasn't going to let him in. Not now. Not again.

The waiter arrived with our food, and the clatter of plates offered a welcome distraction. For a moment, we both focused on the food in front of us, as if it could offer some sort of grounding in the midst of the strange charade we were playing. But Jonah's gaze never wavered for long. He was still watching me, trying to read between the lines of my carefully constructed walls. And it irritated me. He should've known better. He should've known I wouldn't let him see the cracks, not after everything.

"So," I said, after a long pause, trying to keep the conversation light. "Is this what you wanted? Us, back here, pretending we're still the same people we were all those years ago?"

Jonah's smile was a little sad this time, his fork pausing midair. "I don't think we're ever really the same people we were," he said quietly. "I don't think anyone is."

I met his gaze, searching for something in his words. But it was all too cryptic, too layered, and I wasn't sure I wanted to dig any deeper.

"Well, I suppose that's true," I replied, my voice much softer than I intended. "But pretending—this whole game we're playing—it's easier when you know what the rules are."

He didn't respond right away. Instead, he took a slow sip of his wine, his fingers tracing the rim of the glass. When he finally spoke, his voice was low, almost conspiratorial. "And what if you don't know what the rules are anymore? What if there's no clear path back to the way things were?"

The question hung in the air, like a dare. Like he was challenging me to step outside my comfort zone, to risk something I wasn't sure I was willing to risk.

"Then maybe it's better that way," I said, my voice cool, but inside, my heart was racing. "Maybe we're better off with nothing but the past to keep us company."

Jonah didn't respond right away. He just watched me, his expression unreadable. For a moment, I almost wished he would laugh or make some witty remark to break the tension, but he didn't. Instead, he picked up his fork and began to eat, the clinking of silverware filling the silence between us.

I couldn't decide if it was the most uncomfortable meal I'd ever had or the most thrilling. The lines between pretending and something real were starting to blur, and I wasn't sure which one of us was playing the game anymore.

The evening took on a peculiar sort of gravity after that, as if we had somehow shifted from one world into another. Jonah and I fell back into our roles, but there was no mistaking the difference. We were actors, playing parts we hadn't rehearsed, and it wasn't long before the cracks began to show.

A few days later, I found myself standing in front of my bathroom mirror, scrutinizing the reflection that had become more and more unfamiliar. The woman staring back at me wasn't the one I had been before, the one who used to walk out the door with a smile and the confidence of someone who had it all figured out. She was wearing the same clothes I had worn the last time I stood in front of that mirror, but she felt... softer somehow. Weaker. There was something about the way my eyes looked—distant, like I was looking at the world through a fog. I could still hear Jonah's voice in the back of my mind, the way it had sounded the other night, when he'd made me question everything: "What if you're not pretending, Sophie?"

The question lingered, slipping into corners I didn't know existed. I had thought I was perfectly in control of this ridiculous situation. I had told myself I could walk away at any time. But when Jonah's face appeared in my thoughts, with that sad little smile that never quite reached his eyes, I couldn't ignore the nagging feeling that perhaps I wasn't as immune to this game as I'd convinced myself.

"Pull yourself together," I muttered to my reflection, turning away from the mirror before it could suck me in any deeper.

I wasn't about to let this... thing between us get out of hand. Jonah's proposition was absurd, and I would make sure we both stuck to the script. No real emotions. No crossing boundaries. I'd played this game before, and I was good at it.

But when I arrived at the bar the following Friday, things felt different. Jonah was waiting at the end of the room, leaning casually against the wooden beam that framed the door like he had every right to be there. And God help me, he looked good. The same dark shirt, sleeves rolled up, the collar slightly undone—nothing too fancy, but enough to make my pulse do that irritating little dance it always did when he was near. I could feel the eyes of the crowd flickering over him, then over me, but I forced myself to ignore the sinking feeling in my stomach. We were just pretending. Nothing more.

He turned as I approached, and that familiar, devil-may-care smile crept across his face. "There she is," he said, the low note of amusement in his voice causing a stir of heat to spread across my skin. "I was beginning to think you'd changed your mind."

I lifted my chin in mock defiance, my voice too steady for the turmoil swirling inside me. "I don't change my mind. You should know that by now."

He smiled, but there was something in it that made me pause. It wasn't the smile of the old Jonah, the one who used to bring me coffee in the mornings or play with my hair while we talked about everything and nothing. This was different. This was deliberate, like he was trying to see how far he could push me before I cracked.

"Good," he said, his voice a little too low. "Let's make sure we both remember that."

I fought the urge to fidget as we found our seats, the same old booth tucked away in the far corner of the bar. We had always liked it here, away from the noise, where we could talk without being overheard. The bartender nodded as he brought over two glasses of wine, setting them down between us without a word.

"So," I said, breaking the silence with a note of artificial lightness. "Tell me, Jonah, do you have a script for our little charade tonight? Or are we just improvising?"

His eyes glinted, dark and thoughtful, like he was considering whether to tell me the truth or play along with the game. "I think we're well past the point of pretending, don't you?"

The words hung there, charged with an intimacy that made my heart skip in a way that wasn't entirely unwelcome, but also entirely unwarranted. He didn't blink, didn't even seem to register the shift in the air between us. I couldn't tell if he was toying with me or if something real was slipping through the cracks, but whatever it was, I didn't like it.

I took a sip of my wine, the cool liquid sliding over my tongue, but it didn't do much to calm the thudding in my chest. "So, what's the plan?" I asked, trying to keep my voice level. "Are we going to act like this is all normal? Like we're still... whatever we used to be?"

His lips parted slightly, as if he were going to say something, but then he just... stopped. For a long moment, he didn't speak. He studied me, his eyes narrowing, his expression shifting to something unreadable.

And then, without warning, he reached across the table and took my hand. His grip was firm, but not painful. The touch was familiar, comforting, and yet it shocked me to the core, as though he had just flipped the switch on something I thought was off.

I froze, my breath catching in my throat. Jonah's gaze softened for just a second, his thumb brushing over the back of my hand in that slow, deliberate way that made my pulse race.

"You think this is easy, don't you?" he asked, his voice barely above a whisper. "You think you're just playing along, keeping it all in control. But I'm telling you, Sophie... this is not a game. Not anymore."

I couldn't move. I couldn't breathe. Every part of me screamed to pull away, to cut the tension in the air like a knife, but I couldn't. I was frozen in place, caught between the past and the present, between who I had been and who I might become.

And then, before I could even gather my thoughts enough to respond, Jonah leaned closer, his lips brushing against my ear as he whispered, "We've only just begun, Sophie. And you're already in deeper than you know."

The words sent a shiver down my spine. But it wasn't the thrill of anticipation that took over me. It was something much more dangerous.

Something that would change everything.

Chapter 4: A Game of Pretend

The noise of the market surrounded us, a wild chorus of vendors hawking their wares, children's laughter floating above it all like an afterthought. The scent of sweet pastries, roasted meats, and the sharp tang of citrus mingled with the dust of the cobblestones beneath our feet. It was a world full of color—vibrant silks hanging in the stalls, the deep red of fresh cherries gleaming like rubies, and the warm gold of the late afternoon sun spilling over everything like melted honey. But none of it was real to me. Not anymore. Not when I was here, with him.

I had always hated this market. The smells, the noise, the way it made me feel like a small fish in a vast ocean, lost in the sea of faces. But now, walking beside him, I found myself thinking that maybe I didn't hate it at all. Maybe it was just that when we had shared this place years ago, it hadn't been this place, not really. Not the one I was in now.

"Do you remember the rose vendor?" he asked, his voice low, teasing, as if we were children again. His thumb brushed against the back of my hand, and I swore the world around us stilled for a moment.

I glanced up at him, his face still as infuriatingly beautiful as I remembered. His jawline was sharper now, a few more days of stubble gracing his chin, but his eyes—the same deep, impossible shade of green—were unchanged. The corner of his mouth twitched as if he was waiting for me to crack, waiting for me to remember.

"I remember," I said, my voice a little too cold, a little too calculated, but I couldn't let him know how much it hurt to speak those words. I remember everything.

He chuckled, a soft sound, but it didn't reach his eyes. "I thought you might." His gaze lingered on my face for a fraction of a second longer than necessary before he turned his attention to the bustling market again. We moved past the flower stall—roses, daisies, sunflowers all stacked in careful rows—before I could stop myself, my feet halting. My eyes locked onto a single, crimson rose tucked into the corner, its petals vibrant against the dark green of its leaves. It was so like him. So unlike him.

"What do you think?" he asked, already taking a step toward the stall, his hand slipping from mine as though it didn't matter. He was already lost to the game we were playing, the one where everything was just a performance, a charade.

"You know I've never liked roses," I said, my voice a little more biting than it should have been. "Too perfect. Too... predictable."

His eyebrows arched slightly, a smile curving at the edges of his mouth. "That's what you said the last time we were here. You hated them then, too."

I stared at the rose, its soft petals almost mocking me, remembering the last time we'd stood in this very spot. That day, I had been wearing that ridiculous pink scarf he'd insisted looked good on me, even though I had been suffocating in it, fighting the wind. And I had told him, as I had told so many others, that I didn't care for roses. It wasn't the flower, though, not really. It was everything else—the way we had been, the way I had been—before the weight of the world had crashed down on us both.

"I guess I haven't changed much, then." His voice was quieter now, as if he knew I wasn't talking about the flowers anymore.

"People don't change, Mason," I said, my tone sharp as I stepped back, away from the rose, away from him, away from whatever this was. He was too close again, and I wasn't ready for that. Not yet.

I turned my gaze away, searching the crowd for something, anything, to latch onto. I wasn't going to make this easy for him. Not again.

"Is that what you think?" He didn't follow me. Not immediately. I could hear the faint rustle of fabric as he leaned against a nearby cart, the soft clink of something metallic as he shifted his weight. "That people don't change? That we're all just stuck in the same roles we've played since we were kids?"

I shook my head, pretending I hadn't heard him. The noise of the market was swallowing him up. But I could feel the tension between us thickening, a tightrope drawn too taut between us. The game of pretend was starting to slip, and I didn't like it. I didn't want it.

"You know better than anyone," I said, my voice lower now, forced, like I was holding something in. "You know how these things go."

He was silent for a moment, his words hanging in the air like smoke. "Maybe that's what I'm afraid of," he finally admitted, the edge of his voice cutting through the noise. "That I don't know what's going to happen. And that scares the hell out of me."

I glanced at him, but only for a moment. His green eyes were still locked on me, no longer filled with the playful arrogance I had once known, but something different—something far more vulnerable. It made my chest tighten in a way I didn't understand. He'd always been able to do that to me, stir something that didn't belong.

"Why did you come back, Mason?" I asked, the words slipping out before I could stop them. My voice barely rose above the hum of the market, a whisper meant only for him. "After all this time, why come back now?"

For a second, he didn't answer. And then he did, softly, with a hint of something unspoken behind his words.

"I didn't know what I was supposed to do without you."

He didn't wait for me to respond. Instead, his fingers brushed against mine, and it was as though the entire world contracted into that single, electric moment. My breath caught, but I quickly swallowed it down, as if doing so would keep the tide of emotions from crashing over me. He was always like this—so effortlessly there, as though the years hadn't passed, as if we hadn't drawn lines between us with every argument, every betrayal.

"What are you so afraid of?" His voice was low now, threaded with an urgency I couldn't quite place. I could feel him studying me, his gaze tracing every line of my face, searching for something—some sign, some crack in the armor I had built around myself. But he wouldn't find it. I was better than that.

I forced a smile, one that didn't quite reach my eyes. "I'm not afraid," I said, turning away from him. "Not of you."

The truth, of course, was much more complicated than that. I was terrified of everything that had brought us here—the undeniable magnetism that still seemed to pull at me when he was near, when his voice touched the edges of my thoughts like a soft, familiar refrain. I had spent so many years convincing myself that I had moved on, that I had put this entire mess behind me. But now, with him standing just a breath away, I felt the years melt away. As if time had been nothing but a pretense.

"You never did answer my question," Mason pressed, still beside me, his voice a touch more insistent now, as though he were digging for something. "Why now? Why come back into my life after all this time?"

The question lingered, settling between us like the dust from the marketplace, too thick to ignore, too heavy to move past. I could feel the weight of it in my bones, a reminder of everything we had been through—the lies, the misunderstandings, the ache of silence that stretched for years between us.

I glanced at him, meeting his gaze for the first time in minutes, and for a split second, it felt as though the ground beneath my feet was shifting. It was the way his eyes softened when they caught mine, the way the tension in his shoulders seemed to ease just a little. He wasn't just asking because of some curiosity, some desire to patch things up. No. He was asking because he needed to know.

"Maybe I came back for the same reason you did," I said, my voice surprisingly steady despite the riot of feelings swirling inside me. "Maybe because I couldn't let go either."

There it was, the confession I hadn't meant to give him. The one that had been locked away for so long, sealed behind the door I'd bolted shut with all the quiet heartbreak I could muster.

Mason exhaled sharply, a laugh that didn't sound like laughter escaping him. "That's just it, isn't it?" He took a step closer, his eyes now burning with something darker. "We're both here, playing some game we're not even sure we can win. But we can't seem to stop, can we?"

I wanted to say something biting, something that would distance myself from him again, push him back into the corner where I had left him years ago. But I couldn't. Not now. Not when every fiber of my being seemed to want to reach for him, to acknowledge that this—this tension, this undeniable pull—was real. The kind of real that people tried to bury, tried to convince themselves didn't matter. But it mattered. It mattered in ways I couldn't articulate.

"I never asked for this," I muttered, more to myself than to him, my gaze falling to the worn cobblestones beneath our feet. The market had grown quieter around us, as if the world was holding its breath, waiting for something, waiting for us to do what we had never quite done.

"Neither did I," he replied softly, his voice surprisingly vulnerable. "But here we are."

I was still holding onto his arm—my fingers wrapped around his forearm with a tension that mirrored everything we were pretending to be. We looked like two people who were simply enjoying the market, lost in the soft hum of conversation, the warm embrace of the fading afternoon light. But in truth, we were two strangers who had once known each other too well, now trying to pretend we could pick up the threads of a life that had long since unraveled.

And then, just as I thought I had the upper hand, just as I was about to pull away again, his hand brushed against mine once more, this time lingering just a second longer. There it was again—the charge between us. A simple touch, but the weight of it pressed down on me in ways I hadn't anticipated.

"You think I don't know that?" he asked, his voice now almost too soft, a touch of a smile playing at the edges of his words. "That we're pretending to be something we're not?" His fingers curled around mine for just a moment, holding me there, as though he knew I wouldn't move even if I tried. "You're right," he continued, his words now a whisper, but there was a sharpness to them, a challenge. "But the thing is, I think you like pretending, Rowan."

I froze. The words hit me harder than I'd expected, catching me off guard. How dare he? How dare he see through me so easily, to call me out on something I hadn't even fully realized myself?

"Stop it," I snapped, shaking my head as if that would shake the truth from my chest. "You don't know what you're talking about."

But I knew it wasn't true. Deep down, I knew he was right. I had spent so long running, so long pretending I could live a life without him, without what we had been. But I had never been able to truly leave. And the truth was, I didn't want to.

Mason just watched me, a knowing look in his eyes, as though he could read the secrets I thought I had buried. His lips parted as if he might say something else, but the words died in his throat. Instead, we just stood there for a moment, two people caught in the middle of a game neither of us knew how to end.

It was funny how life could move around you, bustling forward, while you stood still in one place, suspended in time. And for the first time in years, I wasn't sure I wanted to move.

I could feel the heat from his body pressing against mine, the warmth of his arm where it brushed against my own, sending tingles that sparked through my skin. For a moment, I could almost forget that we weren't supposed to be here, doing this, walking through the market like two people in love instead of two people caught in a web of half-formed promises and unspoken truths.

I looked up at him, and for a heartbeat, I didn't recognize him at all. Not the man who had shattered everything, not the man I had sworn to forget. This version of Mason was softer, more vulnerable, as if life had chipped away at the sharp edges of who he used to be. His eyes held something deeper now, something harder to read, and the thought that I might be the reason for it made my stomach twist uncomfortably.

"You're looking at me like you're seeing a ghost," he remarked, his lips curling into a smile that didn't quite reach his eyes.

I laughed—short and clipped, the sound unnatural in the space between us. "Maybe I am."

It wasn't the right thing to say. Not now, not when every part of me was caught in the pull of a past I couldn't seem to outrun.

"Rowan," he started again, but this time, his voice was more tentative. "Tell me you're not still angry with me."

For a moment, I didn't answer. How could I? The anger, the hurt—it was buried so deeply within me, layers upon layers of it. The resentment I had spent years perfecting, making sure it remained a shield between us. I wasn't ready to let go of it, even though it was getting harder to hold onto.

"You don't get to ask me that," I replied finally, my voice sharper than I intended. "Not after everything. Not after you—"

"After I what?" he interjected, his tone raw, almost desperate. "Tell me, Rowan, because I don't think you even know anymore."

I stopped walking, pulling my arm out of his grasp. My chest tightened, the air thick with tension. I wanted to scream at him, to tell him exactly how much he had broken me, how much I had given up trying to fix things. But instead, I did what I had always done when faced with this kind of pressure. I shut down.

"You don't get to do this," I said, a breathless laugh escaping me. "We're not friends. We're not lovers. We're not even acquaintances anymore, Mason. We're just two people who have to be in the same space for a while."

His face fell, his hands balling into fists at his sides. It was as though I had slapped him, and for a brief, guilty moment, I wondered if maybe that was exactly what I had meant to do. To hurt him the way he had hurt me, all those years ago.

But he didn't let me have the satisfaction. Instead, he reached out again, grabbing my wrist and pulling me toward him, his grip firm but not unkind.

"Then why are you here, Rowan?" he asked, his voice a whisper now. "If it's all just a game, why do you keep playing?"

I should have pulled away. I should have told him that it didn't matter, that I was done with this dance of pretend. But the way he was looking at me, the way his fingers tightened around my wrist, made it impossible to lie.

"I don't know," I whispered, the words slipping out before I could stop them. "Maybe because it feels too hard to stop."

His expression softened, and for a moment, we stood there, the noise of the market swirling around us, the world moving in fast-forward as we stayed frozen in place. But then, just as quickly as it had come, the moment passed.

"Don't," he said, his voice thick with an emotion I couldn't quite place. "Don't pretend with me. I can't do it anymore."

I didn't know what to say to that. How could I? What was left to say when everything between us had already been said and done? When we had already broken each other too many times for words to matter?

I yanked my wrist free, stepping back quickly, as if distance would make the confusion and the hurt go away. But it didn't. It only made the space between us feel even wider, like some invisible chasm that neither of us could bridge.

"You should go," I said, the words barely above a whisper, but they were final, as though by saying them, I could somehow erase him from this moment, from my life once and for all. "It's over, Mason. You have your answer."

I turned on my heel, determined to leave, determined to pretend that the air between us wasn't charged with a thousand unsaid things. But just as I started to walk away, I felt a sharp tug at my sleeve.

"Rowan, please," he called, his voice desperate now. "I need you to hear me out. Just one last time."

I stopped, the ground beneath my feet feeling unsteady. What was it about his voice—something so raw, so real—that made it impossible to ignore?

I turned slowly, meeting his eyes for the first time in what felt like hours. His face was a mixture of frustration, regret, and something else—something deeper, something that scared me.

"What do you want me to say, Mason?" I asked, my voice breaking just slightly. "That I'm sorry? That I still care? That I want things to be the way they were?"

His gaze flickered to the ground, and for a second, I thought he might give up, might let me walk away. But then, he looked back up at me, and I saw it in his eyes—something that felt like a final plea.

"I want you to know that I didn't mean to hurt you," he said quietly. "I never wanted to."

I took a shaky breath, the words choking in my throat. There it was, that crack in the armor I had built. And just as I was about to say something—anything—something made me stop. I looked over Mason's shoulder, and for a brief moment, I thought I saw something in the crowd. Someone. A figure, barely visible among the people, but enough to make my pulse quicken.

It was him.
The man I had been trying to forget.

Chapter 5: Revelations Under Starlight

The night air wrapped itself around us like a velvet blanket, cool yet soothing, the kind of evening that beckoned with promises of new beginnings—or perhaps the ghosts of what had been lost. Above us, the stars twinkled like scattered diamonds, indifferent to the weight of secrets we carried. Jonah sat beside me, a silent silhouette against the dim glow of the city beneath, his gaze fixed on the horizon, where the lights of Paris flickered like a dream. It should have been a night like any other, a moment of peace. But there was something different in the air—something in the way the shadows clung to him, something in the way his silence spoke louder than any words.

For the longest time, neither of us said a thing. The faint clinking of glasses from the street below, the distant murmur of voices—those were the sounds that filled the quiet, almost as if the world had decided to hold its breath. I had no idea why I was here, why I had agreed to join him on this rooftop when every instinct screamed for me to stay away. Maybe it was the city, maybe it was the inexplicable pull of Jonah's presence, or maybe it was simply the unspoken promise that things could still be different, that somehow, after all that had passed, we could still find a way back to something that resembled... hope.

I was about to say something, anything, just to break the suffocating tension between us, when his voice cut through the quiet like a whisper from the past.

"I never told you," Jonah began, his words slow, deliberate, as if testing the weight of each one. "What happened with Leah." His name—Leah—felt heavy, unnatural on his tongue. He said it like he didn't want to, like it was a name that carried too much history, too much heartbreak.

I turned toward him, eyes searching his face, waiting for him to continue. Jonah's jaw tightened, and his fingers drummed nervously on the edge of the stone wall, a faint tremor betraying the calm facade he was trying so hard to maintain.

"She lied," he said flatly, his gaze distant, somewhere beyond me, as though speaking to the shadows. "She said she loved me." The words seemed to hang in the air, like smoke from a fire that had burned out long ago but still left behind an acrid memory.

I swallowed, unsure of how to respond. I had always known Jonah carried scars from that relationship, though I hadn't realized the depth of them until now. It was a story I had only ever heard in fragments, pieced together in conversations whispered behind closed doors, and now, it seemed, he was finally ready to tell it. To let me in.

"She never loved me," he continued, his voice raw, rough around the edges. "Not really. Not the way I thought she did. She... she betrayed me. With someone I called a friend." He let out a short, bitter laugh, his fingers curling into the stone as if holding on to something that wasn't there. "I trusted her. Trusted him. And when it all came crashing down, they just... walked away. Like I was nothing."

A silence fell between us, thick and suffocating. My mind raced to piece together the bits of information I had gathered over the years, but it felt like trying to hold water in my hands—slippery, elusive. I wanted to reach out to him, to tell him that he wasn't alone in this, that he didn't have to carry that weight all by himself, but the words lodged in my throat, tangled in the mess of our shared history.

"And me?" I finally managed to ask, my voice quieter than I'd intended. "Did I make it worse?"

His eyes shifted toward me then, and for the briefest moment, I saw the rawness of his emotion reflected there—like he was holding a door open just enough to let me in, but not wide enough to fully step through.

"At the time, I thought you were different," Jonah confessed, his words hanging between us, a confession that seemed as much to himself as it was to me. "But you weren't. You..." His voice faltered, and he took a long, slow breath, his eyes meeting mine with an intensity that felt like a warning. "You were a distraction. You made me forget, and I let you. But in the end, it was just another lie."

The sting of his words hit me like a slap, sharp and jarring, though I had no right to be surprised. After all, what did I expect? That somehow, the years apart would have erased the distance between us? That I could step back into his life and expect anything other than the remnants of a broken past?

I should have left then. Walked away and never looked back, letting the ghosts of our failed love remain buried where they belonged. But there was a spark in me, something reckless, something desperate for redemption. I couldn't bear the thought of leaving things unresolved. Not when I felt this strange, magnetic pull between us—like the earth itself was coaxing me closer, daring me to stay and see where this broken road might lead.

His hand brushed against mine then, a fleeting touch that sent a shock through me, as if his warmth could dissolve the weight of everything unsaid. My heart skipped a beat, and for a moment, all the hurt, all the betrayal, all the mistakes of our past seemed to vanish under the quiet glow of the Parisian night. But only for a moment. The reality settled back in, heavy and oppressive.

Jonah was broken, yes. But so was I. And maybe, just maybe, we could fix each other.

The moment his hand lingered against mine, I felt something shift—something that hadn't been there before. It wasn't just the warmth, though it seeped through my skin and into the parts of me I had long thought frozen. It was the way the air between us seemed to crackle, as if the rooftop itself held its breath, waiting for one of us to make a move. I could feel the weight of his words in that touch, the confession still hanging in the air, a heavy thing neither of us was willing to address directly, but both of us were undeniably aware of.

I opened my mouth to speak, to say something, anything, to fill the space he'd carved between us. But the words caught in my throat. What could I say? What was there left to say after all the time that had passed, after the mess of lies and unspoken truths that had tangled us in knots we hadn't bothered to untangle until now?

The city stretched before us, a blanket of twinkling lights and faded dreams, indifferent to the turmoil brewing in the space just a few inches between us. The hum of distant traffic, the occasional shout of a drunk tourist, the quiet lapping of water against the Seine below—it all seemed so far away, like we were the only two people left in the world. I could almost forget everything else in that moment, could almost believe that we hadn't been strangers, that we hadn't once broken each other's hearts.

Almost.

"Why didn't you ever say anything?" I asked before I could stop myself, the question tumbling out as if it had been there all along, buried under layers of pride and fear. "Why didn't you tell me what happened? If you felt this way... if I hurt you—"

Jonah cut me off with a soft exhale, shaking his head, the motion barely visible in the dim light. "I didn't want to hurt you, too." His voice was barely a whisper, yet it felt as though it struck through me, the words landing with unexpected force. "You were so... you were so sure of everything. Of me, of us. I couldn't shatter that for you. Not then."

I swallowed, the lump in my throat making it hard to breathe. He had been protecting me. From the truth. From the fallout of everything that had gone wrong. But in doing so, he had shielded me from him, from the part of him that had loved me enough to keep that secret buried. I had never asked for it, but somehow, I couldn't shake the feeling that I'd missed something vital, something I could never get back.

"Jonah, you—" I stopped myself, suddenly aware that I was clenching the edge of the stone wall, as if holding on to something that might slip away if I let go. "You didn't have to protect me from this. I'm not the same person I was before. I can't be that person anymore. Not after everything that happened." The words felt foreign as they left my mouth, like someone else was speaking them. I wasn't the girl who had walked away without a second glance. I wasn't the girl who had broken his heart and left him in the dust.

Jonah's gaze softened, and for a moment, I could have sworn I saw a flicker of the man I had once loved in his eyes. The man who had been so full of fire, so full of dreams and promises and possibilities. The man I had destroyed with my selfish choices.

"I didn't want you to think that I was still... hung up on her," Jonah said, his voice tight, but steady. "It wasn't about Leah. Not really. It was about me, and about what I let myself believe. I let myself believe that I could have it all. That I could have her, and you. And that if I just kept pretending, I wouldn't have to face the truth."

I shook my head, the confusion threatening to swallow me whole. "What do you mean? What truth?"

Jonah turned to face me fully then, his eyes locking onto mine with a sudden intensity that made my heart stutter. "The truth is," he began, his voice low and rough, "I've spent so much time trying to outrun everything, trying to outrun you, that I never stopped to wonder what it would be like if I stopped running."

The weight of his words settled over me, the full gravity of them making it hard to breathe. For a moment, I thought he was going to say something more, something that would explain everything, something that would make the puzzle pieces click together, finally offering clarity. But the silence stretched between us, thick and painful, as if we both feared what the next breath might bring.

"I don't know if I can do this again," I whispered, my voice trembling despite myself. "I don't know if I can risk it. Not after everything. Not after what we've done to each other."

Jonah's expression flickered, a flash of vulnerability that almost made me falter. He reached for my hand again, his touch warm and steady, the contrast between his calmness and my chaos only making my heart race faster. "I'm not asking you to trust me," he said softly, "at least not yet. But I'm asking you to believe that I'm here. That I'm not the man I was before, and that you don't have to be the woman you were before, either."

I pulled my hand away slowly, the sensation of his warmth lingering like a brand on my skin. I wanted to believe him. God, how I wanted to believe him. But the truth was, I wasn't sure who we were anymore, not when everything had been broken down and rebuilt in a way that felt foreign, unrecognizable.

We were standing on a rooftop, but it felt like we were both standing on the edge of something else entirely. The danger wasn't in the fall, but in what we might become if we let ourselves slip, if we let the past slip through our fingers and sink into the night.

The quiet that had settled between us felt like a living thing, heavy and expectant. I couldn't tell if Jonah was waiting for me to say something or if I was waiting for him to take a step closer, to fill the space that had become too large, too awkward between us. The touch of his hand was still warm on my skin, though it had been several moments since it had lingered there. I could feel the ghost of it, a quiet promise I wasn't sure I could trust. The truth was, I had no idea what I was supposed to do next. He had shared his heartache, his betrayal—so why was it still so hard to share mine?

I wanted to say the right thing. I wanted to be the woman who could stand there and fix everything with the simple, elegant precision of an apology. I wanted to tell him that I hadn't meant to hurt him, that the words I had spoken, the choices I had made, had never been about him—only about my own inability to understand what we were, what we could have been. But the words stuck to the back of my throat like thick, bitter honey, refusing to leave.

Instead, I turned my attention to the Paris skyline, hoping the city would somehow provide the answers I didn't have. The lights shimmered in the distance, twinkling like stars that had fallen just a little too close to earth. I could almost hear the laughter of people spilling out from cafes, the clink of glasses, the murmur of conversations happening in another world—one where things were simpler, more uncomplicated.

"I used to love this city," I said, the words slipping out before I could stop them. "The way it always feels like you're on the verge of something extraordinary, like all the possibilities are right there, waiting for you to reach out and take them."

Jonah didn't respond right away, and for a moment, I thought he hadn't heard me. But then his voice came, low and thoughtful, almost as if he were speaking more to himself than to me.

"Do you think that's what happened with us? That we thought there was some kind of possibility just out of reach? Something we couldn't quite grasp?" His words hung in the air like smoke, curling and twisting around the quiet space between us.

I was surprised by the question, and for a moment, I didn't know how to answer. Was that what had happened? Had we truly believed in something that wasn't there, something intangible that we had clung to, convinced it could save us both?

"I don't know," I said finally, my voice almost a whisper. "Maybe we were too scared to admit that we weren't what we thought we were. That maybe there was nothing extraordinary about us, nothing left to find." The admission made me feel raw, exposed. I couldn't believe I was saying it out loud, let alone to Jonah, the man who had once been everything to me, only to become a stranger in the years that followed.

Jonah turned to face me then, his eyes searching mine with an intensity that made my heart beat faster. "You think we're nothing extraordinary?" His words were a challenge, a dare I hadn't expected.

I opened my mouth to respond, but the words I had prepared fled, scattered like dust in the wind. Instead, I found myself staring at him, really seeing him for the first time since that fateful moment years ago when we had decided to go our separate ways. He hadn't changed, not entirely—there was still that spark of defiance in his eyes, that fire I had fallen in love with—but something had shifted. He wasn't the boy I had once known. And I wasn't the girl who had walked away from him, convinced that love couldn't fix what was already broken.

"I don't know what I think anymore," I confessed, the words feeling strange, foreign. "Everything's so complicated now. It's like we're both holding on to something that might not even be real."

His expression softened, just a fraction, and for a moment, the tension between us seemed to ease. But only for a moment.

"I think," Jonah said slowly, his voice unsteady, "that sometimes we have to risk believing in things, even if they scare the hell out of us."

The words landed like a weight on my chest, a challenge I hadn't been prepared for. Believing in things, even if they scared you? Wasn't that exactly what I had been running from all this time? Wasn't that the very reason I had walked away from him in the first place?

The city felt impossibly close now, the sound of the Seine's gentle current reaching us, the rustling of distant trees mingling with the hum of the city. And for the first time, I felt the pull of something stronger than the fear that had kept me locked in my own head for so long. It wasn't a promise, not exactly. But it was the possibility of one, and I couldn't help but wonder if maybe we had been wrong all along, if maybe we had underestimated the power of what we could still be.

I opened my mouth, ready to say something—anything—but the words were lost when I heard it: the sharp crack of a door slamming open behind us. The sound of footsteps, the unmistakable presence of someone else on the rooftop with us.

I turned, my heart in my throat, already dreading what was coming next. The silhouette of a man appeared in the doorway, his figure tall and unmistakable. It took me a moment to place him, but when I did, my breath caught.

It was Jake. Jonah's best friend. The one I had never expected to see here.

And he wasn't alone.

Chapter 6: The Dance of Old Flames

The soft hum of the orchestra filled the air, every note wrapped in velvet as it swept over the guests, coating the room with its languid charm. The ballroom shimmered under the weight of its extravagance—gold-leafed trim along the windows, the ice-glass chandeliers dangling like diamonds, catching the light and scattering it across the marble floors. It smelled of roses, an air thick with expensive perfume, mingling with the musky undertones of men's cologne and the faintest trace of champagne.

I could feel the cool, almost imperceptible tension in the air, something that only existed at places like this—where every step, every glance, was calculated for perfection. It was a dance of more than just bodies. It was the dance of status, power, and grace, and I, somehow, was dancing in the middle of it.

Jonah's hand rested at the small of my back, and I could feel his warmth through the crisp fabric of my dress. The connection between us was magnetic, a pull I couldn't quite describe, but one I certainly felt with every step. His hand was steady, guiding me with an ease that made me wonder if this was just another part of his world, one he could navigate without a second thought. Yet, with every step, he seemed more like a stranger than the man I'd known. He moved differently in this space, like the music was woven into his bones, like the tempo of his life was set to its rhythm. And I? Well, I was an interloper, a wild card that didn't belong.

I glanced up at him, catching the briefest glimpse of something unreadable in his eyes, something too quick for me to fully grasp. His lips quirked slightly, as though amused by some private thought, and in that fleeting moment, the distance between us seemed almost... impossible. The orchestra swelled, and his eyes found mine, dark and filled with unspoken words, a language I almost understood, but not quite.

"You're quiet tonight," he murmured, his voice low and smooth, the words trailing like a caress.

I looked away, focusing on the intricate embroidery on his tuxedo, anything to avoid the intensity in his gaze. "Just thinking," I replied, my voice sounding foreign in my own ears, unsure. The truth was, my thoughts were not as composed as I wished they were. They were tangled up in him, in his presence, in the way he made everything feel just a little too real.

His grip on me tightened slightly, a subtle question in the shift of his fingers. "About what?"

"About the music," I said, laughing lightly, trying to ignore the twinge in my chest. "How it's kind of like life, you know? Every note, every rest, a moment that leads you somewhere. But sometimes the beat changes unexpectedly."

Jonah smiled, that half-smile I had never quite figured out. "I like how you think," he said, but his voice faltered just slightly. Something hung in the air, as if his words were merely a dance of their own, one where neither of us knew what the next step would be.

I turned my attention back to the floor, hoping to ground myself in the rhythm, to take my mind off the knot tightening in my stomach. But just as I did, something shifted—like a breeze that wasn't supposed to be there. A figure appeared at the edge of my vision, moving with an elegance that could only belong to someone from Jonah's world. I felt a coldness that contrasted sharply with the warmth of his body beside me. She was there, standing just beyond our circle, her presence pulling at the edges of the room.

Her name echoed in my mind before I could stop it. Ava. I'd heard about her before—stories Jonah's friends liked to drop like breadcrumbs, teasing him with the ghost of a past that never seemed to quite let go. Ava. The one who had once been his everything.

I couldn't help it. My gaze flicked over, catching her silhouette as she greeted a few prominent guests with a charming smile, her posture immaculate, her confidence palpable. I watched as Jonah stiffened beside me, just the slightest, almost imperceptible tension in his jaw.

I swallowed, my mind racing. There was something about the way she moved, the way she held herself, that seemed to command attention, even in a room full of people who were used to being noticed. And Jonah? He was looking at her too, though his expression was harder to read than ever. There was something... guarded, something buried under layers of politeness and history that made my chest tighten.

I had known this moment would come. The moment when the past would come crashing in on the present, when the quiet scars of old loves would rise to the surface, pushing everything else aside.

Jonah cleared his throat, and I felt his fingers flex gently on my back, a signal that he was aware of the sudden change. "I should go say hello," he said, his voice soft, distant. I nodded, a strange lump forming in my throat as he gently withdrew from me, stepping away with that familiar grace, his gaze still lingering on me for just a moment before it was absorbed by the woman who had entered his past with such devastating clarity.

I watched as he walked toward her, their conversation starting with small, polite exchanges, but I could see the history between them hanging in the air like a dense fog. I tried to focus on the music again, but the weight of his absence was unbearable. The room had grown too small, and every breath I took seemed to be drawn from a deeper, more fragile place.

My thoughts were interrupted by the flicker of a smile from a stranger nearby, a fleeting attempt at conversation that felt hollow against the throb of my own racing heart. Jonah was talking to her now, his words soft and measured, but the look in his eyes was different from the one he gave me. It was a look that spoke of unfinished conversations, untold stories, and a history that refused to fade.

I told myself that I could handle it. I told myself that I could let him navigate his past without it breaking me. But as the music played on and the people around me swirled like ghosts, I couldn't help but wonder if this would be a dance we could ever finish without someone's heart breaking.

I stood frozen, my pulse thrumming in my throat, as Jonah spoke with Ava. The words between them were too polite, too neutral. I could see that in his eyes—the careful, deliberate mask he wore when the past had a way of reappearing. He was distant, but not quite. The air between them crackled, charged in a way that had nothing to do with anything I could see or hear. It was the quiet space between their gazes, the way they both held their breath for a moment longer than necessary, before one of them spoke again.

The room seemed to stretch, the hum of conversation and clinking glasses fading into a background murmur as I stood there, suddenly very aware of how alone I was. Alone, even surrounded by people. I found myself drawing back, stepping away from the bustle of the crowd, the noise too loud now in contrast to the quiet tension that enveloped Jonah and Ava. It wasn't even jealousy that gripped me—it was the weight of a thousand questions, none of which I could voice.

The polished wood of the ballroom floor felt cool beneath my heels as I moved away from the center of the room, my feet carrying me in no particular direction, not really wanting to know where I was going, but not wanting to stand still, either. It seemed like every corner of the room held some memory of him—of the man Jonah used to be before he stepped into my life, before everything changed between us. Before I knew too much, maybe, or knew too little.

I found myself near the edge of the terrace, a shadowed refuge from the gleaming interior, and I exhaled, watching the mist roll in from the distant ocean. The air was crisp, a contrast to the warm, heady atmosphere inside. The faint smell of saltwater carried on the breeze, mingling with the remnants of floral perfume and faint echoes of laughter. I leaned against the stone railing, the cool touch of it grounding me, steadying me.

The last few months with Jonah had been dizzying, a whirlwind of connection, sparks, and new beginnings. Yet, in moments like this, those sparks felt more like something that could burn, a fire left untended, flickering dangerously. I could hear the laughter from inside, muffled by the heavy glass doors, but the outside air was mercifully quiet, and for a moment, it felt like I could breathe again.

Then I felt it—a presence at my back, a shift in the air. Jonah's footsteps approached, the subtle rustling of fabric as he drew near. He didn't speak at first, not in the way I was used to. His silence was heavier than normal, and when I turned, his eyes met mine with that same guarded expression, the one that didn't seem to want to let me in, not fully.

"Ava's... here," he said, his voice soft, the words coming out slower than usual, like he was trying to find the right way to say them.

I nodded, even though I was pretty sure he knew I already knew that. I wasn't blind, and I hadn't missed the weight in his voice, the way his smile had faltered for just a second when she'd called his name.

"She's... she's important to you, isn't she?" The words slipped from my mouth before I could stop them, my voice barely above a whisper, like I was testing the waters, afraid of what the answer might be.

He hesitated for a moment longer than I would've liked, and then nodded, a single, almost imperceptible gesture. "Yeah," he said, looking away as if he were already trying to move past the conversation. "She was. In ways I don't talk about much."

I swallowed, pushing down the lump in my throat. "And now?" I asked, my gaze dropping to my hands, where my fingers clutched the fabric of my dress a little too tightly.

Jonah took a deep breath, running a hand through his hair, a motion I'd seen countless times before, a signal that he was thinking too much and not saying enough. "And now... things are different. I'm different."

My heart stuttered, but I couldn't tell if it was in relief or disappointment. The words seemed so final, yet they didn't answer anything. His past hung in the air between us like a ghost, and I wasn't sure how to make it vanish.

"I guess I'm not used to people knowing my history," he continued, his voice soft, but a little more open. "Not in the way you do. Not in the way I've let you."

The admission hung there, suspended between us, like it was too raw to put into motion, too heavy to settle. And for a second, I wondered if maybe that was the problem. That maybe the spaces between us—the ones we never spoke about—were what made this feel fragile, like something made of glass. I wasn't sure how much more weight it could take.

The silence stretched, but it wasn't as uncomfortable as it had been before. Jonah's eyes met mine again, this time with something different in them. A softness, a vulnerability that surprised me. But then, just as quickly, the moment shifted. A shadow passed over his expression, and the distance between us grew once more, as if he had sealed himself up again, tucking whatever he had just revealed into some secret, inaccessible corner of his mind.

"I think I need to go," I said, the words surprising me as much as they seemed to surprise him. It wasn't what I had intended to say, not really. But in that moment, it felt right. Like a necessary step.

Jonah looked at me, his brow furrowing, his mouth opening as if to protest, but then he stopped. He took in a breath, letting it out slowly, like he was weighing something inside himself, something I couldn't read.

"I'll walk you out," he said finally, his voice steady, though there was something in his eyes—something that said this wasn't the end, but it might be a pause, a hesitation that neither of us could quite shake.

The night stretched before us, but the evening didn't feel as grand as it had when we'd entered. Now, it felt like we were stepping away from something, from the promise of something, and I wasn't sure if I could bring myself to turn back and try again.

Jonah's hand remained at the small of my back, but it felt like an anchor, tethering me to a place I wasn't sure I wanted to be. The warmth of his touch had melted away in the cool shadow of the terrace, replaced by the soft edge of inevitability. Neither of us spoke as we walked back toward the ballroom, and the silence between us seemed to grow, swelling with all the things we didn't say. I had never been particularly good at reading people—maybe because I was too busy reading myself—but even I couldn't ignore the disquiet that hung between us now, thick and impossible to shake. It was as though the evening had shifted on its axis and I was just a reluctant passenger.

Jonah's hand brushed mine as we walked through the glass doors, the quiet gesture striking me with an almost painful clarity. It wasn't that I didn't want him to touch me. I did. But there was something different about it now. A kind of gentleness that came with the distance between us, the realization that I wasn't exactly the one he was thinking about.

Inside, the lights were still dazzling, the guests moving in a slow, glimmering parade, but everything seemed a little farther away, a little blurrier. Ava was gone, vanished into the crowd like some wisp of a past life, but her presence still hung in the air, like smoke from a fire that had been extinguished but left its trace behind.

I wanted to pull Jonah closer, to find some way to bridge the gap between us, but I wasn't sure where to begin. His thoughts were still tangled in the past, and I—well, I had learned that being part of someone's history wasn't always as simple as showing up and expecting the rest of the world to fall into place.

He stopped abruptly, and I looked up, startled, as he turned toward me. His expression was unreadable, eyes narrowed slightly, jaw clenched in that familiar way that made me wonder if he was wrestling with something. He opened his mouth to speak, but then, just as quickly, closed it again. The words weren't coming easily, and that alone made me feel like I was on the edge of something much bigger than I had bargained for.

"Maybe we should talk about this," he said finally, the words careful, slow, as though each one was being measured. "About Ava. About—" He cut himself off, shaking his head slightly. "I don't know what I'm trying to say."

The air around us thickened, and I realized I wasn't the only one caught in the pull of unresolved feelings. Jonah had never been an open book—not in the way I wanted him to be—but I had hoped, at least, that we could find our way around the pages, navigating through the spaces between what we had said and what we hadn't.

"I'm not asking for a full explanation," I said, my voice steadier than I felt. "But I need you to be honest with me. I can't stand in the shadows of people I don't know."

He winced at my words, but didn't pull away. "It's not that simple," he said, his voice low, the tension thick in his tone. "Ava and I—what we had, what we were—" He paused again, dragging his hand through his hair as though frustrated by his own inability to put it into words. "It's hard to explain. I'm not who I was back then, and I don't want to drag you into all that. But I—"

I cut him off, suddenly tired of the half-formed sentences and unspoken promises that hung in the space between us. "But you're still carrying her with you," I said, the words coming out sharper than I meant. "And I'm just here, trying to figure out if I'm something new or just a distraction."

Jonah's eyes flashed with something—hurt, maybe, or frustration—and he took a step back, his gaze flicking away for a moment before meeting mine again. "I'm not trying to make you feel like that," he said quietly. "I don't want you to feel like second best. I'm just—this is... complicated."

I swallowed, my throat suddenly tight. "I get it," I said, though I wasn't sure if I did. "But what am I supposed to do with all this uncertainty? I'm not looking for your past. I'm looking for now. For us."

He looked at me, his expression softening, but there was still something buried under his eyes, something he wasn't ready to let go of. The truth lingered in the air between us like smoke—something we both inhaled but didn't speak about.

"I'm sorry," he said, his voice quiet. "I need time to figure out what this is. I just—" He shook his head again, frustration marking the line of his jaw. "I don't want to lose you, but I don't know how to untangle all the mess inside my head."

I felt my heart sink at the honesty of his words, even as they rang with a kind of finality. There was something in him—some hidden thread that had never quite been cut, something that tied him to her, something I couldn't touch. And for the first time, I realized that maybe, just maybe, I wasn't the one who could make him let go.

I took a deep breath, the ache of that realization settling heavily in my chest. "You don't have to untangle everything. I just need to know if you're here with me. Or if you're still somewhere else."

Jonah didn't speak for a long moment, and when he did, his words were soft, almost imperceptible in the hum of the room around us. "I'm here," he said, but the way he said it made my heart question if that was the whole truth.

Before I could say anything else, I caught a flicker of movement out of the corner of my eye. A woman's laugh, sharp and familiar, cut through the murmur of the room. And as I turned, I saw her. Ava. Standing there, a few feet away, her gaze locking onto mine with a coldness I hadn't expected.

"I thought I'd find you here," she said, her smile wide and calculated.

Chapter 7: Confessions in a Midnight Garden

The moon hung low in the sky, a pale sliver of light that spilled across the cobbled paths like forgotten memories. We didn't speak much as we walked, the soft rustling of our steps blending with the quiet hum of crickets hidden somewhere in the darkened hedges. The air smelled of earth and something sweeter—a hint of jasmine, if I wasn't mistaken, but it could've been the roses that stretched out in every direction, their heavy perfume drifting lazily on the warm summer breeze.

We had slipped away from the gala unnoticed, escaping the buzz of laughter and the clink of champagne glasses, the ostentatious clamor of society playing out under the glimmering chandeliers. I don't know why I'd agreed to leave, or why I felt so compelled to follow him into the garden, but something about the quiet invitation in his eyes had rendered my willpower useless. His hand had brushed against mine for just a moment, warm and firm, and though I hadn't wanted to, I found myself stepping away from the world of polished faces and tight smiles, into the silence that surrounded us like a velvet cloak.

"I didn't expect to find peace in a place like this," he murmured, his voice low, almost hesitant, as if the words were coming from a place long buried. "The noise, the laughter... it's all just a mask."

I glanced at him, the outline of his face softened in the dim light. He looked... different here, unguarded in a way that didn't seem to belong to him. His usual confident air had given way to something more vulnerable, something I hadn't expected to see. It struck me how little I truly knew about him, despite the endless hours spent in conversation, despite the way he'd captivated me with his charm and those sly, wicked smiles. The way he managed to make everyone around him feel like they were the most important person in the room, myself included. But now, the façade was cracked. He was just another man wandering through the dark, searching for something he couldn't quite name.

"I don't think anyone's ever found peace in places like that," I replied, my voice softer than usual. The moonlight caught on the delicate curve of a rose petal, and I paused, inhaling the air as if it could cleanse something deep inside me. "It's all just noise. It's the silence that's dangerous, isn't it?"

His gaze flicked to me, a flash of understanding in his eyes. "Dangerous? Maybe. But it's the silence where the truth lives. The truth we're all too afraid to face."

I felt a tightness in my chest. He wasn't wrong. How many times had I found myself drowning in the noise, running away from what I couldn't bear to confront? How many times had I let the world blur into something simple and acceptable, when beneath the surface, everything was slowly crumbling?

"What truth?" I asked, though I was almost afraid to hear the answer.

The corner of his mouth lifted into something that might've been a smile, though it didn't reach his eyes. "The one we try to bury. The regrets. The things we've done... and the things we didn't."

I swallowed hard, and the words came unbidden, my own voice betraying me as I finally let the walls crack. "And the things we're still running from."

He didn't say anything to that, but his silence felt like an acknowledgment. We walked deeper into the garden, the path now winding through a cluster of towering willows, their long branches swaying gently in the breeze, casting shadows on the ground that seemed to move with us. The garden, it seemed, was its own world—one where nothing could be hidden. Every bloom, every crack in the stone, every flicker of the moonlight felt like a whisper, a confession made in secret.

"So," I said after a while, forcing a lightness to my voice that didn't quite belong, "what is it you've been running from, then?"

His lips pressed together as if he were carefully considering the question. "I'm not sure I know how to answer that," he said, his voice almost too quiet to hear. "It's not one thing. It's a thousand little mistakes... things I should've said, things I shouldn't have. People I hurt without meaning to. People I hurt because I didn't know how to do anything else."

The rawness of his words hung in the air between us like the thick scent of the roses, cloying but undeniable. I wanted to reach out, to comfort him, but I didn't know how. And maybe, just maybe, I didn't want to. There was something about the way he bared his soul—something about the way his darkness resonated with my own—that made me want to retreat, to wrap myself in the solitude I'd always sought. But I couldn't leave, couldn't stop listening, as though his confessions held some kind of key to unlocking my own buried truths.

"It sounds lonely," I said after a long moment, my voice faltering despite myself. "Being that lost."

His gaze shifted to me then, and for the briefest of seconds, something shifted between us. It wasn't pity, or even sympathy, but something far more dangerous—an understanding. A bond forged in the kind of silent recognition that only those who had walked the same dark path could truly know.

"I suppose it is," he murmured, his words trailing off into the night. "But maybe... maybe we've been lost together all along."

The silence between us stretched for what felt like hours, heavy with the weight of things unsaid. His words hung in the air like a mist, clinging to everything, and I couldn't help but wonder if they would vanish the moment we stepped back into the light. It was a silly thought, I knew. The truth doesn't dissolve in daylight, no matter how hard you try to hide it.

I reached up to push a stray lock of hair behind my ear, though I wasn't sure why. My fingers brushed against my skin, and the simple gesture felt grounding, like I might be able to anchor myself in something—anything—before this moment could slip away. "So, you think we've been lost together?" I asked, though the question wasn't entirely for him. It was more for me, a way to force my mind to make sense of the strange pull between us.

He didn't immediately answer, but instead, his gaze seemed to wander, taking in the shadows of the garden and the moonlight that filtered through the trees. The flickering light played tricks on the leaves, making them look as if they were trembling, caught between the warmth of the world and the coolness of the night.

"I think," he finally said, his voice low, almost a whisper, "we're all looking for something. Some way out, some way in. We just don't always know it until it's too late."

I studied him, the way the shadows played on his face, the way his hands moved restlessly at his sides. He wasn't looking at me now, and that told me more than his words ever could. It wasn't about redemption. Not in the way he'd said it before, not in the way I thought it was.

"You're right," I said slowly, my heart pounding in a way that felt both foreign and familiar. I wasn't sure if I meant the words, but I couldn't stop myself from speaking them. "We spend our whole lives searching for something—meaning, purpose, connection—and it's never clear what it is we're really after until we find it... or realize it was there all along."

I saw his jaw tighten, a flicker of something in his eyes before he turned back to me. "Do you think that's true? That it's always right there in front of us?"

"I think it's the hardest thing to see when you're busy running in the opposite direction."

The words came out sharper than I intended, and I regretted them the moment they were out. There it was again—the truth. The thing I'd been avoiding for far too long. I had been running, hadn't I? Running from the very thing I had craved for so long.

"You think I've been running?" he asked, his voice laced with a wry amusement, but there was something darker in it, something I hadn't expected.

I bit my lip, feeling the sting of his question in my chest. "Maybe we're all just running from different versions of the same thing."

He took a step toward me, closing the space between us in a way that felt sudden, almost deliberate. The air around us thickened, the roses, now more than just fragrance, seemed to trap the words we hadn't said. I could feel the pull of the moment, as though time had slowed, but my heart hammered faster than it should have.

"What is it that you're running from?" he asked, and there was no teasing in his voice, no distance. Just an unspoken invitation to speak the truth.

I hesitated, only for a moment, before I let the words spill out, as if the confession could break the hold he had on me. "I'm running from the idea that I might be exactly what I'm afraid of becoming."

The vulnerability in my own voice caught me off guard, and for a second, I wished I could take it back, stuff the words back into the corners of my mind where they belonged. But I didn't. I stood there, rooted to the spot, letting them hang between us.

He was quiet for a long time. Too long. His eyes, dark and intense, didn't leave mine, and I could feel the tension building, pressing against my ribs. Finally, he spoke, his voice a little rougher than before. "You don't have to be afraid of becoming something. You just have to decide who you're going to be when you get there."

The words struck me like a sudden gust of wind, unexpected but strong enough to knock me off balance. I wasn't sure how to respond to that, how to acknowledge the strange familiarity in his voice—how he seemed to understand, in a way no one ever had, the complexities of my own fears.

I took a shaky breath, stepping back, just enough to break the intensity of his gaze. "Maybe that's the problem. I've spent my whole life deciding who I need to be for other people. I've never really thought about who I am for myself."

There it was. The heart of it. The reason I couldn't seem to find peace, no matter how much I tried to chase it down.

He didn't move, just watched me, and then, with a subtle shift, his hand reached out—not to touch, but just close enough to feel the warmth radiating from my skin. "Maybe it's time to start."

For a moment, everything seemed to stop. The garden, the moonlight, the soft brush of leaves against one another—all of it faded into the background as I stared at him. The weight of his words pressed against me like a quiet challenge, something I hadn't expected, but something I couldn't escape, not anymore.

I swallowed hard, the reality of it settling in around me. I wasn't sure if I was ready. I wasn't sure if I ever would be. But for the first time in a long time, I felt like I could finally breathe. Like maybe, just maybe, this—whatever this was—was exactly where I needed to be.

"I think..." I started, my voice trembling slightly, but with more conviction than I'd ever spoken before, "I think I've been waiting for someone to remind me it's okay to stop running."

He didn't smile, but there was something in his eyes then—something soft, something almost tender. "I think it's time for both of us to stop."

We stood there for a long moment, the night thick with the weight of our shared silence, as though the very air around us had suspended time. His words, still echoing in the space between us, clung to me like an invisible thread, pulling me closer to him without any real effort. I could almost hear the unspoken words in his quiet stare, a challenge and an invitation all wrapped into one, daring me to step into the light with him—or to stay hidden in the shadows, as I'd always done. The tension between us was palpable, crackling in the air like static, making my skin prickle.

And yet, despite the pressure, I couldn't bring myself to move. I stood there, feeling as if I had been waiting for this moment my entire life, though I wasn't sure for what. Was I waiting for him to make a move? Or was I waiting for myself to do the unthinkable—to reach across the gap between us and finally acknowledge the connection I had been pretending wasn't there?

He took a step forward, his eyes never leaving mine. There was no hesitation in his movement, no sign of uncertainty. He was already certain of the path he was about to take, and I realized with a jolt that I wasn't certain of anything, except that I wanted him to stay close.

"I think," he said, his voice low and husky, as if the weight of his own words made them harder to form, "we've both been afraid of the same thing. Afraid of not being enough. Afraid of what might happen if we stop running from the things we've done, or the things we haven't done."

I couldn't stop myself from smiling, though it was a sad, knowing smile. "That's funny," I said, almost too casually. "You've been running, too? I always thought you had everything figured out. You always seemed so... sure."

He let out a short, almost bitter laugh, a sound that felt like it should've been softer, more forgiving. "I think we both know how well pretending works." His eyes flicked over me briefly, but they lingered too long to be anything but searching. "But it's easier to stay in motion than it is to face what's really inside."

His words felt like a punch to the gut, striking too close to the truth I hadn't wanted to face. I wasn't the only one hiding, after all. Neither of us had figured out how to stand still, how to exist in the world without the crutch of distraction. The gala, the smiles, the endless small talk—these were all just ways to fill the empty spaces we didn't want to acknowledge.

"What if we stopped pretending?" I said before I could stop myself, my voice suddenly so small, so fragile in the face of everything we were tiptoeing around.

He was close now, his breath warm on my face, his presence more than just a physical thing—it was like he had wrapped himself around me, almost like he was daring me to breathe him in. "Then I guess we'd have to face it. Everything."

I could feel the pull of him, something magnetic and dangerous, something that both frightened and intrigued me. I wasn't ready for this. Not for him. Not for any of it. But when had I ever been ready for anything?

"Maybe I'm not ready," I said, my voice shaking slightly, despite my best efforts to hold it together. "Maybe I'll never be ready."

He took another step forward, closing the gap between us until we were so close I could feel the heat radiating from his skin. It felt impossible to breathe, impossible to think, as the world around us seemed to shrink, leaving only the two of us standing at the center of something much larger than either of us.

"Then don't be," he whispered, his words a promise and a warning all at once. "But you're still here. You're still with me."

I didn't know what to say to that, so I said nothing at all. Instead, I took a deep breath, my chest rising and falling in a rhythm I didn't recognize. It felt too intimate, too raw to keep going like this, and yet I couldn't stop myself.

And then, before I could say anything, his hand reached out, just grazing my wrist with the lightest of touches. It was barely there—an accident, perhaps, or maybe a question—but it was enough to send a shock through me, enough to make my pulse race.

For a moment, I couldn't think. I couldn't move. The world narrowed to the sound of my breathing and the gentle pressure of his fingers against my skin. And in that moment, I realized something I hadn't wanted to admit to myself: I was standing on the edge of something I couldn't control, something that was far too dangerous for either of us.

But I didn't pull away.

Instead, I looked at him, my heart thundering in my chest as his gaze softened, just a little, a fraction of a moment where the man in front of me wasn't hiding anymore. His eyes, the ones that had always been a little too guarded, a little too sharp, held something different now. Something real.

"I think…" I started, but my words faltered, too unsure, too much of a risk. I couldn't find the right thing to say, couldn't find a way to bridge the gap between us.

He didn't give me time to finish the thought. His hand, still warm against my skin, shifted slightly, his thumb brushing over the delicate curve of my wrist, sending a shiver through me. And for the first time, I wasn't sure if I was going to stop myself from crossing the line that had been so carefully drawn between us.

Just as I opened my mouth to speak, the sharp crack of a branch breaking underfoot echoed through the garden, and both of us turned sharply, the moment shattered as quickly as it had formed. My breath caught in my throat, and I couldn't see where the sound had come from—only that it had changed everything.

And that was when I saw the shadow.

Standing at the edge of the garden, just outside the circle of light, was someone I hadn't expected to see at all.

Chapter 8: The Call of Temptation

The theater was a relic, a crumbling monument to something long past, its faded grandeur tangled in the vines that snaked up the decaying walls. I could feel the ghosts of old performances lingering in the air, the soft echo of forgotten applause and murmurs of admiration from an audience long since disappeared. It was as if time had been paused here, the curtains forever frozen mid-drift, the stage still holding secrets in its dust-covered folds.

Jonah led me through the rows of broken seats, each one creaking under our weight, as though they were protesting the intrusion. The light from the crack in the ceiling filtered through the broken glass, casting jagged shadows that danced across the worn velvet. The smell of mildew hung heavy, but there was something oddly comforting about it—like a memory of things that had been cherished before time got too busy. Jonah's steps were careful, almost reverent, as though he was walking in the presence of something sacred. His voice, when it finally broke the silence, was hushed, almost as if the theater itself might be listening.

"This place," he said, his gaze sweeping over the decaying grandeur, "has a way of making you feel like you're part of something bigger than yourself. It's... peaceful here." His words settled around me like a spell, and for a moment, I wondered if he was talking about the theater or something else entirely—something between us.

I glanced over at him, watching the way the dim light softened the sharp angles of his jaw, the way his fingers brushed the edge of a broken armrest as if testing the weight of history. Jonah was always like this—careful, restrained. As if every movement carried some hidden meaning. I couldn't help but wonder what it would take to unravel him, to see the parts of him that he kept buried beneath layers of mystery and distance.

I wanted to ask him what this place really meant to him, why it was a secret he kept close, but the words stuck in my throat. The air between us was already thick with something unspoken, something that had been growing ever since the first time our eyes had met across the crowded room at that bar. Something electric. Something dangerous.

"Do you ever feel like you're standing on the edge of something you can't explain?" I asked instead, my voice quieter than I intended, almost like a confession.

He turned to me, those dark eyes of his catching mine, holding me in place. "All the time," he replied, his lips curling into a slow, enigmatic smile. "But some edges are worth standing on."

The way he said it sent a shiver down my spine, a thrill of anticipation that twisted in my stomach. There was a promise in his words, a dangerous invitation. I wasn't sure if I was ready to accept it, but it was hard to ignore the pull, that magnetic force between us, making it impossible to look away, impossible to walk away.

I took a step closer, the sound of my boots on the broken floor the only noise between us. As I reached out, my fingers brushed the back of his hand, light as a whisper, and the moment I made contact, I felt it—a current running between us, something sharp and alive. My heart stuttered in my chest, and I could feel his breath quicken, just the slightest hitch. The distance between us, once so carefully measured, vanished in an instant.

He didn't pull away. Instead, his hand shifted slightly, as if testing the waters, before he covered mine with his own. The warmth of his skin against mine sent a pulse of heat through my veins. For a second, the world outside the theater ceased to exist. All that mattered was the touch of his hand, the weight of his palm pressed against mine, and the way it felt like we were both holding our breath, waiting for the other to make the first move.

I couldn't help it. I wanted more. My gaze dropped to his lips, the temptation so strong I could taste it. The words I'd been holding back—the questions I didn't want to ask, the fears I didn't want to voice—were all forgotten. All that mattered was the sensation of his fingers tracing the back of my hand, the pressure building between us, drawing us closer, inch by intoxicating inch.

But just as I was about to close the distance, a sharp noise echoed through the theater—something falling, a chair scraping across the floor in the darkness. The sound shattered the moment, splintering it into a thousand jagged pieces. I jerked back, my pulse racing, as if I'd been caught doing something wrong.

Jonah's hand dropped from mine, and we both froze, our breath coming faster, the air suddenly too thick with tension. I felt the loss of his touch like a physical ache. But I couldn't deny it—there was something more between us, something undeniable, even if we were too afraid to name it.

The silence in the theater stretched, the weight of unspoken words hanging between us like a heavy curtain. Jonah's eyes never left mine, but there was a shift in them, something guarded. He took a step back, his gaze flickering toward the shadows, where the sound had come from, as if daring whatever it was to reveal itself.

"Maybe we should go," he said, his voice rougher now, tinged with something I couldn't quite place. It wasn't fear. Not exactly. But there was an edge to it, a sharpness I hadn't heard before.

I nodded, though I didn't want to leave—not yet. The feeling of him so close, the promise in the air, was still too real, too tangible to ignore. But something had changed. Something had been set in motion, and I wasn't sure if we were ready for whatever came next.

As we made our way out of the theater, the floor creaking beneath our feet like the sigh of a forgotten world, I couldn't shake the feeling that we were both running from something—something neither of us fully understood but both knew was waiting for us just around the corner.

We barely spoke as we left the theater, our footsteps hurried, and the world outside felt a thousand miles away. The late afternoon sunlight was just beginning to stretch across the sky, casting long shadows that seemed to stretch endlessly before us. Jonah was walking ahead, his shoulders stiff and his hands shoved deep into the pockets of his jacket. There was a tension in his posture that I couldn't ignore, something I hadn't seen before. And it wasn't just from the sudden disruption we'd encountered in the theater. It was as though the weight of the unsaid had finally caught up to him, and I couldn't tell if he was angry or merely avoiding the inevitable.

I wanted to ask him what was wrong, to pull him back from whatever place his mind had wandered to, but the words felt hollow in my mouth. So, I stayed silent, watching as he quickened his pace, clearly needing the distance between us, as if the silence might fill the void that had opened between us with something else. I hadn't meant to cross that line, but somehow, I had.

"Jonah," I called, more forcefully than I'd intended, and he stopped, turning slowly. His face was unreadable, but his eyes—they were different. Darker, maybe, or maybe it was just the reflection of the late sun on his face, casting shadows where there had been none before. "Are you okay?"

He didn't answer right away. Instead, he shifted on his feet, his gaze flickering toward the horizon before landing on me. There was something indecipherable there, something that made my heart tighten. It was the same way I'd felt when we were in the theater, inches away from crossing a line we both knew would change everything.

"I'm fine," he said, but there was no conviction in his voice. It was the kind of fine that wasn't fine at all. The kind of fine that only came with the weight of a thousand unspoken things, and I had a feeling that none of them would be addressed anytime soon.

I wasn't sure what to say next, and I think he could tell. So, he turned and started walking again, slower this time, as though he was giving me space to catch up, but not enough for me to feel like I had a chance to follow. The distance between us felt intentional, and the silence thickened around us, pressing in like the heat of a storm that's just waiting to break.

It wasn't until we reached the edge of the street that he spoke again, his voice quiet, almost reluctant. "I should've told you before. About the theater, I mean." He kicked at a pebble on the sidewalk, watching it skitter across the pavement. "It's—well, it's my place. My escape." He paused, his hand coming up to ruffle his hair, a gesture I recognized as one of frustration. "I don't usually let anyone in. Not like that."

I wasn't sure what to say. The vulnerability in his words caught me off guard, but it wasn't the first time Jonah had surprised me. I had learned quickly that there were layers to him—more than anyone might see at first glance. But now, it felt like I was standing at the edge of something deep and dark, something I wasn't sure I was ready to see.

"You don't have to explain yourself," I said, the words tumbling out before I could stop them. "It's just—"

"Just what?" He turned to face me again, his expression a mixture of exhaustion and something else—something raw and sharp, like he was on the verge of saying too much but was holding back. "What do you think it is? All this—us? You think it's just a... a mistake?"

"No," I said, quickly, the word almost too loud in the quiet between us. I wasn't sure what I was answering, but I knew one thing for certain: this wasn't a mistake. It wasn't a mistake to feel the way I did about him. It wasn't a mistake to want whatever this was to unfold, no matter how complicated or terrifying it seemed. "I don't think it's a mistake."

Jonah took a deep breath, exhaling slowly, as if trying to shake off a weight that had been on him for too long. He didn't look at me when he spoke again, his voice barely above a whisper. "I don't know what this is, but it's not simple. It can't be. Not for me."

I wanted to argue with him, to tell him that it didn't have to be complicated, that maybe he was making it harder than it needed to be. But I didn't. Because, deep down, I knew he was right. Nothing about this was simple, least of all the way my heart felt when he was near. I could pretend it was easy, but it wasn't. There was too much history, too much baggage that both of us carried around like invisible weights.

"Then let's figure it out," I said, my voice steady, even though I could feel the uncertainty creeping in. I wasn't sure how to make sense of any of it, but I knew I didn't want to walk away. Not now. Not when things had started to feel like they were finally falling into place.

Jonah's gaze flickered to me, his lips pulling into a wry smile. It wasn't much, but it was something. "I'm not sure I'm the right person to make things easy."

I let out a small laugh, but it wasn't a laugh of amusement. It was the kind that bubbled up when you weren't sure if you were about to fall or fly. "Trust me," I said. "Neither am I."

The tension between us still hung in the air, thick and undeniable, but for the first time since we'd left the theater, I didn't feel like we were walking in different directions. We were both standing on the same edge, just looking down, unsure of what might be waiting for us on the other side. The only thing that seemed certain was that neither of us was willing to turn away.

By the time we reached the street corner, the late afternoon had bled into a bruised purple, the air rich with the smell of rain that hadn't quite fallen yet. Jonah's hands were shoved back into his pockets, his jaw set in that familiar, determined way. It was the kind of posture that made him look as if he were bracing for something, but I wasn't sure if he was preparing for a storm or just trying to weather the one we'd started between us.

I wasn't sure how I felt about the sudden distance between us. I'd never been someone to shy away from confrontation, but I could tell Jonah wasn't the type who let things unravel too quickly. His control, his stoic façade, was both comforting and maddening. And right now, it felt like a wall I was too stubborn to scale, but not entirely ready to dismantle.

"You want to get coffee?" I asked, the question hanging awkwardly between us, as if it might bridge the chasm or deepen it.

Jonah looked at me, his expression unreadable for a moment. Then he nodded, though there was hesitation in the movement, as if he was waiting for the right words to come out. "Sure," he said, his voice distant, as though he were already somewhere else. "Let's go to that place you like."

The familiarity of the request felt like a lifeline, and I latched onto it, offering him a small, tentative smile in response. "You know it's my favorite because they're the only ones who don't screw up a cappuccino."

"That's one way to choose your spots," Jonah replied with a dry chuckle, though it didn't quite reach his eyes.

We walked in silence toward the café, the kind that had the aesthetic of an artist's dream—quirky, mismatched chairs, dim lighting, and walls covered in abstract art that made you wonder whether the painter had known where he was going when he started. It was cozy and familiar, a sanctuary for both of us, though for different reasons. I came here because it was close, because it was comfortable, and because I didn't have to think too much about why I needed a moment to breathe. Jonah, on the other hand, I wasn't sure about. The way he had suggested it, as if the place held some kind of personal significance for him, made me curious, but I didn't ask. Not yet.

We stepped inside, the warmth wrapping around me like a soft blanket. The scent of fresh coffee mingled with the faint traces of vanilla from the pastries, grounding me. Jonah ordered for both of us, as if this small act of normalcy was enough to restore some balance between us. It wasn't. The tension still clung to my skin, making every breath feel like I was holding something back, waiting for it to slip through my fingers.

The barista called our names, and we moved to the counter. As I took my cappuccino, I felt the weight of Jonah's gaze on me. It was heavy, not in a bad way, but in a way that made me hyperaware of every small shift in the room. He hadn't said a word since we'd walked in, but there was an unspoken question hanging in the air, one that neither of us seemed ready to ask.

"I don't know what you want from me, Jonah," I blurted out before I could stop myself. "But I need to know what's happening here. I need to understand why I can't stop thinking about the way your hand feels in mine, why I keep wondering if there's more between us than just—" I stopped myself, suddenly aware of how raw the words sounded. The coffee cup in my hand felt far too hot, my fingers wrapped tightly around it to keep them from shaking.

Jonah's gaze softened, but only slightly. He studied me for a long moment, his expression unreadable. Finally, he took a slow sip of his own drink, as though buying himself time, letting the silence stretch between us.

"What do you want me to say, Emma?" he asked, his voice quiet but firm, like a challenge wrapped in a question. "You want me to tell you that it's just a bad idea? That we're too messed up to make anything work? Because I can say that. I can tell you it's not worth it. I can tell you it's going to hurt."

My pulse quickened at his words, not from fear, but from the undeniable truth in them. He was right. We were both carrying baggage. We had too much history, too many things unsaid. But that didn't mean I could walk away, not when I was already too far in.

"I didn't ask for a list of reasons why it won't work," I shot back, my words sharp, even though my throat was tight. "I'm asking if you're willing to even try. I'm asking if you're willing to figure out if we're worth it."

Jonah was silent for a beat, his eyes searching mine, like he was trying to read something in me that I wasn't sure I was ready to show. The way he looked at me, as if he could see all the pieces of me that I kept hidden, made my heart stutter. He wasn't just looking at me. He was looking through me.

"You don't get it," he said, his voice low now, almost a whisper. "I can't just be what you need. I'm not that guy."

"And I'm not asking you to be," I said, my voice trembling with a mix of frustration and something softer, something desperate. "I'm just asking for a chance. One chance to see if we can figure this out. Because I can't walk away from it, Jonah. Not now."

The words hung in the air between us, raw and unguarded, like a thread pulling us closer, whether we were ready for it or not.

Jonah set his coffee cup down with a soft clink, his gaze never leaving mine. His lips parted, and for a moment, I thought he was going to say something, something that would either make everything click or break it all apart. But then, just as I thought I had him, the door to the café slammed open, and a rush of cold air swept through the room.

A figure stood in the doorway, their silhouette framed by the light from outside. I couldn't see their face, but the tension in Jonah's body was instant, his posture stiffening, his jaw tightening.

The figure took a step forward, and I felt the hairs on the back of my neck rise. Something had just shifted, and I had no idea what it meant, but I knew, without a doubt, that whatever had been building between Jonah and me was no longer the most pressing concern in the room.

Chapter 9: The Return of Old Ghosts

It wasn't the way she stepped off the sidewalk that caught my attention, nor was it the way her laugh slipped easily into Jonah's ear as if she hadn't been away for years. It was the familiar tilt of her head, that subtle gesture that spoke more than any word could ever hope to. She was the kind of woman who didn't need to ask for attention—she simply commanded it. Her presence lingered like smoke, curling up into the corners of my mind, leaving a taste on the air that felt both sweet and acrid, like honey turning sour on the tongue.

I saw them before they saw me. Jonah's back was turned, and there she stood, as if plucked right out of his past. I hadn't seen her in the flesh before, but I recognized her all the same—her features were more vivid than any photograph. A little older, perhaps, but still achingly beautiful. The kind of beauty that turns heads without even trying. Long, auburn hair framed her face in waves that seemed too perfect to be natural, but that only made it more captivating. Her eyes were dark pools that sucked the light from a room and never gave it back, and when she spoke, her voice was low and smooth, as if every word was crafted with the intention of ensnaring whoever listened.

My heart gave an unexpected lurch, not because I feared she might be a threat—Jonah was mine, or so I told myself—but because she seemed like the kind of woman who could take him away with a single glance. I wasn't entirely sure how to handle the rush of emotions that swept through me. Jealousy, certainly. Anger, yes. But also a strange sense of inadequacy, like I wasn't enough. It was absurd. I wasn't a child. I was an adult with an established career, a life, and a reason to stand tall. So why did I feel like I was shrinking, like I didn't quite belong?

Jonah turned at the sound of her laugh. That easy, familiar laugh. It reached him like a soft breeze, and his face softened in that way I'd seen a thousand times before. But this time it felt different. He didn't just smile—he beamed.

I hated how that smile made my chest ache, like a balloon inflating to the point where it might burst.

He walked toward her with that quick, confident stride of his, the one that always seemed to signal he was at ease in his own skin. He didn't see me standing there, frozen in place, watching him greet her with a warmth that hadn't been reserved for me in months. Maybe longer.

"Lila," he said her name with a quiet reverence that made the hairs on my neck stand up. I swallowed, telling myself to breathe. To think clearly. But everything felt clouded, as though the world were suddenly painted in shades of gray, the colors leaching out of it, leaving me with nothing but the sharp lines of their reunion.

Lila. Her name was soft, lilting even, like a melody he could never quite forget. She stepped forward with a grace that was almost too deliberate, her heels clicking on the cobblestones as if the sound itself had been choreographed. She embraced him briefly—no lingering kiss, nothing inappropriate, just the type of hug that spoke volumes about the history between them. I could almost feel the weight of it, the unspoken words pressing against the spaces between their bodies. The years apart had only made their connection stronger, more effortless. That was clear enough from the way he leaned into her, as if there was no question of where he belonged.

I blinked and stepped back, feeling suddenly out of place in a city I'd once felt so at home in. Paris, the city of romance and endless possibility, had begun to feel like a cage, with the bars slowly closing in around me. I'd always known Jonah had a past—what man didn't?—but seeing it standing in front of me, flesh and bone, was a different matter entirely. There were things I didn't know about him. Things I wasn't sure I wanted to know.

I turned away, giving them a moment of privacy, though I hated myself for it. I could have stayed, watched them, demanded an explanation, but instead I walked. My shoes clicked too loudly on the pavement, the noise grating on my nerves, the echo of my own insecurity ringing in my ears. It was silly. Ridiculous. I was no longer that naive girl who was haunted by every woman from a man's past. But for some reason, with Lila, I couldn't shake the feeling that I was losing him.

I found myself in a small café on a side street, far enough from the river so that the sound of water didn't intrude on my thoughts. I ordered a coffee, though I couldn't say why. I wasn't thirsty, I wasn't hungry, but I needed something to hold in my hands while I tried to sort through the messy knots of emotions coiling in my stomach. My thoughts skittered, unwilling to settle long enough for me to make sense of them. Why did Jonah's past feel like a shadow that had come to life?

The café buzzed with a muted energy as the late afternoon sun filtered through the windows, casting long shadows on the floor. I sat near the back, deliberately out of sight, watching the street outside as I sipped my coffee. And then, in a moment of bitter irony, I saw her.

Lila. She walked past the window, and her gaze flicked through the glass. For just a second, our eyes met, and in that brief exchange, she gave me nothing. No recognition. No challenge. Just a blankness that made my heart skip a beat. And I wondered if she knew exactly what she was doing. If she was aware of the game she was playing with Jonah's heart, or if she had simply returned to Paris because she couldn't help herself.

I wanted to believe Jonah had moved on, that he had chosen me. But the lingering question in my mind remained unanswered: would she draw him back into a past he'd long since outgrown? Or would I be the one left behind?

I tried to ignore the gnawing feeling that had taken root in my chest, but it wasn't as easy as it had been before. I had once believed myself impervious to the sting of jealousy. After all, I had lived a life that required me to build walls around my emotions, to construct safe places where no one could reach me. That had always been the way. Keep everything at arm's length, and I'd be fine. But Lila—she had wormed her way through those walls before I even realized it was happening.

I wasn't sure when Jonah's presence had shifted from a warm comfort to an ache I couldn't quite soothe. It could have been the night we first kissed, or maybe the morning I found him staring out the window, his face lost in a memory I couldn't touch. But now, with Lila back in the picture, the space between us felt wider than ever, and every inch of it seemed to be filled with the heavy weight of unspoken history.

I didn't want to be the type of woman who spent her days worrying about a man's past, especially when I was fully aware of the fragile nature of the bond we were building. But it didn't stop the worry from creeping in, nor the self-doubt that had become an unwelcome companion. I had never felt insecure before Jonah, but in the shadow of his past, I found myself questioning everything. Was I enough? Would he choose me, with all my baggage and imperfections, or was I just a fleeting moment—a distraction to fill the void until something more familiar came along?

I spent the next few days carefully avoiding Lila. Not that it was hard; she had a way of making her presence felt without ever actually making an appearance. Jonah spoke of her sparingly, a few casual mentions here and there, as though he were treading carefully around a topic that might ignite something neither of us were ready to face. I was thankful for that. I didn't need to hear about her, not yet. Not until I figured out what this thing between Jonah and me really was.

But the pull of that ghost—Lila, a name that seemed to haunt every room she entered—was impossible to shake. I found myself wondering about her in ways that were far too consuming. What had she been like? What had Jonah seen in her that had made her different from the rest of the women he had dated?

The Parisian nights were no longer filled with the same excitement, not when every corner seemed to whisper her name. Jonah had become more distant, though in subtle ways. His smiles no longer reached his eyes the way they once did, and there was a quietness to him, a space between us that hadn't existed before. I'd like to think it was just the weight of the city pulling him under, but I knew it had more to do with the return of someone he had once loved deeply. It wasn't a matter of whether he still felt anything for her—it was a matter of what she represented. And I wasn't sure I could compete with that.

I decided to confront him, though I wasn't sure what I expected to find. What I did know was that the uncertainty was driving me mad. The nights spent tossing in bed, tangled in sheets and tangled thoughts, had to stop. I needed to know where I stood, or I would keep circling around this fear until it strangled every part of me.

The chance came one evening when we were sitting in a small bistro off the Rue de la Huchette. The table was set for two, but I felt a strange tension in the air, something between us that hadn't been there before. Jonah was leaning back in his chair, absently toying with the rim of his wine glass, his gaze elsewhere, and I knew it wasn't because the wine was particularly fascinating. I watched his fingers, the way they flexed against the glass, and I felt an inexplicable weight settle over me. I cleared my throat.

"So," I said, trying to keep my tone light, though it trembled with something I couldn't name, "How's she doing?" The words slipped out before I could stop them, and I immediately regretted them.

Jonah looked at me, his eyes searching mine, a flicker of something I couldn't quite place behind them. I thought for a moment that he might apologize, might try to reassure me, but instead, he gave a soft sigh, one that carried all the weight of the years that had passed between them. "Lila's... Lila," he said with a small, rueful smile, as if trying to keep the truth from me but failing. "She's still the same. Still the one who can charm the world, if that's what she wants to do."

I laughed, though it didn't reach my eyes. "Sounds like a charm I'd like to avoid."

Jonah's gaze softened then, and for the first time in what felt like days, his attention was fully on me. "You don't need to worry about her," he said, his voice low and earnest. But his words felt like a balm that had no real healing power.

"I'm not worried," I lied, forcing a smile. "I just... I don't know. It's hard, you know?" I paused, unsure of how to continue, of how to put into words the jealousy that had begun to creep into my veins. "It's hard to watch someone from your past just show up like that. Like nothing's changed."

Jonah leaned forward, his fingers brushing mine across the table, a gesture that felt more comforting than I wanted it to. "Things have changed," he said quietly. "I'm here, with you. Not her. Don't let her become a ghost between us."

His words were sweet, but they did little to settle the restlessness inside me. Lila wasn't just a ghost—she was a living, breathing reminder of a past that Jonah had once embraced, and maybe still did in some way. But no matter how many times he reassured me, I couldn't help but wonder if it was only a matter of time before I became a shadow myself, nothing more than a distraction, a fleeting phase he'd soon forget.

I squeezed his hand, forcing myself to smile despite the fear clawing at my insides. "I just want us to be something real," I said, my voice a little too shaky. "Something that lasts."

He smiled, but I saw the flicker of uncertainty in his eyes before it disappeared. And in that moment, I realized we were both pretending we knew what the future would hold. But in truth, neither of us did. Not with ghosts like Lila hanging in the balance.

I watched Jonah from across the room, the dim light from the candles casting shadows on his face, but no amount of soft glow could mask the tension that lingered between us. We had always been good at filling silences with words, but tonight, neither of us seemed to know what to say. The comfortable ease that had once marked our conversations had vanished, replaced by something sharper, something unspoken.

I shifted in my seat, adjusting the glass of wine in my hand, but the slight clink of it on the table sounded far too loud in the quiet. "You've been distant," I said, my voice barely above a whisper, even though I knew I didn't need to tread lightly anymore. What was the point in pretending there wasn't a crack in the air between us?

Jonah didn't look up at first, his gaze fixed somewhere over my shoulder, as though his thoughts were drifting in a place I could never reach. The tip of his finger traced the rim of his own glass, and for a moment, I wondered if he even realized he was doing it.

"I'm not distant," he finally replied, but the words felt like they were being pulled from him, like they were coated in something thick, something he didn't want to say. "Just... distracted. I'm figuring things out."

"Things?" I echoed, unsure if I wanted the answer. My pulse quickened, and I pressed my lips together to stop them from trembling.

His eyes met mine then, and there was a softness in them that only made everything worse. "You've been distant, too."

I swallowed, the lump in my throat tight and uncomfortable. I had to give him credit—he wasn't wrong. We had both become experts at building walls between us, each of us retreating into our own spaces, trying to make sense of everything that had shifted.

"I'm not distant," I said, a little too quickly. "I'm just... thinking. About things. About us."

He raised an eyebrow, a small smirk playing on his lips, but there was something bitter behind it. "Us. That's what this is about, isn't it? What we are, what we've become."

I felt the sting of his words, the way they made the air around me feel heavier. "It's not a bad thing," I shot back, my words snapping sharper than I'd intended. "What we've become. But it's hard to ignore... her."

Jonah's gaze dropped again, and the familiar tightness in his jaw returned. "Lila."

I nodded, the name like a stone in my mouth. "She doesn't even have to be here to make her presence felt."

Jonah exhaled sharply, as if bracing himself. "You know it's not like that. She's a part of my past, but you... you're my future."

My chest tightened at his words, though I wasn't sure if it was relief or something darker that curled inside me. I wanted to believe him. I did believe him, at least in part. But Lila wasn't just a shadow from his past. She was an answer to a question I hadn't yet learned how to ask. And every time I looked at him, there was a flicker in his eyes—something familiar, something that wasn't meant for me.

I reached for my glass again, taking a sip of wine to calm my nerves, but it didn't help. It never did. The words were right there, bubbling under the surface, and I didn't know how much longer I could hold them back.

"Jonah," I said slowly, "What happens if you can't leave the past behind?" The words tasted bitter as they left my mouth, but I couldn't stop them. "What happens if Lila's pull is too strong?"

His expression shifted, a flash of something—hurt, maybe, or guilt—crossing his face before he masked it again with a look of indifference. "You think I'm going to leave you for her?"

I shook my head, my heart pounding. "I don't know what you're going to do. I don't know what she is going to do. I don't know if I can compete with her ghost."

His hand reached across the table, and I stiffened as his fingers brushed against mine. "You don't have to. You're not competing with her," he said, his voice rough, but there was a desperation in his tone that I hadn't expected. It caught me off guard, and for a moment, I almost believed him.

Almost.

But something in me couldn't let it go. "It's not just her. It's everything that came before her. Everything she represents. All the things you can't seem to let go of."

Jonah's face hardened, and he pulled his hand back, the distance between us growing again. "I don't know what you want me to say," he muttered, his voice tight. "I can't erase my past, but that doesn't mean it controls me. I'm here. With you."

I looked down at my hands, twisting them in my lap, and then forced myself to meet his gaze again. "You're here. But how long will you stay?"

Jonah didn't answer, but the silence between us stretched longer than either of us was comfortable with.

Then, just when I thought the conversation might end in more quiet, his phone buzzed from the pocket of his jacket, sharp and insistent. He glanced at the screen, and I saw his entire demeanor shift, the weight of his past descending over him like a storm cloud.

His fingers hovered over the phone for a moment before he slid it back into his pocket without saying a word.

"Is everything okay?" I asked, a knot forming in my stomach.

He didn't respond immediately. He just sat there, staring at the table.

"I need to go," he said quietly, the words hanging heavy between us. "I'll be back soon. I promise."

Before I could say anything, he stood, his chair scraping the floor, and without another word, he walked out of the bistro, leaving me behind.

And just like that, I was alone again, with the growing feeling that maybe the ghost had come to stay.

Chapter 10: Letters Never Sent

The letters were tucked beneath the floorboards, their yellowed edges curling like delicate petals of a forgotten flower. I hadn't meant to find them, but I suppose there's always something about the past that refuses to stay hidden. They were tucked away in an old wooden box, one I had forgotten about entirely until my foot kicked it while moving a chair across the living room. For a moment, I debated ignoring the box, letting it stay buried where I had left it. But curiosity clawed at me, and I couldn't stop myself from pulling it out, dusting it off, and prying open the fragile lid.

The weight of nostalgia was immediate, and the air in the room thickened as if the past itself had decided to settle in beside me. I pulled the first letter from the stack, its paper soft to the touch, worn in a way that made me feel like I was touching a memory more than anything tangible. The words, scribbled hastily as though I feared the ink might run out, were mine. I recognized the messy scrawl—the kind of handwriting you never let anyone else see. The words were raw, angry, and vulnerable all at once. And they were all meant for Jonah.

I closed my eyes for a moment, bracing myself as if I were about to step into a room where every single piece of me had once lived and breathed. Jonah. The name alone was a knife in my side. He had been my everything, or at least, I had let him be. For years, I had told myself that I was better off without him, but reading these letters now, I realized how much of him had stayed with me, embedded like a tattoo I could never erase.

The letter began simply, a mess of sentences strung together with the kind of intensity that only youth can produce:

"Jonah, I'm angry with you. I think I've always been angry with you. But it's not because of what you did. No, it's because of what you didn't do. You didn't fight for me, and that's something I'll never forgive you for. I can't let go of you, even though I know I should. Even now, when I should be over it. Over you. But I'm not. I don't know how to be."

I stopped reading for a second, my heart thumping in my chest. My anger at him, my grief for what we had lost, all of it came rushing back. The way he had kissed me under the stars and promised me a future—one that never came to pass. I didn't even know how to mourn him properly. Our goodbye had been nothing more than a quiet phone call on a Tuesday morning, the words spoken without meaning, because neither of us truly knew how to end something so beautiful and broken.

I grabbed another letter. This one, written in a slightly more composed tone, made my chest ache with a familiar longing. I could almost hear Jonah's voice in my head, the way he would talk when he wasn't sure of what to say but still tried anyway.

"I don't know how to tell you that I miss you. How can I miss someone who is supposed to be in my past? It's been too long, and I don't have the words for what I feel anymore. Maybe it's because I'm afraid of what might happen if I tell you the truth. Maybe I'm afraid of loving you again."

The vulnerability in his words, the hesitation, made me ache in places I thought had long healed. I ran my fingers over the edges of the paper, my breath catching in my throat as I read those lines again, this time with the clarity of someone who had already lived through the story. Jonah had loved me, I knew that now. But he had been afraid, terrified of the future we could have had, and too blind to see how the past was chaining us both.

I didn't realize I was crying until I felt the warm tears drop onto the paper, soaking into the ink, blurring the edges of his confession. I couldn't help it. Maybe it was because reading these letters had torn me open in ways I hadn't expected. Maybe it was because, in the time since, I had learned to live without him—only to realize that I had never really let him go.

The letters kept coming. There was one after another, all of them different versions of the same message: confusion, regret, hope, pain. I read them all, each one pulling me deeper into the maze of what could have been. There were no answers, only questions that had lingered for too long.

By the time I reached the last letter, the evening was slipping away, the candle beside me flickering in the dim light. The words on the page were almost too much to bear:

"I don't know how to write this without sounding like a fool, but here it is anyway. I never stopped loving you. I don't know if you'll ever read this, and I don't know if you'll even care if you do. But I need to tell you, even if it's too late. You were my first love. My only love. And I've never stopped thinking about you. Maybe I never will."

I could feel the weight of those words in my chest, like a brick had settled inside, too heavy to lift. I had moved on, or at least, I had convinced myself I had. I had told myself over and over again that Jonah was just a chapter in my life, a part of me that had faded with time. But here, in the flickering candlelight, it was impossible to deny the truth any longer.

I didn't want to leave these words behind, a ghost of the love we once shared. So, I did the only thing I could think to do. I lit the last letter on fire, watching it curl and burn, the smoke rising in delicate spirals until it was nothing but ash. And as the flame consumed the paper, I made a decision that felt both terrifying and necessary: this time, I wouldn't let the past remain silent. I would tell him. Tell Jonah everything. No more hiding. No more regret.

The letters were gone now. And with them, so was the weight of everything I had kept buried.

The decision hung in the air, heavy and undeniable. In the hours since the last letter had turned to smoke, I had let the silence around me grow thick, each second pulsing with the weight of unspoken words. Paris had softened the edges of who I was, or so I had convinced myself. The city's constant hum, the subtle brush of its ancient history against my life, had made me believe I could outrun my past. But there was no outrunning Jonah. Not now, not when I had seen the words he never said, the things he had buried the same way I had.

I stood by the window now, looking out over the rooftops, watching the evening light fade into the velvet of night. It was a familiar scene, one that had once been comforting in its steadiness. But tonight, it felt like a promise of change, something in the air electric and poised, waiting for the first spark.

I had promised myself that I wouldn't leave this unsaid. The problem, of course, was that the courage to reach out to Jonah had always been a fickle thing. It was there, lurking beneath the surface, bold in moments of defiance, then gone the moment doubt crept in. And doubt always did.

I had told myself for years that we were better off without each other. He was better off. I was better off. I had built a life that didn't require him—my own apartment, my own world of small joys, quiet mornings with coffee that tasted like comfort, afternoons where I could wander the streets of Paris without fear of being stopped in my tracks by a familiar face. I had even gotten good at pretending that I no longer needed the echoes of Jonah's laughter in the back of my mind.

But tonight, as I stood there, the city lights blinking like distant stars, I realized that maybe that wasn't true. Maybe I wasn't better off without him. Maybe I had just built a world without him out of fear. Fear that I'd never be enough for him. That he'd slip away again, like sand between my fingers. That maybe we weren't supposed to have forever. But I had to know.

I reached for my phone, my fingers trembling slightly as I scrolled through my contacts. There he was, at the top of the list, his name so familiar it burned, a ghost of an old life. My heart stuttered, my thumb hovering over his name. How does one begin after all this time? How do you just pick up where you left off, as if no years had passed, no painful goodbyes whispered in the shadows?

I sighed and put the phone down again. This was absurd. There was no script for this. I had no idea how to say what I wanted to say without sounding like a fool. It had been so long, so much had changed, and the thought of hearing his voice again—of hearing him tell me how much he'd missed me—felt like a dream too fragile to touch.

But then, the letters came back to me. The words I had written, raw and unfiltered. I could do this. If I could write them, if I could pour out my heart onto paper, then surely I could find a way to say it all to him.

I pulled out my laptop, the keys clicking beneath my fingers as I began to type. I didn't bother with an introduction or any formalities. There was no need for that. This wasn't a business letter or a polite note. It was my heart, laid bare.

"Jonah, I don't know why I waited so long to write to you, or maybe I do. Maybe it's because I've been afraid of what it would mean if I let you back in. Afraid of how much I would need you, how much I would want you again. But I miss you. I miss you in ways I never thought possible. I've spent years pretending that I didn't, but I was only fooling myself."

I paused, running my fingers through my hair as I read over the words. Too much? Not enough? Was I laying it on too thick? I shook my head. I couldn't second-guess myself now. The words had been buried too long for me to edit them now.

"There are so many things I never said, things I buried deep because I thought that was the right thing to do. But I'm tired of pretending. I'm tired of living in the 'what-ifs' and 'maybes.' You were the best part of my life. And even though I've learned how to live without you, there's still this empty space. You were always supposed to be part of it."

The screen in front of me blurred, my eyes stinging with sudden tears. I wiped them away quickly, frustrated at how easily the past could still slip through the cracks of my composure.

"I don't know where you are now, what your life looks like, but I can't keep pretending that I don't care. I think of you every day. I think of you when I pass by the little café where we used to meet, and I think of you when I'm walking along the Seine at dusk, and I hear the music coming from the bars by the river. Every song feels like it's meant for us, and it breaks my heart all over again."

I let out a breath, the words spilling faster now as the weight of the past lifted just a little bit. I wasn't just writing to Jonah; I was writing to the girl I used to be, the one who had loved so completely that she had forgotten how to protect herself. I was writing to the woman I was now, the one who had learned that the heart doesn't break once; it breaks over and over again, until you're left with nothing but the shattered pieces.

"I don't expect anything from you. I don't even know if I want a response. But I needed you to know. I needed you to know that I've never stopped loving you, and that I always will. Even if we never see each other again, even if our lives have taken us down separate paths. You will always be part of me."

I hit send before I could change my mind.

The next few hours were an exercise in self-inflicted anxiety, and my mind seemed to race in circles, the buzz of Paris outside my window competing with the frantic thrum in my chest. I had sent the email, but I hadn't expected the immediate weight of it to feel so unbearable. Why had I done it? Why hadn't I just kept those damn letters buried in the past, where they belonged? Was I out of my mind? I had spent years convincing myself that Jonah was just a chapter in my life, a brief but beautiful distraction, and that I was better off without him.

But the truth settled into my bones as soon as I pressed "send." I wasn't better off. I was empty.

I stood up abruptly, pacing the apartment as if I could outpace the doubt that gnawed at me. The city outside looked different now—every corner, every shadow seemed to hum with possibility and dread all at once. I could still feel the faint heat of the candle flame against my fingertips, could still smell the burnt paper lingering in the air like a faint perfume. I tried to shake off the feeling, but it clung to me. My chest was tight, my breath shallow, like the calm before a storm that I knew was coming.

The hours passed. Time seemed to stretch and contract as I waited for any sign that Jonah had received my message. I tried to focus on anything else, from the half-finished bottle of wine on my counter to the odd assortment of books lining my shelves—none of them could distract me long enough to keep my mind from racing. How had he changed? What was he doing now? I couldn't even remember the last time I heard his voice, his laughter. Had it been a lifetime ago, or just yesterday?

When the email notification finally pinged in the corner of my screen, I froze, staring at it as if it might bite me. For a long moment, I didn't open it. Instead, I let my finger hover above the mouse, my thoughts tumbling into the void. Was this a mistake? What was I even hoping for? A reunion? Closure? Apology? Did I even deserve any of it?

I clicked.

The message was short. So short, in fact, it almost felt like a slap. Just four words, but those four words shook me more than the entire weight of the years between us.

"I never stopped loving you."

I blinked, once, twice, wondering if I was reading it wrong, if my mind had played some cruel trick on me. But no, there it was—uncomplicated, honest, and achingly raw.

"I never stopped loving you."

I closed my eyes, trying to push the flood of emotions away, but they rushed at me anyway, a relentless tide that swept through my chest. I hadn't expected him to write back so soon, and I certainly hadn't expected words so heavy. I had prepared myself for indifference, maybe even for some bitterness, but this? This felt like a sharp blow, like he had taken the weight of our unfinished business and dropped it into my lap without warning. Now, I had to face it.

I let out a breath, clicking open the message to respond, but my fingers didn't move. There was nothing I could say in that moment that wouldn't feel like a betrayal of everything I had promised myself over the years. I had already opened the door to the past, and now I wasn't sure I could close it again.

I stood up abruptly, the chair scraping noisily against the wooden floor, my hands trembling with the need to do something, anything, to shake off the overwhelming emotions that seemed to pull me under. The windowsill called to me, and I found myself walking towards it, leaning against the cool glass as I looked out over the city that felt both so distant and so immediate. The faint sound of traffic, the distant hum of chatter from nearby cafés, all of it settled over me like a blanket, and for a moment, it felt as though I was completely alone in the world.

I wanted to forget everything—Jonah, the letters, the past. But I couldn't. Not anymore.

There was a knock at the door.

It wasn't just any knock. It wasn't the polite rapping of a neighbor or a deliveryman. No, this knock had a sense of urgency to it, a rhythm I immediately recognized, even before I opened the door. My heart skipped a beat, then hammered against my chest as I stood there, paralyzed for a moment by the sound. My brain didn't even have time to register what was happening before the door swung open, and there he was.

Jonah.

I blinked, unable to process what I was seeing. He was standing there, looking just as I remembered, but somehow, impossibly more real. His hair was a little longer, more windswept, and the lines around his eyes were deeper, as though he had spent the last several years trying to make sense of his own heart, just as I had tried to make sense of mine. His eyes met mine, and for a moment, the world outside disappeared. There was only the two of us, standing in the doorway of my apartment, as if no time had passed at all.

"Hi," he said, his voice rough, as though the word itself had been a long time coming. "I thought you should know... I never stopped loving you."

I swallowed, my mouth suddenly dry. It felt like the entire universe was holding its breath, waiting for me to say something, anything, that might break the fragile tension between us. But I couldn't find the words.

Before I could speak, Jonah took a step forward, his presence overwhelming in the small space of the apartment. My heart thudded loudly in my chest, and I felt myself instinctively retreat. It wasn't that I didn't want him here, but the emotions, the years of wanting him and pushing him away... it was too much.

"I wasn't expecting you," I said, my voice barely above a whisper.

"I know." Jonah's gaze softened. "But I think we need to talk. Really talk."

I opened my mouth to respond, but then—just as quickly—something shifted in the room. The door creaked.

Chapter 11: Unmasking the Heart

The cool breeze brushed my cheeks as I waited at the edge of the old stone bridge, the Seine glittering below in the soft afternoon light. The sound of water, like a whispered secret, drifted up from the river, and I closed my eyes for a moment, allowing the rhythm of the current to calm the restless knot in my chest. Jonah was late—he often was—but I didn't mind. Not today. Today, I had enough weight in my heart to drown an ocean, and the last thing I needed was company to share that burden before I was ready to unburden myself.

When I opened my eyes, he was there, stepping out of the shadow of the trees with the easy grace that had always seemed to come so naturally to him. His dark hair ruffled by the wind, his brown eyes glinting with some thought I couldn't quite place. I remembered the way he used to look at me—like I was the center of his world, and for a time, I had convinced myself that I was.

"Had you forgotten what time it is?" I said, half-smiling. The edge of sarcasm was intentional, a shield. If I didn't speak first, he might do what he always did—shift the conversation to something trivial and safe. I couldn't let that happen today.

Jonah's mouth quirked at the corner. "I thought I'd leave the timing to you," he said, stepping closer. "It's your world, remember?"

I didn't laugh. I just shook my head, turning away and looking out at the river again. "Maybe," I said quietly. "But not anymore."

A small silence fell between us, one that stretched and coiled tighter, suffocating me with every passing second. His presence felt so familiar, like the warmth of a blanket you no longer wanted but kept wrapped around you out of habit. The smell of his cologne—spicy, woody, like rain on dry earth—tugged at memories I'd buried deep, and for a moment, I wondered if I could just ask him to leave, let the ghosts of what we were settle where they belonged.

But I had never been good at avoiding confrontation, and today, the truth had teeth.

"You've been avoiding me," he said, his voice surprisingly soft, like he knew something was coming. Jonah never had to raise his voice to make me listen. It had always been his power over me, and we both knew it.

I took a breath, steeling myself for the words that had been crowding my chest. "I'm not avoiding you. I've just been trying to figure out how to say it."

He raised an eyebrow, his hands slipping into the pockets of his coat. "Say what?"

I met his gaze then, trying to read the calm that radiated from him—an effortless ease that still held me in its grip, despite everything that had happened. "I'm not the same person you left behind, Jonah. I haven't been for a long time."

A flicker of something crossed his face—pain, regret, maybe even hope. But it was gone too quickly for me to hold on to. "Is this about..."

"Yes," I interrupted, cutting off whatever vague trail he was going down. "It's about everything. It's about us, and what we were, and what we never could be. And it's about the fact that no matter how much I try to lie to myself, I'm still in love with you."

The words spilled out of me like a dam bursting—so fast, so sudden, that they left me breathless and shaky, as though I had never once spoken them aloud. I watched Jonah's face as I said it, watching for the flinch or the recoil that would confirm what I already knew—that I was just another chapter in his past, one he had long since closed.

But Jonah didn't flinch. His expression, however, was unreadable. He took a step closer, close enough now that I could feel the warmth of his body against the coolness of the air, close enough to smell the faintest trace of whiskey on his breath. He opened his mouth to speak, then closed it again, as though searching for the right thing to say.

"I don't know what to say to that," he confessed, his voice rough, raw. "You never said anything like this before. You always just... moved on."

"Maybe I didn't know how to say it then," I said, shaking my head as I stared at the river, desperate to hold onto my composure. "Maybe I was too scared, too proud. But I can't keep pretending anymore. You were my everything, Jonah. Even after all this time. And now—now it's too late."

A beat passed, heavy with the weight of everything unsaid. Jonah didn't look away, but I could see the confusion, the conflict flickering behind his eyes. His lips parted once more, but this time, when he spoke, it was not with the easy confidence I was used to. "It's never too late, not for us."

I shook my head, finally turning to face him fully, allowing my gaze to meet his. There was a pain in me, but it was no longer a quiet ache—it was a fierce thing, raw and unforgiving. "It is. It has to be. Because you left me once, Jonah. You didn't just walk away—you ran. And I was too stubborn to follow. Too proud to ask you to stay." My voice cracked on the last part, but I held his eyes, daring him to deny it.

For a long time, Jonah just stood there, his expression unreadable, as if weighing my words. But then, to my surprise, his mouth softened, and he exhaled a sharp breath.

"You think I ran?" His voice was a low murmur, almost like he was talking to himself. "You think I walked away from you?"

I opened my mouth to respond, but my throat was suddenly tight, my words stuck, as if they were tangled in the spaces between us, waiting to be set free.

Jonah's eyes held mine with an intensity that made the air between us feel charged, like the kind of electric hum you feel when you're standing too close to something volatile, just waiting for a spark. I had always thought I knew him, or at least, I thought I could read him as easily as I could a novel I'd read a dozen times. But in that moment, I realized how utterly wrong I had been. There was a quiet strength behind his gaze now, something deeper than the easy charm he used to wear like armor, and it made my chest tighten in ways I didn't know how to handle.

"You left," I repeated, my voice softer now, no longer accusing, but hollow with the weight of the truth. "You walked away. You don't get to pretend it didn't happen, Jonah."

His jaw tightened, and for the first time, I saw the tiniest crack in his composure. A flicker of regret? Shame? Maybe both. But instead of responding immediately, he took a step back, letting the distance grow between us, and ran a hand through his hair, like he was trying to physically shake off a memory.

"I didn't run," he said slowly, each word measured, careful. "I stayed longer than I should have. Because I knew—knew that if I didn't walk away then, I would've stayed forever. And you would've hated me for it."

I blinked, the ground beneath me suddenly feeling less stable, like a hidden chasm had opened up beneath the surface. "What? Why would I have hated you for that? For staying?" The confusion in my voice was unmistakable. I couldn't make sense of his words, couldn't connect them to the man I'd known, the man I'd been in love with.

Jonah's eyes darkened, but there was no anger in them. Just a weary sorrow, a kind of resignation I hadn't seen from him before. "Because, Tessa," he said, his voice low, almost fragile, "I wasn't who you thought I was. And I knew that if I stayed, you would've eventually seen it. I couldn't—no, I wouldn't let you do that to yourself."

I felt the words like a physical blow. "What are you talking about?" My breath caught in my throat, and I almost stumbled backward, grasping for something to steady myself. His revelation, or whatever it was, wasn't making sense. How could the man I had loved—who I had believed was as real as the earth beneath my feet—suddenly become a stranger?

Jonah met my gaze with a tenderness that felt like a lie. "I was a coward, Tessa. And I knew you deserved more than the version of me I was willing to give. You deserved someone who could give you all of themselves, without hesitation, without fear of ruining everything."

I stared at him, my mouth dry, unable to find the words that could undo the sting of his confession. The wind swept across the bridge, ruffling the edges of my coat, and for a long, unbearable moment, we both stood there in silence, trying to make sense of the pieces of us that had shattered.

I should have felt something—anger, perhaps. Or maybe disbelief. Instead, I felt hollow, like a vast, empty cavern had opened up in my chest, and all the emotions I had been carrying for years had just poured into it, leaving me cold and empty.

"So, what? You thought that if you disappeared, I would just forget about you? Like some kind of... fairy tale where the prince vanishes and the princess forgets his name?" My voice was rising now, and I couldn't stop it. I had been drowning in these emotions for far too long, and they were spilling out like a flood.

Jonah's expression softened, his lips curling into a faint, bittersweet smile. "No," he said, almost to himself. "I thought you'd hate me. I thought you'd be better off without me. I couldn't give you the life you wanted. The life you deserved."

I shook my head, my thoughts a tangled mess, and took a step toward him, though it felt like the hardest thing I'd ever done. "You're still doing it," I said, my voice shaking with frustration. "You're still running from me. You don't get to decide that for me,

Jonah. You don't get to tell me what I deserve. That's not your choice."

He flinched, like my words had struck him with a force he hadn't expected. And for the first time in what felt like an eternity, he looked small, vulnerable—like the man who had once loved me so fiercely had vanished entirely, leaving behind a version of him I didn't recognize.

"I didn't want to hurt you," he whispered. His voice cracked, raw with emotion. "I was afraid. Afraid of being everything you needed and then failing. Afraid of not being enough."

I didn't know what to say to that. How could I answer a man who had spent years running from his own fears, leaving me to pick up the pieces of a broken heart? How could I reassure him when I felt just as lost as he was?

"You're not a failure," I finally said, my voice steadier now, though the sting of his words still burned in my chest. "You never were. But you walked away anyway. And I couldn't—" I stopped myself, unsure of how to finish the sentence. How could I possibly explain the years of wondering, of waiting for him to come back, only to realize that I had built a life without him? How could I tell him that I had convinced myself that maybe I didn't need him after all?

Jonah's gaze dropped to the ground, his shoulders sagging. "I never wanted to leave you," he said, the words barely audible, like he was speaking to the air, to the river, to everything but me. "But maybe leaving was the only thing I could do, because I wasn't strong enough to stay."

The tears stung at the back of my eyes, but I refused to let them fall. Not now. Not after everything he had just said. "Well, I'm not waiting anymore," I said, forcing the words out with a finality I didn't quite feel. "You can't just walk back into my life and expect everything to be the same."

For a long moment, Jonah didn't speak. Instead, he reached into his pocket and pulled out a crumpled piece of paper, something I hadn't expected. He unfolded it slowly, as if it was something fragile, something precious. When he looked back at me, his expression was unreadable, but there was something dangerous in his eyes—something that made my heart race, despite myself.

"You should read this," he said, holding out the paper to me. His hands trembled just slightly, and I realized with a sudden, jarring clarity that this moment, whatever it was, was about to change everything.

The paper trembled in my hands, as if the words it held were somehow more dangerous than I was prepared for. Jonah's gaze didn't waver, though his mouth had gone tight, the lines around his eyes deepening, like he was bracing for something neither of us could control. The air between us felt dense now, too thick to cut through, and I hesitated, that ever-present doubt rising in my throat. What if I wasn't ready for what this piece of paper had to say? What if it shattered whatever fragile semblance of understanding we had left?

But I had asked for the truth, hadn't I? More than that, I had demanded it.

"You said you didn't want to hurt me," I said, my voice a little too sharp, a little too desperate. "So, what is this? Is this going to make it worse?"

Jonah's eyes flicked down to the paper, then back to me. "I don't know," he said softly. "But you deserve to know."

The words struck me harder than I expected, like a punch to the gut. I had spent years convincing myself that what we'd had wasn't worth salvaging, that I was better off moving on, even as I carried him with me everywhere, even in the spaces where I didn't want him. And yet here he was, giving me a choice that felt like an unspoken invitation to either dive deeper or walk away for good.

I took the paper from his hands, unfolding it with trembling fingers. The ink was smudged in places, like it had been carried around for far too long, constantly shifting between pockets and bags, never meant to see the light of day until now. I read the first line, then the second, then the third—each word bleeding into the next, pulling me deeper into a story I had never known, one that twisted itself around the core of everything I thought I knew about Jonah.

"I—" I stopped myself, my breath catching in my throat. The words felt foreign, like they were being written not by him but by someone else entirely. I couldn't reconcile the man I had loved with the one who had written these words. How could I?

Jonah's voice broke through the confusion. "It's a letter I wrote years ago, when I thought I was going to lose you for good."

I swallowed hard, reading the lines again. This time, the meaning hit with the force of a thunderclap, and I felt the ground shift beneath me. He had written this letter with the intention of telling me everything—everything he had never said. The things he had kept locked away because he didn't believe I would understand.

But I understood now.

The words on the paper weren't just confessions. They were apologies. Regrets. They were him, raw and stripped of the bravado he'd always worn like armor. I could almost hear his voice, shaking and uncertain, as if he were standing beside me, reading it aloud. It was so personal, so intimate, I almost wanted to crumple the paper and throw it into the river, to drown it and pretend I never saw it.

Instead, I folded the paper neatly, my hands steady despite the maelstrom inside me. "You wrote this?" I asked, my voice quieter than I intended. "For me?"

Jonah nodded, his eyes dark with something I couldn't quite place. "I thought I was running out of time. That I had to say everything before I lost you for good. But by the time I was ready, I had already convinced myself that it was too late. That I had waited too long."

A bitter laugh bubbled in my throat, but I swallowed it down, my mind racing. "You're telling me this now? After everything? After years of silence?"

Jonah's face hardened, his jaw clenching as he turned away, like he couldn't bear to look at me anymore. "I know," he said, his voice tight. "I know it's too late for apologies. But this—this is the truth. The one thing I've never been able to give you."

For a moment, we both stood there in the shadow of our past, the Seine flowing beneath us like an ancient witness to everything we had been and everything we had lost. The sound of the water, usually soothing, now felt like a steady reminder of time we couldn't get back, of chances we had missed.

I wanted to ask him why. Why had he stayed away? Why hadn't he fought for me? But the questions felt too heavy, like they were questions I wasn't prepared to answer myself, let alone ask him.

I folded the paper back into a neat square, then handed it back to him. "What do you want me to do with this, Jonah?"

He took the letter from me, his fingers brushing mine, and for a brief, painful moment, I let myself remember what it felt like to be close to him—to feel the warmth of his touch, the comfort of his presence. But then it was gone, just as quickly as it had come.

"I don't expect anything from you," he said, his voice rough. "I just needed you to know."

I nodded, though I wasn't sure what I knew anymore. "It's a lot to take in."

He smiled, though it wasn't a happy one. "Yeah. It is."

Another silence stretched between us, this one heavier than the last, filled with unspoken words and shattered dreams. Finally, I looked at Jonah, really looked at him, and saw the man who had once been my whole world—so full of hope and promise—and I wondered how much of him was still here, buried beneath the layers of regret.

"What happens now?" I asked, my voice barely above a whisper.

He didn't answer right away. Instead, he turned away from me, staring out over the river, his expression unreadable. I couldn't tell if he was fighting back emotions, or if he simply didn't know the answer to my question.

And then, just when I thought he was about to speak, when I thought he might finally break the silence that had haunted us both for so long, he looked back at me with a mixture of fear and resolve in his eyes.

"I can't tell you what comes next," he said, his voice low and steady. "But I can tell you one thing—"

Before he could finish, a sharp cry split the air, and in that instant, everything changed.

Chapter 12: The Bridge Between Us

The sun was still a hesitant glow behind the ancient rooftops, casting a pale, golden hue that seemed too shy to fully embrace the city. Paris had the ability to look different at every hour of the day, yet it never failed to captivate. The streets were barely stirring, the promise of life just on the edge of waking. But I knew I would remember this moment, even if I could never quite piece it together into something coherent. My mind, like the morning air, was clouded with uncertainty.

Jonah was already there when I stepped onto the bridge, his figure outlined in the soft light. The Seine flowed beneath us, so quiet and slow as if it too was holding its breath. The cobblestones beneath our feet felt uneven, the bridge creaking softly in the silence that hung between us. I had been expecting this moment for days, weeks, maybe even longer, and yet now that it was here, I was unsure of how to approach it.

"You're late," he said, the edges of his lips lifting slightly, a playful tilt to his voice that suggested he wasn't quite as serious as his eyes told me. The words were easy, but I could hear the tightness behind them, the undercurrent of everything unsaid.

I couldn't help the smile that tugged at my mouth. "You're early. I'm just fashionably late."

Jonah laughed quietly, the sound mixing with the soft murmur of the river below. He reached up to adjust the collar of his jacket, the movement almost too calculated, like he was trying to pretend that the tension between us wasn't obvious, even in the chill of the morning.

"I didn't think you'd show up," he said after a moment, his voice turning a little softer. "I wasn't sure if you'd... what's the word? Run? Disappear?" He met my gaze then, his eyes not hiding the vulnerability that he usually tried to keep behind that sardonic smile.

The world felt smaller in that instant, like the bridge between us was nothing but a fragile thread. "And yet, here I am," I said, the words coming out in a whisper I didn't expect. I was aware of the way the cool air skimmed over my skin, the sudden realization that every small thing around us—the birds beginning to chirp in the distance, the faint rustle of wind through the trees—seemed to hinge on this conversation.

He turned to face me fully then, his gaze steady, unwavering. "You've been running from this," Jonah said, his voice dropping lower, serious now. The playfulness was gone, replaced by something I couldn't quite name. "I've seen it. Felt it, even. I've tried to tell myself that it's just... this thing between us—this pull. But it's not just a pull, is it?" He paused, and I watched as his breath formed mist in the air, hanging there before dissipating.

I swallowed, the space between us narrowing. "You don't have to do this." My voice betrayed me, cracking in the middle of the sentence like I was fighting to hold back something larger, more consuming.

Jonah's expression softened, but he didn't look away. "I think I do."

And there it was—the thing neither of us had dared to voice, the thing that had always lingered, unspoken but never ignored. The way we were both too afraid to acknowledge it, too afraid to let ourselves fully feel it. The bridge beneath our feet felt like the last safe place, the last moment before everything changed.

"You want me to say it out loud, don't you?" I said, my words coming out sharp, but not with anger. It was something else, something I couldn't quite understand.

Jonah took a step forward, the air between us thickening with every inch that closed. "You think I want you to say it?" His voice was low now, a little gruff, a little more raw. "I don't need you to say anything. I just need you to stop pretending that you don't feel it too."

The words hung there, like they belonged to another world, another version of me, the version I tried to avoid but couldn't anymore. I felt my heart stutter in my chest, the weight of everything pushing down on me in a way that almost made me want to retreat.

The hesitation was there, thick as fog, clouding my thoughts, but then he did the thing that made it impossible to ignore. He reached out, the warmth of his hand finding mine before I even realized he was moving. The touch was gentle but insistent, and when our fingers brushed, the jolt of it shot straight through me, breaking through every wall I'd carefully built.

Jonah was close enough now that I could see the small lines at the corners of his eyes, the ones that appeared when he smiled, and even the faint shadow of stubble on his jaw. I didn't know how to explain it, but in that moment, I couldn't imagine a life where I didn't see those small things every day.

"I don't know how to do this," I said, the words tumbling out before I could stop them. "I don't know how to fix... whatever this is."

Jonah's grip on my hand tightened, and his voice softened. "We don't have to fix it. We just have to stop pretending it's not there."

The bridge beneath our feet groaned softly, but the world around us was still—suspended in the delicate space between everything we had been and everything we could be. The air between us, thick with unspoken truths, shimmered as the first rays of sun touched the water, sending a ripple across the surface. It felt like a kind of quiet surrender, but the kind I didn't mind. Not when Jonah was standing here, his hand in mine, offering me something I wasn't sure I was ready to take.

But that didn't stop me from wanting to.

His hand felt warm against mine, a contrast to the crisp morning air that tugged at the edges of my coat. For a moment, neither of us moved, as though the very act of stepping forward could shatter the delicate space between us. The sound of the river was soothing, but the thoughts in my head were anything but calm. Jonah's fingers tightened around mine just slightly, and the warmth of his touch seemed to wrap itself around me like a blanket, stirring a flutter of something I wasn't sure I was ready to feel.

"You make it sound so easy," I said, my voice quieter now, soft as if I were afraid to break the fragile moment. My gaze dropped to our hands, the way they were perfectly intertwined, as if they had always belonged there, as if I'd always known the exact shape of his fingers.

He let out a small, surprised laugh. "Nothing about this feels easy to me. Trust me." His thumb brushed against the back of my hand, and the gesture was almost too intimate for the space we were in—too personal for the fragile thread that connected us.

We stood there for a moment longer, a silence hanging between us that was anything but awkward. It was heavy, charged, full of all the things we had yet to say. The soft hum of the city in the distance was at odds with the stillness of our small world, as if the universe had paused, watching, waiting for us to make a decision.

"So what now?" I finally asked, breaking the silence, not sure what I expected the answer to be, but knowing I couldn't leave it unanswered.

Jonah's smile was small, thoughtful, as though he'd been expecting the question but didn't have an immediate answer. "Now we stop pretending that we're fine. That this—" He gestured between us with his free hand, "—isn't something we can just walk away from."

I swallowed hard, trying to ignore the knot in my throat. The idea of walking away had always seemed so simple, so logical. And yet, standing here with him, the weight of that decision felt like it could crush me. I wanted to say something, something smart and sharp to break the tension, but the words stuck in my throat.

"You're really not going to let me off the hook, are you?" I asked, my attempt at humor coming out with more breathlessness than I intended.

Jonah's grin deepened, and his eyes twinkled with a teasing light. "Not even a little bit. You know me better than that."

I should have pulled away right then. Should have laughed it off and stepped back into the safety of distance. But instead, I found myself drawn closer, the pull between us undeniable, like the current of the river beneath us—strong, relentless, and impossible to ignore.

"Jonah," I said his name softly, almost as if I was testing it out on my tongue, trying to figure out how to say the rest. I could feel my heart pounding in my chest, each beat reverberating through me in a way that made it impossible to think clearly. "You're asking for something I don't know how to give. Something I can't give—not like this. Not when it feels like everything else is so broken."

Jonah's gaze softened, his thumb continuing its slow, soothing motion against my skin. "Nothing about us is broken. It just feels that way because we're too afraid to see the whole picture." He paused, his eyes searching mine. "I'm not asking you to fix anything, Lia. I'm asking you to stop running. To see us, and maybe... just maybe, let us be something we've never had the courage to be."

I pulled my hand back slowly, more from instinct than intent, needing space, needing time to breathe, to make sense of what he was saying. The words were so simple, so raw, but they carried weight that made my chest ache. He was right, of course. I'd been running for so long, from him, from this, from the possibility of us. I'd convinced myself that it was easier to bury it, to pretend it didn't exist, than to face the truth of how much it hurt to even think about what might have been.

The sound of footsteps echoed behind us, sharp against the stone of the bridge, reminding me that the world was still turning, that Paris was still waking up, indifferent to the little dramas playing out on its streets. A couple walked past, their laughter light and easy, a stark contrast to the heaviness that hung between Jonah and me. The mundane reminder hit me like a splash of cold water.

"You think I'm ready for this?" I asked, the question slipping out before I could stop it. "I'm not sure I am."

Jonah didn't flinch at the doubt in my voice. "You don't have to be ready. You just have to stop being afraid." His tone was gentle, yet insistent, like he was guiding me through a door I'd been too frightened to open. "I can't do this alone, Lia. I need you to meet me halfway."

The words hit me harder than I'd expected. The thought of meeting him halfway—of giving myself up to this, to us—was terrifying. But for the first time, the fear didn't feel paralyzing. It felt like a call to action. A challenge. And maybe I needed to face it head-on.

I took a deep breath, the cool air filling my lungs, and when I exhaled, I realized that I hadn't been breathing properly in a long time. Not really. Not since the first time I'd met Jonah, not since this thing between us had started to take root. Maybe he was right. Maybe this was what I'd been running from all along—what I was meant to face, even if it scared me more than I was willing to admit.

"You make it sound so simple," I said, my voice a little shaky but determined.

Jonah's eyes softened, the intensity of his gaze never wavering. "It is simple. You just have to take the first step."

I didn't know if I was ready, but I did know one thing—I didn't want to stand here forever, stuck in the silence. And for the first time in a long while, I was beginning to think that maybe it was time to stop running.

The wind picked up slightly, sending a playful chill through the air, rustling the leaves of the trees along the banks of the Seine. My mind was spinning, the sharpness of the moment pulling me in every direction. The softness of Jonah's hand in mine felt like a tether, a connection I didn't know I needed until now. His touch was a quiet promise, but the promise of what, exactly? The future? A chance at something real?

I blinked against the rising sun, my gaze drifting to the shimmering water below. For a moment, I wondered if it could all be as simple as Jonah was making it out to be. Maybe, just maybe, I could take that first step, forget the past and the tangled mess of feelings I had spent so long running from. Maybe we could really be something more than the fragments of time we had stolen from one another over the past few months. But what if it wasn't enough? What if the bridge we stood on, this precarious balance, was nothing but an illusion?

"You really don't get it, do you?" I said, my voice suddenly sharper than I intended.

Jonah's eyes flickered, a momentary flash of surprise, but he quickly regained his composure. "Get what?"

"How much I'm afraid of this," I said, gesturing between us, the words tumbling out before I could stop them. "How much I've been running from this. How much I want it, and how much it terrifies me."

Jonah took a step closer, his face softening. "I get it more than you think." His voice was low now, the teasing gone. "But you're never going to know unless you take the leap. You're always going to wonder what if."

I felt the weight of his words settle into my chest, pressing against my ribs. It wasn't that I hadn't thought about what could happen between us—it was that the thought of losing what I had left to give, of exposing myself to something that could crumble beneath me, was almost too much to bear.

"You don't think I've wondered?" I asked, the words catching on the edge of my throat. "You don't think I've imagined how this could go wrong? How it could fall apart the moment we stop pretending?"

Jonah didn't hesitate. "I think you're imagining a failure that hasn't even happened yet."

I shook my head, a nervous laugh escaping me. "Is that your expert advice? To just... stop thinking about it? To stop worrying about what could go wrong?"

"Exactly," he said, his grin returning, just a little crooked at the corners, as though he were daring me to argue. "But here's the thing: you're never going to stop worrying about what could go wrong unless you take the chance to see if it could go right."

There it was again—the push and pull between us, the stubbornness that had always been there. It was maddening, really. Jonah's unwavering confidence, the way he seemed so sure that this—whatever this was—was worth the risk, left me feeling like I was caught in a current I couldn't escape.

"You make it sound like an easy choice," I said, taking a deep breath. The words felt heavier now, as if they had been waiting for a moment like this, to be said aloud, to settle between us like the first drop of rain before a storm. "But you don't know what I've lost before. You don't know what it feels like to be afraid to hope."

Jonah's face shifted, the warmth in his eyes dimming just slightly. "Maybe not," he said quietly. "But I know what it feels like to wonder what it would be like to love someone who's too afraid to love themself."

The words stung more than I expected. The truth of them was raw, too raw, and it hit me square in the chest. My breath caught, and for a moment, I forgot how to speak, how to move. I wanted to say something—anything—to deny it, to push it away, but I knew deep down that he was right.

"I'm not afraid of you," I said, almost as a whisper. "I'm afraid of what happens when I let myself believe that this—" I gestured between us again, the invisible thread that connected us, "—could actually be real."

Jonah's hand reached out, his fingers brushing against my cheek, the touch as gentle as the morning breeze. "You can't hold on to the what-ifs forever, Lia. You have to choose to let them go."

I swallowed, the lump in my throat threatening to choke me. "And what if I can't? What if I can't let go of the fear? The fear that maybe I'm not enough, or that you'll leave like everyone else?"

Jonah's hand lingered at my cheek, his gaze steady, unwavering. "Then you'll learn. You'll learn that you're stronger than you think. You'll learn that I'm not going anywhere, not unless you push me away."

I looked up at him, the words hanging in the air between us, thick and heavy. The bridge beneath our feet groaned softly, as if urging us forward, but the fear in my chest felt like a weight that was hard to lift. Could I really do this? Could I really take the leap, risk everything, knowing that the fall could be far more painful than I was willing to admit?

"I don't know if I can," I said, my voice barely above a whisper. "I don't know if I'm ready for this."

Jonah's smile was slow, but it was there—an understanding that made my heart ache. "Then I'll wait. I'll wait for you to be ready. But know this, Lia: I'm not going anywhere. Not unless you tell me to."

For a moment, I couldn't move, couldn't breathe, as the weight of his words pressed into me, sinking deeper than I ever expected. The bridge beneath us felt more fragile now, as if the decision we were about to make could shatter everything, leaving only the pieces of what could have been.

And just as I opened my mouth to say something, to finally make a choice, a loud, unexpected sound cut through the stillness—the unmistakable screech of tires on the cobblestones behind us.

I turned, my heart skipping a beat as a black car screeched to a halt just feet away, its headlights glaring into the mist of the morning. And then the door slammed open.

I knew before the figure stepped out what this meant.

Jonah stiffened beside me, his eyes narrowing.

"Stay behind me," he muttered, his hand pulling mine firmly.

And just like that, everything we had built in this fragile moment was about to be tested—by something neither of us could control.

Chapter 13: A Tempest of Doubts

I woke up to the distant sound of traffic—a soft hum, almost like the heartbeat of the city, but beneath that steady rhythm, a quiet tension pulled at my chest. The sunlight filtered through the curtains, weak and hesitant as if unsure whether it was welcome. Paris had always felt like a place of endless possibility, but this morning, it felt as though the city was holding its breath. I could hear Jonah in the kitchen, moving around, the clink of dishes marking the passage of time, but we both seemed to be running on opposite clocks—his, hours ahead, and mine, stuck in some bewildering loop of yesterday.

We hadn't spoken much since the bridge, save for the occasional murmur of polite pleasantries. The night before, I'd watched him carefully, noting the way his shoulders tensed at the slightest touch, how his jaw clenched when I asked a question that pried too deeply. It was all so out of character for him, and it gnawed at me, leaving a trail of unanswered questions. He had been so open on the bridge, so full of honesty and emotion. It felt like a confession, like we'd shared a piece of something real. But then, the silence. The kind of silence that could break a person. It was thick, heavy, like fog pressing in from all sides, suffocating.

I pulled on the first pair of jeans I could find, the fabric cool against my skin, and made my way into the kitchen. Jonah stood by the counter, his back to me, his fingers resting lightly on the rim of a coffee mug, staring out the window as though the world outside held all the answers. I watched him for a moment, unsure of how to approach him. The man who had been so open with me on the bridge now seemed like a stranger, a silhouette of someone I knew, but not quite.

"Coffee?" His voice was low, like he was testing the sound of it, unsure if it would fit in the space between us.

I nodded, sliding into the chair opposite him. The air between us felt thick, heavy with things left unsaid. I knew I was overthinking, but how could I not? Jonah's moods were never easy to decipher, but this... this felt different. He wasn't just distant—he was untouchable. And that terrified me.

I watched as he poured the coffee, his hands steady despite the tension in his body. The way he moved seemed almost mechanical, as though he was on autopilot, going through the motions without truly engaging. My stomach twisted with a quiet sense of unease. I wanted to ask him what was going on, but the words were trapped somewhere between my brain and my tongue, tangled up in the fear of pushing him further away.

He set the mug in front of me, the steam curling up into the air like a phantom. "I'm sorry," he said, his voice quiet. He didn't look at me when he spoke, as though the apology was something he could throw out without making eye contact.

"For what?" I asked, lifting the mug to my lips, the rich bitterness of the coffee sliding across my tongue.

"For this. For... for how I've been. I didn't mean to shut you out."

The words hit me like a slap, though he had spoken them softly, almost too softly. His eyes were dark, shadowed, his gaze still refusing to meet mine. Something in his posture—his hunched shoulders, his clenched hands—spoke volumes, more than any words could ever convey. I wanted to reach out to him, to tell him it was okay, but I wasn't sure anymore if it was.

"You don't have to apologize," I said, trying to keep my voice steady, though it wavered at the edges. "I just... don't know what happened, Jonah. One moment, you're here, and the next, it's like you've disappeared."

He finally met my eyes then, but there was nothing in his gaze to anchor me. I felt like I was sinking into something I couldn't escape.

"It's not you," he said, his voice thick, like he was wading through the words. "It's me. I—I don't know how to explain it."

I leaned forward, feeling the desperate need to bridge the gap between us. "You don't have to explain anything. Just... talk to me. We're in this together, remember?"

He shook his head slowly, his lips pressing into a tight line, his eyes narrowing slightly. "I don't know how to do that. I've spent so long convincing myself that I could handle everything on my own, that I could fix things myself. But... I can't. And I don't want to drag you down with me."

His words cut through me like glass, sharp and jagged, and for a moment, I was speechless. I hadn't realized how much of him was wrapped up in this quiet, stubborn determination to keep everything locked away. I had thought he was the kind of person who wore his emotions like a badge of honor, never afraid to share what was on his mind. But now I saw him—really saw him—and I understood that beneath all the bravado, he was just as lost as I was.

"You're not dragging me down," I said softly, my voice breaking through the tension in the room. "You never have been. I'm here. I'm always here, Jonah."

He looked at me then, really looked at me, and for a fleeting moment, the distance between us seemed to shrink. But just as quickly, it returned, a wall as thick and as unyielding as ever. He swallowed hard, his expression flickering with something I couldn't name. "I don't deserve you."

The words were out before he could stop them, and they hung in the air like a confession, like a truth too painful to ignore.

I didn't know how to respond to that. The hurt in his voice felt like a blow, but it was his self-doubt that stung the most. I wanted to shake him, to tell him that he was enough, that he was worthy of everything good in this world. But I was no better. I had my own doubts, my own fears, and I wondered if they would always hold us apart—if we would always be just two people standing on opposite sides of an ocean of unspoken words, afraid to take the leap.

"I think we both need some time," I said, my voice quieter than before, the weight of his words pressing down on me.

He didn't argue. Instead, he simply nodded, the storm still raging in his eyes. The silence settled between us again, deeper this time, as if the words we had said had only dug a deeper trench. And for the first time since I'd met him, I didn't know if I could bridge the gap.

The morning dragged on, a slow, suffocating march of silence. Jonah and I moved around each other like ghosts, tiptoeing through the motions of what once felt like a familiar rhythm. The way we had laughed over dinner, the way we had walked along the Seine hand in hand, had all been so easy, so light. Now, it was as if the air had changed, thickened with something heavier, something neither of us could name.

By the time the sun had crawled high enough to pierce through the curtains in soft beams, I knew I couldn't pretend everything was fine any longer. There was no denying it—whatever had settled between us was something I wasn't equipped to understand. His silence was a physical presence, one that seemed to follow me around the apartment like an unwanted guest. I was suffocating in it.

The worst part, though, was that I knew he was fighting with himself. I could see it in the way he avoided looking at me, in the way he always stood with his back just a little too straight, like he was bracing against something that wasn't there. I hated that I wasn't the one he turned to, that the walls between us were growing higher and thicker by the hour.

I found myself pacing around the apartment, my feet light on the hardwood floors as if the act of walking could somehow shuffle the weight from my shoulders. In the corner of the room, an old record player sat silent, its dust-laden surface a reminder of what once felt like effortless fun—Jonah spinning songs late into the night, his laugh echoing in the quiet. I wondered if he even remembered that part of us, or if it had already begun to feel like a distant dream.

A soft knock at the door startled me, and I froze, my hand still gripping the back of the chair I had been leaning on. I wasn't expecting anyone. Jonah was still holed up in the kitchen, his presence so large it was as though he filled the space entirely. I opened the door slowly, half-expecting it to be a trick of the mind, a knock that existed only in the tension of the room. But there, standing on the threshold, was a woman I had never seen before.

She was tall, with dark hair that cascaded down her back in waves, and an air of elegance that could have been sculpted by the light itself. Her eyes, a striking green, seemed to shimmer with the kind of confidence that came only from knowing you were in the right place at the right time. She was dressed in a chic Parisian ensemble—black turtleneck, slim trousers, and a scarf that had likely cost more than my monthly rent.

For a moment, neither of us spoke. She studied me with an intensity that was hard to ignore, her gaze sweeping over my face as though she were trying to piece something together. The silence stretched, becoming a taut wire between us.

"Is Jonah here?" Her voice was smooth, rich with an accent I couldn't quite place—French, but with an undertone of something else, something more refined.

I stood there for a beat too long, trying to formulate some sort of response that didn't involve outright confusion. "Yes," I said finally, stepping aside. "He's in the kitchen."

She nodded but didn't move immediately. There was something in her eyes, a flicker of recognition—or maybe it was just curiosity—before she spoke again. "He asked me to come by."

"Jonah asked you?" I echoed, my mind scrambling to keep up. "When?"

"Yesterday," she replied smoothly. "He said we needed to talk. That it was time."

Time for what? I wanted to ask, but the words stuck in my throat, thick with something I couldn't quite explain. The woman was so poised, so confident in her own right, but the air around her was suddenly fraught with an unfamiliar edge.

I glanced over my shoulder, where I knew Jonah was, and for the first time in days, I felt a cold prickle of unease. "I don't—"

"It's fine," she cut in, stepping inside without waiting for an invitation. "I'll only be a moment."

There was a quiet authority in her movement, as though she were accustomed to taking up space in a room and making her presence felt, regardless of who was already there. I stood frozen, watching her walk past me with an ease that made my stomach twist. This wasn't a conversation I was prepared for.

The woman's heels clicked on the hardwood as she moved toward the kitchen, her every step slow, deliberate. I followed behind her, my thoughts spinning in circles as I wondered what this was all about. What did Jonah need to talk to her about? Was I even supposed to be here for this?

I reached the kitchen just as she stood across from Jonah, her arms crossed in front of her, her posture impeccable. Jonah hadn't looked up yet. His eyes were fixed on the counter, his hands gripping the edge as if he could pull the world back together with just the force of his hold.

"Jonah," the woman said, her voice gentle but firm, like a doctor delivering news of a diagnosis that couldn't be avoided.

At the sound of her voice, Jonah finally looked up. His face went through a dozen expressions in less than a second—surprise, recognition, guilt—and then settled into something I couldn't quite place. He seemed both relieved and wary, as though he'd been expecting this moment for far too long.

stand there, waiting for him to explain what had been buried
eath all the silence.

Jonah stepped forward, his voice breaking the thick tension.
"I didn't want to tell you like this," he began, his words stumbling.
"I never meant for you to find out this way."

I leaned forward, my heart hammering in my chest, my breath
low. "Find out what, Jonah?"

His lips parted, but before he could speak, the doorbell rang. A
p, insistent ring that shattered the moment like glass. And just
hat, everything froze.

I turned toward the door, my stomach dropping.

"Clara," he said, his voice low, almost apologetic.

Clara. The name rattled in my head, but before I could make sense of it, she stepped closer to him. Her fingers brushed against his arm lightly, and I felt something in my chest tighten.

"We need to talk," she said simply, her gaze flicking over to me, briefly, before returning to Jonah. "It's time to stop pretending."

I didn't know what she meant, but I could feel the weight of her words hanging in the air. Jonah's expression shifted again, like a door closing quietly but firmly behind him, and I was left standing on the outside, with only the cold chill of uncertainty to keep me company.

I stood there, frozen in place, as Clara's presence seemed to expand, filling every inch of the room with a quiet certainty. She was stunning, the kind of woman who could walk into a room and make everything else fade into the background. There was no dramatic fanfare to her arrival, no sudden bombshell. It was all just a gentle, deliberate move—a whisper in the air that still managed to shake everything inside me.

Jonah didn't look at me as Clara stepped closer, her fingers still grazing his arm, her touch so light it almost felt like an unspoken promise. She was a stranger, and yet her familiarity with him, the way she anchored herself in the space beside him, felt far too intimate. I swallowed hard, the tightness in my throat growing with each passing second.

I had been prepared for a thousand things: for Jonah to pull away from me, for him to open up about whatever was tormenting him, even for him to end whatever we had. But this? This was an entirely different beast. I hadn't prepared for her—Clara. Whoever she was.

Jonah's gaze shifted to me briefly, his eyes meeting mine, but there was no apology there. No explanation. Just the same unreadable look he had worn for the last few days, that quiet storm brewing behind his eyes. It was as though he was bracing himself for something, but I couldn't figure out what. I wanted to reach out to him, to shake him and demand some kind of answer, but instead, I stood rooted to the spot, fighting back the sharp edge of jealousy and confusion clawing at my insides.

Clara, as if sensing the storm inside me, finally turned to face me fully. "I'm sorry for the intrusion," she said, her voice calm, almost too calm. "I didn't mean to cause any discomfort." She said it like a rehearsed line, but the way she said it made my skin crawl. There was nothing innocent about her apology.

I forced a smile, though it felt more like a twitch at the corners of my mouth. "No, it's fine. I'm just a little... surprised. I didn't know Jonah was expecting company."

She didn't flinch at the pointedness of my words, her green eyes remaining steady on mine. "It's not what you think," she said, her tone still polite, but there was an edge to it now, like she was carefully choosing her words, not wanting to upset the balance. "Jonah and I... we go way back."

Her words should have meant something, but all they did was spin a hundred more questions in my head. Go way back? How far back? Was there something between them that I didn't know? I felt a gnawing sensation in my gut, a slow, insidious realization creeping in that maybe I had been living in a fairy tale. And like all fairy tales, this one had its monsters hiding in the shadows.

Jonah, for his part, didn't intervene. He just stood there, silent, watching Clara and me like we were two pieces of a puzzle he was too tired to fit together. I could feel the weight of his silence pressing down on me, suffocating me.

Finally, I couldn't take it anymore. I crossed my arms and stepped forward, my voice unsteady but firm. "What is it that you need to talk about, exactly?" I asked, directing my question to both of them. There was no point in playing nice anymore. I wasn't going to sit here, twisting in the wind, waiting for answers that felt more like half-truths than anything solid.

Jonah opened his mouth, but Clara spoke first, her almost rehearsed. "It's not something we planned to she said, her gaze flicking back to Jonah, "but I thin know, don't you?"

Jonah didn't reply. Instead, his eyes seemed to s his expression a mixture of uncertainty and resignati the back of his neck, something he always did uncomfortable, when the pressure of a situation beca

I couldn't breathe. What the hell was going on looking at her like that? Like he was torn between couldn't let go of and something he didn't want to fa

Clara took a step forward, her heels clicking sh floor. "Jonah's been carrying a burden, and it's everything between you two. He didn't want to a time has come."

Her words hit me like a slap to the face. A burden? And why was she talking like she knew ever

"What are you talking about?" I said, my voic blend of anger and confusion. "What burden?"

She turned her gaze back to me, her smile th "Jonah's been hiding the truth. Hiding it from both

Jonah's eyes went wide, and in an instant, the a charged. His mouth opened, but he was too late. (said it. The words hung in the air like poison, slowly

"Hiding what?" I demanded. I couldn't stop were spilling out now, faster than I could control you hiding, Jonah?"

The room went deathly still. Clara's ey something—a hint of satisfaction? I couldn't tell. me, his gaze dark and troubled, and for the firs saw something that might have been guilt. But it damage had been done. The veil had been lifted,

Chapter 14: Unveiling the Mask

The walls of Celeste's apartment were a soft shade of lavender, the kind that made you think of dusk—quiet, reflective, and deeply comforting. The worn velvet armchairs, tucked beneath crocheted throws, seemed to sigh under the weight of years, of secrets shared and lives lived. Her home smelled faintly of jasmine and old books, the kind of scent that told you this was a woman who read between the lines. The air was thick with history, each crack in the paint telling a story I wasn't sure I was ready to hear.

Celeste herself was a striking figure. Her silver hair, though pulled back into a loose knot, still had a sheen of its former luster. Her eyes were sharp, like a hawk's—glowing with knowledge that she would part with only when it suited her. She was dressed simply, but with a grace that most women half her age would have envied. A cardigan, draped carefully over a loose blouse, paired with slacks that whispered of timeless fashion. It wasn't the kind of outfit that screamed for attention; it demanded it instead, in the way her presence seemed to fill every space she occupied.

"Jonah's always been a stubborn boy," she murmured, pouring the tea with a quiet reverence that felt like a prayer. She didn't look at me, not at first, as though the conversation was something that required a delicate opening, like the turning of a page in a book so fragile that its story might slip away if you weren't careful.

I leaned in, the scent of the tea—dark, with hints of honey and spice—rising into my senses as I prepared myself for whatever she was about to reveal. "Tell me about him," I asked, my voice tentative, unsure if I even wanted to hear the answers she might give. I had loved Jonah for so long, seen him as something both tragic and extraordinary. But I didn't know the first thing about the shadow that clung to him like a second skin.

Celeste's gaze drifted to the window, out into the small garden below, where the sunlight danced over the leaves of an overgrown rose bush. There was a long pause, and I wondered for a moment if she was considering whether or not to answer. But then she spoke, each word laden with a weight I could feel pressing down on my chest.

"He was a quiet child, mostly," she began, her voice soft but firm, like someone recounting a story that they wished they could forget. "Raised in foster homes after his mother abandoned him when he was no more than five. Jonah learned early that people leave. It was the only lesson that stuck." She took a slow sip of tea, as though the act of drinking allowed her time to gather the words she needed. "It wasn't just the absence of a mother—though that was part of it, of course. No. It was the way he was left behind, discarded like a forgotten toy. I don't think anyone ever truly looked at him. Not really. Not the way he needed."

My heart twisted at the thought of Jonah, all those years alone, a little boy too young to understand what it meant to be abandoned. I had always assumed that Jonah's aloofness, his tendency to keep the world at arm's length, was just part of who he was. But now I wondered how much of it was a defense mechanism, a wall built brick by brick from the kind of loneliness that could eat a person alive if they let it.

Celeste seemed to sense my turmoil. She didn't look at me, but she didn't need to. She knew.

"There was a man once," she continued, her eyes growing distant, "a man who was like a father to him for a time. Jonah must have been ten or eleven when this man came into his life. For a while, Jonah believed that maybe—just maybe—he had found someone who would stay." Her voice dropped, as though the very mention of the man's name tasted bitter on her tongue. "But the man betrayed him. Took everything Jonah had given him, every shred of trust, and used it to destroy him. Took from him more than he could ever begin to understand at that age."

I felt a chill crawl down my spine, the weight of her words sinking deep into my chest. A betrayal. A loss like no other. And suddenly, everything about Jonah—the guarded silences, the distance in his eyes—began to make sense. He was a man who had learned that trust was a currency in short supply, and love was an illusion that could vanish in an instant.

"The betrayal was cruel," Celeste continued, now looking at me, her gaze sharp and unflinching. "Not just because it broke his heart, but because it shattered any semblance of hope he had left. Hope that someone, somewhere, might love him the way he needed to be loved. After that, he became a man who believed that he didn't deserve happiness. He convinced himself that he wasn't worthy of it. And that's the Jonah you know—the one who pulls away, who won't let anyone get close enough to hurt him again."

I swallowed hard, her words cutting through me like a blade. She was right, of course. I had always known that Jonah had walls. But I hadn't realized how thick they were, how deep they ran, or how much pain was buried beneath them. Celeste's warning echoed in my mind, louder than the steady ticking of the clock on the wall. "Love alone might not heal him." How could it? Could anything heal a heart that had been broken so many times it no longer believed in the possibility of being whole?

"But you," Celeste said suddenly, her voice steady, a quiet conviction that I had yet to find in myself. "You are different. You see him, don't you? Not just the man he shows the world, but the boy he used to be. The one who wanted to believe in love. You can help him, if you can prove to him that he is worthy. Not just of your love, but of his own happiness. But it will take more than just patience. It will take everything."

Her words lingered in the air, heavy with the responsibility she had placed on my shoulders. I wasn't sure if I could carry it. I wasn't sure if I could be the one to heal Jonah, when so much of his past was a landscape I couldn't even begin to understand. But Celeste was right about one thing: I loved him. I always had. And if there was a way to reach him, to help him see the worth he so easily ignored, then I would find it, no matter the cost.

I stood up, my resolve solidifying in my chest. "Thank you," I said, though it seemed far too small a phrase for the weight of her revelation. She simply nodded, her eyes soft but knowing.

"You'll need it," she said, her voice almost a whisper. "The journey ahead won't be easy. But nothing worth having ever is."

The drive back was a blur. The city's busy streets passed in a haze of light and shadow, like a painting I couldn't quite focus on. My hands gripped the steering wheel too tightly, my knuckles white against the dark leather. I could still feel the weight of Celeste's words pressing on me. They were both a comfort and a challenge, a map to the heart of Jonah but also a warning that I wasn't sure I was strong enough to follow. She'd said it would take everything, and as I turned the corner onto the street that led to his apartment, I realized how little I knew about what that really meant.

Jonah's building loomed ahead, the familiar structure almost unrecognizable in the dark. Its brick façade had once seemed imposing to me, like a fortress. Now, I saw it differently. Now, it was just a place. A place where he lived, a place where he hid. The thought of that made me feel small, like an intruder on some private battlefield that wasn't mine to fight.

I parked in the space across the street, the headlights cutting through the night, momentarily illuminating the sidewalk in stark shadows. I sat there for a moment, just staring at the building, trying to summon the right words. But nothing came. How do you speak to someone whose scars you can't see, whose pain is buried so deep, it almost feels like you're speaking to a ghost?

I had loved Jonah for so long, but it felt like we were standing on opposite sides of a canyon that no amount of hope could bridge. It wasn't that I didn't believe in him; I did. But somewhere, deep inside, I wasn't sure I believed in myself enough to fix what had been broken before either of us had ever met. Love, I knew, was never the answer to every problem. I'd spent too many years living in the kind of fairytale where love was enough to save everyone. But Celeste had shown me that Jonah's story wasn't one where love alone could write the ending.

I pushed open the car door and stepped out onto the sidewalk, the chill of the evening air prickling against my skin. The sound of my boots tapping on the pavement seemed too loud in the silence, too much like a countdown. Each step toward Jonah's door felt heavier than the last, as if the weight of everything I had learned from Celeste was pulling me backward.

When I reached the door, I hesitated. I'd spent hours wondering how I was going to do this—how I was going to approach him, how I was going to say what I didn't even know I needed to say. And yet, here I was, standing in front of his apartment, uncertain as ever.

I took a deep breath, one of those shaky breaths that only came when I was about to do something I wasn't sure I was capable of. I knocked, three firm taps, but even as the sound echoed in the hallway, I felt the moment slip away from me. Jonah would open the door in his own time, just like he always did—quietly, expectantly. Like nothing had changed. But everything had changed. Everything was different now.

When the door finally creaked open, I saw him. He stood there, his frame tall and solid, his hands shoved deep into the pockets of his hoodie, the familiar darkness in his eyes betraying none of the storm that had raged inside me all evening.

"Hey," I said, my voice betraying the uncertainty I'd tried so hard to bury.

Jonah didn't smile. He never did. Instead, he just nodded, his lips twitching slightly, as though he was unsure of what to say. It had always been like this—this unspoken tension between us, like we were two halves of a whole that could never quite find each other. His presence was magnetic, pulling me in even when I knew I shouldn't get too close.

"Can we talk?" I asked, my throat tight with the weight of everything I'd learned.

His gaze flickered to my face, like he was trying to decide whether or not he should let me in, whether or not I was safe to be around. The truth was, he didn't know what to do with me anymore. And I didn't know what to do with him, either. Not after what Celeste had told me. Not after the way his past had unraveled in front of me, revealing the cracks in the man I had once thought invincible.

He stepped aside and I walked past him, the familiar scent of his apartment—wood and leather and the faint hint of something spicier, like his cologne—filling my lungs. Nothing had changed in here. The furniture was still the same, the open windows still let in the same soft night breeze. And yet, everything was different now. I wasn't just a visitor anymore. I was carrying the weight of his history with me.

Jonah closed the door behind us, and for a long moment, neither of us spoke. The silence was so thick, it almost had a texture. I could feel the tension between us, thick as smoke, as if any word, any movement, could make it burst into flames.

Finally, he broke the silence, his voice low and uncertain. "What's going on? What did Celeste say to you?"

I met his gaze, my heart pounding in my chest. His eyes were searching mine, looking for answers, but I wasn't sure I had any. "She told me about your past. About how it shaped you into the man you are now. About everything you've lost." The words came out in a rush, like a dam breaking, but I couldn't stop them. I had to say them, had to give him the space to hear what I couldn't keep hidden any longer. "Jonah, you don't have to keep hiding from me. I see you. I see everything you've been through. And I'm not going anywhere."

There it was—the truth, laid bare between us. It felt raw and real, but also fragile, like it could shatter if I wasn't careful. Jonah didn't speak right away, his face unreadable. But his eyes—those eyes that had always seemed so distant—softened just a fraction. Enough to make me wonder if maybe, just maybe, he was finally starting to believe it. Believe in me.

Jonah didn't speak for what felt like an eternity. His gaze lingered on me, his eyes flickering with something—maybe suspicion, maybe curiosity, but more than anything, the kind of wariness I had come to recognize as his first defense. When he finally broke the silence, his voice was tight, measured, like he was weighing every word before it slipped past his lips.

"So, Celeste told you everything, huh?" His words hung in the air, thick with an edge that made my stomach tighten. He was waiting, watching, like a man on the verge of throwing up a wall I couldn't climb. I didn't know how to answer him. Part of me wanted to reach out, to close the distance between us, to make him understand that I wasn't some stranger peering into his past. But the other part, the one that Celeste had awakened in me, told me that maybe now wasn't the time to try to fix him, to convince him everything would be okay.

"Not everything," I said finally, my voice steadier than I felt. "But enough to understand that your past... it's not something you can bury anymore. You can't keep pretending it's not there."

His eyes darkened, and for a moment, I thought he might retreat—like he had so many times before, like he always did when things got too close. But instead, he stood there, motionless, his jaw tight. There was something raw about the way he looked at me then, as though he was waiting for me to back away, for me to change my mind.

"I don't need your pity," he said, his words coming out sharper than I expected, cutting through the fragile silence between us. "I don't need you to fix me."

I flinched, the words stinging more than I'd anticipated. Of course, he would say that. Of course, he would push me away before I had the chance to get too close. It was the only way he knew how to protect himself.

"I'm not trying to fix you," I said, my voice softer now. I stepped closer to him, but I didn't reach out. I didn't want to crowd him, to make him feel cornered. "I just want you to know that you don't have to hide. Not from me."

Jonah's eyes softened, just a little, like the cracks in the armor he'd so carefully built were starting to show. But it wasn't enough. Not yet. I could see the hesitation in his gaze, the part of him that wanted to believe what I was saying, but couldn't bring himself to. Not after everything that had happened.

He ran a hand through his hair, the motion both frustrated and desperate, like he was trying to untangle the mess of emotions he refused to confront.

"I don't know how to let someone in," he muttered, his voice quieter now, almost a whisper. "I don't know how to trust anyone anymore."

The words landed like a punch to my chest. It was as though I could feel every ounce of the weight he carried pressing down on me, the years of scars, the years of believing that no one could ever be there for him the way he needed. How could I ask him to trust me, to believe in me, when he'd been let down so many times before?

"Then let me show you," I said, and it was more a plea than anything. "Let me show you that you don't have to do this alone."

Jonah's eyes flickered to mine, a brief spark of something there—something like hope, or maybe the memory of it, before it vanished just as quickly as it appeared. He looked away, his shoulders sagging with the weight of a thousand unspoken words. I could see the fight in him, the resistance. But it was there, too—the small, almost imperceptible shift that told me he was on the verge of something. A breaking point, or maybe a breakthrough.

"I don't deserve it," he said finally, his voice barely audible. "I don't deserve someone like you."

The words hit me like a cold wind, sharp and biting, but I refused to let them break me. I refused to let him push me away again, not when I was so close, not when I could see the man he could be, if he only let himself believe it.

"Jonah," I said, my voice steadier now, with a quiet certainty that I hadn't known I had in me. "You do deserve it. You just don't see it yet. But I'm not going anywhere. Not this time."

He turned to face me fully then, his gaze intense, searching mine like he was trying to gauge whether I meant it, whether I could be the one to make him believe the truth about himself. For a moment, we just stood there, the space between us charged with everything unspoken. Everything I wanted to say but couldn't quite find the words for.

Then, as if the weight of everything had suddenly become too much to bear, Jonah took a deep breath and walked toward the small kitchen, his footsteps heavy and deliberate. I stood still, watching him, waiting for him to say something, anything. But all he did was reach for a glass, fill it with water, and down it in one quick motion. It was a gesture so small, so ordinary, that it almost felt like a distraction. But I knew better. It was the way he avoided facing me when he couldn't face himself.

"I don't know how to fix this," he muttered, turning to lean against the counter, his back to me. "I don't know how to fix me."

I could feel the walls he was trying to build between us, and for a moment, I almost let him. I almost stepped back, afraid that if I pushed too hard, I'd lose him forever. But then I remembered what Celeste had said—love alone wouldn't heal him. He needed to know that he was worth something more than his past. And I needed to show him that.

"I'm not asking you to fix anything," I said, taking a tentative step toward him. "I'm asking you to let me in. Just a little. Let me see you."

Jonah didn't answer right away, but when he finally turned to face me, his eyes were full of something I couldn't quite read. A mix of pain, disbelief, and maybe the faintest glimmer of something else—something he hadn't allowed himself to feel in a long time.

And then, just as I thought we might finally break through, his phone buzzed on the counter, loud and insistent, cutting through the fragile moment we had created. Jonah's eyes flickered to the screen, his face hardening instantly as he reached for the phone without a word.

"Not now," he muttered under his breath, but it wasn't to me. It was to the message, the interruption that had come at the worst possible time.

His expression shifted, a new tension creeping into his shoulders. And just like that, the moment we had shared—however brief—seemed to slip right out of our grasp.

"Who is it?" I asked before I could stop myself, my voice tinged with a sudden suspicion that I couldn't shake.

Jonah's gaze flickered toward me, his jaw tightening. He didn't say a word, but his silence told me everything I needed to know.

And then, without warning, he turned and left the room, phone still clutched in his hand.

Chapter 15: A Night of Broken Promises

The air in the bar was thick with smoke and the hum of muffled conversations, like the city had exhaled its last breath and decided to exhale no more. The low lighting cast flickering shadows across the brick walls, where the paintings seemed to stretch and sag with time, much like the souls who lingered inside. It was the kind of place where secrets were traded as easily as drinks, and I, feeling the pulse of the world outside the door, had to admit that for all its quiet charm, it was a little too easy to drown in this place.

Jonah sat in the corner, hunched slightly, like the weight of his own thoughts might crush him if he stood too tall. His jaw was tight, and there was a slight tremor in his fingers as he twirled the glass between them. The amber liquid inside was nearly gone, but his eyes remained fixed on it, as though it held the answers to a riddle he couldn't solve.

I took a step toward him, and the sound of my heels against the polished floor felt unnervingly loud. He didn't look up at first, but the way his shoulders stiffened told me that he knew I was there, that somehow, he was already bracing for the inevitable conversation we both had been avoiding.

When he finally looked up, I could see the storm clouds in his eyes, the ones he tried so hard to hide. His gaze met mine with an intensity that made my breath catch, and for a moment, we just stood there, tethered by some invisible thread that neither of us dared to break.

"You should've left, you know," he said, his voice low but harsh, like gravel being ground underfoot. He took a long sip of his drink, swallowed, then set the glass down with a gentle clink. "You should've walked away when you had the chance."

The words hung in the air between us, slicing through the dim light like a blade. I sat down across from him, my fingers curling around the edge of the table as if to anchor myself to reality. I didn't want to believe what he was implying, but the sting of truth already seeped into my skin, a slow burn that I couldn't ignore.

"You think I should have run?" I said, my voice lighter than I felt. I had to laugh, even if it was bitter. "I didn't run, Jonah. I stayed. And I'm here now."

He leaned forward, and there was a vulnerability in his posture that made my stomach tighten. He was trying so hard to keep it together, to keep his walls up, but I saw past them. I saw the cracks, the fragility that he refused to acknowledge.

"I don't know how to do this," he confessed, the words spilling out before he could stop them. "Love. Relationships. Hell, I'm not even sure I know how to trust anyone anymore." His voice broke, just for a second, but it was enough to make my heart ache. "I've made too many mistakes, and I don't think I can undo them. I don't deserve... this. Not you."

A bitter laugh escaped my lips before I could stop it. "Do you think I'm some sort of saint? Because trust me, Jonah, I'm not. I've made my fair share of mistakes too."

He shook his head, looking away as if the weight of my words hurt him. "No, you haven't. You're too good for me. You don't even know what you're getting yourself into."

I reached across the table and took his hand, forcing him to look at me. His skin was warm and rough under my touch, his pulse racing beneath my fingers. "I don't need saving, Jonah. And I'm not here because I think you're some broken project that needs fixing. I'm here because I want you. For all the parts of you—the ones you keep hidden and the ones you show the world. All of it. You're enough. And I'm not going anywhere."

For a moment, he didn't respond. His chest rose and fell with a ragged breath, his lips pressed into a thin line, as though he couldn't decide whether to believe me or not. I could see the battle raging behind his eyes, the fight between the man who wanted to hold onto me and the one who was convinced that he'd destroy everything good in his life.

I didn't know how to fix it, didn't have the perfect words to make everything right. But I would try. For us, for what we could be. Even if it wasn't easy.

As the night stretched on and the conversations around us blurred into a dull hum, I tried to believe that this was enough, that love could survive the past. That maybe we could survive it together.

But then, as the first light of dawn began to filter through the small windows of the bar, I turned my head for a moment to take in the sleepy atmosphere of the room. When I looked back at Jonah, the chair where he had sat was empty.

I blinked, my pulse quickening as I scanned the room, the cold dread settling in like a thick fog. No sign of him. Not a trace. Not even a whisper of his presence. My heart dropped into my stomach, and I stood up quickly, the world tilting beneath me as I stumbled toward the door, barely noticing the curious stares of the other patrons.

Outside, the streets were still damp from the night's rain, the city slowly waking from its slumber. I stood there, feeling the chill of the morning air cut through me, as I searched the streets. Nothing. No Jonah. Just the endless hum of cars and people going about their lives, oblivious to the storm that had just torn through mine.

I stood there, frozen, my heart a jagged mess of confusion and heartbreak. Had he really just disappeared? Had he really left without a word? Without even the decency to say goodbye?

I didn't know. But one thing was clear—nothing had prepared me for this. And yet, somehow, I knew this was just the beginning.

The following days felt like walking through a fog, each step muffled and uncertain. I kept replaying the moment Jonah had vanished, as though if I examined it enough, if I dissected each second with the precision of a surgeon, I might find some hidden explanation for his disappearance. But the more I thought about it, the less it made sense. He had been there, and then he wasn't. No goodbye. No note. Not even a trace of his jacket or his keys left behind, like he'd never even existed in that dimly lit bar at all.

I couldn't sleep. The bed felt too large, like the space between the sheets was mocking me with its emptiness. My mind was a whirlwind, spinning around that last conversation, his confession still echoing in my ears. Love only ever ended in ruin for people like him. What had that meant? He was so sure of it, but I refused to believe him. I couldn't. I wouldn't.

Every place I went, I found myself looking for him, half-expecting to see him leaning against a lamppost, or maybe standing in the doorway of the cafe we had passed that one Saturday morning, the sun bright and the world ahead of us. It was irrational, I knew that. But the thought of him, of his absence, gnawed at me like a hunger I couldn't sate.

I couldn't bring myself to call his phone, not yet. I needed to feel like I had some control over this mess, like I wasn't completely at the mercy of whatever ghost he had decided to become. I needed to take some time, some space, to put myself back together.

But space didn't help. Time didn't help.

By the third day, I found myself standing in front of his apartment building, my breath caught in my throat as I stared at the door like it might open at any moment. The silence between us had stretched too far for comfort, and I couldn't let it stand. I had to know.

I buzzed the intercom. His voice came through, distorted and muffled, but unmistakable. "Who is it?"

It took every ounce of my willpower to keep my voice steady. "It's me. Let me in."

There was a long pause before the buzz of the door unlocking sent a shock of relief through me, a strange mix of dread and hope swirling together in my chest. I let myself inside, moving up the stairs as if every step was weighted with the promise of something—either salvation or heartbreak. I couldn't decide which.

Jonah's door was slightly ajar when I reached it, the faint scent of cigarettes lingering in the air, mingling with something else I couldn't quite place. My heart hammered against my ribs as I pushed it open, stepping into the apartment.

It was empty.

Everything was still and silent, like the whole space had been waiting for something to shift. There were no signs of him, no half-empty coffee cups, no abandoned shoes by the door, no stray jackets tossed over chairs. The place was perfectly in place, like he'd stepped out for a moment and would return any minute.

But the longer I stood there, the more it felt like a lie. The stillness of the room was too sharp, too deliberate. There was a message in that silence, something unsaid, and I couldn't shake the feeling that I wasn't meant to be here. I wasn't meant to know what had happened.

The temptation to leave was there, strong and insistent, but I resisted. My feet felt glued to the floor, my mind whirling with the need to understand, to piece together this jigsaw puzzle he'd left behind. I walked deeper into the apartment, past the sparse furnishings and cluttered desk, until I reached the bedroom.

I stopped in the doorway, breath catching. It was just as silent, just as still, except for a single item on the bed. A crumpled envelope, the edges worn and frayed as though it had been handled too many times. I could feel it calling to me, as if it were the one thing Jonah had left behind on purpose, a final message for me.

I picked it up with trembling hands, flipping it over to see the messy scrawl of his handwriting on the front. My name. Just my name, written in all caps like he was shouting across a void. I slid my finger under the flap and opened it, pulling out a piece of paper that was slightly crinkled, as if it had been folded and refolded over and over again.

The words on the page hit me like a punch to the gut.

I didn't want to leave you like this. You deserve better than me, than my ghosts. I've already hurt you more than I should. I won't be the one to ruin what you've got. I can't be the man you want me to be. Please understand. I love you, but not enough to stay.

My vision blurred, the words swimming in and out of focus as I read them again and again, each time hoping that somehow, the meaning would change, that I'd missed something important. But it never did.

He was gone. For good.

I dropped the letter, letting it flutter to the floor as if the paper itself held the weight of his absence. I stared at the spot where it lay, feeling an overwhelming mixture of anger and hurt rise up inside me, a cocktail so bitter I could taste it at the back of my throat.

How could he? After everything we had shared, all the promises made, the laughter, the tenderness, the quiet moments where it had felt like we were building something real... how could he just walk away?

I wanted to scream, to throw something, to tear apart this whole apartment and demand answers. But instead, I sat down on the bed, pressing my face into my hands. The tears came then, hot and uncontrollable, as if all the heartbreak I'd been holding inside finally had nowhere to go but out.

The truth was that I had never truly understood Jonah. Not really. He had let me in, just enough to make me think I knew him. But in the end, he had always been a shadow—elusive, untouchable.

And now, with him gone, I was left with nothing but the hollow echo of his absence.

I wasn't sure what hurt more—the fact that he had left or the fact that, deep down, I had known he would.

The days that followed felt like swimming against an unforgiving tide, each breath I took coming slower than the last. The apartment felt colder, quieter. My thoughts reverberated around the echo of Jonah's departure, sharp, relentless, and hollow. I kept trying to find meaning in the letter he'd left, but the words never changed. They sat there, mocking me, reminding me of how little I had really known him, despite everything we had shared. It was like trying to read a novel where the pages kept shifting, the plot constantly rewriting itself, leaving me frustrated and desperate for an ending that made sense.

I couldn't understand it. The words were clear, but they weren't the full truth. I had seen the way he'd looked at me, the quiet moments when he'd seemed to let down his guard. I had seen glimpses of something—something real—that he hadn't let anyone else see. So, why had he run?

The city around me was unchanged. People still hurried through their routines, the hum of the streets so ordinary, so unaffected by the storm that had already churned through my life. It felt wrong, like the world should pause for a second, hold its breath, as if to acknowledge the weight of what had just happened. But it didn't. It moved on, as it always did, without a second thought for the hearts that were left broken in its wake.

I couldn't move on. Not yet.

A week passed, and I still found myself waking up with his absence pressing down on me like a weight I couldn't escape. It was in everything. The coffee that didn't taste right without his quiet comments about how much sugar I used. The silence that stretched between me and everyone else, as if they could sense the gaping hole where Jonah used to be. I had to do something. I had to find him.

I'd tried the obvious routes first. His phone was disconnected. His social media accounts locked down tighter than Fort Knox. No one had heard from him, not even his closest friends. It was like Jonah had vanished off the face of the Earth, leaving nothing but questions in his wake. But I wasn't about to give up. Not on him.

The next step was more desperate, more reckless: I was going to visit his hometown. The one place he had only ever spoken of in vague terms. It was the place he'd run from, and now it was the place I thought he'd run back to. Maybe it wasn't logical, maybe it didn't even make sense, but I had to try.

The road to the small town was long and winding, the sort of place where the trees and fields stretched on forever, and the sky felt impossibly wide. It wasn't a place I would have ever imagined Jonah coming from—there was nothing wild or reckless about it. It was quiet, too quiet, like the kind of place where nothing ever changed. And yet, there was something about it that seemed to hold answers, as if the place itself had the key to unlocking everything Jonah had kept hidden.

I pulled into a parking lot in front of a small diner at the edge of town. The building was weathered, the sign hanging crooked above the door, but there was a warmth to it, a familiarity that made my heart ache. Inside, the smell of coffee and fried bacon hit me immediately, and for a split second, I thought I might find Jonah sitting at a booth by the window, waiting for me to show up. But of course, he wasn't there. He wasn't anywhere.

I approached the counter, where an older woman with gray-streaked hair was busy scrubbing a mug. She looked up as I stepped closer, her expression friendly but guarded, as if she had seen strangers come and go all her life.

"I'm looking for someone," I said, my voice steady despite the nerves twisting in my stomach. "Jonah Rourke. Do you know him?"

The woman's hands froze mid-scrub, and for a brief moment, I thought she might laugh. But she didn't. Instead, she wiped her hands on a towel and nodded slowly.

"Jonah, huh?" She leaned in slightly, her eyes narrowing with a certain kind of knowing. "I'm afraid you've come a little too late for that."

I felt a jolt in my chest, the words ringing louder than they should have. "Too late?"

The woman nodded, but there was something in her eyes that made my skin prickle, something that told me she wasn't talking about time.

"You'd better sit down," she said, motioning to an empty booth in the corner. "I don't think you're going to like what you hear."

I took a seat, trying to steady my breathing as she set a cup of coffee in front of me. The warmth from the mug seeped into my fingers, but it couldn't chase away the cold creeping into my veins.

"He came back here about a month ago," the woman said, lowering her voice as though someone might be listening. "Said he needed to settle something. He was quiet. Withdrawn. Spent most of his time walking around town, going to places he hadn't been in years."

I leaned forward, my pulse quickening. "Did he say why?"

She shook her head, the memory of Jonah seeming to weigh heavily on her. "He didn't. Not to me, anyway. But there's one thing I do know."

I waited, holding my breath.

"Jonah wasn't just running from something. He was running to it."

The words hung in the air, heavy with meaning. Running to it. What did that mean? Who or what could Jonah possibly have been chasing after, even after all this time? My mind raced, but I couldn't form a clear picture.

Before I could ask more questions, the door to the diner opened, a gust of cold air sweeping through. And there, standing in the doorway, was someone I hadn't expected to see—someone I had hoped I wouldn't.

Jonah.

Chapter 16: Whispers in the Wind

The scent of fresh croissants from the bakery at the corner wrapped itself around me like a familiar, albeit bittersweet, embrace. Paris, in all her glory, seemed to hold her breath as I stepped into the morning fog. The damp cobblestones beneath my feet were slick with the remnants of an early rain, and the city hummed its usual lullaby—distant voices, the clink of a bicycle bell, the soft shuffle of shoes against stone. But none of these sounds brought the comfort they once had. No, the city now felt like a stage where I was both the lead actress and the unwitting audience, trapped in a performance with a script I didn't understand.

His absence was a weight in the air—heavy and suffocating. The kind that settles into your lungs when you breathe too deeply, reminding you that something vital has been stolen away. His name flickered in my thoughts like a neon sign, impossible to ignore yet harder to decipher. Luc. Just the thought of him made my fingers twitch with the need to find him, to uncover whatever tangled mess he had left behind.

I passed a café, its outdoor tables empty save for a couple sipping their espresso in the shadow of the large, leafy trees lining the street. The aroma of roasted beans and sugar-dusted pastries drifted from within, but I didn't stop. I had a destination now—an address scribbled on the back of a crumpled napkin, handed to me by a woman who spoke of Luc with such reverence that it both disturbed and intrigued me. "He was a man of mystery, mademoiselle," she'd whispered, her fingers trembling as she passed me the note, "but his secrets were never his own. They were ours, too." The words had settled uneasily in my stomach, as though I had bitten into something that was both sweet and spoiled.

Turning onto Rue des Martyrs, I kept my eyes trained on the streets ahead. The café where I had last seen him, laughing with that carefree smile that seemed to suggest the world was merely a puzzle he was willing to solve on a whim, was tucked between two bookshops. I could almost picture him now, leaning against the window with his usual air of indifference, watching the world spin by as if he were above it all. But Luc had never been above anything—except, perhaps, the truth.

I stood in front of the café, the large glass windows reflecting my own image, slightly askew, as though I were a stranger to myself. The table we had shared was still there, its chipped surface wearing the marks of too many quiet conversations and the passing of days. My fingers brushed the edge of the table as I stepped closer, and I could almost feel him beside me. But he was gone. The seat across from me was empty, as it had been for days.

A voice cut through the silence, low and familiar. "You're looking for him, aren't you?"

I turned sharply, heart leaping into my throat. A man, his features sharp and inscrutable, stood just behind me, his dark coat blending with the shadows. His eyes, cold and distant, studied me as though I were a puzzle he was piecing together, but I wasn't sure if I wanted to be solved.

"Who are you?" I asked, my voice coming out harsher than I intended.

The man smiled, but it didn't reach his eyes. "Someone who knows what it's like to search for a ghost." His gaze flicked to the empty chair at the table. "And I'm guessing you're not the only one who misses him."

I straightened, my pulse quickening. There was something in the way he spoke, a subtle hint of familiarity that tugged at the edges of my mind. "I don't know what you're talking about."

"Don't you? You think he just disappeared, but Luc isn't the type to vanish without a reason." He took a step closer, lowering his voice. "People like him don't leave without leaving something behind, mademoiselle. And it's not always a trail of breadcrumbs."

I swallowed, my fingers tightening around the strap of my purse. The tension in the air thickened, a storm building just out of sight. "What do you know about him?"

The man studied me for a moment, then nodded, as though making a decision. "More than you think. But that doesn't mean you'll like what you hear."

I crossed my arms, refusing to let the doubt creeping into my thoughts show. "Try me."

He stepped back, his gaze never leaving mine. "Luc wasn't a saint. And he certainly wasn't the man you thought he was. But he did care, in his own way. Just not enough to keep the promises he made."

I felt a pang in my chest, the words too sharp, too raw. "You don't know what he promised me."

The man's lips quirked, almost imperceptibly. "Maybe not. But I know he made promises to others, too."

He turned, glancing down the street before meeting my eyes again. "You want to find him? Follow the money. It's always where the answers are."

I opened my mouth to respond, but the man was already gone, swallowed up by the fog that clung to the street like a secret.

I stood there, the words echoing in my mind. Money. Promises. Lies. Each of those had a weight, a weight that now threatened to crush me under its heaviness. But in that moment, I realized something—something that made my chest tighten and my legs tremble with the intensity of the revelation. Luc had left a trail. I didn't know where it would lead, but I was about to follow it, no matter where it took me.

And the truth? That was something I wasn't sure I was ready to face.

I had spent the better part of two weeks haunting the same few streets, hoping for a sliver of a lead, a whisper of his name in the back alleys where the locals lingered. There was something about Paris that made it easy to believe in ghosts—perhaps it was the shadows that stretched long across the cobblestones in the fading light, or the way the city seemed to wrap itself in its own mysteries. Each café, each bookshop, each narrow lane had become a part of the puzzle I was trying to solve, the piece that would finally explain where Luc had gone. The puzzle, however, remained frustratingly out of reach.

I was on the edge of giving up, my hands clammy as I tried to smooth the crumpled napkin with the address I had been given. It was a place I hadn't visited before, a part of the city far from the tourist crowds, and there was something about it that felt too obscure to be real. A nondescript office building on Rue de la Concorde, tucked behind an overgrown hedge and an iron gate so rusted it looked like it might collapse under the weight of its own history. The address had led me here, but now I found myself standing before it, unsure whether I should be here at all. There was a peculiar tension in the air, as though the building itself was holding its breath.

I glanced around. No one seemed to notice me, a solitary figure lost in the sea of passersby. The usual buzz of city life continued unabated—people huddling under umbrellas, arguing with their baristas, hurrying along to their next appointment. But I felt a distinct shift when I turned back to the building. The quietest of movements caught my eye—a figure slipping inside through the gate, disappearing behind the heavy iron bars. It was too quick to be certain, but I had the sinking feeling that it was no coincidence.

Heart thudding in my chest, I followed. Not too quickly—too much haste might make me look suspicious—but not too slowly, either. I had come too far to lose my nerve now. The gate creaked as I pushed it open, its rusted hinges protesting my intrusion. I winced at the sound, but kept moving, slipping past the entrance and into the darkened courtyard.

The air here felt different—thicker, as though the weight of so many untold stories hung in the atmosphere like a fog. Every step echoed off the old stone walls, but I didn't dare turn back. I pressed on, my pulse a drumbeat in my ears, until I reached the building's door, which loomed before me like an ominous sentry.

The door was ajar. A sliver of light leaked from the crack in the frame, barely enough to see, but enough to stir something deep inside me. The choice before me was simple: turn around and walk away, or step inside and face whatever awaited me. I didn't know what made my feet move, but before I could second-guess myself, I was inside.

The hallway smelled of old wood and dampness, the floors creaking under my weight as I tiptoed deeper into the building. My eyes adjusted to the gloom, and I found myself standing before a narrow staircase that spiraled upward into the shadows. Every instinct screamed at me to leave, but I couldn't. Luc had always been elusive, and this felt like the final stretch. I had to see it through.

The staircase creaked with every step I took, and the air grew colder, the walls narrower. The faint light at the top of the stairs suggested a hallway beyond, but the closer I got, the more I wondered if I was walking into some elaborate trap. The fear that had clung to me for days now tightened around my chest, a vice I couldn't loosen. But the pull of answers was stronger than my hesitation. It had to be.

At the top of the stairs, I found a door, slightly ajar. The same sliver of light escaped from behind it, and I pushed it open, my heart lodged somewhere in my throat. The room beyond was small, almost claustrophobic, with only a desk and a few chairs. The walls were bare, save for a map of Paris tacked up near the window. I froze.

He was there—Luc.

But not the way I remembered him. This version of Luc looked different—darker, perhaps more worn. His face was streaked with stubble, his eyes shadowed as he stared out of the window, oblivious to my presence. He didn't turn when I entered, and for a moment, I wondered if this was some cruel trick my mind had played on me. But no. The faint scent of his cologne, the sound of his breath, all confirmed it.

My voice trembled as I spoke, barely a whisper, "Luc?"

He turned slowly, as though the weight of my words was too much for him to bear. When his eyes met mine, they were the same—intense, wild, with that same flicker of mischief beneath the surface—but there was something else there now, something unreadable.

"Isn't it a little late for this?" he asked, his voice rough, like he'd been waiting for me for far longer than I cared to admit.

I swallowed hard, trying to find my footing. "I—where have you been? I've been looking for you."

His lips curled into a smile, but it was the kind of smile that never reached the eyes. "You shouldn't have come here. It's not safe."

I took a step forward, my resolve hardening despite the chill in the air. "I don't care about safe. I care about you. And I want the truth."

He sighed, and for the briefest of moments, his gaze softened. "The truth?" he muttered, as though the word were foreign to him. "The truth is a dangerous thing to seek, darling. Trust me on that one."

The silence that followed was deafening. Neither of us moved. I felt a coldness seep into my bones, but it wasn't the chill of the room. No, this was the kind of cold that came from knowing you'd just opened a door you couldn't shut again.

I barely noticed the hours slipping by as I stood there, the air between Luc and me thick with unspoken words. His eyes never left mine, and despite the bravado in his posture, I could see the tension tightening in his shoulders. The city, once so full of life and possibility, now felt like a distant memory. Here, in this dim room with its stark walls, everything seemed suspended, as though time itself had forgotten how to move.

"You always were a stubborn one," he said finally, his voice low, the words heavy with something I couldn't quite place.

"Stubborn?" I repeated, my own voice sharper than I intended. "Maybe I'm just tired of the games, Luc. Tired of not knowing. Tired of chasing after your ghosts."

He took a step closer, and I could almost hear the breath catch in his throat as he hesitated. There was something unspoken between us, a shared history that hung in the air like smoke—dense, suffocating, and nearly impossible to ignore. For all the confusion, the lies, the moments of sharp, biting silence, I realized I had never truly stopped wanting him. Even now, standing in this strange, cold place, I felt the pull of him, like a thread tying me to the past I couldn't escape.

"You think you know everything?" he asked, a sardonic smile curling at the edges of his lips. "You think this is about what you want, what you deserve? It's not, Claire. It's about survival."

"Survival?" I repeated, disbelief creeping into my tone. "You're talking to me about survival?"

"Survival," he repeated, stepping forward as if to punctuate the word. "You don't understand the world I'm in. You never did."

I took a shaky breath, trying to steady the whirlwind of emotions spinning in my chest. "So that's it? You're just going to disappear again, like nothing happened?"

Luc paused, his eyes flicking to the floor before meeting mine again, darker now, colder. "You think it's that easy?" His voice dropped to a near whisper, and the words he spoke were not ones I had expected. "There are things I've done, Claire. Things that... you don't get to walk away from."

The chill in the room deepened, and I felt my heart sink. "What are you saying?"

He didn't answer right away, but his gaze flickered to the map pinned on the wall, as though the answer were written somewhere in the folds of its intricate lines. I followed his gaze, but the map was just a map—no cryptic symbols, no answers waiting to be uncovered. It was ordinary in every sense of the word. Except for the fact that Luc was clearly losing himself in its details, like a man searching for something that was already long gone.

"I'm not the same person you knew," he said, his voice hoarse now, as though confessing a secret too dangerous to share. "And you don't want to know who I've become."

I shook my head, the confusion, the hurt, the anger all mingling together in a storm. "I don't want to know? Are you really saying that? You think you can just pull away from everything we were? Everything we could have been?"

Luc's face twisted, a flicker of regret passing through his eyes before he closed them briefly, as if blocking out the memory. "I'm protecting you," he said finally, his words soft but resolute. "The less you know, the safer you'll be."

"Safe?" I scoffed, stepping toward him, ignoring the warning bells ringing in my head. "You think keeping me in the dark is going to keep me safe? Luc, if you wanted to protect me, you should've never disappeared in the first place."

He flinched, and the expression on his face faltered for a moment, the wall he had built between us starting to crack. I saw the man I had once known, the one who smiled with such wild abandon, the one who kissed like he was stealing something he never wanted to give back. But even as I reached for him, I knew something had changed irrevocably. The distance between us was no longer just physical—it was something deeper, darker.

"You don't understand what you're asking," he said quietly, his voice no longer certain. "You think you do, but you don't."

I crossed my arms over my chest, a bitter laugh escaping me. "I understand more than you think. You think I'm the one who's confused, but it's you who's lost, Luc. Lost in this mess you've made. And I'm not going to sit by and let you drag me down with you."

His eyes flickered, a flash of something—guilt, or maybe fear—passing through them before he stepped back. "You don't get to make that choice. You never did."

Before I could respond, the sound of a door slamming open echoed through the room, making both of us jump. The moment was broken, the fragile connection between us snapping like a thread under pressure. I turned quickly, heart pounding in my chest. A figure stood in the doorway, silhouetted by the dim light of the hallway behind them. I couldn't make out their features, but the weight of their presence was undeniable.

"Luc," the voice called, calm but carrying an edge that made my skin prickle. "We need to talk."

Luc's face tightened. His jaw clenched, and I saw the muscles in his neck strain as he suppressed something—anger, maybe, or fear, or both. "Not now," he muttered under his breath, but it was too late. The person—whoever they were—stepped forward into the room.

And just like that, I was no longer sure of anything. The weight of Luc's secrets was suddenly more than I could bear, and the walls that had been keeping me at arm's length were closing in. Whatever this new person wanted, I knew one thing for certain: it wasn't good.

I barely had time to inhale before the figure spoke again, and their words cut through the air like a blade.

"We need to finish this, Luc. Now."

Chapter 17: A Chance Encounter with Destiny

The rain had a way of turning the world into a watercolor painting—colors bleeding into each other, edges softened by the persistent drizzle. It was the kind of day that made you feel as though the world had paused, just for a moment, allowing you to catch your breath. But I hadn't been breathing for a long time. I'd been holding my chest tight, my heart locked away behind a door I didn't have the key to. Until that moment, when the door swung open with a snap, and the world—my world—took on a sharper clarity.

I had almost convinced myself that I was done. That I had buried whatever it was between us so deep that even the smallest shovel wouldn't be able to unearth it. I had become adept at ignoring the shadows of memories, pushing them into corners of my mind that I rarely visited. After all, it wasn't as if I'd expected anything more. I had learned the hard way that people didn't always come back, no matter how loudly your heart screamed their name.

And yet, there he was. Across the street. His back was to me, but I could feel the pull, a magnetic force I couldn't deny. The world seemed to contract around him, as though even the rain held its breath, waiting for me to make the first move. The old bookstore, with its faded sign and heavy wooden door, stood beside him like a silent spectator. He was standing still, his hands shoved in the pockets of his worn jacket, looking through the misted-up glass of the window, oblivious to the traffic splashing past him. I could tell it was him—there was no mistaking that dark, untamed hair or the sharp, almost angular line of his jaw.

I hadn't seen him in months. I hadn't seen anyone in months. I'd made it a point to pull away from everyone I once knew. People always came and went, but no one ever stayed. That was the lesson life had taught me. And so I had hidden, curled up in a cocoon of my own making, keeping to the edges of the world, trying to keep it from unraveling any further.

But here he was, unbidden, and suddenly everything felt wrong. He should have stayed a ghost, a memory, someone I could haunt in my dreams. Not flesh and blood, standing in front of me like an apparition come to life.

My legs moved before I could talk myself out of it. The pavement was slick beneath my feet, each step a small gamble that the rain-slicked surface would betray me. But I couldn't stop now. I was too close. The air between us felt charged, like a storm that was about to break.

"Why are you here?" My voice came out more broken than I'd intended, a trembling question that I had no right to ask. He turned at the sound of my voice, his eyes locking with mine. And for a second, everything stopped.

His eyes—once so full of fire, so full of promises—were now dull, like the last embers of a fire that had burned too long without attention. There was something different about him, a weight to his gaze that hadn't been there before. It took me a moment to gather myself, to even understand the wave of emotion crashing through me. He looked... smaller. Not physically, no. It was as if the world had pressed in on him so hard that it had caved in some part of his soul, leaving only the outer shell of the man I once knew.

"Why am I here?" His voice was hoarse, rough from something deeper than just the weather. "Maybe because I couldn't stay away."

I blinked, trying to absorb the words as they fell from his lips, like stones dropping into a quiet pond, creating ripples I wasn't prepared for. His gaze didn't waver, and for the first time, I saw the truth in his eyes. The vulnerability that had always been so well-hidden behind walls of bravado was now exposed, raw, and so painfully human that it made my chest ache.

I had almost forgotten what it felt like, the feeling of something real, something unguarded. The kind of rawness that burned, that forced you to confront things you weren't ready to face. But there it was, standing right in front of me.

"You left," I said, more firmly than I felt. My pulse quickened, and I almost stumbled over the words. "You didn't even—"

He raised a hand, silencing me with a gentle gesture. "I know," he said, his voice strained, like he was dragging the words from a place that had been closed off for too long. "I left, and I shouldn't have."

The apology hung between us, awkward and too large for either of us to fully hold. The weight of what was unsaid pressed in on me, suffocating any immediate words. I had never expected an apology. I had never expected anything.

But here he was, standing before me, and somehow, the questions I'd buried beneath the surface over the months found their way to my tongue.

"Why?" The word felt heavy, as though it carried the weight of the years we'd spent apart. "Why did you go? Why couldn't you tell me? Why couldn't you—"

"I couldn't be the person you needed me to be," he said, his words barely above a whisper. "I didn't know how to be that person. And I thought... I thought leaving was the only way to protect you from the storm I was dragging behind me."

There was a crack in his voice at the end, and for the first time, I realized how much he had been holding back. How much he had been carrying alone.

I almost took a step back, my heart both angry and aching at the same time. "And you think leaving me was protecting me?" I couldn't keep the bitterness out of my tone, but I couldn't keep the hurt from spilling over, either.

He nodded slowly. "I do. I thought it was the only way."

I wasn't sure whether to laugh or cry. There was something absurd about it—the idea that he'd thought his absence would somehow shield me. The world didn't work like that. It never had.

But here we were, standing on the edge of something I wasn't ready for, and yet couldn't turn away from.

The rain continued to fall, the world around us still blurred by the soft, gray mist.

The moment stretched between us, taut and trembling, as though the universe itself was watching, holding its breath. I couldn't quite trust myself to speak, to move, to do anything other than stand there in the rain with him. I had spent so many months perfecting the art of pretending he didn't matter, of convincing myself I was better off without him, that now, faced with the reality of him standing there, I didn't know how to be. The irony was not lost on me. All that time, I had built a wall high enough to keep him out, but I hadn't accounted for the possibility that he might try to climb it again.

He ran a hand through his hair, disheveled now in the way it always was when he was lost in his thoughts. "I didn't think you'd want to see me," he muttered, his voice low, tinged with the kind of regret that seemed to echo across the space between us. "I thought I could just disappear, and you'd forget me."

Forget him. If only it were that simple. Forgetting him was like trying to forget the way the sun feels on your skin in the summer, or the taste of the first sip of coffee in the morning. There were some things you couldn't erase, no matter how much time you spent trying.

But that wasn't the point now, was it? The point was that he was here, and the anger I had wrapped so tightly around my heart was already starting to slip. I couldn't hold onto it anymore, not when I saw the raw, unfiltered truth in his face. "You think you could just vanish? You think that's how it works?" I could feel my own voice shaking, the cracks in my own armor becoming more apparent by the second. "I waited for you. I didn't know where you were, or if you were okay, and I didn't—" I stopped myself before I could spiral further. There were things I didn't want to say, things that hurt too much, things that I wasn't ready to admit, even to myself.

He took a slow step closer, as though he was testing whether the space between us would allow him. "I'm sorry. I should've told you what was going on, but I was too proud, too lost in myself."

His voice cracked on the last word, and it was a sound I hadn't expected. It caught me off guard, tangled itself in my chest like the branches of an overgrown tree, and suddenly, I wasn't angry anymore. I was tired. So damn tired of carrying all of this alone.

The rain was falling harder now, the sound of it growing louder, like a drumbeat in the background of this small, fragile moment. I didn't know what I wanted from him, or from this encounter. What did I want from a man who had left me without a word, without a trace? But then, maybe that was the thing—this wasn't about wanting anything. It was about letting go of everything I thought I needed, everything I thought I deserved, and allowing myself to just feel.

"I never wanted you to disappear," I said quietly, more to myself than to him. "I just wanted you to stay. To fight for us. But you didn't. And that hurt more than anything."

He nodded, the movement slow, deliberate, as though each acknowledgment was a weight he had to carry. "I don't know how to explain it," he said, his voice barely above a whisper, "but I couldn't be the man you needed. Not then. Not with everything I was running from."

I tilted my head, studying him, searching for the man I had once known beneath the layers of exhaustion and defeat that seemed to hang around him like a second skin. "And now?" I asked, trying to steady my own breath. "Now that you've run out of places to hide, what happens?"

The question was reckless, unexpected, but it felt necessary. The truth hung in the air between us, more present than the rain itself. He looked down for a moment, his hand resting on the back of his neck, and for a brief second, he looked like a man who had forgotten how to look anyone in the eye.

"I'm tired of running," he said finally, his voice steadying. "I didn't want to hurt you. I was trying to protect you from myself. From the mess I'd made. But I know now that was a mistake. I can't fix it, but I'm not running anymore."

Something in me broke then. Not in the way I'd thought it would, not in the way I'd imagined when I'd replayed our last argument over and over in my mind. It wasn't a violent break, but a quiet one. Like a thread snapping loose from a delicate weave. The anger, the hurt—it all unraveled, leaving only a raw, open space. And in that space, there was room for something new. Not forgiveness, not yet. But maybe—maybe there was room for something else. A chance. A possibility.

I inhaled deeply, feeling the rain soak through my coat, my hair, my skin. "You can't just come back and expect everything to be the same," I said, the words falling from me before I could stop them. "I've moved on. I've built a life without you in it. And maybe that's what I needed. Maybe that's what we needed."

His eyes locked onto mine then, and there was something fierce, something unspoken in them. "Maybe," he said, his voice low, but steady, "but I don't think we're done yet."

The world around us seemed to shrink, the space between us tightening as the moment held us captive. The rain continued to fall, but neither of us moved. He stood there, soaking wet, his breath coming out in slow, deliberate puffs, and I could almost hear the words he wasn't saying. I wasn't sure what came next, but I knew one thing for certain: whatever happened, it was going to change everything.

I wasn't sure if I was ready for that change. But when I looked into his eyes again, all I could think was that I might never be ready for it. And yet, somehow, I was going to have to be.

The words hung in the air between us, delicate and fragile, like the last thread of a tapestry being pulled too tightly. "I'm not running anymore," he had said, and while the sentiment should have been comforting, it only served to increase the weight pressing down on my chest. The space between us crackled with unanswered questions, each one heavy and looming, but there was one question I couldn't shake.

"How do I know you mean it this time?" I asked, my voice barely a whisper, barely even my own.

He swallowed hard, a muscle working in his jaw as if the question had struck him deeper than any words I could have chosen. For a moment, he didn't answer. Instead, he simply stared at me, those dark eyes of his unreadable—too full of memories, too full of things left unsaid. I wanted to look away. I wanted to be strong enough to walk away. But I couldn't. I wasn't strong enough, not when the storm in his eyes was a mirror of the one inside me.

"Because I'm here now," he said quietly, as if that should settle everything. As if his presence, in all its weariness and quiet desperation, should erase the months of silence, the weight of his absence.

I almost laughed, the sound caught in my throat, bitter and mocking. "And that's supposed to make up for everything?"

His gaze softened, a faint trace of remorse flickering beneath the surface. "No. It's not. But it's all I have to offer. The only thing that's left, really."

I had no response to that. What could I say? That the pieces of me that had been left behind had long since turned to dust?

That I had learned to live without him, without us, and the idea of rebuilding it all felt like too much? I should have walked away then, before my heart could say anything my mind couldn't quite catch. But instead, I stayed.

He took a hesitant step closer, and my pulse quickened, my heart rebelling against the stillness I had tried to cultivate around it. The rain continued to fall in steady sheets, the city now a blur of reflections and dampened colors. His hand, so close yet so far, hovered in the air between us, as if uncertain whether to reach for me, to bridge the gap that had stretched for so long.

"You don't owe me anything," he said, his voice low and strained. "I didn't deserve your forgiveness. And I still don't. But I—" His voice faltered, and he looked away for a moment, as though he couldn't bear to meet my eyes. I knew what he was about to say, but it didn't make it any easier to hear. "I want to try. If you'll let me."

The weight of those words settled over me like a blanket—heavy and suffocating. Try. I wanted to laugh again, to ask him just how he intended to try when the foundation of everything we had built had crumbled. How could you try to rebuild something that had shattered? But I didn't laugh. I didn't scoff. I simply stood there, drowning in the unspoken tension between us.

"I'm not the same person I was when you left," I said, each word careful, deliberate. I had to make that clear. I wasn't the same version of myself who had waited, who had hoped, who had believed. "I've changed. And maybe you have too." The words stung as I spoke them, because I knew that change wasn't always for the better. Sometimes, change only left scars where something beautiful had once been.

"I know," he said, his voice tight. "I've been... different, too." The sadness in his eyes was a weight I couldn't ignore, and something twisted deep inside me, something that had lain dormant for so long. For a moment, I wondered if I could forgive him. Not because he asked, but because I was tired of carrying the burden of resentment.

Tired of the constant ache that had accompanied his absence. I wanted to let it go, to let him go, to be free of the heaviness of our shared history.

But the words were harder to say than I had imagined. They caught in my throat, tangled with the fear that maybe, just maybe, forgiving him would open a door that neither of us were ready to walk through.

"Do you think we can ever go back?" I asked, the question slipping from my lips before I could stop it. It felt like the kind of question that shouldn't have been asked, that shouldn't have been possible after everything that had happened. But there it was, hanging between us like a silent prayer.

He closed his eyes for a moment, as if the question itself was a weight too heavy to bear. "I don't know," he said, and his answer, simple and honest, was more than I had expected. "But I think we have to try. I think we have to let go of the past in order to move forward."

His words hung in the air like smoke, lingering and elusive, and in that moment, I wasn't sure if I believed them. I wanted to. God, I wanted to believe that we could somehow find our way back to the beginning, to the version of us that hadn't been broken. But I wasn't sure if that was even possible.

"You can't just ask me to forget," I said, the bitterness creeping back into my voice despite myself. "You can't just ask me to erase everything and pretend like it never happened."

He flinched, a slight, almost imperceptible movement, and it was enough to make my heart twist. "I'm not asking you to forget," he said, his voice softer now, more sincere. "I'm asking you to trust me. Just this once."

Trust. The word felt foreign, a relic of a time I didn't quite recognize. How could I trust him after everything? After the lies, after the silence? I wanted to say no. I wanted to say that trust wasn't something you could demand, that it had to be earned. But the words caught in my throat, and I found myself unable to speak them.

"Please," he whispered, his voice rough now, like it hurt to say it. "I'm not asking for your forgiveness. I'm just asking for a chance."

And as I stood there in the rain, staring into the eyes of the man who had once been everything to me, I wondered—what was the price of that chance? And was I willing to pay it?

Just as I opened my mouth to answer, the sound of a car's screeching tires cut through the air, sharp and sudden, and I turned in time to see a flash of headlights. The world seemed to tilt for a moment, everything spinning in a dizzying blur, before the unmistakable screech of metal against metal echoed through the street.

My heart leapt into my throat as I looked back at him—only to find that he wasn't looking at me anymore. His eyes were wide with something I couldn't place. And then, without warning, he pushed me.

Shoved me.

And everything went black.

Chapter 18: Secrets Beneath the Surface

The rain had been coming down in sheets for hours, drenching the city, a relentless patter against the windows. It was the sort of rain that makes everything feel both claustrophobic and expansive, like the world outside was too big and too small at the same time. Jonah and I sat across from each other in the dim light of my kitchen, the silence between us more comfortable than it should have been. His eyes kept flitting to the window, tracing the storm's rhythm, but his thoughts seemed far away.

I poured a second cup of coffee, the rich scent filling the room, and studied him. He had always been so unreadable, a fortress wrapped in layers of sharp angles and worn-down edges. But tonight, he was softer somehow. A storm brewed inside him, I could see that in the subtle tightening of his jaw, in the way his hands gripped the mug like it was the only thing keeping him tethered. It made me want to reach out and pull him closer, though I had no idea what I was doing, or what he needed.

"Are you always this quiet?" I asked, trying to break the tension. It came out sharper than I intended, a challenge of sorts, but the only sound in the room was the hiss of the rain. I almost regretted the question, but Jonah didn't seem to mind.

"No," he said quietly, eyes locking with mine for a split second before looking away again. "Not really."

It was then that I noticed the tightness in his shoulders, the way his fingers twitched nervously at his side. The man was wound so tight, it was like watching a live wire about to snap. But what was he running from? What kept him so far away from me, even now when we'd started to close the gap?

I hesitated, wondering if I should press further. But Jonah wasn't the kind of man to open up easily. It had taken weeks to even get him to show up at my door when I asked for help with the car, and even then, he had been all business. But now... now there was something else in his eyes. Something fragile. Something that made my chest tighten.

"You don't have to talk about it," I said before I could stop myself, my voice soft, almost a whisper. "But you can, if you want."

There it was. The offer hanging between us like an unspoken promise. The truth, or some version of it, finally coming to light. I could almost feel the heat of it, sizzling like the rain hitting the pavement outside. For a long moment, Jonah didn't move. He didn't even breathe.

And then he spoke, his voice low, rough like it had been dragged over gravel. "I wasn't always like this." He paused, the words thick and hard to swallow. "I used to think I knew what love was. Until I didn't."

I felt my stomach tighten at his words. The vulnerability in them was almost more than I could bear. Jonah, this man who had built himself up to be unbreakable, was now revealing something raw, something torn open.

"Tell me," I urged, though I didn't know what exactly I was asking. "What happened?"

His eyes flickered to mine, and for the briefest moment, I saw it—something dark, something painful that I had never seen before. But before I could read it fully, he looked away.

"It was a long time ago," he muttered, running a hand through his hair. "A woman... We were everything to each other. Or at least, I thought we were." His voice cracked, and I could see the anger that bubbled beneath the surface, the years of resentment and hurt that he had buried so deep. "But she... she left. Without a word, without a trace. She just disappeared."

I leaned forward, my heart pounding in my chest. "She just—"

"Vanished," he finished for me, his voice hard as stone. "And it took me years to even begin to understand why. Turns out, I wasn't the one she wanted. She found someone else—someone who could give her what I couldn't. And I couldn't stop her." He exhaled sharply, his breath coming in uneven waves. "That's when everything changed. That's when I learned not to trust. Not to... care."

There it was, the core of him—the reason he was so closed off, so resistant to everything that even hinted at real connection. He had loved deeply once, and someone had taken it all from him. And now, he was a man running from that pain, trying to protect himself from the wreckage of something he could never reclaim.

"I'm sorry," I said softly, my voice barely above a whisper. "That sounds... awful."

Jonah didn't respond right away. He just stared at the floor, his hands still gripping the coffee mug, his knuckles white. "Yeah, well," he muttered after a long pause. "It is. But it's also made me who I am." He looked at me then, his gaze steady and unreadable. "And I don't know how to change that. How to be... anything different."

Something inside me stirred. It was a mixture of pity and understanding, but also something else. A quiet, undeniable pull toward him, a desire to find whatever light he had buried so deeply.

I didn't know how to fix him, or if he even wanted to be fixed, but I knew one thing—this man had scars deeper than I could imagine, and if I was going to keep him close, I needed to understand them. Because Jonah, for all his anger and bitterness, was still someone I cared for. Someone I didn't want to lose, even if I didn't yet know how to navigate the dangerous waters of his heart.

I leaned back in my chair, not knowing what to say, but knowing I had to say something. Because the last thing I wanted was for Jonah to disappear too.

The quiet between us stretched longer than I was comfortable with, and the tension settled like fog in the room, thick and persistent. Jonah wasn't looking at me anymore. His eyes were trained on the steam rising from his coffee cup, as if it were the only thing left in the world that could make sense to him. I could feel the weight of the moment, as if we were standing at the edge of a cliff, staring down into something deep and murky. The silence was suffocating, but I wasn't ready to let it consume us entirely.

"You know, you never told me how long it took you to get over her." The words slipped out before I had a chance to stop them. I hadn't meant to go that deep, but it was like something inside me couldn't help but push forward. To understand him fully, I needed to know the true cost of the wreckage he'd just confessed. And maybe, just maybe, he needed to say it out loud.

Jonah's eyes snapped up to meet mine, sharp, like he hadn't expected the question, or perhaps didn't want to. He looked at me with something that almost seemed like a challenge, but there was a flicker of vulnerability underneath, something softer than the armor he usually wore.

"I never got over her," he said, his voice a little too cold, a little too tight. He ran a hand over his face, the exhaustion in his movements too raw to hide. "You don't just get over something like that. You learn to live with it. But that's the thing, right? You keep moving forward, pretending you're okay until one day you wake up and realize you're still stuck. The past isn't behind you—it's tangled up in your bones, in the way you look at people, at relationships. You think you've got it figured out, but you don't. You never do."

I let his words sink in, feeling the weight of them settle on my chest. I didn't want to feel sorry for him—I didn't think pity was what he needed—but I couldn't help it. The fact that he was sitting here, with me, sharing this much of himself, made my heart ache. How had I not seen this before? How had I missed all the small signs, the cracks beneath his tough exterior?

"I get it," I said softly, pushing aside my own confusion to meet his gaze with a steady look of my own. "You think moving on means forgetting. That's how it works, right?" I let the words linger in the air between us. "But forgetting doesn't erase. It just... buries it deeper."

Jonah let out a long breath, nodding, but there was something restless in the way he shifted in his chair. "Exactly," he murmured, his voice a little strained. "And after a while, it becomes easier to just live with the weight of it all. Easier to shut people out, keep them at arm's length, than risk going through that again."

The room felt colder then, though the heat from the coffee was still there, swirling in the air like the smoke from a long-forgotten fire. He was talking in circles, trying to protect himself by pushing me away before I could get too close, before he could fall for the very thing he feared. I wanted to understand. I needed to. But I couldn't let him hide from me—not now.

"I'm not asking you to forget, Jonah." I reached across the table, my fingers brushing lightly against his. It was a simple gesture, nothing more, but it felt like an invitation to something more. To the possibility that there might be more to his story than the grief he kept locked away. "I'm asking you to remember, but let it go. Not for her, but for you. Because you're not that man anymore, and you don't have to keep living like you are."

He stared at my hand for a moment, his eyes flicking between my fingers and my face, as if weighing whether or not to take that small leap of faith. Then, he took a deep breath and pulled his hand back, though the distance between us felt more like an ocean than a few inches of empty space.

"It's not that simple." His voice was firm, but there was something uncertain underneath. A crack in the armor, though barely visible. "You can't just forget the way someone can break you. You can't erase the way it feels to have your trust shattered."

I nodded, understanding his reluctance. Of course it wasn't that simple. Trust wasn't something you could build and tear down at will. It wasn't a structure you could just reconstruct whenever you felt like it. But I wasn't trying to get him to forget. I was trying to help him see that there was more to life than the scars he carried around like armor.

"I know," I said, my voice barely above a whisper, not wanting to push him further than he was willing to go. "But I'm not asking you to forget. Just... to let someone in. Even if it's just a little bit."

Jonah's gaze was intense now, like he was seeing me for the first time. I wasn't sure what he saw exactly, but the way he was looking at me made my stomach flip in ways I couldn't quite explain. He was testing me, I could tell. Seeing how far I was willing to go, how much of myself I was offering without expecting anything in return.

"You're asking a lot," he said, a slight edge to his voice, but the challenge wasn't harsh anymore. It was a kind of quiet acknowledgment.

I smiled, trying to keep it light, trying to make him feel less like he was standing on the edge of a cliff. "Maybe. But not everything that's worth it comes easily, right?"

Jonah's lips curled into a faint smile, the first real one I'd seen in a long time, and for a moment, the weight of everything between us seemed to lift, if only a little. "I guess not."

I let that silence stretch again, but this time, it wasn't uncomfortable. This time, it felt like something was shifting. Something that had been stuck for too long was starting to move, and maybe—just maybe—we were both beginning to understand what it meant to trust again. To open up, even if only a crack, to let the light in.

The rain had slowed to a trickle, but the humidity in the air hung thick, like everything was holding its breath, waiting for something to change. Jonah and I remained in that space between words, that delicate silence where everything was still unresolved. I could feel the walls he'd built for so long, each layer an unspoken promise to never let anyone in. But with every look, every hesitant touch, it felt like something was cracking. The air around us was charged, not with tension, but with the possibility of something more.

Jonah shifted in his seat, running a hand through his hair, his eyes briefly meeting mine before darting away again. He was trying to fight something—his instinct to close off, to pull back—but it was slipping. I could see it in the way his body language softened, the tiny shift in his posture when he finally turned to face me more fully.

"You know, this wasn't what I had in mind," he said, his voice still rough but carrying a certain bite. It made me smile, the teasing note barely hidden in his words.

"Really?" I leaned back, matching his playful tone. "Because I was under the impression that sharing painful, traumatic experiences over coffee was exactly how you imagined this night going."

He snorted, the sound catching me off guard, like the tension had cracked just a little, letting some humor sneak through. "Oh, absolutely. You know me. My ideal date is a long, drawn-out therapy session."

I couldn't help but laugh. "Well, you're in luck. I'm a fantastic listener. And I'm practically certified in making awkward silences bearable."

Jonah's eyes flickered with something—amusement, relief, maybe both—and for the first time in what felt like forever, he let out a breath that wasn't full of restraint or frustration. He actually relaxed a little, the tightness in his jaw easing. It was a small change, barely noticeable, but enough to make my heart skip.

"You're weirdly good at this," he muttered, though there was something almost affectionate in his tone.

"I know," I replied, matching his mock-seriousness. "It's my superpower."

There was a beat of silence before he shifted, his expression becoming more guarded again. "You shouldn't... You shouldn't be here, you know. Not with someone like me."

I raised an eyebrow, leaning forward just a fraction. "Someone like you? Care to explain that? Because I'm pretty sure you've been exactly who you are this whole time. And I think I like the guy you're trying to convince me doesn't exist."

Jonah shook his head, his eyes suddenly distant. "It's not about who I am. It's about what I can't be. What I can't give. I'm—" He stopped himself, the words choking off like they didn't belong.

"You're what?" I pressed, unable to help myself. I could see him retreating, pulling back, like I was edging too close to something he wasn't ready to face. But I wasn't going to back off this time. Not when he was this close to letting something real slip out. "Jonah, you can't keep pretending like you don't want to say it. Whatever it is."

He looked at me for a long moment, his expression unreadable. Then, almost imperceptibly, he shook his head. "I can't offer you any of the things you think you need. Not right now."

I felt a sharp twist in my chest, the words sinking in like they were meant to make me back away. But they didn't. They didn't do anything but make me more certain, more determined to break down the walls he'd surrounded himself with.

"I don't need anything from you, Jonah," I said, the words coming out more softly than I intended. "But I want to understand. I want to be here, in whatever this is, without all the pressure. Without any promises."

Jonah's gaze dropped to the table, and his hands, clenched tightly, slowly unfurled. It was as if he had been waiting for someone to call his bluff, to tell him that it was okay to stop pretending. That the burden of his past didn't have to define him forever.

"Maybe that's the problem," he muttered, almost to himself. "Maybe I'm not sure how to stop pretending anymore."

His words were like a shudder through the air, an admission that was both too heavy and too fragile. It was like he had just placed a thousand-pound weight in my lap and expected me to handle it with the care of someone who had never been broken. I didn't know how to respond to that.

Instead, I reached across the table and gently touched his hand, feeling the tension in his fingers as he froze under my touch.

"I'm not asking you to change overnight," I said, my voice calm, but with an undercurrent of something deeper—something that felt like it had been building for longer than either of us had realized. "But you can't keep running from it forever, Jonah. You have to face it. Whatever it is. Or else you'll end up..."

"Alone?" he finished for me, his voice laced with bitterness.

I met his gaze, steady. "I wasn't going to say that," I lied. "But yeah. Alone."

He was silent for a long moment, and I could feel the weight of his thoughts pressing down on him. He was a man at war with himself, caught between a past he couldn't shake and a future he didn't believe he deserved. And here I was, trying to be the bridge between the two, unsure if I could carry the weight of both.

Then, just as I thought he might pull away again, he looked up, his eyes meeting mine with something different in them. Something that made my heart stop, just for a beat.

"I'm not used to being this close to anyone," he said quietly. "It's... it's terrifying. But it's also... tempting."

I swallowed, trying to steady my breath. "You don't have to be scared of it, Jonah."

And then, just like that, the doorbell rang.

We both froze. The sound of it was so jarring, so completely out of place in that fragile moment, that it felt like an interruption from another world entirely. I glanced at Jonah, and he was already standing, the careful mask slipping back into place. The moment had shattered.

"Who the hell..." I began, but Jonah was already walking toward the door, his shoulders tense, his steps swift.

I stayed rooted to the chair, confusion swirling. Whoever it was, they had no idea what they were walking into. And neither did I.

Jonah hesitated just before opening the door, his back to me, but then he turned, his expression unreadable once again.

"I'll be right back," he said, the words heavy, like there was something he wasn't saying. Something that had just arrived, and I had no idea how much it would change things between us.

Chapter 19: An Oath in the Moonlight

The moon hung low, its light spilling over the lake like a silver blanket, soft but penetrating. It caught the surface of the water in shimmering arcs, the ripples small but deliberate, echoing in the silence that stretched between us. Jonah's hand was warm in mine, the kind of warmth that seeped into your bones, even on the coolest of nights. Yet, there was a chill that lingered, just beneath the surface, something that gnawed at the edges of my thoughts.

Jonah had always been a mystery, a man made of shadows and silence, whose past was tucked away like an old photograph, edges frayed and fading. But tonight, as we stood together on the rocky shore, I could see a flicker of something different in him. A promise, maybe. A raw honesty that made the night feel both fragile and infinite.

"I'm not asking for forgiveness," Jonah's voice was steady, low. It matched the night—calm, yet full of undercurrents. "I'm asking for the chance to move forward. With you."

I wanted to believe him, truly. There was something about the way his words hung in the air, thick with conviction, that made my heart beat faster, like the first step toward something undeniable. But there was also a small, stubborn voice inside me, the kind that never quite shut up, that told me things weren't as simple as they appeared. I glanced down at our intertwined hands, the weight of the past heavy between us.

"I don't know if I can just forget it all," I murmured, not because I wanted to throw his past in his face but because the truth of it—of what he'd lived through—still hung between us, a ghost of things that had never been fully said. "You think you can erase it?"

Jonah exhaled, the sound like a soft wind through the trees. He shook his head, his dark hair catching in the moonlight. "No. I don't think I can. But I can try. For you. For us."

I wanted to tell him that trying wasn't enough. That the weight of the things he carried—grief, regrets, all the parts of him he'd never shown anyone—wasn't something you could just shake off with a vow. But the tenderness in his touch, the rawness in his eyes, made it impossible to dismiss him outright. Jonah had always been a man of contradictions, and tonight, he was no different.

I looked out over the water, the smooth, glassy surface reflecting the full moon, now rising higher in the sky. Its light seemed to wash over everything, lending a sense of clarity, but I knew better than to trust its illusions. The moon, in all its beauty, had its dark side, just like Jonah. I could feel it—his past, like a storm brewing just out of sight, just beyond the horizon.

"You really think this... us... can work?" I asked, the words tasting unfamiliar on my tongue. The fear, the doubt—it was all there, swirling just beneath the surface.

Jonah tightened his grip on my hand, his thumb brushing over the knuckles, slow and deliberate. "I have to believe it can. Or I'm nothing."

His gaze was unwavering, the sincerity in his words wrapping around me like the first signs of spring—hopeful, soft, but fragile. I wanted to believe him. But something in the way the shadows stretched beneath the trees told me that the past wasn't done with us. Not yet.

The air was still, save for the occasional rustle of the trees, and I could feel the weight of his gaze on me, asking for something—permission, maybe? I didn't know what to give him, not yet. Not when the specters of what he had lived through still clung to him like a second skin.

"I'm not perfect," he said, breaking the silence with a small, rueful smile. "But I can promise you this—I'll never ask you to be."

I wanted to laugh, but the ache in my chest tightened, pulling me deeper into the moment. Jonah had never understood the way

I carried my own burdens—how I had built walls around myself to keep the world at bay, to keep from being swallowed whole. He was a man of extremes, but I was something else entirely. I was a woman who had learned to hide in the quiet, to shelter myself in the corners where no one could find me. But standing here, with Jonah, under the ghostly light of the moon, I felt like I was being drawn into something I didn't know how to escape.

"I don't know if I can do this," I whispered, almost to myself. "I don't know how to trust without wondering when the other shoe will drop."

Jonah stepped closer, his presence surrounding me like the earth itself. His hands reached for my shoulders, and for the first time that night, his touch felt grounding, solid.

"You don't have to know everything," he said, his voice soft but firm. "Just take the next step with me. No more, no less. We'll figure it out as we go."

I looked up at him then, really looked at him, and for a moment, I could see the boy beneath the man—the boy who had been scarred by the world, whose heart had been shattered by things too dark to speak of. And in that moment, the weight of my own fears seemed small, insignificant compared to the enormity of what we were standing on the edge of.

"Alright," I said, my voice barely a breath. "One step. Together."

Jonah's smile was the first real one I had seen that night, full of light, full of possibility. And just like that, the ghosts of the past didn't feel quite as close. Not yet, at least.

Jonah's smile lingered, but there was a nervous flicker in his eyes that hadn't been there before. I noticed it, because it mirrored the unease stirring deep in me. It wasn't that I didn't believe him—God knows, there was something about him that made me want to believe every word. But this wasn't something as simple as a fresh start. The past, like a stubborn shadow, always had a way of creeping back in, no matter how brightly the present tried to shine.

He reached for my face, his fingers cool against the heat of my skin, and for a moment, everything else blurred. The rustling trees, the far-off croak of frogs, the hum of the night air—all faded into the background, leaving just him and me standing on the edge of something we both feared but couldn't resist.

"I know it's not going to be easy," Jonah said, his voice rough, like he was fighting for the words. "I'm not asking for an easy life. I'm asking for a chance. To fight for us."

The sincerity in his voice tangled with something I couldn't quite name. The words sounded perfect. Too perfect. My heart fluttered against my ribs, uncertain whether to leap toward him or retreat back into the safety of silence.

"Fighting is a lot easier than winning," I said, my own voice a little too sharp, a little too distant. It wasn't intentional, but the walls I'd spent years building weren't quite as forgiving as I liked to believe.

Jonah's hand lingered on my cheek for a moment longer, his thumb brushing my skin in slow, deliberate circles. "I'm not asking for a guarantee," he replied, his voice low, the way it always was when he was serious. "Just... don't make me fight this alone."

I swallowed hard, the knot in my throat tight enough to choke me. I wasn't used to this. I wasn't used to people asking for something from me—not like this. Sure, I'd offered my heart, my trust, my everything to people before. But somewhere along the way, I'd learned to keep it locked up tight, under wraps.

But Jonah? He had a way of making me feel like maybe, just maybe, I could unlock it again. That hope I'd felt earlier, that flutter between us, was still there, just underneath the skin. But hope always had an ugly cousin. And right now, its name was doubt.

"I'm not exactly the easiest person to be around," I said, my voice quiet now, almost like I was testing the words before letting them fully slip out.

Jonah's smile softened, and there was something in his gaze that made me feel a little less like a puzzle with missing pieces. "We're both broken," he said with a slight shrug, "in different ways. But if we're being honest, I think I'd prefer to be broken with you than to be whole without you."

His words hit me harder than I expected, and I had to blink away the sudden rush of emotion that threatened to overtake me. That strange mixture of warmth and fear. I wasn't sure which was more powerful.

"So," I said, taking a half-step back, pretending the distance between us would stop the tide of feelings rising in me. "What now?"

He chuckled softly, a quiet sound that made my stomach flip. "Well, now we go back to town, I guess. Pretend like everything's normal. Get some sleep. Wake up in the morning and figure it out."

"Pretend?" I arched an eyebrow, letting a wry smile slip past my lips. "Is that your idea of romance?"

Jonah's grin widened, but I saw the subtle shift in his posture, like he was testing the waters. "What can I say? I'm a fan of low-key dates. You know, a bit of moonlight, some heart-to-heart. A couple of ghosts lurking in the background." He winked. "Really sets the mood."

I laughed, the sound of it surprising me more than it should've. There was something disarming about him, something that made me feel a little less like a soldier on guard and a little more like a woman just trying to figure out if she was willing to risk it all again.

But that's the thing, isn't it? The risk. The uncertainty of it. Everything Jonah said made sense, and yet, a small part of me was still holding back, hesitant to fully dive in. Maybe it was the fear of repeating past mistakes. Maybe it was the fact that in my experience, good things didn't come without their price. And Jonah? He had a price. One I wasn't sure I was willing to pay.

I cleared my throat, feeling the weight of the conversation shift, becoming heavier. "You know, the past doesn't just disappear because we decide it should. There's no magic reset button. No quick fixes."

Jonah took a step closer, closing the gap between us again, his hand slipping to the small of my back, warm and steady. "I know," he said, his voice firm, but with a tenderness that made my chest tighten. "But maybe, if we're lucky, we can find a way to move forward without it suffocating us."

I didn't respond right away. Instead, I looked up at the moon, the same one that had bathed the water in its silver light, casting long shadows over the rocks and trees. It felt distant, untouchable. Much like the future I wasn't sure I could reach.

"So," I said after a long pause, glancing at Jonah, my voice teasing to cover the uncertainty, "does this mean we're officially on some kind of... romantic adventure? Or are we just two people who are hopelessly bad at saying no to each other?"

Jonah's smile tugged at the corners of his mouth, but there was something more behind it. Something more real than I was willing to admit. "Honestly? It means we're two people who are about to make one hell of a mess together."

I laughed, the sound escaping before I could hold it back, and in that moment, I felt the first flicker of something hopeful bloom between us again. It wasn't perfect. But maybe, just maybe, perfect wasn't what we needed.

We didn't move right away. Instead, we stood there for a while longer, side by side, letting the night stretch out around us. The air was cool, but it didn't feel cold anymore. The future, though unclear, didn't seem quite so impossible to face.

And for the first time in a long time, I let myself believe that maybe, just maybe, we were both exactly where we were supposed to be.

The world seemed to hold its breath as we stood there, Jonah and I, in that fragile space between promises and reality. The moon above us continued its silent vigil, casting its pale glow over the land, but beneath its soft light, there was nothing quiet about what was rising between us. The weight of the past, of everything unspoken, lingered like a shadow, casting doubt in places where hope had only just begun to bloom.

Jonah's hand still held mine, firm but gentle, as if trying to convince both of us that this was the moment—the moment—when everything would shift, when the ghosts would finally slip away. But I couldn't shake the feeling that they weren't gone. Not yet.

"You think we can just move on, don't you?" I asked, the words escaping before I had a chance to soften them. It wasn't what I meant, not exactly. But the question hung in the air like a challenge.

Jonah's jaw tightened slightly, and for a moment, I saw something in him—vulnerability, maybe, or the start of doubt. "I'm not asking for an easy fix. I know it's not that simple," he said, his voice low but steady. "But I am asking for a chance. For us."

His words were like a balm, soothing some of the raw edges of my own fears, but it was a fleeting comfort. I knew what it was like to fight for something, to work so damn hard to make it right, only to watch it unravel anyway.

"I can't promise I won't have moments when I'm not sure," I said, voice catching a little. "I can't promise I won't look over my shoulder, expecting to see the past coming up behind us."

Jonah's thumb grazed my wrist, a gesture so simple, yet it carried the weight of everything unspoken. His gaze softened, and for a heartbeat, it felt like maybe we were both speaking the same language.

"Then we'll deal with it together," he said simply. "One step at a time. The past doesn't get to dictate our future. Not if we don't let it."

I wanted to argue, to tell him that it wasn't that simple, that the past wasn't something you could just banish with a couple of good intentions. But then he smiled at me, a quiet thing, full of understanding, and something inside me unraveled. The fear, the hesitation, the doubts—they all slipped just a little bit, giving way to something warmer, something that made my pulse quicken.

But before I could say anything else, the unmistakable sound of footsteps crunched through the gravel nearby. I froze, the sudden interruption like a cold splash of water in the middle of something intimate and delicate. Jonah's hand moved instinctively to my waist, pulling me closer, his posture shifting to one of alertness.

"Who's there?" he called, his voice low and controlled, but there was no mistaking the tension in it.

From the shadows, a figure emerged, tall and lean, their face partially obscured by the brim of a hat. The way they moved, too smooth and purposeful, made my stomach tighten with unease.

"You should be more careful, Jonah," the figure said, their voice smooth, but with an edge to it, like a blade just beneath the surface.

Jonah's grip tightened on my waist, and I could feel the change in him—something darker, more guarded. "I've been careful enough," he replied, his tone clipped, but not without an underlying warning.

The figure stepped closer, just enough for the moonlight to catch their features. A familiar face. A face I never expected to see again. My breath hitched in my chest, and for a moment, I couldn't quite place it.

"You," I whispered, my voice barely audible, as recognition flickered through the fog of my thoughts.

The man smiled, a slow, calculated curve of his lips that made my blood run cold. "Long time, no see, Eve."

His words were like a slap, and my stomach churned at the sound of my name on his lips. Eve. The last person I ever expected to come across again. And the last person I wanted to see tonight, of all nights.

Jonah stiffened beside me, his body going tense as if preparing for something. "What the hell do you want, Remy?"

Remy's smile never faltered, but there was something predatory in it now, a glint of satisfaction in his eyes. "Nothing much. Just a little chat. About old times. And, you know, some unfinished business."

The air between us felt suddenly too thin, the weight of his presence pressing down on my chest. I couldn't breathe. Jonah's hand on my waist seemed to be the only thing anchoring me to reality. And yet, in that moment, all I could think about was how easily Remy had appeared out of nowhere, like a shadow from a past I'd tried to leave behind.

"I'm done with you, Remy," I said, the words coming out sharper than I intended. "Whatever you think you're here for, it's not happening."

Remy chuckled, but it wasn't a sound of amusement. It was dark, taunting. "Oh, I think you'll want to hear me out, Eve. You've got no idea what's coming."

Jonah moved to step in front of me, a protective gesture, but Remy raised a hand, silencing him with a look.

"You might want to keep your distance," Remy said to Jonah, his voice as smooth as silk. "I wouldn't want to make things... complicated."

I stepped closer to Jonah, a surge of protective instinct rising within me. "What do you want, Remy?" I demanded, my voice trembling slightly, though I refused to show it. "You think you can come back after all this time and scare us into doing your bidding?"

Remy's grin widened, a cruel, knowing smile. "No, Eve. I'm not here to scare you. I'm here to remind you that the past never really lets go. Not until it's ready."

The words hit me like a punch, knocking the wind from my chest. Something cold slid into my veins. Something I couldn't shake.

And as Remy stepped back into the shadows, his final words hung in the air like a curse, their meaning still unclear but heavy with promise.

"You'll find out soon enough," he said, his voice fading into the darkness. "The past isn't done with either of you."

Chapter 20: Shadows of an Old Flame

The moment she stepped into the café, the whole room seemed to shiver in a collective breath, as though the air had been suddenly weighted with something dark and unspoken. I was sitting at a table near the window, Jonah opposite me, the sunlight slanting in just enough to make his eyes gleam with that familiar warmth that had become my anchor. I was in the middle of telling him about a client who'd tried to pull a fast one on me, laughing over the ridiculousness of it when the bell above the door chimed.

At first, I didn't think much of it. People came and went in the café all the time—tourists, students, the occasional businessman with his head down in a desperate attempt to avoid eye contact. But then, her voice—rich and honeyed with an underlying sharpness—cut through the noise. "Jonah."

It wasn't the way she said it that struck me, but the way he reacted. His smile faltered. For a fraction of a second, he looked like a man who had just glimpsed the very thing he thought he had buried. His face, once so open, closed like a book, the pages snapping shut with a finality I hadn't expected.

My gaze snapped to her. She stood just inside the door, a tall, striking figure, framed by the soft glow of the café's interior. Dark hair, pulled back into a loose knot at the top of her head, revealed a long neck and a face that was sharp, almost cruel in its beauty. Her eyes were a striking blue, cold and calculating as they locked onto Jonah before flicking over to me with a slow, deliberate scan.

Jonah cleared his throat, the sound rough, as though it had to fight its way through something lodged in his chest. "Eva," he said, the name falling from his lips like an old memory, dusted off and offered up reluctantly.

She smiled then, but it was the kind of smile you might see just before someone strikes. "I didn't think I'd find you here, Jonah," she purred, her eyes glinting with some private joke. "What's it been? A year? Two? I had to take a chance when I saw your car parked outside."

A year. Two. My fingers tightened around the edge of my coffee cup, the warmth doing nothing to thaw the cold knot that had formed in the pit of my stomach. I could feel the shift in the room—the weight of history that hung between them, thick and heavy like a storm cloud. But I wasn't ready to fold. Not this time.

I gave Jonah a half-hearted smile, the kind that you flash when you're pretending not to care. "Do you want me to leave?" I asked her, my voice steady, though the nerves were starting to creep in. There was no need to make this dramatic, I told myself. It was just an ex. Right?

Her eyes narrowed slightly, the smile still in place but now more calculated, the kind of expression that signals someone who isn't used to being challenged. "I didn't think you'd be the type to back down so easily," she said, her words a slow, deliberate burn. "But it's nice to know that you're already showing your true colors."

"Eva," Jonah warned, his voice soft but firm. He wasn't looking at me anymore—his attention fully on her now. "This isn't the place for this."

The tension between them crackled, and for a moment, I wondered what exactly had happened between them. What was it that made Jonah tense in her presence, as if he were bracing himself for a storm?

Eva took a step forward, drawing my attention back to her. Her heels clicked sharply against the floor, the sound unnervingly deliberate. "Oh, I know exactly what I'm doing," she said, a hint of mockery in her tone. She shifted her gaze back to Jonah, her eyes narrowing as she softened her voice, a dangerous sweetness replacing the earlier edge. "I'm just here to remind you of what you're missing. After all, it wasn't just the distance that drove us apart, was it?"

I watched Jonah's jaw tighten. He shifted in his seat, running a hand through his hair, the unease in his posture like a flag waving in the breeze. Whatever history they shared, it wasn't something I was prepared to unpack in a café, not with the air thick with her presence and the weight of unsaid things pressing in on all sides.

My stomach churned, the uncertainty gnawing at me. What did she mean by that? Was I missing something here? Was there something Jonah hadn't told me?

But I couldn't ask. Not yet. Instead, I turned to Eva, my voice slipping into something smooth, a calm that didn't match the storm brewing inside. "If you're done here," I said, "maybe we could all pretend like this never happened." I offered her a smile—one that could have been friendly if I weren't about a half-second from losing it.

Jonah shot me a look then, one that was too heavy to ignore. He wasn't angry, but there was something there—something unspoken that made me hesitate. Could it be guilt? Regret? Whatever it was, it made my breath catch, and I suddenly found myself fighting to keep the smile in place.

Eva tilted her head, studying me. Her gaze was a sharp, calculating thing, but she didn't seem to want to make this easy for me. Her lips parted, and she looked about to say something, but Jonah cut her off.

"Enough," he said, his voice sharper now, a crack in the calm that had defined him moments before. He stood abruptly, knocking his chair back in the process. "I'm not doing this with you, Eva."

I watched the change in her. The sudden stillness, the way her mouth pressed into a tight line. For a moment, she looked less like a woman and more like a predator that had just realized its prey was no longer scared.

"Fine," she said, turning on her heel with a flick of her wrist. "But don't think I won't be back. I'll always be back." Her voice floated in the air, a lingering threat that hung between us, heavy and ominous.

Jonah was already sitting down again, his face drawn and tired as he placed his hands on the table, staring at them like he was searching for answers that weren't there. But all I could think about was the sharpness of Eva's presence, the weight of her words. And the cold, bitter taste of insecurity that she had left behind.

The café door swung shut behind Eva, and the quiet that followed felt like a sudden drop in temperature, as though the room had been holding its breath for too long. Jonah sat back down, his fingers still curled around his cup, but now, it seemed like he was holding on to it for dear life. He didn't look at me at first, his eyes fixed somewhere just beyond the rim of his coffee, as if the answers to all the unspoken things between us might appear in the steam curling up from the mug.

I felt a weight press into my chest, heavy and uncomfortable. Something about her, about the way she walked in with the same effortless grace that she'd clearly wielded over Jonah's past, unsettled me in a way I hadn't expected. The sharpness of her words still echoed in my ears. I told myself it was ridiculous, that I was being ridiculous. She was just a ghost from his past, and we had more than enough in the present to build on. So why did her presence feel like a sudden rupture in the fabric we'd so carefully stitched together?

"I'm sorry," Jonah said, finally breaking the silence, his voice a little too strained, a little too quiet. He didn't meet my eyes, though. "That was... not how I planned for today to go."

I let the silence stretch for a moment before responding, my tone as light as I could make it. "I don't know. I thought it was pretty entertaining."

Jonah chuckled, but it was hollow, the sound barely reaching his lips. He finally looked at me, but there was a distance there, a hesitation I hadn't seen before. "I didn't expect her to show up like that. She's... been in and out of my life for years, but I thought she'd moved on."

"Clearly, she hasn't," I said, forcing the words out with more bite than I intended. The words tasted bitter on my tongue, and I didn't quite know why. Was I jealous? I didn't like the taste of that, not one bit.

Jonah's gaze softened, and he leaned forward, setting his cup down on the table with a gentle clink. "I don't know what she's trying to do. I really don't. It's been... complicated."

"Complicated," I repeated, more to myself than to him. "That's a word. What exactly does that mean?"

He sighed, rubbing a hand over his face, as though the simple act of explaining this would require him to peel back years of history he wasn't quite ready to share. "It means that she and I... we've had our share of good times and bad times, but nothing that should have kept her holding on to the idea that there's anything left for her here."

I crossed my arms, sitting back in my chair, studying him. He seemed so certain, so convincing, but something about the way he said it made me wonder. How could someone like Eva, who carried herself with such quiet power, still be lingering around, casting shadows on everything Jonah and I were trying to build? What had really happened between them? And why did I feel like he was still holding something back?

"So, she's just a bad memory, right?" I asked, my voice careful, like I was testing him for cracks.

Jonah paused, his gaze flickering for a moment, and I saw something dark pass over his face. "I guess you could say that. But..." He hesitated again, and I could see the words fighting their way through his resolve. "But the truth is, Eva has a way of... pulling people back into her orbit. And I guess, for a long time, I was one of those people."

I tilted my head, feeling my stomach do a strange little flip. "You're telling me that she had that kind of hold over you? Enough that you couldn't just shake it off?"

"It's not that simple." Jonah's voice dropped, quieter now, as though he were confessing something he hadn't shared before. "She knew how to get under my skin. She knew the parts of me that were... vulnerable."

I raised an eyebrow. "Vulnerable?" The word tasted strange coming from him. Jonah wasn't exactly the type of man who wore vulnerability like a comfortable sweater. He wore confidence, like a second skin.

Jonah ran his fingers through his hair again, looking somewhere past me, like he was seeing something in the distance that wasn't there. "I was younger. Stupid. We were both just... lost, in a way. She made me feel like I mattered when everything else felt like it was falling apart."

His words hung in the air between us, a heavy silence settling in. I wanted to say something—anything—to ease the sudden tension, but the words caught in my throat. So, instead, I just stared at him, watching the way his jaw tightened, the way his shoulders tensed.

Eva had known exactly how to slip back into his life, hadn't she? She wasn't just an ex; she was a shadow, one that seemed to cling to him no matter how far he'd come. And I hated that, in some small way, it worked.

"You don't have to explain anything to me, Jonah," I said, my voice gentler now. "I get it. She was part of your past. You don't owe me an apology for something that was long gone before we even met."

But I didn't get it. Not entirely.

Jonah finally met my gaze again, and there was something in his eyes—something raw—that made my chest tighten. "I don't want you to feel like I'm still holding on to her, because I'm not," he said, his voice almost pleading. "But I'm not perfect, and I know that some of the things she said... might have made you feel like there's something more there."

I wanted to laugh—just a little, because I was trying to make light of it. But the tightness in my throat stopped it before it could escape. "I'm not some naïve girl, Jonah. I know how exes work. You don't just forget about someone who mattered once. But if you want me to believe that there's nothing left there, then I'm going to need more than just your word."

There. The words were out. I'd said it aloud, and there was no taking it back now.

For the first time since she'd walked in, Jonah actually looked shaken. He looked at me as though he'd just realized how deep this could go, how much was hanging in the balance between us.

"I'm not asking you to trust me blindly," he said, his voice soft but firm. "I'm asking you to trust what we have now. And to know that I'm not running back to someone who's already shown me exactly who she is."

That was the thing about Jonah, I realized then. He wasn't perfect, not by a long shot, but in this moment, he was offering me something I hadn't expected: honesty.

I looked at Jonah, really looked at him, and for the first time since he sat down across from me, I felt like I was seeing him clearly. He wasn't just the man who had made me laugh or held me in the dark or even the one who knew the exact right moment to kiss me with that delicious mix of tenderness and fire. He was layered, as everyone was, with all his messy, complicated parts that didn't always make sense. He was more than I'd known, and somehow, Eva had scraped away the illusion I'd been holding onto—that he could just be the perfect partner, unaffected by his past.

I had thought we'd already settled the terrain between us, thought we understood each other's boundaries. But with every word he spoke, it was like watching a veil lift, and the more I saw, the more I questioned whether I was prepared to navigate the darker places that Eva had just tossed into the light.

"I don't know if I can just take your word for it, Jonah." My voice was quieter now, the playful edge from earlier gone. It wasn't that I didn't believe him, but the threads between trust and insecurity had become tangled, and I wasn't sure how to untangle them without pulling something important loose.

Jonah opened his mouth as though to speak, then closed it, running a hand through his hair again, clearly at a loss for words. There was nothing left to say, was there? He had given me his version of the story, the truth as he saw it. But the truth felt slippery, hard to grasp. I could almost see Eva's voice in the space between us, echoing with her confident, biting commentary. "Nothing left there," I repeated softly, tasting the words again. "You really want me to believe that?"

"I do," he said, his voice rough. "I want you to believe that. I need you to believe that."

The frustration in his voice mirrored the tightness in my chest. He wasn't angry, not at me. But it wasn't just the past he was trying to move on from. It was everything—everything he had been holding inside since Eva had walked in. I could feel the weight of his regret pressing down on him like the afternoon sun beating on us through the windows. We were still in the café, surrounded by people who were oblivious to the storm building at our table. But it was as though the space had shrunk, closing in around us. The clatter of plates and coffee cups, the hum of conversations, all faded into the background.

"I don't know if I can do that, Jonah," I said finally, my voice trembling now. I wasn't sure if I was speaking to him or to myself. "I can't pretend like her presence doesn't bother me. Like this isn't some... some war between old ghosts that I'm not even a part of."

Jonah's face softened, but there was something in his eyes—something that made me feel small, like I was suddenly standing on the edge of something dangerous and uncertain. He reached across the table, his hand hovering over mine, as though asking permission to make this moment feel real. To bring it back from the brink of something neither of us could control.

"I'm not asking you to ignore it, or pretend it doesn't matter," he said quietly, his voice dipping into something raw, something almost desperate. "I just need you to understand that this isn't about her. It's about us. About what we've built."

His words were like a lifeline, but they also felt like a trap, pulling me into a place I wasn't sure I could handle. The sharpness of his touch was a promise, but also a reminder that promises were delicate things—fragile. I wanted to believe him. I wanted to pull him into my arms and reassure him that everything would be fine, that I could shake off the weight of this strange competition between his past and our present. But something in the pit of my stomach told me that wasn't going to happen. Not without a fight. Not without something breaking.

"I'm not sure I'm the right person to fix this, Jonah," I whispered, suddenly finding it difficult to breathe. "Maybe I'm just not cut out for this—being part of a life that has so many... layers, so many shadows."

His hand tightened around mine, his fingers warm against my skin. "You don't have to fix anything. You just have to be here. With me."

And in that moment, I thought I might crumble, right there in the middle of the café, my heart shattering beneath the weight of his words. But I didn't crumble. Not yet. I just sat there, holding his gaze, trying to convince myself that what we had was enough. But the truth was, I wasn't sure. The whole thing felt like walking a tightrope with no net beneath me, teetering between trust and doubt, between everything I wanted and everything I feared.

"I don't know if I can do this, Jonah," I said finally, my voice barely more than a breath. "I don't know if I can compete with the ghosts of your past."

Jonah opened his mouth, but before he could say anything, the café door swung open again. I didn't have to turn around to know who it was. That feeling, that cold weight pressing down on my chest, told me everything I needed to know. Eva was back.

I could hear the click of her heels, the sound sharp, deliberate, like she was walking straight into a battlefield. The air shifted, the temperature dropped, and Jonah's hand withdrew from mine as he straightened, his posture suddenly rigid, his eyes flicking nervously toward the door. I didn't need him to tell me what was happening. I saw the way he tensed, the way his body went still, like a soldier preparing for another wave of attack.

She stood at the entrance, her gaze sweeping over the room, her eyes landing on us with a slow, deliberate calculation. A smile tugged at her lips, and I felt the room shift once again. This time, it wasn't just an interruption. It was an invasion.

"Did I miss something?" she called out, her voice dripping with sweetness that made my skin crawl.

I didn't know whether to laugh or scream, but in that moment, I realized this wasn't going to be as simple as walking away from her shadow. It was going to take more than that.

And before I could even begin to process what was happening, Jonah stood up, his face suddenly unreadable, his posture a wall of tension.

"I need to go," he said, his voice firm, but there was something else there, something I couldn't quite place.

And as he turned to leave, I was left staring after him, my heart pounding in my chest, unsure if I had just lost him for good.

Chapter 21: The Price of Jealousy

The storm had started long before the thunder cracked through the sky. Jonah and I had been circling each other for weeks, like two wolves testing the boundaries of a new territory, each of us wary, each of us wanting but unable to fully trust the other. I knew this about us—knew how the cracks in our foundation widened with every unspoken word, with every half-formed glance that veered too close to accusation. And there it was, hanging between us, that name—Lena. It was always Lena. Never just a fleeting mention. Always lingering on his lips like a secret lover he could never quite forget.

I had tried to push it aside, to breathe through the tension whenever it surfaced. I'd smile, nod, let him sweep me into the present moment, but Lena's shadow was never far. And when I'd ask, when I'd gently prod him about the past, his eyes would close in on themselves, and his smile would falter just enough to break my heart. Something about her, something about the way she made him smile with his whole face, the way his eyes softened in a way that I hadn't seen for years, pricked the rawest parts of me, those jagged bits of insecurity I'd tried so hard to bury beneath the surface.

That evening, though, the dam broke. I hadn't planned for it—oh, no, no plan at all. I simply had enough. Enough of waiting, enough of pretending, enough of allowing myself to shrink in the shadows of a woman who no longer existed but still haunted me like a ghost in the room. I had a drink, too many, maybe. The amber liquid burned my throat, filling the hollow in my chest where my confidence should have been. Jonah sat beside me, his hand stretched across the table toward mine, fingers tracing the edge of my palm like a gentle caress. But I wasn't having it anymore. I wasn't having him dance around this.

"Jonah," I said, my voice barely a whisper at first, just a tremor in the air. "Tell me about Lena."

He stilled. That perfect, practiced smile fell away, and I saw a flicker of something—fear? Guilt? His hand faltered, then pulled back, not in an overtly dramatic gesture but in that quiet way he withdrew when he was on the defensive. My stomach knotted. This wasn't going the way I had hoped.

He shifted, his fingers tapping out a rhythm on the edge of his glass. I noticed, for the first time, how nervous he looked, his eyes darting away from me, anywhere but my face. A flash of doubt seized my heart, and for a split second, I wondered if I even knew this man sitting across from me at all.

"I don't think this is a conversation we need to have right now," he said, his voice strained, as though he were carefully considering each word before letting it slip. His eyes were averted, his shoulders stiff as though bracing for an impact he was certain was coming.

"No." I leaned in, the words coming faster now, propelled by something hot and dangerous deep inside me. "I need you to tell me about her, Jonah. Because every time you say her name, it feels like you're handing me a page from a book I'm not in. Every time you smile when she comes up, I feel like I'm the one being forgotten. I'm the one who's just—" I stopped myself, the words choking on the edges of a bitterness I didn't know I was capable of.

Jonah's face tightened, the muscles in his jaw clenching, and I saw a flash of frustration cross his eyes—frustration with me, with himself, with all of it. I knew I was pushing him further than I should have, but there was something raw and real about the way my emotions bubbled up from a place I didn't want to acknowledge. I could feel myself unraveling, the tightly wound threads of patience and restraint slipping one by one, leaving me exposed.

His voice came out as a low growl, thick with emotion. "You're imagining things, Mia. You're making a story where there isn't one.

Lena was a part of my life. A chapter. That's all. It's done." He wiped his hands on his jeans, his gaze flickering back to mine, and for a second, it almost seemed like he was pleading with me—begging me to believe him.

But I didn't believe him. Not then. Not after everything that had passed between us.

"You don't get to just erase things," I shot back, my heart pounding in my chest. "Not after everything. I need to know, Jonah. I need to know how much of you is still hers. How much of you is left for me."

I saw him flinch, and the words felt like a slap, ringing in the space between us. For a moment, the room was dead silent, the tension between us so thick I could taste it on my tongue. And then—without warning—he stood up. The chair scraped across the floor in a sharp, jagged sound that cut through the heavy air.

"Maybe it's better if I go," he said quietly, his voice barely above a whisper. His eyes met mine, but there was nothing soft about the way he looked at me then. No warmth. No understanding. Only something cold and final, like the last page of a book you never wanted to finish.

I wanted to call him back. To pull him back into the space we shared. But I was too late. Jonah was already gone.

The silence that followed Jonah's departure seemed to fill the room like smoke, curling into every corner, suffocating any trace of warmth we once shared. I stood there, frozen in the middle of the kitchen, the remnants of the argument hanging in the air like an ugly stain I couldn't scrub away. My heart was still racing, but now it was sharp with regret. I could still hear his last words echoing in my ears, and the quiet desperation in them made my stomach turn. How had we gotten here? How had my desperation to understand him—understand us—turned into something so toxic?

The weight of the night pressed on my chest, every breath I took a struggle against the tension that refused to dissipate. I walked to the window, pulling aside the heavy curtains just enough to peer into the darkness outside. The street below was lit by a single flickering streetlamp, casting long shadows across the pavement. It was as though the world had gone still, as though even time itself had stopped to wait for me to fix the mess I had made.

But I didn't know how. I had pushed him too far, exposed the rawness of my own insecurities without thinking about the toll it would take on him, on us. In my desire to claim him, to possess him in a way that felt secure, I had torn open a wound I couldn't close. I had become that thing—the thing I feared most: the jealous woman, the one whose suspicions consumed everything in its path. I'd never thought of myself that way.

I sank onto the couch, my hands trembling in my lap. I had to make it right. But how? Jonah wasn't the kind of man you could just smooth things over with a quick apology. No, Jonah was careful, deliberate, and whatever I had done had pushed him so far back that I wasn't sure how to reach him again.

The night stretched on, endless and suffocating. I stared at the clock on the wall, watching the minutes crawl by, each tick a painful reminder of how much time had passed since he left. I thought about calling him. I thought about running after him, but the pride that had gotten me here in the first place—this stupid, stubborn streak that had held me back—now kept my fingers firmly planted by my side.

It wasn't until the early morning light began creeping in through the cracks in the blinds that I realized I hadn't moved. Not once. I hadn't even thought to sleep.

The buzzer on my phone startled me out of my daze, and I grabbed it quickly, as though it held the key to the whole situation. It was a text from Jonah.

"I'm sorry for leaving like that."

The words were simple, almost too simple, but they hit me like a lifeline thrown from the other side of a chasm. I let out a breath I didn't realize I'd been holding, feeling the knot in my stomach loosen, if only slightly. I stared at the screen for a long moment before responding, unsure of how to begin. How do you apologize for breaking someone's trust while you're still in the middle of doing it?

I wiped my palms on my jeans, the fabric worn and soft from too many washes. My thumb hovered over the keyboard, the words coming slowly, too carefully. My first instinct was to beg, to make him come back and fix everything. But that wasn't what this needed. What it needed was honesty.

"I shouldn't have pushed you like that. I was just scared, Jonah. Scared of losing you. But I'm not proud of the way I acted. I never wanted to be that person."

I hesitated before hitting send. The moment the text was sent, I felt the weight of it—felt exposed, as though every thought I had ever tried to bury was now on display for him to read.

It didn't take long for him to reply. I could see the dots appearing on my screen as he typed, then disappearing. Over and over. My heart sped up with every beat, wondering what words he would choose, wondering if he even wanted to speak to me at all.

When the text finally came, it was simple, but there was something in it that made the breath catch in my throat.

"I'm here, Mia. Come over."

I didn't need any more than that. I didn't care if I looked a mess or if the air between us was still thick with uncertainty. I grabbed my jacket and left.

By the time I reached his apartment, the early morning had settled into a soft, sleepy haze. The streets were quiet, the world still half asleep, but my heart was pounding in my chest, a steady drumbeat that kept time with the rhythm of my footsteps.

I knocked on his door, my breath coming in quick, nervous gasps. Jonah opened it almost immediately, as though he had been waiting for me. He didn't say anything at first, just stood there for a moment, his expression unreadable, his eyes searching mine. Then, slowly, his mouth twisted into the barest of smiles, and he stepped aside, opening the door wider.

"I'm sorry," he said quietly, his voice a whisper in the stillness of the room.

I stepped inside, but I didn't know what to say. We were both standing there, two people who had crossed lines we shouldn't have, and now, all we had left was the awkward space between us. A space we both knew we needed to cross, but neither of us knew how.

"I don't know how to fix this," I said after a long pause, my voice fragile, tentative. "I don't know if I can fix it."

Jonah looked at me for a moment, his face softening. "You don't have to. Just be honest. That's all I need."

And so, there we were—two people who had torn each other apart and now stood in the wreckage, unsure of how to rebuild. But for the first time in a long time, I didn't feel the panic rising in my chest. We still had time. Time to figure out what came next. And maybe, just maybe, that was enough.

Jonah had always been the kind of man who carried silence like a second skin. It was one of the things I found so intriguing about him in the beginning. The way he could sit in a crowded room, absorbed in his thoughts, but still present, as if his mind were a place no one could trespass. It made him mysterious, even alluring. But now, that silence felt different. It was an absence. A void where his warmth used to be.

The quiet stretched on between us, like the long pause before a storm hits. Neither of us spoke as I stood there in the middle of his apartment, staring at him, my pulse racing. I had apologized, but it didn't feel like enough. Words had never felt like enough. It was the silence that worried me, the way we could still stand within a few feet of each other and yet feel a million miles apart.

Jonah didn't step forward, didn't reach for me. Instead, he just stood there, his hands in his pockets, his face unreadable. I watched the way the light caught the sharp lines of his jaw, the way his eyes seemed to darken with thoughts I couldn't access. It felt like we were two strangers trying to find a way back to something we had once shared so easily.

"So," I began, my voice quieter than before, "What now?" The question hung there, awkward, tentative. "How do we fix this?"

He let out a breath, a soft sound that seemed to deflate the tension, but only just. "I don't know, Mia. I wish I did." His gaze softened slightly, though it didn't reach the warmth I was hoping for. "I've never been good at this—at any of this," he added, a self-deprecating smile tugging at the corner of his mouth. "I don't know how to make it right."

I nodded, forcing my own smile. It was shaky, uncertain, but it was the best I could manage. "That makes two of us," I muttered. "I've spent so much time trying to protect myself, building walls around everything. And now..." I trailed off, shaking my head. The mess of emotions I felt was overwhelming. I didn't know how to untangle them, and I wasn't sure Jonah could either.

He glanced at me, his eyes softening, as if the weight of my words were finally starting to land. Then, unexpectedly, he took a step forward. "Mia," he said, his voice rough, the sound of it stirring something inside me, something I had almost forgotten was there. "I'm not asking for anything big. I'm not asking for you to just forgive me and move on. I can't expect that from you."

I swallowed hard, trying to steady myself. My heart beat louder in my chest as I waited for him to continue. "But I think... I think if we can stop trying to control everything, if we can let go of these stupid, pointless games we keep playing with each other..." He paused, shaking his head, clearly frustrated with his own inability to find the words. "Maybe we can figure out what comes next."

I stood there, still as a stone, absorbing the weight of his words. "And what's that?" I asked, the question hanging in the air between us, my voice barely above a whisper.

Jonah didn't answer immediately. Instead, he stepped closer, his presence overwhelming in the small space, the air between us crackling with something unspoken. His hand reached out, tentative at first, then more assured. His fingers brushed against my arm, sending a jolt through me. It was as if his touch was a lifeline, a promise that maybe, just maybe, we could figure this out.

"I don't know what it looks like yet," he admitted, his voice low and raw. "But I'm willing to try. If you are."

There was something vulnerable in his tone, something rare and fragile that made me want to reach for him, to close the distance between us. And yet, I hesitated. There was so much left unsaid, so many things we hadn't yet faced. Could I trust him again? Could I trust myself not to tear us apart with my own fears?

I took a step back, needing the space to think, to breathe. "You want me to let go of all the doubts, the insecurities that have been eating me alive?" I asked, more to myself than to him. "You want me to just... trust you? After everything?"

Jonah's gaze held mine, steady, unwavering. "Yes," he said quietly. "But not because it's easy. Not because you owe it to me. You don't owe me anything, Mia. I'm asking because I want to be with you. Not because of what happened with Lena or anything else from the past. But because I want this to be real. I want this to work."

The sincerity in his voice was undeniable, but I still couldn't shake the feeling that something was off. The air between us still felt charged, like it was on the edge of exploding, waiting for one more mistake to tip it all over the edge.

I opened my mouth to respond, but the words got caught in my throat, as though they had nowhere to go. My chest tightened, the weight of the situation too heavy to carry.

Jonah noticed my hesitation, his brows furrowing in concern. "Mia?"

I couldn't answer him. I couldn't find the words, and just as I opened my mouth again, the sound of a door opening from down the hall broke through the tension. Jonah's eyes darted toward the noise, and I followed his gaze just in time to see a figure step into the doorway—Lena.

I froze, my blood running cold, my pulse racing in my ears. Jonah's face shifted the moment he saw her, his entire demeanor changing in an instant. Lena smiled, a knowing, almost smug expression on her face, and I felt the weight of the past slam into me. This wasn't over. Not by a long shot. And in that moment, I realized the stakes had just gotten much higher.

Chapter 22: A Letter Never Sent

The sun had barely started its slow descent when I sat at the old oak desk by the window, the worn wood under my fingers cool against the heat of my palms. The room smelled like dust and lavender, an odd combination that always managed to calm me, even as my heart pounded in my chest. I hadn't planned to write to him. I hadn't planned on feeling anything, to be honest. But the words started spilling out—uninvited, messy, like a flood I couldn't dam.

Jonah. Just his name felt like a secret I kept locked inside my ribcage, and now it was spilling onto the page with a vengeance.

I hadn't seen him in months. Not since the night everything fell apart. The memory of it was sharp, like broken glass underfoot. There were words said in haste, things that should never have been spoken, and in the end, the silence between us had stretched so wide, I wasn't sure there was enough room to bridge it. But here I was, sitting at this very desk, putting down the words that had tangled inside me for too long.

I wrote about the way he used to make me laugh, the way his fingers would brush against mine in the dark, as if even then, in the quietest moments, he was still trying to hold on. I wrote about the nights we spent together—how the weight of him beside me had always felt like home, and how, somehow, without him, I didn't know where I belonged anymore.

The letter wasn't for him. Not really. It was for me, for the girl who had lost herself in his eyes, in his smile, in the tangled mess of us. It was an apology, and it was a goodbye. Maybe that was the most honest part of it. A goodbye I wasn't ready to say, but one I had to.

I didn't know what I was expecting when I wrote it. Maybe a sense of closure. Maybe peace. But all I got was a letter that, in its messy, raw honesty, felt like a weight I could barely carry. I folded it carefully, sealing it in an envelope that I tucked away in the drawer of the desk, hidden away where no one could find it. I couldn't give it to him—not like this. Not when I was still trying to figure out if I could forgive myself.

It was then, of course, that Jonah walked in.

He didn't knock. He never did. His presence filled the room like a gust of wind, and for a moment, everything else in the world faded away. He was wearing that dark jacket he always liked, the one with the worn cuffs, and his hair was messy in that way that made him look too damn good. It was a small thing, the way his eyes softened when he saw me, but it was enough to make my stomach twist.

"You left this on the desk." His voice was low, calm, like he hadn't just dropped a bombshell in my lap. He held up the envelope, the one with my handwriting on it, and my heart stopped dead.

I opened my mouth, but nothing came out. My fingers, still frozen on the chair, felt too numb to move. How had he found it? Why was he holding it?

"Jonah—" I began, but he didn't let me finish.

"I wasn't snooping," he said, his voice so level, so steady. "I was cleaning. And I found it. But I didn't mean to pry."

I almost laughed. A bitter, sharp thing. Of course, he wasn't snooping. He was just Jonah. Always the type to stumble into things—whether he meant to or not. But now, with the letter in his hand, it didn't matter what he had meant to do. He had it, and he was reading it, his eyes scanning over the words that felt like they had been ripped from my soul.

"I'm sorry," I whispered, though I wasn't sure what I was apologizing for. Was it for the letter? For the words I couldn't keep hidden any longer? For the fact that he was holding my truth like a fragile thing?

Jonah didn't say anything. He just stared at the paper, and I could feel the heat of his gaze, like a fire burning through me. I wanted to turn away, to shrink into the shadows where I could hide, but I couldn't. Not now.

Slowly, he lowered the letter, his fingers still curled around the edges like he didn't know what to do with it. His eyes met mine, and I saw something there—something I hadn't seen in so long. It was that same intensity I remembered from the nights we used to spend together, the kind of look that made my breath catch in my throat.

"I didn't know," he said softly. "I didn't know you felt that way. About me. About...us."

And then, in that quiet, fragile moment, he did something I hadn't expected. He took my hand. His fingers brushed against mine, tentative at first, as if he was unsure if I would pull away. But I didn't. I couldn't.

Our hands fit together like they always had, like they were meant to.

"You don't have to say anything," he added, his voice thick with something I couldn't quite place. "But I need you to know, I don't regret what we had. I never will."

It wasn't a promise, not exactly. It was more of a plea. A plea that echoed in the air between us, hanging there like a question I wasn't sure how to answer. But Jonah didn't wait for an answer. Instead, he simply held on. And in that moment, with his hand in mine, the world outside seemed to pause—just long enough for me to breathe.

Jonah's fingers curled around mine, steady and sure, as if he were offering a lifeline in the midst of a storm. My heart, which had been trapped in a cage of uncertainty for so long, thudded harder, but not in the way it used to. It was no longer frantic or desperate. There was no fight for survival in the rhythm of my pulse. It felt like something else entirely—like the slow exhale of a breath I hadn't realized I'd been holding for too long.

I should've pulled away. I should've yanked my hand from his and made some excuse to end this quiet, fragile moment. But I didn't.

I couldn't. There was too much between us, too many things unsaid and so many things that couldn't be fixed with a simple apology.

But Jonah... Jonah was a force. The kind of man who walked into a room and filled it with the weight of his presence. The kind who could make you feel both small and important at the same time, like you were the only thing that mattered in his world. And in this moment, as his gaze held mine, I realized something: he hadn't come here to fight. He hadn't come to dig into the past or demand answers I wasn't ready to give. No, Jonah had come for something else entirely. He'd come for the piece of me he knew still belonged to him.

"I wasn't ready for you to see that," I said quietly, my voice barely above a whisper. The words slipped out of me before I could stop them, though I instantly regretted the vulnerability in them. It was a foolish thing to say. He'd already read the letter. What did it matter now? Still, I couldn't help the rush of heat that spread across my cheeks.

Jonah gave me a crooked smile, the kind that made his eyes crinkle at the corners, and for a moment, I forgot how much time had passed. "You really think I wouldn't find it?"

I winced, trying not to let the amusement in his voice twist something deep inside me. "I wasn't exactly hiding it under the couch cushions."

His smile faded just enough that I could see the shift in him—like a switch had been flipped. He looked at me with something deeper than the playful teasing that usually defined his expression. Something older. Something raw. "Why didn't you want me to read it?"

I swallowed hard. My mouth felt dry, my tongue useless, as if the words I wanted to say had caught themselves on the tip of my tongue. But they wouldn't come. The confession I had written—the one that had bled out of me when I thought no one would ever see it—now felt like a strange artifact, an alien thing I was no longer sure how to explain. The love, the regret, the rawness of it all—how could I make him understand?

"I didn't think you'd want to," I managed, my voice quieter this time. "After everything."

Jonah's grip on my hand tightened slightly, a subtle reminder that he was still here, still holding on. "I can't speak for the past, but right now, I want to hear everything." His voice had softened, but it still carried the weight of that steady, unwavering conviction. "All of it. No matter how ugly it is."

I could see the sincerity in his eyes, but it wasn't just the sincerity that made my chest tighten. It was the depth of what lay beneath it. Jonah had always been a man of few words, but when he spoke, it was always with a certainty that made me feel like he had already figured out all the things I was still fumbling to understand.

There was no point in running from it. No point in pretending the feelings I had buried for so long weren't still alive, trying to claw their way out.

I sighed, pressing my free hand to my forehead, trying to stave off the dizziness that had settled there. "I wasn't ready to face it. Face you. Not after... not after everything."

He was quiet for a moment, just enough to make the space between us feel like a chasm. Then, with the kind of quiet confidence I had come to expect from him, Jonah slid his chair closer to mine, until our knees brushed. He didn't try to rush me. Didn't ask me to explain everything all at once.

"It's okay," he said, his voice low. "You don't have to fix it all right now. I'm not going anywhere. I'm right here."

But he didn't let go of my hand either. And that, I realized, was the part that mattered. The part I had missed more than anything. Jonah had always been the kind of person who didn't need to force a thing to happen. He simply... existed in a way that made it impossible to ignore him. And now, in this strange, tender space we had created, he wasn't asking for anything except my honesty. My truth.

And maybe that was the hardest part—because the truth had been so tangled in fear, regret, and hurt, I wasn't sure how to unravel it.

"I still love you," I whispered, barely audible, as if speaking the words out loud would break the fragile thread between us. "I don't know how to stop."

Jonah's thumb brushed over my hand, a gesture so small but so significant it made my breath catch. "You don't have to stop." His voice was steady, unwavering. "I don't want you to."

The words hung between us, almost too heavy to breathe in. It wasn't a promise, not exactly. But it was enough. Enough for now. Enough to make me wonder if maybe, just maybe, we had more than a fragile chance at something that had never truly been broken.

Jonah's hand was warm against mine, but it wasn't the warmth that caught my attention. It was the way he held on—steady, like he had always known the exact pressure to apply, the exact distance to keep. Like he had learned the rhythm of my pulse long before either of us could admit it. His thumb stroked over my knuckles, sending little sparks of electricity through my veins. I wanted to pull away, wanted to step back and keep myself intact. But somehow, with him standing there, with that steady presence of his filling up every corner of the room, it felt like it was too late for that. Too late to pretend I was fine.

"I've always been good at pretending," I said quietly, the words slipping out before I could think better of them. "But you're right. This—this thing between us—it's never been something I could hide from. Not really."

Jonah's eyes never wavered, still locked onto mine, as if he were waiting for me to unravel myself completely. As if he knew exactly what I needed to say before I even realized it. His gaze didn't carry any judgment, just patience. And that was enough to make me feel like I could finally breathe again, even if only for a moment.

"I never wanted you to pretend," he replied, his voice quiet, rough at the edges. "I just wanted you. The real you."

That was when the dam I hadn't even known I'd built started to crack. There was something in his voice, something in the way he was looking at me, that broke down whatever resistance I had left. Jonah had always been this way—steady, relentless, and somehow softer than I deserved. And no matter how hard I tried to keep him at arm's length, he never stopped coming closer.

"I'm not sure I know who that is anymore," I whispered, the admission tasting like ash on my tongue.

Jonah's hand tightened around mine, the heat of his fingers grounding me as if he could somehow pull me out of the haze I had been living in. "You don't have to know right now. I'm not asking for answers. I'm just asking you to be here. With me. Like this."

It was the "like this" that sent the last of my composure crumbling. Like this, with him close enough to feel the pulse of his heartbeat, close enough to drown in the intensity of his eyes. Like this, with everything between us hanging by the thinnest thread, waiting for me to decide whether or not I could trust him again.

"Jonah, I—" I started, but the words failed me again. My throat had closed up, like it always did when I tried to speak the things that mattered most.

He leaned in slightly, his breath warm against my skin, and for a moment, I thought he might kiss me. I almost wanted him to. Almost. But then he paused, just a fraction of an inch from my lips, and I could hear the steady beat of his pulse in the quiet space between us. His voice was soft, barely more than a whisper. "You don't have to say anything. Just... just stay with me. For now."

For now. The phrase echoed in my mind like a siren's call. It was an invitation, but it was also a warning. A quiet acknowledgment that we were both standing on the edge of something we couldn't predict. I had learned the hard way that nothing—nothing—was ever as simple as it seemed with Jonah. He had this way of making you feel like you were floating, suspended in air, just above the ground. But at any moment, if you weren't careful, the ground could slip away, and you'd fall.

I wasn't sure if I was ready for that kind of fall again.

"I wish I knew how to fix this," I said, my voice trembling just a little, betraying the calm I was desperately trying to project. "I wish I knew how to make all of it—everything—go away."

Jonah's gaze softened, and for a moment, I saw the raw, unguarded version of him—the one that hadn't been afraid to love me, to fight for us, even when it seemed like I didn't deserve it. "You don't have to fix anything. We're not broken, M—"

A loud crash interrupted him, followed by the unmistakable sound of glass shattering. My heart stopped.

Jonah's hand jerked away from mine, and I barely had time to register the confusion in his eyes before I was on my feet, adrenaline surging through my veins. My heart raced as I scanned the room, my eyes darting around in search of the source of the noise.

"What the hell was that?" Jonah demanded, his eyes narrowing as he stood up beside me. He was tense now, his posture shifting from the softness of just moments before to something alert, protective. I could see his mind racing as he moved to the door.

"I don't know," I said, my voice shaky. I took a step forward, but before I could move further, Jonah caught my arm, his grip firm but not unkind.

"Stay here. Lock the door."

I barely had time to nod before he was moving, fast, through the house. Every instinct told me to follow, to make sure he was okay, but something inside me told me to stay put. Something was wrong.

I closed my hand around the door handle, my pulse thumping in my ears. I could feel the weight of the silence closing in around me, pressing in from all sides. And just as I locked the door and stepped back, there was another sound—a shadow moving across the window, and then, a voice.

"Maya?"

Chapter 23: Revelations in the Rain

The rain hit us like an unexpected slap, cold and relentless, splattering against our skin with a sound that drowned out everything else. It wasn't the gentle kind of rain you'd imagine on a warm spring day, the kind that carries with it the sweet smell of earth and the promise of something soft. No, this was an untamed downpour, a thing that seemed to have no mercy or intention other than to remind us of our vulnerability. The kind of rain that soaked through layers of clothing, chilling you to the bone in a way that felt personal, like nature itself had decided to press the reset button on your world.

Jonah had stopped in the middle of the sidewalk, his hands hanging limply at his sides, his head tilted slightly back as though he was trying to catch raindrops with his face. There was something about the way the rain clung to him, as though it was holding him in place, forcing him to stay, to listen, to speak. And for a long moment, neither of us said anything. It wasn't that we were shy, or even that the rain had stolen our words. It was more like we both needed to feel the weight of the storm, to let the air crackle with the tension of things unspoken before we could finally break the silence.

"I never told you about my mom," Jonah said suddenly, his voice rough, low, as though the words were being dragged out of him. "She died when I was eleven. Just like that. One day she was there, and the next she wasn't. No goodbyes, no explanation. Just gone."

I watched him as the rain clung to his hair, dripping down the back of his neck, his shoulders hunched as though trying to keep himself small, to make himself disappear. I wanted to reach out, to say something comforting, but the words caught in my throat. How do you comfort someone who's lived through a loss so profound, so stark? How do you tell them that everything's going to be okay when the world had already shown them how easily it can take everything away?

His gaze flickered to mine, and for the first time, I saw the cracks in his eyes. The things he'd buried deep within him—guilt, anger, confusion—now out in the open like a storm cloud that had finally broken apart. "I wasn't there when it happened. I was at a friend's house, and when I came back, they told me she was gone. I didn't even get to say goodbye. It was like... like she had been erased, and no one could explain why. Everyone just kept telling me I was lucky to have had her for as long as I did. But I wasn't. I wasn't lucky. I was just angry."

I took a step toward him, my own heart breaking for the boy he used to be, the one left standing in the rain, the one who had to grow up too fast. But still, I didn't know how to help him, how to take the weight of his words and make them lighter.

"I don't think I ever stopped being angry at her," he continued, his voice shaking now, though he tried to keep it steady. "Not really. It's easier to stay angry than to admit I miss her. Easier to blame her for leaving me than to face the fact that she's never coming back." He closed his eyes, as if shutting out the rain, as if shutting out the memory.

I stood there, in the middle of the storm with him, the sound of the rain like a drumbeat in my chest, and I knew, right then, that I wanted to be the person who could give him peace. The person who could help him put down the weight of all those years, all that grief, that anger, and make him feel like he could breathe again. But I also knew I couldn't do it all at once. People like Jonah, the ones with so much pain tucked into their hearts, didn't open up overnight. They needed to do it in pieces, like peeling back layers of a wound that had never fully healed.

"I can't fix this for you," I said, my voice steady now, despite the rain pouring down, "but I'm here. For as long as you need. To listen. To be angry with you. To just be here."

He gave me a strange look then, one I couldn't quite place. A mix of confusion and gratitude, maybe even something deeper, something rawer that he wasn't sure how to name. For a second, I thought he might say something else, might tell me he didn't need me or that it was too much, too soon. But then he stepped closer, his chest brushing mine, and he let out a breath that felt like he had been holding it in for a long, long time.

"I think," Jonah began, his voice breaking just a little, "I think I've been waiting for someone to say that. To say it's okay to not be okay, that it's okay to just be... angry."

I smiled, even though I could feel the sting of the rain in my eyes, blurring everything around me. "It's okay to be angry. You don't have to carry it alone."

For a long time, we just stood there, letting the rain wash over us, and in that strange, fleeting moment, I felt something shift. The weight of all the things he had never said, the weight of all the things I had never known, seemed to lighten, just enough to make room for something new—something that didn't need words or explanations. Just us, standing together, two people who had both been broken, but were learning how to be whole again, one step at a time.

The rain was no longer just a nuisance; it had become something we could no longer ignore, each drop marking the passage of time, washing away the pretense that had kept us standing apart. Jonah's hand brushed against mine, a subtle shift in the way he stood, his posture less rigid now, almost like he was testing the waters—testing me. I took the hint and slipped my fingers into his, letting the connection be as much about the warmth we shared in that moment as the rain that pelted us with its cold, indifferent ferocity.

"I didn't know what to do with it all, you know?" Jonah's voice was softer now, quieter, like the rain had somehow unlocked something deeper within him. "My dad wasn't much help. He never talked about it. After my mom died, he just... closed up, like a man who didn't know how to grieve, but didn't want to admit it."

I didn't ask questions, because I knew this wasn't a story that needed interruptions. Jonah had spent years burying parts of himself in silence, and I could feel how heavy it must have been, how deep those memories ran. I couldn't offer him a cure for what had happened, but maybe I could give him the space to feel what he hadn't let himself feel before.

There was an ache in my chest, the kind that only comes when you realize just how much someone has carried alone for so long. It wasn't pity, not at all. It was the sharp, strange feeling of wanting to be the one who could make it better, who could share that burden without taking it away. Maybe I wasn't supposed to fix him. Maybe he wasn't even broken. But that didn't stop me from wishing I could somehow make it easier.

Jonah took a deep breath, like he was bracing for the next wave of memory, and then he spoke again, his words a little less guarded now. "I remember when I was sixteen, I tried to fix things. I thought if I was the man of the house, if I stepped up... maybe things would change. But nothing did. My dad was just... distant. And I wasn't enough to fill the space my mom had left behind. I guess I spent a lot of years thinking I had to be someone else to make it work, to make people stop looking at me like I was broken."

I squeezed his hand, not to offer reassurance, but because I knew, deep down, that I understood what he meant. That feeling of not being enough, of not fitting into the mold that life had thrust upon you, was something I could relate to in ways I hadn't expected. We were both caught in the tension of our own expectations, but neither of us had ever dared to face them head-on until now.

"What changed?" I asked, not because I thought he'd have a neat answer, but because I was curious about the shift that had taken place in him. The Jonah I knew now wasn't that angry boy, wasn't the one who had been stuck in the past, frozen in a moment where nothing felt like it would ever get better. I had seen him laugh, had seen him take risks, had seen him care about things he'd never let himself care about before.

He exhaled sharply, as if the question had caught him off guard, and for a moment, his expression softened, something like nostalgia flickering in his eyes. "I guess I realized that trying to be something I wasn't only made it worse. You can't force yourself into a role that doesn't fit, not for long. And maybe... maybe I had to learn to let go of all that guilt, to stop thinking that I was responsible for fixing things that weren't mine to fix."

The rain had lessened, its intensity fading into a soft drizzle, but the cool air still held a weight that lingered on my skin. I leaned in slightly, just enough to close the space between us, my voice barely more than a whisper. "You don't have to fix everything, Jonah. Not for anyone. Not for me. And certainly not for your dad. You're allowed to just be... you."

He turned to look at me then, his expression shifting into something a little more vulnerable, a little more open than it had been before. For a second, I saw the remnants of the boy who had been left to pick up the pieces, the one who had built walls around his heart and never asked for help. But he wasn't that boy anymore. And I wasn't the girl who needed to hold it all together, either.

"I don't know how to be this person," he admitted, his voice a little ragged now, as though the weight of his words had drained him. "I've spent so long pretending I was fine, convincing myself I didn't need anyone, that I didn't even know what to do with... whatever this is. Whatever I'm feeling now."

"Maybe you don't have to know right away," I said with a soft smile, brushing a wet strand of hair from my face. "Maybe you just have to let yourself feel it first, without trying to figure it out."

Jonah gave a small, almost reluctant smile, the kind that said he wasn't sure he believed me, but he wanted to. "I think you might be right," he said, his voice still carrying that raw honesty, but there was a hint of something lighter there, too. Something like relief, even if he wasn't ready to admit it fully.

I laughed, a light sound that didn't feel forced. "I know I'm right. I've got an uncanny ability to be wise when it's absolutely necessary."

He raised an eyebrow, the shift in his mood evident now. "Uncanny, huh? I'm starting to think you might be a little more than you let on."

I grinned, feeling a spark of warmth spread through me despite the lingering chill of the rain. "Well, I am full of surprises."

We stood there for a moment, letting the silence settle between us, but it wasn't uncomfortable. It was... comfortable, in a way I hadn't expected. Jonah wasn't asking for anything more than what I was willing to give, and I wasn't trying to make him into someone else. Maybe, just maybe, that was enough.

The air between us felt thicker now, almost electric, as though the rain wasn't the only thing that had changed in the last few minutes. Jonah had pulled back, just slightly, and for the first time since we'd started walking, I could see the wheels turning in his mind, like he was trying to piece something together, trying to reconcile the parts of himself he'd kept hidden for so long. I stood there, letting him work it out, the weight of the rain like a backdrop to this fragile, unspoken shift between us.

There were no promises. No grand declarations of love or comfort. But there was a kind of understanding, a quiet knowing that, despite all the brokenness we carried, we were still standing here, together.

"I haven't said those things out loud in years," Jonah said finally, his voice a little hoarse, but there was something lighter about him now, something that made the air feel less heavy. "I don't know why I said it now. Maybe because… because you're here. Because it doesn't feel so wrong to say them out loud with you."

I nodded, not trusting myself to speak. He didn't need to hear the reassurance, not yet. He just needed space, and I was more than willing to give it to him. His eyes flickered down to my hand, still entwined with his, and for a moment, the rain seemed to blur everything else out, like we were the only two people left in the world.

But then, as quickly as the moment had arrived, it was gone. The tension between us shifted once more, and I could see that Jonah was already pulling himself back, retreating into that place where he kept everything locked away. It was so subtle that if I hadn't been paying attention, I might've missed it. His shoulders tightened, his jaw set, and there was that familiar, defensive look in his eyes, like he had suddenly realized that he had shared too much, been too honest.

"Don't," I said softly, stepping forward. The rain seemed to lessen again, almost as if the world was giving us a chance to breathe. "You don't have to shut down. Not with me."

Jonah's gaze was stormy, unsure, like he was caught between wanting to pull away and wanting to stay. "I don't know how to do this, to… let people in. I don't know how to just… be. To stop pretending that I have everything under control, that I'm fine." His voice cracked on the last word, and for a split second, I thought I might actually see him crumble.

"Then don't," I said, my voice gentle but firm. "You don't have to. Not with me." I let my hand slip away from his, not because I wanted to, but because I could feel the space between us widening, the invisible barrier he always built when things got too real.

"I'm not asking you to fix me," he said quickly, his eyes darting around, like he needed something to focus on other than me. "I'm just... I don't know, I guess I'm afraid that if I let anyone in, they'll see how messed up I really am."

"Jonah," I said, stepping closer again. "No one is perfect. You don't have to be perfect for me. You never did." I paused, letting my words sink in, and when he met my gaze again, there was a flicker of something—maybe hope, maybe disbelief—shifting behind his eyes. "You're allowed to be messy. I don't need you to be anything else."

The rain had all but stopped now, leaving the world feeling oddly quiet and still. The only sounds left were the occasional drip from a nearby tree and the steady beat of our heartbeats, racing just a little too fast. The moment stretched between us, full of unsaid things and things that could never be said aloud, and it felt like everything was hanging in the balance.

But Jonah was still holding back. I could see it in the way his fists clenched at his sides, in the way he kept glancing over his shoulder, like he was calculating an escape. And I knew. I knew he wasn't ready to stay, not yet. Not with all the ghosts he carried.

Before I could say anything else, a sharp voice interrupted us, slicing through the moment with an unexpected jolt.

"Well, well. What have we here?"

I turned quickly, my stomach flipping with unease. Standing on the edge of the alleyway, framed by the dim light from a flickering streetlamp, was someone I hadn't expected to see. My heart lurched in my chest.

It was Ben.

Jonah stiffened immediately beside me, his whole body going taut as if he'd just been caught in some sort of trap. I could see the flash of recognition in his eyes, and then something else—something colder, something guarded. The world seemed to shift, like we had stepped out of one reality and into another, and suddenly the space between us felt fragile again, a thin thread about to snap.

Ben took a step forward, a smug grin pulling at the corners of his mouth. "Didn't know you two were... close," he said, his tone far too casual, far too knowing.

I swallowed, trying to steady my racing pulse. "What are you doing here, Ben?" The words slipped out sharper than I meant them to, but I couldn't help it. His presence was like a shadow over this fragile moment between Jonah and me, and I didn't like it. Not one bit.

Jonah's eyes darkened, a storm brewing behind them, but he didn't speak. He didn't even move, his gaze fixed firmly on Ben, as though he were sizing him up, weighing something that wasn't immediately clear to me.

Ben chuckled, stepping closer still, his gaze flicking between Jonah and me. "I could ask you the same thing." His eyes lingered on Jonah, and for a moment, I thought I saw something flicker in his expression—something predatory.

And then, in the blink of an eye, Ben took a step back, his smile fading. "Maybe I'll just leave you two to... work it out." He turned to go, but not before giving us one last look that left a chill in the air.

The silence that followed was thick, heavy, as if the rain had started again inside my head, beating in time with the pounding of my heart. Jonah's jaw was clenched so tightly, I was almost afraid he might shatter something inside himself.

And I knew, in that moment, everything had changed.

Chapter 24: The Silent Reckoning

The air was thick that evening, a strange warmth hanging between the sun's reluctant descent and the chill that came with the first hint of fall. I stood in the kitchen, the scent of rosemary and garlic lingering like an old lover's perfume, coaxing memories out of the shadows. The room felt too quiet, as though the walls themselves were holding their breath. It was an odd feeling—one I hadn't experienced in months, since Jonah and I had found our rhythm, our quiet understanding. But today, as I stirred the sauce, it wasn't just the weight of the spices in the air that pressed on me; it was the knowledge that something had shifted—something unspoken and unsettling.

The knock on the door had come just as Jonah was setting the table, his movements practiced, his easy smile still in place. But it had faltered when I opened the door and saw the stranger standing there—tall, angular, with a sharp edge to him that put me on guard immediately. He didn't introduce himself at first, just a lingering, appraising look that felt as though he were measuring the space between us, calculating something I wasn't privy to.

"Jonah's niece," he had said with a slow, deliberate drawl that made my name sound foreign in his mouth. "I've heard a lot about you." His eyes didn't meet mine when he spoke, but instead, they slid over the room, pausing briefly on the family photos that lined the walls like silent witnesses. Then, just as quickly, he'd returned his gaze to me, an unspoken question hanging in the air between us.

I couldn't place it—what about him made me uneasy. He wasn't imposing, but there was something about the way he lingered at the threshold, like a secret waiting to be uncovered. And as much as I wanted to dismiss him, to brush it off as nothing more than a man with too much time on his hands, I couldn't ignore the way my pulse quickened when Jonah stepped into the hallway, his expression morphing into something unreadable.

"I didn't know you were expecting company," I had said, trying to sound casual, but the words came out stiff, as though they were too big for my mouth. Jonah, usually so open, so free with the details of his life, was oddly silent as the man introduced himself as James, a cousin from Jonah's father's side—someone who, apparently, had been estranged from the family for years.

Jonah's hesitation was enough to make my stomach twist.

I hadn't realized just how much I had trusted him until that moment, when I found myself standing in the quiet, waiting for an explanation that wouldn't come. It was as though the very air had changed around us, thickened with unspoken truths.

James's arrival had been followed by small, scattered visits over the course of the next few weeks, and each time, I couldn't shake the feeling that something was off. Jonah, the man I had known for years, who had shared pieces of his soul with me in the quiet hours of the night, was distant. Not in the way that men sometimes grow distant after too many unspoken things weigh on them—but in a way that made my gut twist in knots, as though there were something—someone—lurking behind his eyes, waiting for the moment to surface.

"What's going on, Jonah?" I had asked one evening after dinner, my voice a whisper that felt too loud in the sudden silence that had fallen over us. He was sitting on the couch, his fingers loosely intertwined with mine, but his mind was miles away.

Jonah had looked at me, his brow furrowing ever so slightly, before he took a breath as though trying to decide whether to say something, to finally explain. But before he could speak, the phone rang, its shrill cry slicing through the stillness like a blade. I didn't need to see the name on the screen to know it was James. Jonah's face twisted briefly before he answered it, his voice low and guarded.

I had excused myself to the kitchen, though I couldn't ignore the feeling that something was unraveling just beneath the surface. The walls felt closer, the warmth of the room suddenly stifling. I was doing the dishes when Jonah's voice came from the doorway, calm and measured, but his words rattled me.

"James says there's something I need to hear."

The casualness of his statement made my stomach lurch, the implications of it heavier than any single moment before it. What could James possibly have to say that Jonah hadn't already told me? What had I missed?

"I didn't think it would come to this," Jonah had continued, his gaze turning inward as though the words were not for me but for himself. "I never meant for you to be caught in the middle of this."

Caught in the middle of what? I had wanted to scream the question, but I didn't. Instead, I simply nodded, my pulse thudding in my ears, the realization creeping slowly through me like a cold, creeping fog. The pieces were starting to fall into place, but none of them made sense.

And now, here I was—standing in the kitchen, stirring sauce I no longer had the appetite for, waiting for Jonah to return. But the quiet felt different this time, not peaceful but strained. Like the calm before a storm, and all I could do was wait for the clouds to break.

I heard the soft click of the door closing, his footsteps slow as they crossed the threshold. I turned, my eyes meeting his, and for the first time in months, I didn't see the man I had grown to love. Instead, I saw a stranger, someone with layers I hadn't known existed, someone whose secrets were unraveling just out of reach. And the worst part was, I couldn't tell if he was hiding from me—or if I had been hiding from him all along.

"James," Jonah said quietly, his voice a rough murmur that seemed to echo in the quiet of the room. "He says there's something we need to discuss. Something that changes everything."

The room seemed smaller the moment Jonah spoke, as though the air had suddenly become too thick to breathe. He looked at me with a sort of hesitation I wasn't used to. It wasn't the kind of pause that hinted at his usual introspection, nor was it the quiet before he carefully chose his words—it was something else, something darker, something that made me feel like an outsider in my own life. His words hung between us, and I didn't know if they were meant to reassure or warn.

I pressed my lips together, trying to read him, to find something familiar in the chaos of his expression. He looked tired, his shoulders slumped as if the weight of whatever James had said was pressing down on him in a way that was far too heavy to bear. I stepped closer, willing him to meet my gaze, but Jonah was lost in some quiet abyss I couldn't reach.

"Jonah," I whispered, my voice shaking just a little. "What is it?"

He sighed, the sound so full of exhaustion that it felt like it should be followed by a collapse. But instead, he only leaned against the back of the couch, running a hand through his hair. It wasn't until his gaze flickered toward me that I saw it—the old, familiar sadness buried beneath layers of frustration and resignation.

"Something happened a long time ago," he said quietly, like each word cost him. "Something I thought was long buried, something I thought I could keep hidden."

The admission hung in the air, teasing the edges of my understanding. I nodded slowly, trying to keep my face impassive, though inside my heart was a violent beat, a silent drum warning me of the storm I could already feel approaching.

"Jonah, if we're going to make it through this—whatever this is—we need to be honest with each other," I said, more firm than I felt. My words felt like a lifeline thrown in a sea of uncertainty. "No more secrets."

I saw the way his jaw tightened at my words, the way he almost flinched as though the truth was something he couldn't face. His eyes wandered to the floor, to the space between us that felt, for the first time, miles apart.

"I never wanted you to be a part of this," he murmured, his voice low and gravelly. "But James... he knows things. Things about my past that I've never shared, things I've kept buried for years."

I waited for him to continue, but he didn't. Instead, there was a long, pregnant silence that stretched between us, until the only sound in the room was the soft ticking of the clock on the wall. I could feel the weight of it, pressing down on me, each second pulling at the threads of my patience.

"What things?" I asked, my voice firmer now, a subtle edge creeping into it. I had to know. If I was going to understand, to make sense of the strange tension that had settled over us, I needed to hear the truth, no matter how ugly it might be.

Jonah shook his head, running a hand over his face as though trying to wipe away the past. "I don't know how to explain it... It's not a simple story, not something that can be wrapped up in neat little words."

"I don't need neat," I said, my voice soft but insistent. "I just need the truth."

Jonah sighed again, his hands running down his face before resting in his lap, his fingers trembling ever so slightly. There was a fleeting moment of hesitation before he finally spoke, each word more reluctant than the last.

"When I was younger, I got mixed up in something... a group of people who weren't exactly law-abiding. I made some bad choices, things I thought I could walk away from. But I couldn't. Not until I was in too deep."

My breath caught, but I didn't interrupt. I let him continue, though every word felt like another thread pulling apart the fabric of everything I thought I knew about him. Jonah had always been the solid one, the dependable one—the man who stood as my anchor when the world was turbulent. But this... this was different. This was a part of him I hadn't known, a part I wasn't sure I could embrace.

"James was involved," Jonah continued, his voice strained, like each word was a struggle. "And he's been holding that over me, threatening to tell you everything if I didn't... well, if I didn't meet him halfway."

I took a step back, the air growing colder as I processed his words. James wasn't just some distant relative. He was a shadow in Jonah's past, a specter he'd been running from—and now, it seemed that shadow had caught up with him.

I felt a wave of anger crash over me, not at Jonah, but at the situation, at the way the past always had a way of clawing its way to the surface, no matter how deep you buried it. I had trusted him, trusted us, and now I wasn't sure what I was left with.

"Why didn't you tell me?" I asked, my voice barely above a whisper, though the hurt in it was unmistakable. "Why keep it a secret? Why keep me in the dark?"

Jonah looked up at me then, and I saw something in his eyes—something raw and vulnerable, a side of him that made my heart ache. "I thought I could protect you. I thought I could keep you safe from all of this... from the mess I created. But now I see that I've only made it worse."

The admission felt like a punch to the gut. He'd kept it from me, not because he didn't trust me, but because he thought he could shield me from the fallout. And in doing so, he had isolated me in a way that felt worse than any secret could.

I took another step back, my mind whirling. The room suddenly felt far too small for all the weight of our tangled pasts. The space between us, once filled with warmth and unspoken understanding, now felt like a chasm I wasn't sure we could bridge.

"What do we do now?" I asked, my voice a whisper as the cold seeped in deeper.

I watched Jonah, his shoulders hunched in defeat, as though the weight of everything that had just been revealed had pressed him down in a way that no apology or explanation could lift. He hadn't meant to drag me into this, he said. He thought he could protect me, shield me from the past he was still running from. But somehow, that felt more like a betrayal than anything else—his silence, his unwillingness to trust me with the full picture.

The air between us had gone thick, like the dense humidity before a summer storm. It was heavy, oppressive, and I didn't know if I wanted the rain to come to break it, or if I was terrified of what the storm would bring. My mind scrambled, replaying his words, looking for the moments when things should've clicked. How had I not seen it? How had I not noticed that the casual way he avoided certain topics wasn't just his way of protecting himself, but a defense mechanism? And the worst part was, he thought he could handle this alone. That he could shoulder the mess of his life and spare me from it. But what was it he didn't understand?

I wasn't some fragile thing to be kept in the dark. I was stronger than that.

"You think I'd walk away from you because of some secrets?" I asked, my voice quieter than I intended, but there was a sharpness to it that even I could hear. The way I said it made the words feel more like a question than a statement, as though I still wasn't sure where I stood in all this, but I couldn't help but feel betrayed by the very idea that he had underestimated me. "Jonah, you're not the only one who's lived through things, you know."

His eyes flickered to mine then, his expression unreadable. "It's not the same," he said, his voice almost pleading.

"Isn't it?" I replied, pushing the words out before I could stop them. "You think I haven't had my own ghosts? That I haven't carried around my own set of secrets, buried under layers of guilt and regret? You're not the only one who has a past, Jonah."

The words were too sharp, too pointed, but I couldn't stop them. They felt like they were clawing their way out of me. I'd spent years hiding pieces of myself—pieces I thought I could bury deep enough that no one would ever find them. But here he was, asking me to shoulder his burdens while he kept his locked away, hidden from the person who loved him most. I wanted to throw that in his face. Tell him that I had my own demons too, and I'd long since learned to live with them.

Jonah's eyes softened, and for a moment, I saw the vulnerability beneath the armor he'd built so carefully around himself. But it was fleeting—gone before I could grasp it fully. He opened his mouth to speak, but the doorbell rang, loud and sharp, interrupting us both.

I froze, unsure whether to answer it. Jonah glanced at me, then at the door, and I saw his jaw tighten again, the shift in him subtle but undeniable. Something in his eyes flickered—an unease, a wariness that made the hairs on the back of my neck stand up.

"I'll get it," I said, my voice tight, unwilling to leave the tension between us unresolved. But as I turned toward the door, I saw Jonah stiffen behind me. He didn't move to stop me, but the way he watched me go made my chest tighten.

I reached for the handle, but before I could even turn it, the door swung open of its own accord. James was standing there, his face still carrying that same calculating, detached expression I'd come to know so well. But this time, his eyes were different. There was something darker in them, something colder that sent a chill running down my spine.

"Jonah told you, then?" James asked, stepping into the doorway without waiting for an invitation. His voice was a blend of curiosity and something far more sinister, like he was the one holding the strings and was waiting to see how far he could pull.

I stepped back, instinctively putting space between myself and him. "Told me what?" I asked, even though the answer was already hanging between us. I couldn't keep up the pretense that I didn't know something was off. The truth was, I was scared. And not just because of Jonah's past, but because James seemed like a man who thrived in chaos, who relished in knowing more than anyone around him.

"About the deal," he said, his voice low, the words coated in something that felt like a threat. "About what I need from Jonah to keep his skeletons in the closet."

I swallowed hard. So, it was a deal then—one I had no part in, one that was apparently being decided without my knowledge. The weight of it crushed me, the realization that I was standing in the middle of something I didn't understand, and that Jonah had been letting this man—this stranger—dictate the terms of our lives.

"You think you can just walk in here, make demands, and we're supposed to go along with it?" I asked, my voice barely containing the edge of disbelief that surged within me. "You think this is some kind of game?"

James's lips curved into something that wasn't quite a smile but something far colder. He took a step forward, close enough now that I could feel the pressure of his presence, the dangerous pull of it.

"I think you misunderstand," he said, his tone smooth as silk, but the threat was unmistakable. "This isn't about me or Jonah anymore. It's about what's left to lose."

Before I could respond, Jonah was there, standing beside me, his eyes locked on James with a kind of silent warning I hadn't seen before. The distance between us felt vast now, the weight of the choices he had made hanging in the air like a noose.

"Leave," Jonah said, his voice low but firm, an authority I hadn't heard in him before. "This isn't your fight."

James's eyes flicked to Jonah, then back to me, before he turned and walked away, leaving nothing but the sound of the door closing behind him.

But as he left, I couldn't shake the feeling that this was just the beginning. And that maybe, just maybe, the fight was only starting.

Chapter 25: The Gathering Storm

I had always prided myself on reading people. It wasn't a gift, exactly, more like a learned skill born of necessity. Growing up in a house where silence was as frequent as the droning hum of an old refrigerator, I learned to watch. To listen. To see what wasn't said more than what was. The way someone shifted in their seat when they were lying, the slight tremor in a hand when they weren't telling the whole truth—it was all there if you knew where to look. Jonah had been easy to read at first. There was a softness to him, an openness that made him feel like a safe place. But somewhere between the late-night talks and lazy Sunday mornings, I'd lost track of him. The man who had been so vulnerable, so raw with me, had built walls higher than I could scale.

When I met his cousin for the first time, something inside me clicked, an instinctive recognition of the kind of person I would want to avoid if given the chance. Elijah. A smile that looked too sharp, like a blade waiting to cut, and eyes that skimmed over you, assessing in ways that didn't sit well with me. He'd come into our lives as if he were some sort of errant knight, full of swagger and claims of loyalty, but I hadn't missed the undertone of something much darker. Jonah had warned me about him in passing, more in jest than earnestness, but I'd brushed it off as typical family nonsense. You know the type—the cousin who's always trying to make his mark, to stand out in a family full of big personalities.

I should have paid attention. I should have taken it seriously.

The dinner that night had been full of strained politeness, my words carefully measured, as if I could somehow hold the balance between Jonah's irritation and Elijah's predatory charm. We sat around the table, passing dishes of food that tasted like cardboard, the clinking of silverware and the hum of conversation filling the spaces that Jonah's silence had created. His cousin was a master of conversation, the kind of person who could pull you into a discussion without you even realizing you'd been swept away. His compliments were too smooth, his laughter too loud. Everything about him seemed designed to charm, to win over, to get you to drop your guard. But there was a sharpness beneath it all—a subtle tension in the way he studied me when Jonah wasn't looking.

As the evening wore on, I could feel Jonah pulling further away. His jaw clenched whenever Elijah said something that struck a nerve, his eyes flickering to me like he wanted to say something, but couldn't. I could feel it, the tension swirling like a storm about to break, and yet, I didn't know how to make it stop. I could only watch, helpless, as the rift between us grew wider, as the questions I had avoided asking piled up between us like bricks in a wall.

Finally, after dessert had been served and the conversation had shifted to something inconsequential, Elijah turned to me, his smile taking on a dangerous edge. "You know," he began, leaning in just enough that his words felt like a whisper meant for only me, "I think Jonah's been keeping something from you."

I froze. My spoon, halfway to my mouth, stalled in midair. I had heard it before—the insinuations, the doubts—but hearing them from Elijah felt different, sharper, like a threat that had been masked as concern.

"Excuse me?" I asked, my voice a little too tight, a little too careful.

His smile widened, but it wasn't kind. "Oh, nothing specific. Just... well, I think it's pretty obvious that he's been hiding something from you. You'd be surprised what people keep locked away."

My heart beat a little faster, an uneasy flutter in my chest. I didn't want to give him the satisfaction of showing that he had gotten under my skin, but I could feel the seed of doubt taking root in my mind. It was ridiculous. Jonah wouldn't lie to me. He couldn't. But even as I thought it, I felt the edge of uncertainty nibbling at the edges of my certainty.

I forced a laugh, trying to sound casual. "And what exactly is it that you think he's hiding?"

Elijah leaned back, his gaze flickering over my face, assessing. "Oh, I don't know. Maybe it's nothing. But then again, maybe it's something. You're a smart woman. I'm sure you've noticed the little cracks, the things he doesn't say, the way he avoids certain subjects."

Jonah shifted in his seat across from me, his fingers curling tightly around his glass of wine. I could feel the weight of his discomfort radiating off of him, and I turned to him, hoping for some sign that this was all just a game, that Elijah was trying to provoke me for some unknown reason. But Jonah wouldn't meet my eyes. He wouldn't say a word.

The silence stretched, suffocating, and I suddenly felt very alone in that room, surrounded by people I should have trusted, but who seemed to be working against me at every turn. My gaze flickered between the two men—one I loved, the other I barely tolerated—and I couldn't decide which one was more dangerous.

The next morning, the house felt too quiet. Jonah had already left for work, and I hadn't been able to sleep much. The tangled mess of thoughts swirled in my mind, like a storm rolling in on a sleepy beach, too loud to ignore but too far off to do anything about. I tried to distract myself, fixing a cup of coffee and walking around the living room as though the rhythmic movement could chase away the weight that had settled on my chest. But every creak of the floorboards, every flicker of the lights, seemed to echo with the question I couldn't ask.

What was Jonah hiding?

I wanted to believe Elijah's words were nothing but the cheap shot of a jealous relative, but they had taken root in my mind. Jonah hadn't been himself for weeks now, retreating into silence the way he always did when something was wrong, yet never willing to tell me what that something was. He had become this unyielding force, so far removed from the man who used to lay beside me in the dark, whispering secrets and dreams. I tried to tell myself that it wasn't anything, that maybe it was just work, stress, life—after all, life could wear anyone down. But deep down, I knew. I knew it was more than that.

I grabbed my phone, my fingers hovering over the screen. I could call him. I could demand an answer, press him until he cracked. But I'd tried that. And every time, he pulled away, retreating further into that stone wall he'd built around himself. My mouth went dry. I didn't want to break something that felt so fragile, but I couldn't keep pretending everything was fine when it clearly wasn't.

The knock at the door startled me out of my thoughts. My heart stuttered in my chest. Jonah? But no, I didn't think he'd be back yet. I glanced through the peephole, and there was Elijah. Of course.

I opened the door, forcing a smile that didn't quite reach my eyes.

"Elijah. What are you doing here?"

His grin was too wide, too knowing. "Just wanted to check on you. You seemed a little... tense last night." He brushed past me before I could say anything, his presence like a shadow that made the room feel smaller.

I closed the door behind him with a quiet click, watching him as he looked around, his eyes far too observant, like he was taking mental notes on every detail.

"I'm fine," I said, though the words felt hollow. "What do you want?"

His gaze flickered to me, sharp and calculating. "What's going on between you and Jonah? It's not hard to see that something's off."

The air in the room thickened, the quiet hum of the refrigerator suddenly too loud. I opened my mouth to speak, but the words wouldn't come. How could I explain what I didn't understand myself?

He didn't wait for an answer, of course. He never did. Elijah took a few steps into the living room, sinking down into the couch like he belonged there. "You're a smart woman. You can figure it out. You know Jonah better than anyone, don't you?" He let the question hang in the air, like a challenge.

I crossed my arms, resisting the urge to step back. "You think I don't know what's going on? You think I'm blind?"

He laughed, a low, almost sympathetic sound. "Not at all. But maybe you're a little too close to it to see things clearly. Jonah's been distant for a while. You don't think that's strange?"

My pulse quickened, the knot in my stomach tightening. I wanted to say something—anything—to dismiss him, to shove him out of the house and lock the door behind him. But the words wouldn't come, and for the first time, I felt the weight of his words settle deep in my chest, planting the tiniest seed of doubt that had begun to sprout faster than I could tear it out.

He leaned forward slightly, watching me with those calculating eyes. "You've noticed, haven't you? He's not the man you think he is. He's hiding something. I just don't know if you're ready to find out what."

"Don't you dare," I whispered, the words slipping out before I could stop them.

He smirked. "Don't what? Face the truth?"

"You're lying. Trying to get inside my head." I moved towards him, frustration surging like a wave crashing on the shore. "If Jonah's hiding something, it's his business. Not yours. So if you think you can manipulate me into believing whatever you've got cooked up, you're wrong."

For a moment, the air between us crackled with tension, the heat of it almost unbearable. But Elijah didn't flinch. Instead, he chuckled softly, as if he knew something I didn't.

"You think he'll protect you? Think again." He stood up, his tall frame looming over me, but there was no warmth in his smile anymore—just cold, empty amusement. "He's got a lot of secrets, and I'm sure he'll keep them all from you. You'll be left standing here, wondering where it all went wrong."

Before I could respond, he turned and walked out the door, his footsteps echoing in the silence he left behind. The door closed with a soft click, but the weight of his words hung in the air, thick and suffocating.

I stood there, my breath shallow, my mind spinning with possibilities, none of them good. Elijah had planted his seed, and now it was growing, taking root in places I didn't want to explore. The worst part? I didn't know how much of it was truth and how much was just manipulation. But I couldn't ignore it any longer. Something was wrong, and Jonah was hiding it from me. I could feel it. I just didn't know how deep the lies went.

By the time Jonah came home that evening, the house felt more like a battleground than a sanctuary. I stood in the kitchen, pretending to be busy with a pot of pasta, the soft hiss of boiling water a thin veil over the simmering tension. My hands were steady as I stirred, but my mind was a whirlwind. Elijah's words echoed relentlessly, like an unwelcome guest who refused to leave. They wrapped around my thoughts, tightening with every passing minute.

I hadn't confronted Jonah yet. Something about the way he'd left that morning—distant, barely meeting my eyes—kept me rooted in place, unwilling to push too far. And yet, the weight of the silence between us felt unbearable now, as if it were a third person in the room, lurking just behind the door, waiting for one of us to open it. The question that had lodged itself deep in my chest—What is he hiding?—was growing like a vine, creeping into every corner of my mind.

The door creaked open, and I didn't have to look to know it was him. The air seemed to shift when he entered, like the atmosphere itself was waiting for something to happen. He dropped his keys on the counter and came over to where I stood, his movements slow, deliberate, like he was calculating the distance between us.

"Hey," he said, his voice low, almost apologetic.

I didn't answer immediately. Instead, I turned the pasta off the burner, the soft click of the knob echoing louder than I expected. Then I glanced at him, trying to gauge how much of the man I loved was still here. He looked tired—there was a weariness in his eyes that hadn't been there before, as though something heavy had settled in his bones. But that was all. No explanation, no easy way to read him. He had perfected the art of silence in the past few weeks, and it seemed to be his shield now.

I swallowed hard. "We need to talk."

His jaw tightened, the muscles in his neck flexing as though preparing for a fight he didn't want to have. I saw the flicker of something in his eyes—hesitation, maybe? Guilt? Whatever it was, it didn't sit right with me. Not after everything we'd been through.

He cleared his throat. "About what?"

I set the spoon down, wiping my hands on the dish towel with more force than necessary. "Don't play dumb, Jonah."

I heard the sharp intake of breath, but he didn't argue. Instead, he stepped closer, the space between us shrinking until I could feel the warmth of his body, the familiarity of him, even though every inch of me screamed to step back. I didn't. I couldn't.

"What did Elijah say to you?" His voice was a little rough, as though he'd been running through something in his mind over and over again, trying to figure out how to say it. But he wasn't saying anything, was he? Not really.

I took a deep breath, trying to steady the nerves that had suddenly flared to life. "It doesn't matter what Elijah says. I don't care about him."

His expression softened, but only for a moment, before his eyes hardened again. "You should." His words were like ice, colder than I'd ever heard him sound before.

I blinked. "What do you mean by that?"

He stepped back, running a hand through his hair, a nervous habit I had come to recognize over the years. But this wasn't the usual stress of work or some trivial misunderstanding. This was different. There was something lurking behind his eyes, something he wasn't saying, and it made my skin prickle with dread.

"Jonah," I said, my voice quieter now, but my heart was racing, thudding in my chest like it wanted to escape. "Tell me the truth. What is going on?"

For a long moment, he didn't answer. The seconds stretched out between us like hours. I could feel the walls closing in, could feel the foundation beneath us starting to crack. The silence was deafening, suffocating.

"I can't." His words were barely above a whisper, and it hit me with the force of a slap. The simple admission was like a blow to the gut, and it left me reeling. He couldn't. He couldn't tell me. Not after everything. After all the years we'd spent together, after all the promises we'd made.

I felt a sickening wave of nausea rise in my throat. I wanted to scream. To demand answers. To tear apart every lie, every secret, and expose him for what he was. But I didn't. Because I knew, deep down, that I didn't want to hear what he might say next.

The seconds ticked by, the silence stretching even further, and I could see him visibly struggling with something, his eyes darting away from mine as though he couldn't bear the weight of them. Finally, he spoke, but it wasn't the answer I expected.

"Don't you think you should know who you're really dealing with before you make any decisions?" His voice was cold now, like the warmth had been sucked out of the room, leaving behind nothing but the sharp, biting chill of something dark and dangerous.

I shook my head, confusion clouding my mind. "What are you talking about?"

Jonah took a step back, his expression unreadable, and just as I opened my mouth to ask him again, he reached for his jacket hanging by the door. "I need to go," he said, the words a finality that slammed into me harder than any argument.

I didn't move, rooted to the spot, my heart a pounding mess in my chest. "No," I whispered, but he was already walking out the door, his back turned to me as he stepped into the night.

The door slammed behind him, and I was left standing in the quiet, the echo of his departure ringing through the empty house. A sudden shiver ran down my spine, and for the first time since I'd met Jonah, I felt like I had no idea who he truly was.

And then, before I could even process the thought, my phone buzzed on the counter. One message. From an unknown number.

"Meet me at the park. 10 PM. You need to hear the truth."

Chapter 26: The Betrayal Unveiled

I felt the breath freeze in my lungs the moment the words left her lips. I hadn't expected her to say anything at all. And certainly not that.

Jonah. The name rang through my mind like a bell struck by an unseen hand, its reverberations harsh and sharp. The world around me seemed to tilt slightly, as if I were no longer standing firmly on the ground but teetering on the edge of something vast and uncharted.

Her eyes were cold as she studied me, sitting across from me in her sterile living room, a place that seemed more museum than home. Everything in the room was pristine—white leather furniture, glass tables reflecting the muted light of early evening, and shelves upon shelves of books that were neatly arranged, unread. I could feel the slight stifling quality of the air, like a room holding its breath. It mirrored my own unease.

"Jonah," she repeated, her voice almost delicate. "He was never who you thought he was."

The words were too calm, too measured. It was as if she had been rehearsing this moment for longer than I'd been aware of the problem. "What are you talking about?" I asked, my voice barely a whisper, afraid that even the faintest tremor in it might give away how completely I was unraveling.

She sighed, a sound too long-suffering for someone who wasn't yet old enough to be weary. "You really don't know, do you?" she mused. There was something in her tone, a note of pity mixed with something sharper—gloating, perhaps? "Jonah's past, darling... He's kept it from you, and for good reason. But I suppose you're owed the truth."

I should have stood up and walked out, should have slapped the heavy envelope of suspicion from my mind and erased the growing knot in my stomach. Instead, I stayed seated, heart pounding harder with every second I let this conversation unfold. It felt as if I were being slowly suffocated by the air between us, and yet, I couldn't tear my gaze away from her.

"What is it?" I demanded, now desperate for answers, any answers, even if they were things I wasn't sure I was ready to hear.

She leaned forward, her fingertips grazing the smooth edge of the table, almost possessively. "Jonah has a family, one he doesn't like to talk about. They're dangerous, Ivy. The sort of dangerous that leaves you in a position you can't come back from."

My head spun. "Dangerous?" I echoed, the word thick on my tongue. "What are you saying?"

"He's not the man you think he is." She straightened in her seat, her tone shifting to something more sinister. "He's been hiding his past from you, and there are things—" she paused for effect, her eyes glinting "—things he's never mentioned, things he doesn't want you to know. Things that, once you understand them, will change the way you see him. It'll change everything, Ivy."

I shook my head, disoriented. "I don't—what does that mean? What could be so bad?"

For the first time, she allowed herself a small smile, but it was a cruel one. "You wouldn't believe me if I told you. Trust me, you'll find out soon enough. Just be careful."

I stood abruptly, the floor beneath my feet suddenly feeling too small for my racing thoughts. "No. I don't—this is insane. Jonah wouldn't—"

"Wouldn't?" she interrupted, her voice a shade too sharp. "That's what you don't understand. He's already told you more than he should have. Now he's making sure you don't ask the questions that could tear apart everything he's worked so hard to build." She stood up, too, then, closing the gap between us with slow, deliberate steps.

Her eyes were fixed on me, dark and heavy with the weight of secrets. "You won't believe me now. But you will."

She watched me turn and leave, her smile still lingering in the air, like a bad perfume.

The walk back to my apartment was a blur, each step feeling like it was being taken through molasses. My mind couldn't focus on anything other than her words, twisting them into knots of confusion. Jonah. Dangerous? Hiding things? What was she trying to say?

I arrived home just as the sky outside was beginning to darken, the first hints of evening settling over the city. The apartment felt too quiet, too still. Jonah's coat wasn't draped over the back of the couch, and the faint smell of his cologne didn't linger in the air. It should have been comforting, in a way—a reminder that we had space in each other's lives. But tonight, the emptiness pressed in on me from every angle, filling me with a gnawing sense of dread.

I walked into the bedroom, half-expecting him to be there, half-hoping that he wasn't.

But he was. Sitting on the edge of the bed, his back to me, his shoulders tense and squared, as if he'd been expecting this moment all along.

I froze in the doorway. "Jonah?" My voice cracked on his name. It felt like a question I shouldn't have to ask, yet the sound of it hung in the air like a confession.

He turned slowly, his eyes locking with mine, unreadable and cool. "I knew you would find out eventually," he said, his tone low and steady.

"Find out what?" I whispered, though I already knew.

"Everything," he answered. "I never meant for you to find out like this."

And just like that, the world I had so carefully built around him, around us, began to crumble, piece by piece.

He didn't move when I walked in, not even to glance up at me, and for a moment, I wasn't sure if he had heard me, if he had even noticed I'd come home. But the stillness of the room was deceptive. The tension between us snapped like a taut wire when he finally spoke, the sound of his voice so soft it might as well have been a knife slipping through the air.

"I didn't want you to be in the middle of this," he said, his back still to me, his shoulders tense. I could almost feel the weight of the words before they hit. "But you've already crossed that line, and I can't stop you from knowing."

My heart thudded painfully against my ribs, the betrayal thickening the air around me, making it hard to breathe. "Stop me from knowing what?" I tried to keep the panic out of my voice, but it was futile. It quivered, betraying me as much as he had.

Jonah finally turned to face me, and the expression on his face wasn't what I'd expected. It wasn't regret or guilt. It wasn't fear. It was something else, something older, deeper, like a man who had been living with his secrets for so long they had become as much a part of him as his skin. Something that made him look like a stranger.

"I didn't want you to have to carry the weight of my past," he said again, his words heavy in the air between us. "I thought I could protect you from it. I thought I could hide it from you forever."

I swallowed, trying to steady myself, but the ground beneath me felt as unstable as sand. "Jonah, what do you mean? What are you talking about?"

He looked at me, and for a brief moment, it felt like we were two strangers meeting for the first time—neither of us quite sure of what the other was capable of. "You know how I told you I've had… complications? Family stuff?" His voice was flat, as if the weight of it had long since crushed any emotion out of him.

I nodded, too stunned to speak. Of course I remembered. But what had seemed like just vague hints, a softening of the truth, was so much more than I had ever imagined.

"I didn't tell you the whole story, Ivy," Jonah said, and for the first time, there was a flicker of something more human in his eyes—regret, perhaps, but only just. "My family... they're not what they seem. I've been keeping you safe from them, and I thought I could keep you safe forever."

I couldn't process his words, not all at once. They collided in my mind like a freight train. A part of me wanted to yell, to demand the truth now, but I couldn't summon the strength to speak. Not when I was so afraid of what I might hear. "What do you mean by 'keep me safe?' What aren't you telling me?"

Jonah's gaze dropped, and the air between us seemed to grow colder, denser, like it was filling with something toxic. "There's a reason I don't talk about them. A reason I stay so far away. They... they have a way of getting to people. They've hurt people in the past. And I didn't want you to be one of them."

The last of my breath left my lungs. It felt like the ground had slipped out from under me, and I was falling, falling through a reality I had thought I understood. "What does that even mean?" My voice was barely above a whisper, the words trembling on my lips. "What did they do?"

Jonah didn't answer right away. Instead, he ran his hand through his hair, a gesture I had seen him do when he was agitated, when he was trying to gather his thoughts, or when he was just too exhausted to pretend everything was fine. But now, it felt like a man preparing to face the music, something too monumental to keep burying.

"I'm not proud of this," Jonah finally said, his voice low, almost lost. "But my family... they've been involved in some things—things I shouldn't have let myself be a part of. But I didn't know how to get out. They control everything. They're ruthless, Ivy. And they don't care about anyone but themselves. Not even me."

I stared at him, unable to reconcile the man I knew with the one he was describing. "You're telling me this now?" I shook my head, my voice finally rising. "After all this time, Jonah? After everything we've been through?"

He nodded slowly, his face drawn and weary. "I didn't know how. I thought I could keep it all buried. I thought I could protect you."

I stepped back, the weight of his confession pressing against me like a physical force. "Protect me? From what, Jonah? From you? From your family? Or from the truth?" I couldn't stop myself. The words spilled out, sharp and accusing. "You think I didn't deserve the truth? After everything, you think I would've walked away if you'd just told me who you really are?"

Jonah's eyes flashed, and I knew then that this was the moment where everything could change. "You wouldn't have understood," he said, his voice more forceful now. "You wouldn't have believed me. I couldn't risk you pulling away from me."

My mind raced, everything he'd said too much to absorb in one moment, but the truth was starting to take shape, like a jagged puzzle I couldn't quite fit together. My legs felt weak beneath me as I leaned against the wall for support, my thoughts scattering in every direction.

"Is this why you've always been so distant? Why you won't let me in?" My voice cracked, the ache in my chest becoming unbearable. "Why you always keep a part of yourself locked away? Because of your family?"

Jonah didn't respond at first, and for one gut-wrenching moment, I thought I might hear nothing at all. Then, in the silence that followed, I heard him speak, his words so quiet they felt like they were coming from someone else.

"I never wanted you to see me like this, Ivy. But I can't hide from you anymore. You deserve more than this."

I closed my eyes, the gravity of his confession crashing down on me. I thought I knew him. I thought we had built something together, something real. But now, I wasn't so sure.

The silence stretched between us, suffocating.

I could hear my breath coming in shallow bursts, the air too thick to swallow, as I stood there, my heart an unholy mess of emotions I couldn't name. Jonah didn't flinch, didn't blink. His gaze was steady, almost too steady, as though he were already bracing for the fallout. The realization hit me then—he had known, all along, that I would find out the truth. He had never expected to keep it from me forever.

But that didn't make it easier to accept. No, if anything, it made it worse.

"You knew," I said, my voice a mix of disbelief and hurt. I felt like I had swallowed something too large to digest, like a stone lodged in my throat, refusing to go down. "You knew I'd find out. And you just... waited for me to."

He nodded, but it wasn't in apology, and it wasn't in relief. It was just a simple acknowledgment of something we both knew too well.

"I didn't want to keep this from you, Ivy. But I couldn't bear the idea of you hating me. Not for this."

The words didn't settle in my chest. They rattled around, mocking the delicate way I had imagined our relationship to be—smooth and easy, built on shared truths and a common understanding. But now it felt more like a house of cards, fragile and ready to collapse under the weight of one wrong move. I stepped back, shaking my head.

"How could you think I'd hate you for telling me the truth?" I was practically whispering, as if the quietness of my voice could somehow make the world stop spinning long enough for me to make sense of it all. "I might not have liked it, but I could've handled it. I should've been the one to hear it from you, not someone else."

"I was trying to protect you," Jonah said, the words barely audible. There was a faint crack in his voice, and it made me hesitate, just for a second. "I thought if I kept you safe from them, safe from this..."

"Safe from what?" I demanded, my hands trembling at my sides. "What could you possibly think I wouldn't understand? I'm not some delicate little thing who can't handle your secrets, Jonah. I thought you knew that."

"I didn't know who I was anymore," he said, and this time, I saw it—the flash of desperation in his eyes, the shadow of someone who had been carrying far too much for far too long. "I thought I could bury everything. Thought I could just leave it behind and pretend it didn't matter anymore." He was pacing now, back and forth in the small space between us, his hands running through his hair. "But it does. It matters. And if I told you, I knew you'd look at me differently. Like I wasn't... who you thought I was."

The words stung, but there was something raw in his voice that I hadn't expected. I swallowed, forcing myself to keep my ground, even when every instinct was screaming at me to run. To walk out that door and never look back.

"But I'm still the same person, Ivy," he continued, his voice softer now, almost pleading. "I haven't changed. What happened, what they did... it wasn't my fault. I'm not who they are."

I watched him, waiting for the words to land, waiting for something inside of me to click, to understand the puzzle I had been trying to piece together. But there was too much missing. Too much I couldn't grasp. "Who are they, Jonah? What did they do?"

Jonah's eyes darkened, and for the first time, there was a fleeting shadow of fear behind them. "They're not like us," he said, his voice laced with something darker than I'd ever heard from him. "And I can't stop them from coming after you, Ivy. Not now. Not with you in this."

"What do you mean by coming after me?" The words twisted in my chest, and I found myself fighting the urge to panic. "What are you saying?"

He closed his eyes for a moment, like he was summoning the strength to speak, to confess something far worse than I had imagined. "They've been watching you. They know everything about you. Every move you've made since I brought you into my life." His eyes snapped open then, locking with mine. "And they won't stop until they have you, too."

I didn't know what to say to that. I couldn't make sense of it, couldn't wrap my mind around the idea that Jonah's past had somehow bled into my present, that this... family, these people I couldn't even begin to understand, had me in their sights now. I thought of the conversations we had shared, the plans we'd made. The quiet nights spent curled up together, talking about everything and nothing. Was any of that real? Or was it all just the calm before a storm?

I shook my head, my thoughts racing in circles. "This is insane. You're telling me that people—your family—are after me? What for, Jonah? What could they possibly want with me?"

He hesitated, then stepped closer, as though the space between us was no longer enough to contain the weight of his words. "They'll want leverage. They'll want to use you against me."

The air seemed to thin as his words sank in. I couldn't breathe. I couldn't think. I felt the sharpness of the fear creeping up my spine, like a chill that was settling deep in my bones.

"No," I whispered, shaking my head as though denying it could make it go away. "No, Jonah. I can't— I can't do this."

He reached for me then, his hand outstretched, but I took a step back, my chest tight, my mind scrambling for clarity. "I didn't ask for any of this," I said, my voice coming out in a raw rasp. "I didn't ask for any of you."

And just like that, the room seemed to tilt. Everything I thought I knew about Jonah, about us, splintered. The tension between us was palpable, like the last thread of a rope that was about to snap. The truth was there, heavy in the space between us, but it was slipping further away with every word.

And then—before I could react, before I could make sense of it all—there was a knock at the door.

A sound that cut through the fragile silence like a knife.

Chapter 27: A Heart Torn Asunder

I couldn't look back, even if I wanted to. The door swung shut behind me with a soft click, the kind that felt louder than a gunshot. Jonah's desperate voice still echoed in my ears, a twisted melody I couldn't escape. "You don't understand," he'd begged, his words breaking like glass with every syllable, as if the weight of them was too much for him to bear. But how could I? How could I understand when everything he'd told me had been a lie?

The night air wrapped itself around me like a cold, damp blanket, biting at my skin, a stark contrast to the warmth I'd left behind. I didn't know where I was going, didn't care, really. The world felt unreal, a hazy blur of streetlights and shadows. My heart beat a frantic rhythm, each pulse another reminder of the pain I'd just walked away from.

I found myself standing at the edge of the bridge, the one I'd always walked across without a second thought. The water beneath it was dark, flowing steadily, relentless, indifferent. If I stood there long enough, I wondered if the river might swallow me whole, take me somewhere far away where Jonah couldn't reach me. But I didn't move. I couldn't.

The wind tousled my hair, the strands sticking to my lips as if even nature itself was trying to keep me grounded. My chest tightened. It hurt, the kind of hurt that made every breath feel like it might be my last. But that was the thing about heartbreak, wasn't it? It wasn't just the absence of love that left the ache behind; it was the way it stayed with you long after the moment passed, like a ghost that refused to fade into the shadows.

I could still see his face in my mind's eye—his eyes, wide with that familiar panic, the way his hands shook as he reached out to me. He hadn't been the man I thought I knew, but wasn't it always like that? We spent years building a life with someone, only to discover the foundation was nothing more than cracked clay. The lie I'd uncovered—oh, God, it wasn't just one. It was everything. Every whisper, every smile, every promise. They'd all been laced with something I couldn't quite name until now.

I stepped away from the railing, my boots clicking sharply on the pavement, each step a tiny rebellion against the storm that brewed inside me. My mind screamed at me to go back, to face him, to demand answers—more answers than he had the nerve to give. But my heart, ever the traitor, whispered something else. Something softer, but far more dangerous. It begged me to forgive him.

Forgiveness, I realized, wasn't something that could be given on a whim. It was a slow, painful process, one I wasn't ready to begin. Not yet. Not when the wounds were still raw and bleeding.

I pulled out my phone, but the screen looked foreign in my hands, as if it might break under the weight of the decision I had yet to make. I'd done this before, reached out to him in moments of weakness, convinced myself that the love we'd shared could patch over the cracks. But not this time. This time, there was no going back. I couldn't unsee what I had seen. I couldn't forget what I'd learned.

And yet, there was this nagging pull, this quiet desperation that made me wonder if maybe, just maybe, I was wrong. I could picture him in my mind now—the way he stood there, half in shadow, half in light, his features etched with something darker than regret. He wasn't a villain, not really. He was just… human. Flawed. He'd made mistakes, terrible ones, but who hadn't? Who hadn't done something unforgivable, only to wish they could take it all back?

I wanted to hate him. I wanted to throw all my anger at him and burn every memory we'd shared. But I couldn't. Because despite everything, there was still a part of me that loved him. A part that wanted to believe the best in him, even when he couldn't see it himself.

With a shaky breath, I stuffed my phone back in my pocket. The cold of the night seeped into my bones, and I wrapped my arms around myself, trying to hold onto the last remnants of who I was before Jonah and I became... this. I thought about the way we'd laughed together, the stupid inside jokes that no one else understood, the way his hand had fit so perfectly in mine. I had believed in us, in him. But now, all of that felt like a lie, like a beautiful illusion I'd created in my own mind.

I wasn't sure where I was going, but I knew I couldn't stay here. Not with the memories of him, of us, still hanging in the air like smoke. I turned and walked away from the bridge, my steps more deliberate now, even though my mind was still spinning. The night was quiet, the city around me oblivious to the storm brewing inside. As I made my way home, I realized I wasn't just running away from Jonah. I was running away from myself. From the person I had been before I knew what he had done, before everything fell apart.

But at least, in the quiet of the night, I had the chance to think. To breathe. To decide who I wanted to be in a world that no longer seemed to make sense.

The following days stretched like an endless winter, each one colder than the last. I kept to my apartment, cocooned in the mess of unwashed dishes and clothes strewn across the floor, trying to escape the thoughts that seemed intent on invading every waking moment. It was like living inside a haze, where even the mundane was tinged with bitterness, and every corner of my home felt like a reminder of Jonah's absence. Or maybe it was more the absence of the person I thought he was, the version of him that had been wrapped in affection, in promises that were now nothing more than ashes in my hands.

The coffee machine buzzed in the background, but I didn't need it. Not really. Not when my body was already on high alert, every muscle tight, my nerves stretched to their breaking point. I wasn't sleeping—couldn't, not when the quiet of the night seemed to echo with the unanswered questions that swirled in my mind. I'd thought about reaching out to him, just once, to ask if there was a sliver of truth in the tangled web of lies he'd woven. But each time I reached for my phone, my hand trembled, and I'd quickly drop it back on the counter as if the mere idea of him was too much to bear.

I knew he was trying, of course. His name popped up on my phone screen like a sick joke, the little notification bright and insistent. He was sorry. He loved me. He wanted to fix things. I hadn't replied. Couldn't, really. Because how could I face him after everything? After the way he had lied to me, betrayed me in the worst possible way?

But there was something in his voice, something raw and vulnerable, that kept tugging at my chest. The part of me that wanted to believe him—the part that wasn't entirely sure I could walk away from everything we had, from everything I thought I knew. Was love enough to mend what was broken? Or was it too late?

I shook my head, pushing the thought aside as I walked toward the living room, staring absently out the window. The city stretched before me, a maze of gray buildings and hurried commuters, each person wrapped up in their own little worlds. I envied them for their oblivion, for their lack of burden. For a moment, I wanted to disappear into that sea of strangers, to blend in and forget who I was and what had happened.

Instead, I pulled a blanket off the back of the couch and wrapped it around myself, as though its warmth might offer me something I couldn't seem to find anywhere else. The silence of the apartment pressed in on me, and I sighed.

I should have been angry, right? I should have been storming around, throwing things, smashing plates. But I wasn't. Instead, I was lost. Lost in the kind of grief that doesn't scream, but quietly gnaws away at your heart, until it's too late to remember what it felt like to be whole.

The doorbell rang, and I froze. For a moment, I wondered if I had somehow imagined it, but the sound came again, sharper this time, followed by a soft knock. I didn't move. Didn't want to.

Another knock.

I took a breath and stood, wrapping the blanket tighter around my shoulders as if it could protect me from whatever awaited me outside that door. I wasn't ready for a confrontation, not yet. But there was something in the way the world tilted on its axis that made me feel like I had no choice.

When I opened the door, there he was. Jonah. Standing there, looking like a man who had been chewed up by the world and spit back out, every inch of him radiating exhaustion and regret. His hair was a mess, his eyes red from lack of sleep—he hadn't shaved in days. But it was the look on his face that stopped me in my tracks.

He didn't speak immediately, just stood there, his lips pressed into a tight line as if the words he needed to say were too heavy to carry. I knew that feeling. The weight of things left unsaid, of wounds too fresh to touch. But then he spoke, his voice low, hoarse.

"I know I don't deserve this," he said, the words like a balm to a wound that hadn't yet begun to heal. "But I couldn't just let you walk away without trying."

I didn't know what to say. I had imagined this moment in a thousand different ways, rehearsed the words I would say in response, in anger, in pain. But now that he was here, the words caught in my throat. He seemed so small in that moment, so fragile, like the man who had once been my rock was nothing more than a pile of rubble at my feet.

"You don't get to come here and act like everything is okay," I managed to say, my voice shaking, though I didn't want it to. "You don't get to just show up after everything. After... everything."

He nodded, like he expected the words to cut through him, and maybe they did. "I don't expect forgiveness," he said, his voice barely a whisper. "I just... I need you to know that I never meant to hurt you. I was stupid, and I—"

"I'm not sure 'stupid' covers it," I interrupted, the words spilling out before I could stop them. But as soon as they left my mouth, I regretted them. Jonah flinched as if I'd struck him.

"I know," he said, his hands clenched at his sides. "And I'm so sorry. I'm so sorry, Kate."

There it was again. That terrible, delicious word. Sorry. A word so often abused it had lost its meaning in my mind. But the way he said it, the weight of it... I didn't know what to do with it. I couldn't just swallow it down. I couldn't just let him off the hook because he said the right thing.

"Then what now?" I asked, my voice softer now. I hated how it wavered, how it betrayed the crack in my own heart. "What are we supposed to do with all of this?"

Jonah looked at me, his eyes dark with uncertainty, with fear. "I don't know. I don't know what comes next. But I'm not ready to let go of us."

I stared at Jonah for what felt like an eternity, the silence between us thick, as if the very air was trying to hold its breath, afraid to disturb the fragile reality we were now both trapped in. His eyes were pleading, still holding that familiar desperation, the one I had once found endearing—now it only made my stomach twist. He wasn't asking for forgiveness. He wasn't begging me to love him again. He was simply... here. And for all his regrets, all the words he said, I couldn't figure out what had shifted. Why did I feel like I was being swallowed whole by a void that had been waiting for me all along?

"Kate," he began, his voice barely above a whisper, but I held up a hand, silencing him before he could say anything more. I didn't want his words to wash over me, not right now. Not when the only thing I could think about was how different this all felt. How the man in front of me didn't match the man I thought I knew. The Jonah I had once believed in, the Jonah I had trusted with pieces of my heart, seemed as lost to me as I was to him.

"What now?" I asked, my voice barely my own. My heart wasn't in the words; it was in the pain that crushed my chest, that turned my breathing into something jagged and broken. "You've broken me, Jonah. And all you have to offer is... sorry?"

His eyes tightened, as if I had slapped him. But I didn't care. My words were raw, and they were real. The hurt was too big to hide, too real to ignore, even if I wanted to.

"I didn't mean for this to happen. I never wanted to hurt you. You have to know that, Kate."

I took a shaky breath, trying to steady myself, but the more he spoke, the more it felt like his voice was dripping with something more sinister than sincerity. Was this what it meant to be deceived? To look at the person you thought you knew and see them for what they truly were? Not just a liar, but a stranger who had somehow crept into your life, wrapped you in illusions, and walked away when the curtains fell?

"You're telling me this now, Jonah? After everything? After the truth came crashing down like a damn freight train?" I wanted to be angry. I wanted to scream at him, to throw my fists into his chest until he could feel the same ache I was feeling. But there was something in his eyes—something that wouldn't let me. Something that made me hesitate. It was as if he had become a mirror, reflecting my own vulnerability back at me, and it left me raw in ways I hadn't anticipated.

"I never wanted to lie to you," he repeated, his voice thick with emotion. "I don't expect you to believe me. But I swear to you, I didn't know how to tell you the truth. I thought—I thought I could protect you from the fallout, from the consequences."

"Protect me?" I scoffed, my lips curling with bitterness. "Protect me from what, Jonah? The truth? The truth is what's destroying us. It's what's destroying me."

I took a step back, pulling my cardigan tighter around my body as if it could shield me from the intensity of the conversation, the weight of his presence. But it didn't help. I still felt exposed. Still felt the sharp edge of everything he had done, everything that had led us here.

Jonah reached out, his hand hovering, unsure, as if asking for permission to touch me again. But he didn't. He didn't make the mistake of touching me without asking. Not this time. Instead, he stood there, the space between us thick with history, with everything we had shared. I could hear the sound of my pulse, beating in my ears, drowning out everything else. The silence stretched longer, more unbearable than any words could have been.

"I thought I could fix it," he said, his voice barely audible. "I thought I could make things right. But I—" He broke off, unable to finish, his eyes filled with the kind of helplessness that only added to the mess we were already in.

I shook my head slowly, unwilling to let myself fall into the pity he seemed to be offering. "You can't fix this," I said, the words bitter on my tongue. "This is broken beyond repair. And you can't just waltz back into my life because you feel bad about it. You broke something inside of me, Jonah. And that's not something you can fix with a few words and a sad face."

I turned away, unwilling to meet his gaze any longer. The sight of him—broken, pleading—was too much. It stirred something in me, something I wasn't sure I could trust anymore. For a moment, the ground beneath me felt like it might shift, like it might swallow me whole if I didn't keep moving.

"You're right," he said quietly, his voice distant now, almost resigned. "I don't deserve another chance. I don't deserve your forgiveness. But I had to try. Because if I didn't, I wouldn't be able to live with myself."

I took another step away, my heart caught in a vice of confusion. There was something in his words, in the sincerity of his voice, that made it impossible for me to turn my back completely. Part of me wanted to forgive him, to let him back in, to believe that we could fix this. But another part of me, the part that had been shattered, knew that to do so would be to sacrifice everything I had learned about myself in the wake of his betrayal.

I heard him take a step closer, his breath shallow. I closed my eyes, not wanting to hear him, not wanting to see what came next. But then—just as quickly as he had moved toward me, I heard a sound from behind. A voice, sharp and insistent, cutting through the tension like a knife.

"Kate?"

I froze. My heart lurched in my chest. The voice was familiar, a voice I hadn't heard in what felt like a lifetime.

Chapter 28: A Solitary Escape

The small cottage I rented perched on the edge of a hillside, nestled in a valley where the wild lavender clung to the earth with reckless abandon. The air smelled like a garden in full bloom, fragrant and heady, with traces of rosemary and thyme carried by the breeze. I had been there for two weeks, but it felt like I had been marooned for months. The kind of exile where time either stretches endlessly or shatters into jagged fragments, neither of which felt comforting.

I had arrived in the village with nothing but a bag of clothes, a mind heavy with thoughts I couldn't escape, and the faint, barely recognizable version of myself that had once known how to laugh without it being a sound of forced release. The locals were polite enough, always greeting me with kind smiles and slightly curious eyes. They didn't ask why I was there, and I didn't tell them. My past wasn't something you share with strangers, especially when your own reflection still feels like a foreign landscape.

The days drifted slowly. In the mornings, I wandered the meandering paths through the lavender fields, where the tall stalks reached toward the sky like dancers in a trance. My fingers brushed against the flowers, their tips soft and cool as if the earth itself were whispering secrets through the stems. I was drawn to their muted purple hues, and the way the sunlight dappled through the clouds, casting shadows that seemed to move with a life of their own. There was a tranquility here that soothed the raw edges of my thoughts. But even as I let the world around me settle, the ghosts of him still lingered in the back of my mind, in the rustling of the leaves and the hum of distant bees.

I couldn't shake the weight of the past. His voice echoed, even when he was far from me—his words, his laugh, those moments of connection that now felt like something out of a dream. There had been a time when I thought we were untouchable, as if nothing could tear us apart. The small apartment we'd shared, the coffee dates that turned into lazy Sunday mornings, and the way he'd kiss the top of my head as if it were the most natural thing in the world—it all seemed so real, so undeniable. Until it wasn't.

I had tried to push him out of my mind, tried to tell myself that this was exactly what I needed. That I was doing the right thing by retreating to this peaceful corner of the world. But the silence of the countryside only amplified the storm inside me. I wanted to be angry, to rage at him for the betrayal, for leaving me alone in a sea of uncertainty, but the anger never came. Instead, all I had were fragments of us—murmurs of tenderness that seemed to mock my attempts at healing.

One evening, as the sun dipped behind the hills and the sky bled into hues of amber and lavender, I found myself sitting on the porch of the cottage, the wood beneath me warm from the heat of the day. The chirping of crickets filled the air, the sound rhythmic and soothing, and for a moment, I thought I might be able to breathe without the tightness in my chest. The world, it seemed, was giving me the space to heal, to breathe, to begin again.

But then the phone buzzed in my pocket. My heart stuttered at the sound, a reflex I hated. It was a text, simple, unassuming. A message from him. I almost didn't open it, almost threw the phone away, tossed it into the field and left it there like an offering. But I couldn't.

"I miss you. Are you okay?"

My fingers hovered over the screen, the words blurring as my vision swam. I had spent days convincing myself that I was better off without him, that this distance was necessary, even healthy. But one sentence, one tiny line of text, and I was back in that place—those late nights spent tangled in the sheets, our bodies speaking in a language only we understood. I could almost hear his voice in my ear, feel his hand on my back as he murmured words of comfort I wasn't sure I believed in anymore.

The phone slipped from my hands, landing on the porch with a faint thud, its screen cracked. The irony wasn't lost on me. It had all been fragile, hadn't it? The way we'd pieced ourselves together, only for everything to crumble when the truth came to light.

But in that moment, I wasn't sure if it was the phone that was broken or me.

I didn't want to think about him. Not now. Not here, in this haven I had built, even if it was only temporary. But I had no control over the pull of memory, over the way the love I had once felt for him could still twist itself into something painful and bitter, like sugar turning to ash on the tongue. I wanted to push it all away, but every time I tried, it returned stronger, more insistent.

I rose from the porch, my feet pressing into the soft earth as I walked away from the cottage, toward the hills that stretched endlessly before me. The path was narrow and winding, each step taking me further into the embrace of nature. The lavender fields were gone now, replaced by stretches of golden wheat and vineyards that shimmered like liquid gold in the fading light. I breathed in deeply, hoping the fresh air would fill me up, make me forget. Make me stronger. But the more I walked, the more I realized that running from him, from us, was an impossibility.

And yet, I couldn't go back. Not yet. Not until I found a way to reconcile the parts of me that still loved him with the parts that knew I had to move forward, even if it meant walking away from the only person who had ever truly understood me.

I wasn't sure what would happen next, but I knew that I couldn't stay in this in-between forever.

The night came swiftly in the countryside, as it always did, with a cool breeze sweeping over the fields, carrying the scent of earth and the distant perfume of night-blooming jasmine. I stood at the edge of the vineyard, my feet half-buried in the soft soil, and watched the last rays of daylight dip behind the horizon, as though the world were sighing and settling into its evening slumber. The stars were starting to take their places in the sky, little pinpricks of light that would soon blanket the expanse above me in a million glimmers. I could feel the tension in my chest, a subtle tightness that wouldn't quite release, like a string pulled too taut.

There was a pull in me, a desire to move, to go somewhere, to do something—anything that would distract me from the ache of his absence. And so I walked. With no destination in mind, I let the path guide me, my feet moving with a mind of their own. The earth was cool beneath me, the first touch of autumn already creeping in. The breeze carried the promise of change, but still, I was rooted in this moment, in this space, trying to separate the woman I was now from the one I had been before. The woman who had believed, blindly, in love that could withstand everything.

The village was quiet as I passed through it, the streets empty, save for the occasional flicker of light behind a window, a family gathering over dinner, or an old man out for his evening stroll. It was all so peaceful, so idyllic, and yet it felt like a world apart from the chaos in my mind. I wasn't sure what I was searching for—perhaps some sense of purpose, or maybe just a way to quiet the voices that swirled in my head. I knew I couldn't keep running forever, but the thought of facing what was waiting for me at home, in the place we'd shared, was unbearable.

I found myself at the local café a short time later, the one with the crooked sign and the faded awning that had clearly seen better days. The door creaked as I pushed it open, a soft jingle announcing my entrance. Inside, the air was warm and smelled of freshly baked bread and strong coffee. The few patrons who lingered in the dim light barely glanced up, lost in their own quiet worlds. The owner, an older woman with a round face and hands that moved like liquid as she wiped down the counter, smiled at me with a knowing look. She didn't ask what brought me here, but her eyes, gentle and kind, seemed to say everything. Sometimes, that was all you needed—someone who understood without a word.

I took a seat by the window, letting the soft hum of conversation wash over me. The café was a refuge for many in the village, a place where time didn't quite matter, where the worries of the world could be pushed aside for a while. As I sat there, my mind wandered again to him, the man I thought I would spend the rest of my life with. The one who had made promises he never intended to keep. He had always been charming, always knew just what to say to make me feel like the center of his world. And for a while, I had believed him. I had trusted him. But trust, like everything else, had its breaking point.

I was jolted from my thoughts by the sound of the door opening, the bell chiming as a man stepped inside, his silhouette framed by the last bits of sunlight from the street. He was tall, with dark hair that had the kind of casual, tousled look that most people would have to try hard to achieve. His eyes, sharp and observant, swept the room before settling on me. There was something familiar about him, something that tugged at the edges of my memory.

He took a seat at the bar, ordering a coffee without a word. The barista, an older man with a thick French accent, responded with a grunt of recognition before turning to prepare the drink. My gaze lingered on him for a moment longer, my curiosity piqued, before I returned to my own thoughts, pretending not to notice how much he stood out in this sleepy little place.

It wasn't until he moved closer to the window, brushing past my table on his way outside, that our eyes met. There was an instant recognition, a flicker of something unspoken between us, but it wasn't until he smiled that I realized who he was.

Adrian.

The name hit me like a wave, a sudden rush of memories crashing over me—hot summer nights on the beach, stolen kisses, the sound of his laugh filling the air like music. Adrian had been part of a life I had left behind, a life before him, before the lies and the betrayal. And now, here he was, standing in front of me as if nothing had changed.

His smile was crooked, a little amused, as if he'd known this moment was coming, though I hadn't. "Fancy running into you here," he said, his voice smooth, with that same trace of humor I remembered so well. "I didn't expect to find you in a place like this."

I blinked, disoriented. "I didn't expect to find you either," I replied, my voice a little unsteady, but I couldn't help the faint edge of amusement that rose in me. This was absurd, wasn't it? Running away to the French countryside to escape the past only to have it catch up with me in the form of someone I never thought I'd see again.

Adrian chuckled, taking a step back and glancing out at the street. "Small world," he mused, his gaze lingering on the fading light of the village as if weighing something unspoken.

There was a silence between us, thick with all the things neither of us said. It wasn't a silence of comfort, but one of unspoken tension, the kind that happens when you share a history with someone you're not sure how to relate to anymore.

The silence between Adrian and I stretched longer than it should have. He was the one to break it, of course, his voice warm but tinged with that hint of something I couldn't quite place—perhaps it was regret, or just the casual ease of someone who thought time had erased the distance between us.

"Looks like the countryside has a strange way of bringing people together, doesn't it?" he said, his gaze flicking back to me, catching my eyes with an intensity that made my breath catch in my throat. "I never thought I'd find you here. Last time I checked, you were..." He trailed off, as though unsure of where to take the sentence.

"Somewhere else?" I finished for him, feeling the sting of his uncertainty like a needle pricking my skin. I hadn't expected to see him, especially not here, of all places. But there he was, looking like the same Adrian who'd once made me feel like I was the only person in a crowded room, and also, somehow, like I was the most expendable.

"Something like that," he murmured, his voice lowering as though speaking louder would break whatever delicate thing was hanging between us.

I stared down at the table, my fingers tracing the rim of my coffee cup, trying to find some ground to stand on. My mind raced, trying to piece together this strange collision of my present and past. I wasn't sure if I wanted to throw myself into this—this him—again, or if I just wanted to walk out of the café, out of the village, out of everything.

"I didn't think you'd come here," I said finally, meeting his gaze. "You're not exactly the 'runaway to the countryside' type."

He laughed, a low, throaty sound that made the hairs on the back of my neck stand up. "No, I'm not," he agreed, his eyes softening. "But sometimes, the world has a way of redirecting us when we least expect it." He leaned forward just a little, his elbows on the table, his voice dropping. "I'm guessing it wasn't the lavender fields that brought you here, was it?"

I pressed my lips together, refusing to let him see how deeply his question cut. He was right, of course. The lavender fields, the vineyards, the quaintness of it all—none of it was enough to pull me away from what had been left behind. I was running from something, but the deeper I ventured into this quiet world, the more it felt like I was running toward it.

"I needed space," I said, my voice steady. "I needed to figure things out. But that doesn't mean I'm ready to sort everything out with you."

The words came out more sharply than I meant, and the slight tinge of defensiveness I couldn't entirely conceal made my stomach tighten. Adrian didn't flinch, though. He just nodded, his eyes searching mine in that way he always did, like he could see straight through my defenses.

"Fair enough," he replied, then after a pause, added, "But you're here now, aren't you? Maybe we should talk. For real this time."

The air in the café seemed to grow denser, as if the walls themselves were holding their breath, waiting for me to respond. I wanted to say no, wanted to retreat into the safe silence of my solitude. But something—something in his voice, or perhaps in the way he'd said "for real this time"—tugged at me. A thread of something old, and something new. The ache of the past mixed with the rawness of a future that felt uncertain, but maybe... not entirely out of reach.

"I don't know," I murmured, the words tasting foreign, even to me. "I don't know if I'm ready to revisit that. I've come so far—this place, this peace—it's all so different." I could feel the tremble in my own voice now, the tremor of vulnerability I wasn't sure I wanted to expose. "I don't want to make the same mistakes again."

He tilted his head, the corner of his mouth lifting in that same half-smile that had once disarmed me in seconds. "You can't make the same mistakes if you're not making any decisions. If you're still stuck in the past, you'll never know what could happen next."

I swallowed hard, my gaze darting to the window, the fading golden light from outside casting shadows in the café. His words hung in the air like smoke, curling and twisting with an unsettling clarity.

"Maybe I don't want to know what happens next," I said quietly, more to myself than to him. "Maybe some things are just better left behind."

But Adrian didn't let the conversation go. "You know, sometimes the things we think we've left behind are the ones that we need to move forward." His voice was soft now, almost coaxing, as though trying to draw me out of the shell I'd built around myself. "We can't change the past, but we can choose what to carry with us. And what to let go."

The sincerity in his voice, the way his words slipped through the cracks of my armor, made me ache. I wanted to hate him for it. For showing up here. For making me think of things I had promised myself I was done with. But I couldn't.

The air between us shifted again, and the distance I had tried to create suddenly felt insurmountable. And yet, in that insurmountability, there was something... alive.

Before I could respond, the door swung open with a creak, and the little bell above it jingled, signaling the arrival of another customer. My eyes shot to the door, but it was as if I had blinked and missed something. Standing in the doorway was a woman, her dark hair pulled into a neat bun, her posture rigid. She was dressed simply, but there was something sharp about her—an energy I couldn't place.

Her gaze flicked between Adrian and me, and for the briefest moment, her eyes lingered on him with something that could have been recognition—or perhaps something more. She hesitated, then stepped forward, her heels clicking sharply on the wooden floor as she moved toward the bar.

I had no idea who she was, but the way she moved, the way her presence seemed to fill the space, made my stomach knot. I turned my attention back to Adrian, but his expression had shifted too—he was no longer smiling, no longer him. He was watching the woman, his jaw tightening.

"Who's that?" I asked, my voice barely above a whisper.

Adrian's gaze flickered toward me, then back to the woman, who was now standing at the counter, ordering with that same sharp, deliberate manner. His response came slowly, but the tension was unmistakable. "Her name's Isabelle," he said. "She's… someone from my past."

I could feel the shift in the room, a pulse of energy that made the air feel too thick to breathe.

Isabelle, with her sharp eyes and cold composure, seemed to bring with her an old ghost I wasn't sure I was ready to face.

Chapter 29: Letters of Longing

The ink felt like an extension of my soul, dragging itself across the pages as if each word bore the weight of every unspoken thought I had stored up for months. My hand trembled slightly, the delicate flow of letters interrupted by the occasional jagged stroke where my anger flared, forcing me to pause and catch my breath. With Jonah's name, written at the top of each page, I began again. The letters were never meant to be sent—at least, that was what I told myself each time I folded one and tucked it into the drawer. But the need to write, to spill my truth into the quiet of my apartment, was undeniable. The weight of unspoken feelings had become unbearable, and this was the only place I could safely unravel it all.

Jonah's absence had created an aching void in my life, one that I had convinced myself I would fill with the simple routine of work, friends, and obligatory distractions. But each morning, when the sunlight hit the edge of the kitchen counter just so, I felt it. That familiar knot in my stomach—the one that tightened every time I thought of the way he'd looked at me the last time I saw him. How his eyes had betrayed him, full of guilt, but also a kind of helplessness that made me want to reach out and fix things, even when I knew better. Even when I knew that I was the one who had been left behind, the one who had been deceived, the one who had watched as everything I had believed in crumbled to dust.

I wasn't proud of how much I still missed him, of how often I found myself replaying the words that had never come. "I'm sorry." That's all he had said. It was all he'd been able to offer before he turned away from me, from us. And though I tried, with all my might, to hate him for it, my heart had no room for anything but longing. The ache, raw and relentless, pushed me to write again.

The letters were nothing special. There were no poetic flourishes or grand declarations of love. They were just words. Honest words.

Simple words. Words I needed to say even if they would never reach his ears. It felt like a desperate attempt to make sense of the chaos that had settled in my chest, twisting the knife of betrayal deeper with each unanswered question. What had happened? Why had we let it all slip away?

I could hear his voice in my head, the rough sound of his laugh, the easy way he always seemed to know exactly what to say to make me smile. And there it was again—the loneliness that came with remembering a version of him I would never see again. I would never hear that laugh in the same way, never feel the warmth of his hand on my back, or the quiet hum of his presence beside me as we made breakfast together on Sunday mornings. Those small moments, those small gestures—what were they worth now? Were they nothing but fleeting illusions, created in my mind to cover the reality of what he had done? Was I fooling myself to keep reaching back into those memories?

I had no answers, only questions. And so, I wrote.

The morning light was creeping through the window as I put pen to paper again, the smell of coffee and the faint buzz of traffic from below grounding me in the present. "Jonah," I began, "it's been a long time, hasn't it? Funny, I thought the days would feel longer, but they pass in a blur, like water running through my fingers. It's like I'm standing on the shore, watching everything slip away, but I'm not really moving. Maybe I'm just stuck in place. Maybe we both are."

My hand stilled as I thought about the words I had just written. "Maybe we both are." Maybe that was the truth. Maybe we had both been trapped by our own mistakes, our own stubbornness. Wasn't that the most cruel part of it all? The knowledge that I had played my part, too? The things I had ignored. The truths I had chosen not to see.

I hadn't always been the easiest person to love. I was quick to react, quick to judge. Maybe that was why Jonah hadn't been able to stay. Maybe that was why the lies had built up until they became a wall between us, one that neither of us knew how to tear down. It was a painful realization, but it was mine. And it was one I had to face before I could move on. But there was something else, too, something deeper that gnawed at me—the feeling that this wasn't the end. That somehow, someway, there was still a thread connecting us, even if I couldn't see it.

The doorbell rang, the sudden sound pulling me out of my reverie. I stood, the letters still scattered across the table in front of me, and walked toward the door, feeling the familiar chill of uncertainty settle in my chest. I hadn't expected company. Maybe it was the neighbor with a misplaced package or, more likely, some well-meaning acquaintance who had come to check in on me. But as I opened the door, the last person I expected to see stood there, eyes dark with a mixture of guilt and hope.

Jonah.

His name was a whisper in the back of my throat, a truth I couldn't even bring myself to say aloud. He stood there, awkwardly shifting his weight from one foot to the other, as if unsure whether he had the right to be here, to intrude on the life I'd built in his absence. I didn't speak, didn't even breathe for a moment. The air between us felt thick with the weight of all the things that had been left unsaid.

Finally, he spoke, his voice quieter than I remembered, and somehow that made the ache in my chest worse. "I know this is the last thing you expected." His eyes flickered to the stack of letters on the table behind me, and for a brief moment, I saw something—something like recognition, like he knew, deep down, how long I had been holding on.

And for the first time in months, my heart skipped a beat.

I had expected him to say something, to fill the silence with the hollow words I had become so accustomed to—an apology, an excuse, something to explain how he could walk away and leave me here, buried under the weight of my own thoughts. Instead, he stood there, and I realized the depth of how much time had passed between us. It felt like years, not just the months since we last saw each other. His presence, though familiar, was also a stranger's. And that made the rush of emotions in my chest all the more disorienting.

"Why are you here?" The words slipped out before I could stop them, sharper than I intended. But the thing was, I was terrified of what I might say if I gave myself a chance to breathe, so I needed to keep this moment in control. It was a fragile thing, this brief encounter, and I could sense how easily it could slip out of my grasp if I wasn't careful. His eyes flickered, like he was preparing for a different kind of reception, but it didn't seem to bother him. He just looked at me, really looked at me, in a way I hadn't felt in so long that I almost forgot what it was like to be the center of his attention.

"I needed to see you," he said simply, his voice tight, almost as if the words weren't enough to hold back something much heavier. I swallowed hard, unwilling to let my heart believe the words just yet.

"And what, exactly, did you think you would see?" My own voice surprised me with how steady it was, how measured. If I had any intention of breaking down in front of him, it wasn't going to happen now. Not when the edges of the wound were still raw and the scabs hadn't even begun to form. Not when every step we took toward the past seemed to pull me back into the tangled mess of feelings I had tried to untangle.

"I didn't know," he admitted, running a hand through his hair in that familiar, restless gesture. "I didn't know what I expected, but I—" He paused, as if trying to find the right words, which only made the moment feel all the more fragile. "I think I just wanted to remind myself of who I used to be when I was with you."

A flash of something stirred in me—something unexpected. It wasn't the anger I had anticipated, nor the bitterness that had kept me up at night, writing letter after letter with no intention of sending them. It was a deeper emotion, something quieter. Maybe regret. Maybe love. Or maybe both, a messy combination of emotions I wasn't sure I could sort through.

"Who you used to be?" I echoed, raising an eyebrow, unable to mask the skepticism in my voice. The words tasted like ashes on my tongue, but I needed him to say more. I needed him to prove to me that he wasn't just here because he couldn't bear the silence any longer.

"Yeah," Jonah said, rubbing the back of his neck, clearly uncomfortable. "I've been thinking a lot about the way things used to be. How easy it was—just... us. The way we talked about everything, how we could spend hours doing nothing and still feel like we were exactly where we were supposed to be. I want to believe that wasn't a lie. I need to believe it wasn't."

I swallowed hard, my pulse pounding in my ears. The words cut through me in a way I hadn't anticipated, like the sharp edge of a knife against skin. Of course I remembered those days—how could I not? They were the ones that had defined me, had shaped my expectations for what love should feel like. And now, to hear him voice that sentiment, it threatened to drag me back into the very thing I had worked so hard to untangle from.

The silence between us grew heavy. I wanted to say something cutting, something clever, to break the tension. But the words were tangled in my throat, caught between the part of me that still longed for him and the part of me that had learned to stand on her own, even if it hurt like hell.

"So, what do you want now?" I asked, the question slipping from me before I could second-guess it. I didn't want him to misunderstand, didn't want him to think that I was inviting him back into my life. But that didn't stop the aching sense of wanting to hear the answer. I needed to know where we stood—or if we stood at all.

Jonah looked at me for a long moment, his gaze steady and searching. "I don't expect anything, not really," he said quietly. "I don't think I deserve anything from you, honestly. But I needed to know if there was still a chance, even a small one, that you could forgive me."

I blinked, the weight of his words pressing down on my chest. Forgiveness. It felt like such a loaded word, one I wasn't sure I was ready to hand out so freely. Because forgiveness meant opening the door to everything that had come before, everything I had been trying to close off. But at the same time, the thought of him—of us—lingered, unspoken and unresolved. And that was worse than anything.

"You hurt me," I said, my voice barely above a whisper. "And that's not something I can just forget. It's not something I can fix with a 'sorry,' Jonah. And you know that."

His face hardened, but I saw the flicker of something softer behind his eyes. He was trying to read me, trying to find the cracks, trying to see if there was any piece of me left that would let him in. But I wasn't sure anymore. The walls I had built were solid, impenetrable, because once someone had torn you apart, how could you ever trust them again?

"I know," he replied, voice low. "I don't expect you to forget. I wouldn't even ask you to. But what I'm asking for... is just a chance. A chance to show you that I can be better. Not for you, but for myself. I owe you that, don't I?"

I stared at him, feeling the weight of his words settle heavily in the room between us. Could I? Could I give him the chance he asked for? Or would I be setting myself up for more heartbreak? The questions circled, dizzying in their complexity, while the answer seemed just out of reach, like the edge of a cliff you couldn't quite see in the fog.

"I don't know," I said finally, the words both a release and a weight. "I don't know if I can."

The air in my apartment felt different now—thicker, somehow, like a veil of unspoken words and unacknowledged feelings settled over everything. Jonah's presence had carved a space in the room that I wasn't sure how to fill. I was used to the quiet of these walls, to the stillness that had become my refuge. But now, the silence seemed to hum with potential, and it was unsettling. Jonah had always been a force—quiet, but magnetic, pulling me in even when I wanted to resist. And now, after everything, he was still doing the same thing. Pulling at me, tugging at that raw part of my heart I had so carefully wrapped up and buried under layers of pain.

We stood there for a long moment, neither of us moving, neither of us speaking. I could feel my pulse thrumming in my ears, and I wondered if he could hear it too, if he felt the tension snapping between us. The clock on the wall ticked away the seconds, but they seemed to stretch into infinity. Jonah's gaze never left mine, and in that silence, I felt the weight of everything unsaid, everything unresolved, hovering between us like a shadow.

"You've had time to think about this," Jonah finally said, his voice tentative, like he was afraid of what might happen if he pushed too hard. "Time to think about me, about us. I get it. I understand if you need more time. I just need to know if there's still a chance. Not just for us, but for you. For you to—" He stopped, visibly struggling to find the right words. "For you to believe in me again."

The vulnerability in his voice caught me off guard. It wasn't what I expected from Jonah. I had prepared myself for deflection, for excuses, maybe even for a confession, but not for this honesty. He wasn't asking for my forgiveness in a way that demanded it. He wasn't trying to rush me, as if he believed time could make everything right. No, he was asking me to trust him again, to believe in something I wasn't sure I had left to give. And that was the hardest part—trusting him with my heart once more, after everything that had shattered it.

I stepped back, my mind a whirlwind of contradictions. I wanted to say something—anything—that would make this easier. I wanted to answer him, but the words were tangled in my throat. How could I explain what I was feeling without sounding like a mess? Without sounding weak? How could I tell him that, yes, I missed him in ways that hurt more than I could admit, but no, I couldn't just fall back into the arms of someone who had let me go so easily?

Instead, I found myself opening the door wider, a signal I couldn't quite read. Was it an invitation, or just an attempt to let the suffocating tension out into the open air? Jonah hesitated for only a moment, then stepped inside, his gaze flickering around the room as if he was seeing it with new eyes. The sound of his footsteps on the hardwood floor was almost deafening in the stillness.

"This place," he said, gesturing vaguely at the apartment, "it's different, but it still feels... like you."

"Does it?" I asked, surprised by the bitterness in my own voice. "Because everything's changed, Jonah. It's not the same place, and it's not the same me anymore." I hadn't meant to say that, hadn't meant to reveal that much, but once it was out, I couldn't take it back. I wasn't the woman who had let him slip away without a fight. I wasn't the woman who had believed that love was something that could fix anything. I was someone who had learned the hard way that you couldn't pour everything into someone who wasn't willing to give anything back.

He looked at me then, his eyes searching, trying to decipher what I hadn't said, what I hadn't shown. I didn't know if it was pity or something deeper—something I couldn't name—that flashed across his face, but it made the hairs on the back of my neck stand up. I didn't need his pity. I needed the truth. I needed something more than vague reassurances and half-formed apologies. I needed him to tell me that he understood what he had done, that he knew what he was asking of me wasn't just forgiveness—it was a chance to rebuild something that might never be the same again.

He took a step closer, and this time, I didn't back away. Not immediately, anyway. "You're right," he said, his voice quieter now. "You're not the same, and neither am I. We can't go back to what we were. But I'm willing to try. I want to try. And if you're willing to give me a chance, I'll prove it to you. I'll prove that I'm not the man who walked away before."

I swallowed, feeling the lump in my throat grow heavier with every word. "You want to prove it?" I echoed, my voice thick with emotion. "You can't prove it, Jonah. You can't just erase the past. You can't just pretend like nothing happened."

"No, I can't," he said firmly, his voice steady now. "But I can show you that I've changed. That I've learned. I can show you that I'm not the person who made all those mistakes. I know I can't take back what happened, but I can make sure it doesn't happen again. If you'll let me."

I shook my head, fighting the tears that threatened to spill over. This was the moment, wasn't it? The one where I had to decide—where I had to choose whether or not to let him back in. My heart screamed yes, but my mind, sharp and cautious, urged me to hold back. I had worked so hard to rebuild my life after he left, after everything unraveled. Could I really take the risk again?

Just as I opened my mouth to answer, to tell him what I was really thinking, the phone rang, sharp and insistent, cutting through the air like a blade.

I glanced at Jonah, and for a brief second, he looked almost... relieved. As if the timing had given us both a reprieve, a moment to collect ourselves before diving into the conversation that was about to change everything. I reached for the phone, but as I lifted it to my ear, something inside me stilled. The voice on the other end was unfamiliar—low, urgent.

"Is this the woman who knows Jonah?" The words hit me like a punch in the gut.

Chapter 30: A Twist of Fate

The scent of old paper and dust filled the air, and the low hum of conversation from a couple of patrons in the far corner was the only sound that broke the quiet. My fingers grazed the spines of worn-out novels, the ones that had become old friends to me, their pages yellowed and fragile from years of being opened and closed. I wasn't looking for anything in particular. At least, that's what I told myself as I let the silence pull me deeper into the maze of towering shelves. The soft creak of the wooden floorboards under my boots felt oddly comforting, as though I had never really left this place, this moment. But then, everything shifted.

I glanced up, my gaze drawn, almost against my will, to the far end of the room. And there he was.

His figure stood out even in the dim light, as though the air itself bent around him. The years had added a fine edge to his features, deepening the lines at the corners of his eyes, but they didn't soften his gaze—they sharpened it. His dark hair was a little longer, a little messier, but the slight wave and the careless way it fell across his forehead made it seem deliberate, as if he hadn't bothered to tame it. My heart gave a lurch, a feeling I had tried so hard to bury, like a forgotten book gathering dust at the back of the shelf. I had thought I was done with him. That our time together was one of those things I could neatly pack away in the past, like one of these old, unread books that nobody would ever pick up again.

But no.

He saw me. Our eyes locked, and suddenly, everything I had buried—the anger, the sadness, the yearning—came rushing to the surface. The world around us dissolved. There was only him, standing there, looking at me with that same intensity, as if he could see right through me, to the person I had tried so desperately to leave behind.

I knew, without a doubt, that he wasn't just seeing me. He was seeing everything I had tried to escape from—every mistake, every wrong turn, every bit of unfinished business that had never been resolved. The fact that I had come back here, to this city, after all these years, seemed almost inevitable now.

He took a step forward. One. Slow, deliberate, as though he had all the time in the world. It felt like my chest had contracted, and I had forgotten how to breathe. The space between us filled with all the words we had never said, all the things we had left unsaid—things we should have said back then, things I should have heard and things I should have done.

The air around us crackled, the silence hanging heavy between us, and I could feel the weight of it in my bones. He stopped just a few feet away, close enough that I could smell the faint trace of his cologne, something warm and woodsy, as familiar as his touch. My pulse quickened, each beat like a drum, announcing his return in a way I could never ignore.

"Well," he said, his voice low and husky, rougher than I remembered, like he hadn't used it in years. "This is a surprise."

A smile tugged at my lips, though I couldn't bring myself to say anything. There was too much to say, too much to untangle in the space of a single breath. So instead, I settled for something less revealing.

"You could say that," I replied, my voice sounding strange to my own ears. It had been too long since I had spoken to him, too long since I had heard him speak my name. The way it felt on his lips—the way he always seemed to make it sound like a secret between us—was a sensation I had forgotten, but not one I could ignore.

"Are you back for good?" he asked, the question hanging in the air like a challenge. His eyes narrowed slightly, as though he were trying to read my every thought, trying to peel back the layers of whatever façade I had carefully constructed.

I shook my head, the motion feeling jerky and almost foreign. "I don't know yet," I said, the words coming out more uncertain than I intended.

He raised an eyebrow, that same mischievous glint in his gaze that I had always found so infuriatingly attractive. "No plans, then?" he teased, a smile tugging at the corners of his mouth.

I crossed my arms over my chest, a defensive gesture that I hadn't even realized I had made until I was already doing it. "I didn't come here for you," I said, though even as the words left my mouth, I knew they weren't entirely true. I hadn't come for him, not specifically. But that didn't mean I wasn't aware of his presence, of how much it affected me, how much I had thought about him in all the time we'd been apart.

He didn't flinch at my words, though. Instead, he let out a soft laugh, one that didn't reach his eyes, but still carried that same warmth I remembered. "Right," he said, "just passing through, then."

I wanted to tell him everything. I wanted to explain why I had left, why I had cut him off, why I had thought I could move on without him. But none of it seemed important now, not with him standing there, his presence consuming me in a way I hadn't expected. The years apart had created a distance, yes, but it also made the memories sharper, more vivid. I had tried to forget, but the truth was, I had never really let go.

Before I could stop myself, I found myself saying the one thing I hadn't planned on. "I didn't forget about you, you know."

His eyes softened just a fraction, but the smile never fully left his lips. "I didn't think you did," he replied, his voice barely above a whisper.

He didn't rush. There was something almost cruel about how slowly he moved toward me, as though he was savoring the way I stiffened with each step. My heart beat too loudly in my chest, a drum that outpaced any thoughts I might have tried to collect. I felt the old patterns forming, the ones where I would smile, pretend I was fine, and walk away without so much as a backward glance. But as I watched him close the distance between us, a part of me knew that I had long stopped pretending.

He stopped just a breath away, close enough that I could hear the subtle intake of his breath, that familiar rasp that still unsettled me. I could smell the coffee and fresh air clinging to his jacket, a scent I had once spent hours memorizing in the quiet of the mornings when I thought time itself had slowed just for us.

"So," he said, his voice a mixture of amusement and something darker that I couldn't place. "Paris, huh? Back for good this time?"

I swallowed, hating how much I wanted to say yes. Hating how easy it would be to pretend that nothing had happened, that we could slip into our old rhythm as if the years apart hadn't existed at all. But that was the thing about him. He could make you feel as though the world had stopped turning, as though every word spoken between us could change the course of history. And I wasn't sure if I was ready for that.

"I told you, I didn't come here for you," I said again, though the conviction wasn't there. It was a half-hearted defense, a shield I hoped would hold long enough to keep me safe from the vulnerability I had long avoided.

He tilted his head, his lips twitching at the corners. "Sure, sure. Just a coincidence, then? After all these years, you find yourself back in the same bookstore we used to fight over?" His eyes darkened a little, like the playful tone was a mask for something deeper. "You didn't answer my question, though."

"I'm not sure what the question is," I replied, not wanting to give him the satisfaction of seeing me falter.

"Are you staying?" He leaned in just enough that his breath brushed against my cheek, a light whisper of warmth that sent a jolt through me, making it impossible to stay composed. "Or is this just another fleeting moment?"

"I don't know," I admitted, hating the word as it left my mouth. It felt like a confession, one that tied me to the past in a way I wasn't ready for. "I don't think I'm good at the whole staying thing."

For a moment, there was nothing but silence, the heavy kind that wrapped around you like a fog, making everything sharper, more fragile. He was watching me, really watching me, in a way that unsettled me. His eyes were searching, not with the impatience of someone trying to hurry you into an answer, but with the quiet certainty of someone who already knew what the response would be.

"I used to think you were the one who'd never leave," he said quietly, and for the first time, there was a trace of vulnerability in his voice that I hadn't heard before. It was raw, open in a way I wasn't sure I was ready to handle.

I laughed, though it came out a little too brittle. "And what did you think, that I was going to drop everything and stay?"

"I didn't think that," he said, but there was a flicker in his gaze, a momentary hesitation, like he wasn't sure whether to press further or let it go. "I just thought... well, never mind."

The words hung in the air like a broken promise. I wanted to fill the space, to say something that would close the gap between us and ease the tension that was thickening with every passing second. But I couldn't. Not when I knew how fragile the balance was, how easily everything could shatter if I allowed myself to slip back into the patterns that had led us to where we were now.

"You didn't come here for me, but you're still here," he said, his tone light, almost teasing, though I could hear the undertone of something deeper, something that felt too much like regret. "It's funny, don't you think?"

"Is it?" I didn't want to get sucked back into this. Into him. Not again. But the way he looked at me, like the last few years had meant nothing, like he could undo the distance between us with a simple touch, made it impossible not to react. "Maybe it's just that the city has a way of pulling you back in."

"Ah," he said with a wry smile, stepping back just enough to give me space, but his eyes never left mine. "So you're saying it's Paris' fault?"

I let out a short laugh, but it didn't feel like one of those laughs that came from humor. It was strained, tight, as though I were trying to hold on to something that was slipping through my fingers. "Maybe," I said, crossing my arms over my chest. "Maybe Paris is just a convenient excuse."

He raised an eyebrow, looking amused, but there was a sharpness to his gaze now, a realization settling between us. "You're not fooling anyone, you know. Least of all yourself."

I shook my head, unwilling to let him see how much his words stung. "I'm not the one pretending things can go back to how they were."

For a moment, he didn't speak. His gaze softened, his lips barely moving as he took a step closer again, lowering his voice. "You know, I never stopped thinking about you. Not once."

I didn't have the heart to tell him that I'd been doing the same. That every place I had wandered through, every time I had felt lost, I had wondered if he was feeling it too. But I couldn't say it. Not yet. Not when the weight of those words felt like too much.

Instead, I took a deep breath and looked away, the flicker of something unspoken hanging between us. The world felt still for just a moment longer, and in that silence, I realized the truth. There was no such thing as running from him—not when everything I had ever wanted was right in front of me.

He shifted his weight slightly, as though testing the waters between us, his gaze never leaving mine. That familiar intensity, the one that used to keep me awake at night, now felt like a weight pressing against my chest. I could feel the tension rising again, like the moment we had once shared, when everything had felt so easy and simple, had returned with a vengeance.

For a second, neither of us moved. I wasn't sure if I was waiting for him to speak, or if he was waiting for me to make the first move. The silence felt heavy, almost suffocating, like something waiting to be broken. I wanted to say something witty—something sharp, something clever, just to deflect the way my heart was racing, but the words wouldn't come.

"Well," he said, breaking the stillness, his voice low, almost too casual, but I could see the way his hands clenched slightly at his sides. "I guess we're both just full of surprises, aren't we?"

I tried to laugh, but it came out more like a sigh, a tired little noise that I hated hearing. The weight of the years, the bitterness that had clung to everything between us, felt like it was settling on my shoulders again, threatening to drag me under. But still, I forced myself to meet his eyes, not wanting him to see how much he still had the power to make me feel out of control.

"You should stop," I said, my voice sharper than I intended. "Stop acting like this is just some chance meeting, like you're not already playing some game here."

He raised his hands in mock surrender, a half-smile curling at the edges of his lips. "I'm not playing any games," he said, though his tone didn't quite match the words. "I thought we were past all of that."

The words hit me harder than I expected. It was as though he had seen right through the layers I had built, the walls I had constructed so carefully over the years. I opened my mouth, wanting to snap back at him, to tell him how much I had suffered while he had moved on, but I didn't. I couldn't. Instead, I took a breath and steadied myself, the space between us now more like an ocean than the few feet it really was.

"And you think I haven't?" I said, voice faltering only slightly. "You think I've just been sitting here, waiting for you to waltz back in and fix everything?"

He didn't reply immediately. His eyes narrowed slightly, and there was something in his gaze that made me wonder if I had just said the wrong thing. If the cracks I'd tried to cover up had suddenly been laid bare for him to see. But then, with a soft chuckle, he leaned back, crossing his arms. "Is that what you think I'm trying to do? Fix everything?"

"Isn't that what you always do?" The words slipped out before I could stop them, sharp and bitter. "You always think you can fix things—fix me."

For a moment, his expression faltered, and I saw a flicker of something—hurt, maybe? Or guilt?—before it was quickly masked by that damnable smile of his, the one I had once loved. The one that had always made me want to trust him, even when I shouldn't.

"Is that what you thought?" he asked quietly, his voice changing, dropping to a gentler register. "That I wanted to fix you?"

I didn't know how to answer. The truth was, I had never really let him in enough to let him fix anything. And yet, there had always been this pull between us, like a tide that I couldn't resist no matter how many times I tried to swim in the opposite direction.

"I don't need fixing," I said finally, though it felt like a lie, the words hollow and incomplete.

He stepped forward, his gaze not leaving mine, but the shift in his demeanor was palpable. It was as if something had clicked—some understanding passing between us that neither of us had been willing to acknowledge before. I took a step back, instinctively, as though moving away would somehow protect me from whatever this conversation was about to become.

But he followed. Of course, he did.

"You're not the same," he said softly. "I can see it."

I raised an eyebrow, trying to keep my voice steady, though my chest felt tight. "And what's that supposed to mean?"

He took another step closer, now standing just inches from me, so close that I could feel the heat of his presence. He wasn't touching me, but it was as though his proximity was enough to send my pulse skittering out of control.

"You've changed," he said, his voice barely above a whisper. "I can see it in the way you stand, the way you look at the world. You don't hide it as much as you used to."

The truth of his words hit me harder than I cared to admit. I had changed. In the time we'd been apart, I'd built walls around parts of myself that I didn't even recognize anymore. I'd become someone who wasn't afraid to walk away, who didn't wait for anyone to choose her. But somehow, in his presence, it all felt like it was unraveling, thread by thread.

"Maybe I had to," I said, my voice rougher now, the emotion I'd kept locked away finally breaking free. "Maybe that's the only way I could survive."

He studied me, his expression unreadable. Then, with a small, almost imperceptible shake of his head, he took a step back. I couldn't decide if it was a relief or a blow to see the distance between us grow.

"Well," he said, his tone changing again, lighter this time, almost teasing. "If you're going to survive, maybe it's time to start living again."

I didn't know how to respond to that. I didn't know if I wanted to respond to that. But before I could form another thought, before I could make the decision to walk away or stay, I heard the unmistakable sound of footsteps approaching us from behind.

A voice, unfamiliar but insistent, cut through the tension like a blade.

"There you are," it said, sharp and unmistakable. "I've been looking everywhere for you."

I turned, my stomach twisting at the sight of a figure emerging from the shadows of the bookstore, someone I hadn't expected, someone I couldn't have predicted would appear in this moment.

And just like that, the fragile balance of the room shattered.

Chapter 31: The Weight of Forgiveness

The restaurant was quiet, the flickering candle on the table casting gentle shadows on the walls. It was a place we had once adored, a small, tucked-away bistro that smelled faintly of garlic and butter, where laughter always hung in the air like an invitation. Now, it felt like an altar, and I, unwillingly, was the priestess, waiting for the confession I hadn't been sure I wanted to hear.

His hands, the same hands that had once cupped my face in gentle affection, were now trembling, betraying the calm mask he'd tried to wear. The deep-set lines in his forehead, which I had once traced with my fingers during quiet mornings, were now etched deeper with guilt. His eyes, which had once sparked with mischief and affection, were clouded with sorrow, searching mine as if he hoped they could offer him absolution without words. But I wasn't sure I could give that to him. Not yet. Not after everything.

I took a slow breath, letting the air settle in my lungs, steadying myself. The urge to flee was powerful, but it was no longer an option. I had stayed when I could have left long ago, and now, I needed to hear the truth—no matter how it tasted, no matter how much it stung.

"I'm sorry," he began, his voice low, thick with the weight of years. "I should have told you everything, from the start." His eyes flickered toward my face, searching, and then dropping away. "But I didn't. I couldn't, not then."

I nodded. I had known, in pieces, in moments of clarity, but hearing him say it out loud felt different. It was the truth, raw and unvarnished, and for the first time, I wasn't sure I could stomach it.

The clink of silverware, the soft murmur of the waitstaff in the background—it all seemed distant, as if I were underwater, the world muffled and faint. The space between us felt infinite, yet the warmth of his hand, hesitantly reaching across the table toward mine, was undeniable. I could feel the magnetic pull of it, but I wasn't sure if I wanted to give in.

His fingers brushed mine, tentative at first, as though testing the waters of forgiveness. It would have been easier, I thought, to push him away, to let the coldness between us grow until it swallowed all the warmth we had once shared. But something in his eyes made me pause, made me reconsider the path of rage that had been waiting for me like a familiar shadow. Maybe it wasn't just him who needed forgiveness. Maybe I needed it too, though I hadn't figured out yet how to ask for it.

"You were right," he continued, breaking the silence that had settled heavily between us. "I didn't trust you enough to tell you the truth. And I lied, not to hurt you, but to protect you. But in the end, all I did was hurt us both." He swallowed, and his voice cracked on the last word. "I wasn't the man you thought I was. And I'm sorry."

The truth hung in the air, thick and sticky, like honey that clung to everything it touched. I wanted to say something, anything, to make this moment—this painful, raw moment—end, but the words were locked in my throat, a jumble of anger, disappointment, and a strange, unfamiliar tenderness.

I had spent so many nights replaying this moment in my head, imagining what I would say, how I would tear him apart with the cold precision of my anger. I had rehearsed it, every line, every possible outcome. But this wasn't the way I had imagined it. It wasn't a confrontation, a battle of who could hurt the other more. It was something else entirely—something quieter, more dangerous.

Because the truth was, I had known, hadn't I? I had known in the hollow spaces between the words we didn't speak, in the way his voice faltered when I asked too many questions, in the way his eyes couldn't meet mine for too long. And I had let it go, hoping that love would be enough to cover up the cracks, hoping that we were stronger than the lies that had begun to seep in. But it wasn't. And I wasn't sure if we were stronger than the weight of the secrets he had buried so deeply.

His hand, now fully resting over mine, was warm, and for a fleeting moment, I wondered if I could forgive him. Forgiveness wasn't something I had ever given freely, not to anyone. It was a gift, something you had to give with intention, with care. And it wasn't something I could offer lightly. Yet, there we were, two people caught in a tangled web of their own making, trying to untangle it without ripping ourselves to pieces.

"I don't know if I can forgive you," I said, my voice softer than I intended. "Not yet. But I need you to know that I'm listening. And that I'm... I'm trying." The words felt foreign in my mouth, like a language I hadn't spoken in years. And still, there was a tenderness that pulled at my chest, something that hadn't disappeared, despite everything.

He exhaled, a breath that seemed to carry years of guilt, of regret. "I don't deserve your forgiveness," he whispered. "But I'll wait. I'll wait for as long as it takes."

And for the first time in a long time, I believed him. There was no more pretending, no more masks. There was just the raw, exposed truth between us, fragile but real. The path ahead was uncertain, but it was the only one we had now.

The restaurant's quiet hum felt like a soft echo of the world outside, distant and faint, as if the life we knew before this moment had already slipped away. His hand lingered over mine, the warmth of it pressing against my skin like a question I wasn't sure I had the answer to. I hadn't expected to feel this pull—this magnetic tether between us, the kind that might have saved us years ago, before the lies and the silences had woven their web around us.

He seemed unsure of what to say next, as if every word he spoke might shatter something fragile that we hadn't yet named. His eyes, still watching me with that desperate vulnerability, made it harder for me to stay mad. I had spent months—hell, years—practicing my indifference, convinced that anger was the only armor I needed. But now, with the truth between us, I could no longer pretend that I wasn't just as broken, just as lost in this maze as he was.

"I never wanted to hurt you," he said, the words rushing out, like a confession that had been locked away for too long. "But I did. I hurt you more than I ever meant to. And I don't know if I can make that right." His voice cracked, the rawness of it like a blade cutting through the tension that clung to the room. He was telling me what I had already known, but hearing him say it, hearing him admit the weight of his guilt, made something inside me shift.

I wanted to scream at him. I wanted to tell him that he had no idea what he'd done to me, to us. How many nights I'd spent lying awake, wondering if the lies would ever come to light, wondering if he would ever just admit what we both already knew. But the anger was starting to feel pointless, like the last embers of a fire that had long since burned out. And as much as I hated to admit it, part of me was already moving past it, moving past him. But that part was so small, so fragile, that I couldn't bear to let it surface. Not yet.

I pulled my hand back, just slightly, enough to create a space between us that felt both comforting and devastating. The space between us had always been there, like a fog that never quite lifted. But now it was different. Now it wasn't just a physical distance. It was a chasm, deep and dark, and I had no idea how to bridge it.

His eyes flinched, a silent plea for me to come back to him, and I almost did. Almost. But there was a voice inside my head that kept reminding me how many times I had tried to close the gap, only to find that he was always a step away, always holding something back. And that—well, that was something I didn't know if I could forgive. Not right away, not with the same open heart I had given him before.

"Why didn't you tell me?" I asked, my voice soft but sharp, a little too bitter for my liking. I tried to keep the edge out of it, but it snuck in anyway. "Why didn't you trust me enough to let me in?"

His shoulders slumped as if my words had weight enough to carry him down, the defeat in him palpable. "Because I was afraid," he said quietly. "Afraid that if you knew, you'd leave. Afraid you'd look at me and see all the things I wasn't—everything I promised I'd be but never could."

I couldn't help the laugh that escaped, dry and harsh, like something long forgotten and unpleasant. "You're really telling me that you didn't trust me enough? After all this time?" My hands were clenched into fists on the table now, nails digging into the wood. I could feel the heat rising in my chest, but this time, it wasn't anger. It was something else—something deeper, something that made me want to reach across the table and shake him. "You think that I would've left you because you weren't perfect? Because you had flaws? God, if only it had been that simple."

He flinched again, as though my words had landed harder than I'd intended, but I couldn't stop now. The dam inside me was breaking, the floodgates opening. "What you don't get is that it wasn't about perfection. It was about honesty. About trusting me enough to let me love you the way you deserve. It was about standing up and saying, 'Hey, I made a mistake,' instead of letting it fester and lie between us. I didn't need you to be perfect. I needed you to be real."

His eyes softened at that, just a fraction, as if my words were starting to break through the barriers he'd built up. But the silence stretched, and the weight of it was unbearable. We were at a crossroads, and neither of us was sure which road to take.

Finally, he stood, slowly, like a man walking through a fog, and moved to my side of the table. He didn't speak at first, just stood there, watching me. His breath was slow, measured, as though he were carefully choosing his next words. And then, without warning, he reached out, his hand resting on mine, a light touch that felt both familiar and foreign all at once. "I don't want to lose you," he said, his voice almost a whisper. "I never did. But I can't ask for your forgiveness if you don't want to give it. All I can do is wait. Wait for you to figure out how to trust me again."

There it was. The simple, heartbreaking truth. He was giving me the space I needed, and somehow, that hurt more than anything else he had ever said. Because in that moment, I realized how much I wanted to forgive him, how much I needed to. But the question wasn't whether I could forgive him. It was whether I could forgive myself for letting it go on for so long. And that, I wasn't sure I was ready for.

I didn't know how long we sat there, the air between us thick and pulsing, every breath heavy with unspoken words. The warmth of his hand on mine had long since ceased to comfort; now, it was just a reminder of everything we had lost, and everything we might never regain. There was something about the way his fingers lingered, the pressure just enough to make me remember that he was still here, still trying—though I couldn't yet bring myself to meet him in the same space.

"You don't have to say anything," he whispered, his voice barely audible over the soft rustle of napkins and the distant clink of glasses. "I'm not asking for your forgiveness. I'm just asking for your understanding. For a chance to make this right."

A sharp laugh escaped me before I could stop it, the bitterness in it curling like smoke in the still air. "Understanding? That's what you want now? After everything?"

I wanted to be angry. I wanted to hurl every accusation at him, every thought I'd kept locked away in a dusty corner of my mind. But instead, all that came out was exhaustion. I couldn't fight the feelings anymore, couldn't pretend that the numbness I'd been carrying around wasn't starting to wear thin.

The truth was, there was nothing left to fight. The lies had already taken root, their tendrils twisting around the foundation of everything I thought I knew. It wasn't just the betrayal that cut me—it was the silence that had followed. The lies weren't even the worst part. It was the not knowing. The feeling of being left in the dark, alone, while he carried on with his secrets like they were his to bear.

I took a deep breath, a shaky one, as if to steady myself. "How long?" I finally asked, my voice a little too soft, too raw for my own liking. "How long were you going to keep this from me?"

His gaze faltered, and for a split second, I saw the guilt flash across his face—the real kind, the kind that only a man who truly understood the depth of his actions could wear. "I didn't want to hurt you. I didn't want to lose you."

I shook my head, my lips pressed tight together. "You already did, though. The moment you chose to keep me in the dark, you lost me."

It was brutal, saying the words aloud, but I didn't regret them. They were true, and truth had become a currency I couldn't afford to waste anymore.

The tension between us had shifted, but not in the way I expected. Instead of retreating, he seemed to lean in, his eyes wide with an intensity that almost bordered on desperation. "I know I've messed up. And I know it's too late to take back what I've done. But please, let me show you that I can be the man you thought I was. The man you deserve."

I didn't know if I could believe him. Hell, I didn't know if I wanted to believe him. But that voice inside me—the one that had screamed at me for so long, for so many things—I heard it again, quieter this time, a plea. It wanted me to listen. It wanted me to remember the man I had loved before all this.

For a moment, I let my guard slip. Just a moment. And in that fleeting instant, I saw the man I once believed in. But only for a second, before the walls went back up, higher this time.

"Don't make promises you can't keep," I said, the warning in my voice sharper than I intended. "I'm not asking for you to be perfect. I'm just asking for you to be real."

I was done with the games. Done with pretending that things could go back to how they were. We had reached the point where we both needed to decide what was worth salvaging and what was too broken to repair. I was no longer sure which category we fell into.

His lips parted, as if to speak, but before the words could form, the door to the restaurant swung open with a gust of cold air, and for the briefest moment, I thought the world had shifted in a way I wasn't prepared for.

I turned instinctively, my body stiffening as a figure stepped inside—a woman, tall, with a confident stride and an all-too-familiar air about her. I felt a rush of unease flood through me as she scanned the room, her eyes locking on us immediately, like she had known exactly where to find us.

And then, my heart sank as recognition hit.

She was beautiful. Of course, she was. The kind of beauty that makes you wonder how it's even possible to look like that. She wore a confident smile, one that radiated warmth, but it didn't reach her eyes. Her eyes were calculating, cold—like she knew something I didn't. Something I wasn't supposed to know.

My pulse quickened, the knot in my stomach tightening. What was she doing here?

She approached our table, her heels clicking against the floor with an almost deliberate rhythm. I couldn't tear my gaze away, and when she finally stopped in front of us, she glanced from him to me, her smile never wavering.

"Hello," she said, her voice smooth as silk, as though she were greeting an old friend. But there was an edge to it, something that didn't belong.

"May I?" She gestured to the empty seat next to him before either of us could respond.

I felt my breath catch in my throat as she smoothly slid into the chair, her presence too much to ignore, too much to dismiss. The world around me seemed to close in, her intrusion creating a jagged crack in the fragile wall we had started to rebuild.

I couldn't decide what was worse—the fact that I didn't know who she was, or the fact that she was sitting so close to him, like she belonged there.

And then she smiled again, this time directed at me, a smile that didn't feel like a welcome at all. "I think we have a lot to discuss," she said softly, her words heavy with meaning.

And just like that, I knew my world had just shifted again. But this time, I wasn't sure if I could hold on for what came next.

Chapter 32: Rebuilding from Ruins

I had never liked the rain. Not in Paris, at least. It made the streets slick and treacherous, turning the cobblestones beneath my boots into little rivers of reflection, where every step felt like an unwanted echo. I wasn't fond of echoes. They made me think of things I had long buried under years of silence, a thousand whispered apologies that were never spoken, and words that never quite reached the heart. But today, I let the rain fall.

We hadn't spoken of it, the thing that had fractured us, that had driven us apart so completely. The space between us—physical and emotional—had seemed too vast to ever bridge. Yet, here we were, side by side, as though it hadn't been months, as though the last time we'd looked at each other hadn't been a standoff, a war waged in silence and sharp glances. But Paris had this way of making everything feel like a second chance, even the impossible. Or maybe it was just that I didn't care anymore about the impossibility of things. I'd learned to let go of expectations, the weight of what should be, and embrace what was.

The cafés we passed were alive with conversation and the clink of porcelain cups, the kind of sounds that usually made me feel disconnected, like I was on the outside looking in. Today, however, there was a comfort in them, as if the world had become a little smaller and the gaps between people just a little less vast. The rain pattered softly against the awning of a café we stopped at, and I followed his gaze as he watched it, almost as though he was seeing it for the first time.

"You don't like the rain, do you?" His voice was softer than I remembered, a contrast to the sharpness it once carried. It made me wonder if I'd imagined all those barbed comments, or if they had simply been weapons we both wielded to protect ourselves from the truth.

I shook my head. "No. Not really." My hand instinctively reached up to touch the damp strands of hair that clung to my face. "But it's better than the heat. The heat always made me feel... trapped."

He chuckled, the sound low and genuine. "I remember you complaining about that every summer."

It was strange, how quickly the past could become a familiar kind of memory. As if it was no longer some sharp-edged wound, but something I could wrap in a blanket, holding it gently and without resentment. It was too early for me to trust that this wasn't just a fleeting moment, but in that one soft laugh, I heard a piece of him that hadn't been there before. It was as if the world had shifted just enough for us to meet in the middle again.

I sat down at one of the small tables outside, the cloths still damp from the weather, but not uncomfortable. The chairs were sturdy, the kind that had been scraped by countless people who had come and gone, leaving traces of their lives in the creases of the wood. I realized I could do the same, leaving pieces of myself behind, scattering bits of me for others to find. But not him. Not now.

"You're not really one for small talk, are you?" I asked, leaning forward slightly, looking at the back of his hand where a scar curved, just below the wrist. He hadn't had that scar before, not when we met. Not when I thought I knew everything about him. The edges of it were smooth now, but it made my heart ache for reasons I couldn't quite understand.

"I'm not sure I ever was," he replied, his voice carrying that same weight, as though it was dragging behind him all the things we'd never said. "But I'm trying. Trying to be... better, I guess."

I couldn't help but smile at that. There was something almost charming about the way he fumbled with words, as if he was still figuring out how to talk to me after everything that had happened. It was endearing in a way I hadn't expected. I'd always liked the easy way he moved through the world, as though nothing could throw him off course. But now, here he was, stumbling through our conversation like a man who didn't know the first thing about me anymore.

"You're doing fine," I told him, even though I wasn't sure what fine even meant anymore. We'd broken each other in ways that could never be undone, but maybe that wasn't the point. Maybe the point was to rebuild, piece by fragile piece, until we understood each other better than we ever had before. "I just…" My voice faltered, not from uncertainty but from the rawness of the thought. "I just want to know if you've changed. If you've really changed."

There it was. The question that had been hovering in the air between us, the one we hadn't dared to voice until now. I hadn't expected him to answer, not really. Maybe I just needed to hear it aloud, to finally give voice to the doubt that had been creeping into my thoughts ever since we'd come back to this city together.

He didn't hesitate, didn't pull away from the weight of it. Instead, he looked at me, his gaze steady, the same as it had always been, and I saw something there—something I hadn't seen before. "I have. I don't expect you to believe it, but I have." The sincerity in his eyes took me by surprise, a jolt that rattled through me, making me wonder just how much I had underestimated him.

"Then show me," I said, leaning back in my chair, my heart pounding against my ribs. "Don't just tell me."

He didn't move for a long moment, his gaze locked on mine, and for the first time in months, I saw something in him that wasn't a shadow of what we used to be. It wasn't a promise, or some grand gesture, but it was enough to make me hold my breath. The kind of look that said, I'm here, and for all the wrongs we'd done, maybe that could be enough to start again.

But he didn't say anything. Instead, he turned his attention to the street, the flow of people passing by in their endless dance of obliviousness. I almost thought he hadn't heard me, but then his hand reached across the table, resting lightly on mine. It was tentative at first, a feather-light touch that sent a spark up my arm, but he didn't let go. I felt the weight of his palm settle against mine, the warmth between us thick and tangible.

"I'll show you," he said, his voice low, almost a whisper against the rumble of the city. His thumb brushed over the top of my hand in a slow, deliberate motion, as though trying to erase the distance that had once stretched between us. "But it won't be easy. You've put walls up, too."

I hadn't realized how true that was until he said it. I hadn't noticed the way I had fortified myself, how the fear of letting him back in had turned me into a fortress with every stone carefully placed, every crack filled with uncertainty. The fear of losing him again was heavier than anything I had ever felt, and yet, here I was, giving him the chance to tear those walls down.

"Maybe I like my walls," I replied, a half-smile tugging at my lips despite the seriousness of what we were discussing. "They keep out the mess."

He raised an eyebrow, the corner of his mouth curving upward. "Or maybe they just keep out the good stuff too."

I wanted to argue. To tell him that the mess had never been worth it, that the good stuff didn't come without its own price. But the way his hand was still resting over mine, the way his eyes had softened into something less guarded, something almost... tender, made the words catch in my throat.

Instead, I squeezed his hand, and the smile that I gave him this time was real—less a facade and more the first hint of something that might, just might, be the beginning of trust again. "I'll let you prove it," I said, my voice steadier now. "But don't expect me to fall for your charm so easily this time."

He chuckled, a sound that felt like a balm on a wound I hadn't realized I was still nursing. "I wouldn't dream of it. Not unless you're ready."

I didn't reply. I didn't need to. There was something in the space between us, something unspoken but understood, a shift in the air that told me we weren't done. Not yet. The rain had tapered off, leaving the streets glistening like the reflection of some secret world, and as the light turned to dusk, we fell into step beside each other without a word, the sound of our shoes against the wet pavement the only music in the silence.

The days bled into one another—slow, tentative, but steadily building. There were moments where I caught myself watching him, really seeing him again, in ways I hadn't allowed myself before. The way his eyes crinkled at the corners when he laughed, the way he brushed his hair back, as though trying to pull his thoughts into some kind of order. There were those little things, those fleeting gestures that reminded me of who he had been before all the destruction.

But there were also the darker moments. The moments when his hand would hover just above my shoulder, hesitant, as if unsure whether I'd recoil or lean into the contact. The way his words would sometimes falter, as if he were afraid of breaking something fragile between us. He was no longer the man who could take up a room with his presence, whose confidence had once made me feel both electrified and unnerved. Now, he was a man who had learned, painfully, that not all things could be fixed with charm and bravado.

We were strangers, in a way. Not the kind of strangers who don't know anything about one another, but the kind who once knew everything and then forgot it all in the fire of their own mistakes.

One evening, we found ourselves walking by the Seine, the sky a deep, velvety blue that stretched above us like some kind of dream. The city was quieter now, and there was a stillness in the air that felt both reassuring and unsettling. I could feel the tension in the way he moved beside me, like he was carrying something he wasn't ready to put down.

"Do you ever wonder if we're just pretending?" I asked, my voice barely above a murmur, the question floating between us like a leaf carried on the breeze.

His gaze met mine, the weight of it almost too much to bear. For a long moment, I thought he wouldn't answer. But then, with a sigh, he shook his head.

"I don't know anymore," he admitted, the truth hanging between us like a forgotten promise. "I don't know if we're pretending or if we're trying to rebuild something that was broken beyond repair."

I stopped walking, my heart giving a sudden, erratic thump. The words were so raw, so open, that it felt like the city itself had paused with me, holding its breath. For the first time, I realized that this wasn't just about healing from the past. It was about confronting what lay ahead, the uncertainty of whether the love we had once shared could survive the damage we had done to it. Whether we could ever truly rebuild.

"You're right," I said finally, the words sounding like they were being pulled from the deepest part of me. "We don't know. But I think..." I hesitated, looking at him, my fingers twitching, wanting to reach for him. "I think we owe it to ourselves to find out."

His eyes softened then, a silent agreement passing between us, as though we had just made some kind of unspoken pact.

The mornings had become easier. I noticed the small things—like the way his coffee now sat just to the left of his plate, where it had once been to the right. Or how he always let me walk a step ahead, not because he was too slow to catch up, but because he knew I needed space to breathe, to think, to exist on my own before the world crowded me again. It was these small changes that made me believe we could maybe, just maybe, fix what had broken us. But even in the quiet moments, I could feel the tension still alive between us, like the electric hum of a wire just before it snaps.

We were at a little bistro tucked on a side street, the kind of place only locals knew about. The clatter of cutlery and murmured conversations was comforting in its normalcy, reminding me that the world didn't stop when we decided to examine our wreckage. The waiter had just set down our plates—chicken with rosemary and potatoes that were crispy in all the right ways—and I was picking at my food, unsure how to fill the space that stretched between us. We were still testing the waters, trying to see if we could swim in the same sea without drowning.

"I don't know how to do this," he said suddenly, his voice low, a note of frustration threading through his words.

I looked up from my plate, surprised. His eyes weren't on me, but on his glass, tracing the condensation on its surface. "Do what?"

"Whatever this is." He gestured vaguely at the table, at the space between us, at the walls that still seemed to exist even in a room full of people. "I don't know how to fix it. I don't know how to make it go back to how it was. I think…" He paused, a hand running through his hair, making the already-messy strands stand on end. "I think I'm terrified of you not wanting me anymore."

The words hung in the air, heavy, suffocating. I hadn't expected them to come out that way—raw, almost desperate—but there they were, a plea for something I hadn't yet figured out how to give. There was nothing in the world I wanted more than to reach across the table and close the space between us, but I couldn't. Not yet. Not when we were still standing on the edge, looking at the abyss below.

"Why are you scared?" I asked, my voice quieter than I intended. I didn't know where the words came from, but once they were out, I couldn't take them back. "You know me better than anyone. I'm not going anywhere unless you push me."

He met my eyes then, and I saw the truth in his gaze—the fear, the vulnerability, the echo of things he hadn't said yet. "I don't know if I trust myself anymore. I don't know if I can get it right this time."

For a moment, I just stared at him, the weight of it all settling like a stone in my chest. "Trust is something we rebuild. It's not a light switch you flick on and off," I said, trying to keep the frustration from creeping into my voice. "It takes time. But you've got to stop expecting perfection."

"Perfection was never the goal," he murmured, almost to himself. "But you... You deserved someone who could give you everything. Who could make you feel safe. I couldn't do that. I couldn't even protect what we had."

I leaned back in my chair, taking in his words, and for the first time in weeks, something in me loosened. A part of me had been holding on so tightly to the hurt, to the wrongs done, that I hadn't been able to see beyond them. But here, now, in the way he spoke, in the way he carried himself as though he had nothing left to hide, I began to understand something. He wasn't perfect. Neither was I. But maybe that was what we needed all along. To be imperfect, together.

"You don't have to be perfect to be enough," I said softly. "And you don't have to protect me from everything. I just need you to show up."

His eyes flickered with a mix of relief and something else—something that, for the first time, didn't seem like regret. He nodded slowly, as if weighing the possibility, then gave a little laugh, the kind of laugh that didn't quite reach his eyes, but it was enough to break the tension. "I don't know if I'll ever be good at showing up, but I'll try."

"You'd better," I said with a grin, the words light but the meaning clear. "Because I'm not going anywhere, but I'm not sticking around for nothing."

The rest of the meal passed in a companionable silence, the kind that was just comfortable enough to make me believe that we weren't beyond repair. That maybe, just maybe, we could learn to trust again, without the weight of the past bearing down on us. We paid the bill, and I stood up first, not wanting to stay in the same place too long, afraid that if I sat too still, everything would unravel again.

As we stepped out into the crisp evening air, the city alive with the rhythm of night, I felt the stirrings of something new between us. Something tentative, but real. He walked beside me, a little closer than before, his shoulder brushing mine in a way that felt more like an invitation than an accident.

We didn't speak as we walked through the streets, but I could feel him beside me, as if he were trying to find his place in this new version of us. The old familiarity was there, like an echo of something I'd nearly forgotten, but now, it was different. He was different. I was different.

I turned the corner onto a quieter street, where the noise of the city began to fade into the background. We'd gotten so far, but I knew we weren't there yet. Not yet. And before I could say anything else, I felt his hand on my arm, stopping me.

"Wait."

I turned, expecting to see that same vulnerability, but there was something else in his eyes—something sharp, something urgent. He opened his mouth, as if to say something, but the words didn't come. And in that moment, the tension between us snapped like a twig underfoot, and I knew, just knew, something was coming. Something that would change everything.

Then, out of the corner of my eye, I saw the figure emerge from the shadows. A figure I had not seen in years. And my heart stopped dead in my chest.

Chapter 33: A Test of Loyalty

It was a quiet afternoon, the kind that fooled you into thinking you could breathe again, like the calm before a storm that didn't yet know it was brewing. Jonah had promised me a break, a day where the world could be shut out and we could exist, just for a moment, in a bubble of peace. I should have known better. The universe has a funny way of slipping a curveball into even the most carefully laid plans.

His mother arrived first, sweeping into the house like a gust of wind, every movement calculated and precise. She didn't even knock. I never understood how she could glide across rooms like that—like a predator testing for weaknesses, eyes sharp and unblinking. The moment her heels clicked against the hardwood floor, I knew. She had come to disrupt.

"Lena," she greeted me with that cold smile, the one that never reached her eyes, "Jonah will be down in a moment."

I barely had time to respond before she was already settling herself into the living room, her gaze darting to the family portraits hanging on the wall. She didn't say anything about them, of course. She was too good for that. But the look in her eyes, as she scrutinized each image, told me everything. She saw us—Jonah and me—as a flaw in the story she had carefully crafted for him. A tear in the fabric of their perfect family. Her son had been her crown jewel, her pride. And I was nothing more than a tarnish she'd have to scrub away, one way or another.

I could hear Jonah's footsteps from the hallway, deliberate but slower than usual, the weight of what was about to happen settling between us. I straightened up, taking a deep breath to steady myself. I knew this wasn't going to be easy, that the next words out of her mouth would be anything but civil, but I wasn't prepared for the bombshell she dropped.

"Jonah," she began, her voice like silk and steel, "we need to talk about this... situation with Lena." She didn't even look at me, her words wrapped in a kind of indifference that made my skin crawl.

Jonah's grip on my hand tightened. I could feel his pulse, rapid and unsure, the same fear that had been haunting us for weeks. He had been doing everything he could to protect me from his family, but now, they had found their way in.

"I'm not a situation," I said, my voice coming out sharper than I intended. But it felt good to finally push back, to not let her dictate the terms of this war she had started.

Jonah glanced at me, a flicker of surprise in his eyes. He had been the buffer between us for so long, but this time, it was different. This time, I wasn't going to cower. I wasn't going to stand there quietly while they played their games.

His mother, however, was unfazed. "I'm sure you think of yourself as something else entirely," she said, her tone dripping with condescension. "But in the end, Jonah deserves better. He doesn't need a distraction. He needs someone who knows how to play the game."

The words stung. Not because I didn't know they were coming, but because they cut so deep. She was right about one thing—I wasn't part of their world. I had never been invited into their gilded cage. And now, I was the reason Jonah's carefully curated existence was on the verge of unraveling.

I opened my mouth to retort, but Jonah beat me to it. "Enough, Mom." His voice was low, dangerous, like the rumble of thunder right before a storm breaks. "I'm not going anywhere. And neither is Lena."

The finality in his words hung in the air, thick with something unsaid, something I couldn't quite put my finger on. His mother's eyes flickered, but only for a second. She was a woman who knew how to wield power, and if Jonah wasn't playing by her rules, then he had just signed himself up for a fight.

"You think this is over?" she asked, standing up with a slow, deliberate grace. "This is just the beginning, Jonah. You can't escape your family. You can't escape us."

I wanted to scream at her, to tell her that no one could make Jonah do anything he didn't want to, but instead, I just squeezed his hand tighter. He needed me more than ever now, and I wasn't going to let her win—not without a fight.

Jonah's gaze softened as he turned to face me. He knew what was at stake. He understood what it meant to stand by me. But the weight of his family's legacy was heavy, and as much as he wanted to tear himself free from it, there was a part of him that still hesitated, still looked over his shoulder, wondering if he could outrun them all.

His mother's departure was as swift and silent as her arrival. She didn't say goodbye, didn't offer a shred of compassion. She simply left, her heels clicking against the floor in a staccato rhythm that echoed long after she had gone.

We were left in the aftermath, standing in the wreckage of what had been a fragile peace. Jonah stood at the threshold, looking at me with something unreadable in his eyes. There was so much I wanted to say, but the words seemed to stick in my throat. Instead, I walked to him, stood close enough that I could feel the heat radiating off him, and looked up at him, searching his face for something—anything—that would tell me what he was thinking.

"I don't want to lose you, Lena," he said, his voice barely above a whisper, as though the words themselves might break him.

I swallowed hard, trying to push back the lump in my throat. "You won't. But we both have choices to make, Jonah. And sometimes, the right choice doesn't come without sacrifice."

His fingers brushed against my cheek, a silent promise, but the storm clouds on the horizon were unmistakable.

Jonah and I spent the evening locked in silence, the weight of his mother's visit pressing down on us like the thick humidity before a storm. I couldn't shake the feeling that something else was coming—another piece to this puzzle that neither of us had fully grasped yet. The air in the apartment was still, save for the occasional creak of the floorboards as Jonah paced in front of the window, his fingers running through his hair.

"I never thought they'd come for us so soon," he muttered, as though the words had only just occurred to him.

I leaned against the back of the couch, watching him, feeling both helpless and hopeful in equal measure. I wanted to reach out, to tell him it would be okay, but the tension was like static in the air. He was holding something back, I could feel it. There was a quiet storm building inside him, too. Something deeper than the surface argument with his mother.

"You don't have to protect me from them," I said softly, my words careful. "I can handle it. I've handled worse."

Jonah stopped pacing, his back to me for a moment before he turned, his face a mixture of frustration and something else I couldn't quite name. "It's not about protecting you, Lena. It's about everything I've spent my life building... and whether I'm willing to burn it all down."

My breath caught. I knew what he meant. He had told me stories of the family business—the empire his parents had built and the weight of expectations that had come with it. Jonah had been groomed to take over, the heir to something vast and intimidating, something I had never fully understood. And now, standing here with me, he was at a crossroads. The future that had once seemed so certain was suddenly a blur. A fog he couldn't navigate.

"Don't make me your sacrifice," I said, the words slipping out before I could stop them. "Because I'll burn everything down too. You and me, Jonah—we're already in this. There's no 'out' anymore."

He looked at me, his expression softening, though there was still an underlying tension in his jaw. "You're not a sacrifice," he said quietly, his voice low. "You're everything."

His words sent a jolt through me, a crackling electric thread connecting us that neither of us could ignore. But the truth was, no matter how much we might want to believe we could choose each other without consequences, the world wasn't going to let us off that easy.

The doorbell rang just as I opened my mouth to reply, and Jonah froze, his gaze darting toward the door.

I felt a pang of unease shoot through me.

"That's probably them," Jonah said, his voice laced with both warning and resignation. He moved toward the door slowly, as though every step was a decision he wasn't ready to make.

I followed him, watching as he opened the door. It wasn't his mother this time. Instead, it was his brother, Ben. He stood in the doorway, his expression unreadable, but the air around him was charged—like he had a secret, and it was one that could change everything.

"Ben?" Jonah asked, his voice taut with surprise. "What are you doing here?"

Ben stepped inside, his eyes flickering toward me for just a moment before locking back onto Jonah. He looked like a man who had been through too much—too many meetings, too many decisions. His suit was impeccably tailored, but there was a slight hunch to his shoulders, as if the weight of his family's world was pressing down on him, too.

"I need to talk to you," Ben said, his voice unusually strained. "Alone."

I opened my mouth to protest, but Jonah gave me a look, the kind that was both apologetic and resolute. "I'll be right back," he said quietly, leading his brother toward the back of the apartment.

I stood there, alone, in the quiet aftermath of their conversation. I could feel the silence settling in like a blanket, thick and suffocating. I tried to push aside the anxiety swirling in my chest, but I couldn't ignore the knot tightening in my stomach. Something was off. Ben's presence here wasn't a coincidence.

I paced the living room, running my hands through my hair, trying to make sense of what was happening. Jonah's family had always been a source of tension between us, but it had always been his mother at the helm. Ben was the one who had kept his distance, the one who had played the peacemaker when things got rough. But now... Now, it felt like he was standing in front of us, a harbinger of something darker.

After what felt like an eternity, Jonah returned, his expression hard to read. "You might want to sit down," he said, his voice taut.

I didn't argue. I sat, feeling the weight of the moment settle heavily on my shoulders.

"Ben's—" Jonah paused, gathering his thoughts, "Ben's been offered a deal."

My heart skipped a beat, the words hanging in the air like a death sentence.

"What kind of deal?" I asked, my voice barely above a whisper.

Jonah hesitated, and that hesitation told me everything. "It's a buyout. The company. They're offering us a way out."

My pulse quickened. A buyout? The entire family business was on the line. "Is that... good news?" I asked, struggling to make sense of the chaos in my head.

"No," Jonah said, his voice sharp. "It's not good news. It's their way of making us choose. Choose between loyalty to the family or loyalty to everything else we've built."

I felt a chill wash over me. I could see the trap, the noose tightening around Jonah, around both of us. Loyalty had never been so loaded.

The silence after Jonah's revelation stretched on, heavy and thick. It clung to the room, wrapping itself around the edges of every thought, every decision we had yet to make. I could feel the weight of the future pressing down on us like an unrelenting tide, dragging us deeper into the depths of uncertainty.

"I don't understand," I said, my voice breaking the tension like a crack in glass. "What do you mean, 'choose'?"

Jonah took a slow breath, rubbing the back of his neck. He looked exhausted, worn down by decisions that weren't his to make. His hand trembled just slightly as he reached for mine, the lightest of touches, but it felt like a lifeline.

"They're offering to buy us out," he repeated, his voice soft but firm. "It's a way to cut us loose, to let us walk away from the company without consequences."

"But you'd lose everything," I whispered, the weight of it settling in. The empire his family had built would no longer belong to him, to them. It was a lifeline extended with one hand, and with the other, it was tightening the noose.

Jonah's jaw tightened. "It's not just about money. It's about the control they want. They're offering us freedom, but only if we walk away completely. If we say goodbye to the business, to the name. To everything."

My mind spun. The decision was monumental. And the cost—what would it be if he walked away? If we walked away? Jonah had spent years building his future within that world, and now it was being offered to him like a poisoned chalice. But even worse—if he refused, if he stayed, he risked losing me, losing us.

"So if you don't take the deal..." I began, but the words felt heavy on my tongue, like the weight of a thousand unspoken things.

"They'll make us pay for it," Jonah finished for me, his voice low, almost a growl. "And it won't be just about the business anymore. It'll be about loyalty. About who we are. And once that happens..." He trailed off, not needing to finish. We both knew what came next.

Loyalty. Always that word. It was the sword they wielded above us, the line they expected us to toe. But loyalty to whom? To them? To a family that thought they could control every part of Jonah's life, from the boardroom to his personal choices? Or was it loyalty to each other—the very thing that had kept us tethered through every storm?

I stood up, pacing the room, the impulse to move, to act, pressing down on me. Jonah watched me with tired eyes, but his hand never let go of mine. He was a man caught in the middle, torn between everything he had been raised to be and everything he wanted to become.

"We have to make a choice," I said, more to myself than to him. The decision felt impossible, the consequences too vast to comprehend. "And we have to do it now."

"I can't lose you," Jonah said quietly, his words cutting through my thoughts like a sharp knife. "Not to them. Not to this."

My heart clenched, the weight of his confession sitting heavy in the air. He didn't need to say more. The choice was clear: I was in this with him. But at what cost?

Jonah stepped closer to me, the distance between us narrowing until I could feel his breath on my skin, warm and steady. "We'll figure this out," he said, his voice steady but tinged with something—desperation? Hope? "Together."

I nodded, squeezing his hand, but there was no certainty in the action, no promise that things would work out. All I knew for certain was that the decision wasn't just his to make. This was mine, too. And no matter how much I wanted to believe in him, in us, I couldn't ignore the gnawing fear that we were about to walk into something neither of us could escape.

The knock at the door interrupted my thoughts, the sound sharp and demanding, pulling me back to reality.

Jonah's expression darkened, his grip tightening on my hand, but this time it wasn't a gesture of affection. It was a warning.

"Stay here," he said, his voice hardening. "I'll handle this."

I watched him leave, my pulse quickening as the door swung open. His family's presence had already been like a shadow hovering over us, but now it was no longer just a shadow—it was a storm. And we were standing right in its path.

I stood frozen, my mind racing as I heard the muffled voices from the hallway, sharp and demanding. Jonah wasn't backing down. I could hear it in the way he spoke, in the edge of his tone. But there was something else, something beneath the surface. A promise that we would fight, no matter what.

I couldn't just sit here and wait. Not anymore.

I made my way to the door, my heart pounding as I pressed my ear against the wood, straining to hear more. Their voices were growing louder, but I couldn't make out the words. Jonah was talking, but the others were shouting now, their words clipped, like the sound of knives being drawn.

I knew one thing for sure: Whatever was happening out there, it was far from over. It had only just begun. And we weren't just fighting for the future we had planned. We were fighting for our lives.

With one last glance at the door, I stepped into the hallway, my heart hammering in my chest.

I couldn't stand idly by anymore. Whatever happened next would change everything.

Chapter 34: The Last Trial

The fog clung to the air like a damp, invisible hand. It wasn't the kind of mist that whispered a promise of morning warmth or welcomed a new day with a touch of romance. No, this fog held something darker, something ancient, swirling like an omen as I stood in the front doorway of Jonah's house, my fingers pressed to the cool brass of the doorknob. The sky was a bruised shade of grey, heavy with the weight of something unsaid, and as I took a deep breath, the chill seeped into my lungs, making my skin prickle with a sense of foreboding.

Jonah wasn't home yet. He'd been gone all morning, pacing through the town, no doubt trying to outrun whatever ghosts had caught up to him. I didn't need to ask what had happened. The news had already spread like wildfire through the small town of Marlowe. A phone call, an unspoken tragedy, and suddenly everything had changed. The life Jonah had carefully tucked away, the one he had kept hidden behind layers of silence and half-truths, had come crashing back into the present, and with it, everything we had fought for seemed to teeter on the edge of destruction.

I knew Jonah was struggling. I had seen it in the set of his jaw, the way his shoulders had slumped under the weight of unspoken memories. I could feel it in the tense silence that often stretched between us, as if the space between us had grown too vast, too filled with things neither of us could say. But I had been patient, waiting for him to come to me when he was ready. I was ready for anything—except this.

The door opened with a groan, revealing the dimly lit hallway inside. My footsteps echoed on the hardwood floors as I stepped over the threshold, the scent of stale coffee and something heavier, something indefinably sad, clinging to the air. I had no intention of sitting and waiting. Not this time. Jonah needed me, and I wasn't going to let him face whatever storm had come for him alone.

I made my way to the kitchen, where the kettle still sat on the stove, a forgotten relic of the morning he hadn't come home to yet. His coffee mug, cracked at the rim and chipped from years of use, sat abandoned beside it. The cluttered counters and half-done tasks seemed to mock me, whispering that nothing was ever as simple as it appeared. Jonah had a way of pretending everything was fine, a façade that even he sometimes believed. But I had seen through it—seen the cracks, the glimpses of the man he had been before, the man he fought to bury every single day.

I heard the door creak open behind me, and before I could turn, his voice sliced through the stillness, low and ragged. "Don't."

I froze, a chill creeping over me that had nothing to do with the weather. The word hung in the air, thick and suffocating, as if he were trying to hold me at arm's length even though we both knew the distance between us had already closed.

"You don't need to see me like this," he continued, his voice tight. "Not today."

I felt my heart ache at the sound of it. His words were a plea, not a command. Jonah didn't want to be seen in his weakness, didn't want to be vulnerable, but what he didn't realize was that I'd already seen him at his lowest. I had seen the cracks in his armor, the way his guard slipped when he thought no one was watching. He didn't need to hide it from me anymore.

I turned to face him, my gaze meeting his with all the determination I could muster. His eyes were darker than I had ever seen them, bloodshot and haunted. The stubble along his jawline looked grimmer than usual, the rough edge of it a stark contrast to his usually well-groomed appearance. He stood in the doorway, a man at war with himself, but I wasn't afraid of the battle he was facing.

"Jonah, look at me," I said, my voice steady even as my insides twisted. "You don't have to fight this alone. I'm here. I want to be here. Whatever it is, we'll face it together."

He stepped back, as if the weight of my words were too much to bear. "You don't know what you're saying. You don't know what this... this is," he murmured, the words dripping with bitterness. "I should've stayed away. It was easier that way."

I crossed the room in two long strides, my fingers reaching for his arm. I didn't let him pull away this time. "No," I said firmly. "It's never easier to run. You're not running anymore. You're standing here, with me, and that's all that matters."

He exhaled sharply, his eyes closing briefly as though he were gathering the strength to say something, anything, to push me away. But when his eyes met mine again, I saw something different—a flicker of uncertainty, a crack in the fortress he had built around his heart.

And that was when the knock came.

It was sharp, insistent, as if the universe had decided our moment of vulnerability needed an interruption. Jonah flinched at the sound, his posture stiffening. I turned toward the door, every muscle in my body tensing with a mix of anticipation and dread.

He didn't move, and I didn't wait for him to. The door swung open, revealing a figure I had not expected.

Detective Webb.

He stood there, looking like he had just stepped out of a storm, his face grim and unreadable. But his eyes—those eyes—were full of things I wasn't ready to face.

"Jonah," Webb said, his voice colder than the fog outside. "We need to talk."

I felt the weight of his words before I understood them fully.

The first hint of daylight barely pierced the gloom, casting a muted glow over the remnants of the world still clinging to its sense of normalcy. In the quiet hum of the city, the usual noise felt distant, muffled, as though the universe itself was holding its breath, waiting for something to unfold. The mist curled around the streets, like fingers reaching from another world, and I couldn't help but wonder if the air itself was laden with secrets. There was something about this morning that felt... wrong. Too still. Too perfect in its imperfection.

Jonah stood at the window, his silhouette framed by the soft, gray light. His posture was stiff, rigid in a way that made my heart tighten. He hadn't spoken in hours, hadn't even moved from that spot since we woke, and I knew the weight of something dark and unresolved was pressing against him. I hadn't pried, hadn't asked him what was troubling him, but I could feel the suffocating pull of it—whatever it was—settling between us like a silent barricade.

He had always been haunted by his past, and there were times when it seemed like the ghosts of his mistakes were just waiting for the right moment to emerge from the shadows. I knew it was inevitable, that the past would find its way back to him eventually. But I hadn't expected it to come crashing in like this. His face was etched with a hardness that wasn't there the night before, as though the man I thought I knew had suddenly been replaced by someone else—someone familiar, yet distant, like a version of himself I didn't fully understand.

"Jonah," I whispered, stepping into the room, my voice barely audible over the sound of my own pulse. It seemed too fragile for the weight of the moment, but I pressed forward anyway. "What's going on? Talk to me."

He didn't turn immediately. Instead, he stared out into the fog, his hands clenched tightly against the cold glass. The muscles in his jaw twitched, but still, he remained silent. I could feel the tension in the room, thick enough to choke on. Every second stretched like a rope tied too tight, threatening to snap.

"You don't have to do this alone," I said, my words sharp with more urgency than I intended. It wasn't just a plea; it was a command. I needed him to hear me. I needed him to see that he didn't have to face whatever was eating at him in the dark recesses of his mind by himself.

Jonah's shoulders sagged slightly, but he didn't turn. Not yet.

"I'm not sure you can understand," he muttered, his voice low and gravelly. There was a bitterness in it, a worn-out edge that scraped against my resolve. "Some things... they don't just go away. No matter how far you run, no matter how much you try to forget, they always come back."

His words hung in the air, and for a brief, treacherous moment, I thought he might shut me out completely. But then, slowly, he began to speak, the words coming out in a rush as if they'd been trapped in a cage far too long.

"It's him," Jonah finally admitted, his voice strained, like the act of saying the name was enough to open old wounds. "David. He's back."

The name hit me like a physical blow, and for a moment, I could taste the bitterness that lingered in the back of my throat. David. The ghost of Jonah's past, a shadow that had loomed over him for years, threatening to undo everything he had fought so hard to build. I had never met David, but I had heard the stories. The lies. The manipulations. The betrayal that had left Jonah fractured, barely holding on.

"Is he..." I hesitated, unsure if I was asking the right question, if I was even prepared to hear the answer. "What does he want?"

Jonah finally turned to face me, his expression unreadable. But there was something in his eyes, something raw and desperate that made my breath catch in my chest. It was as if he were silently pleading with me to understand—to forgive him for whatever would come next.

"He's threatening everything," Jonah said, his voice thick with the weight of his confession. "The life we've built. The peace we've found. He won't stop until he has it all back—until he destroys me, destroys us. He's... he's not finished."

I wanted to reach out to him, to pull him into my arms and tell him it would be okay. But I knew better than to offer false assurances. This wasn't something we could just wish away. This was the reckoning that had been waiting on the horizon, and no amount of love or hope could shield us from the storm that was about to break.

"We'll fight back," I said, my voice steadier than I felt. I met his gaze, locking my eyes with his, willing him to see the truth in my words. "You're not alone in this. We'll fight together."

Jonah didn't respond at first. Instead, he looked at me with a mixture of disbelief and something more—something I couldn't quite place. It was the look of a man who had spent years carrying the weight of his past on his own, never daring to let anyone share the burden. But I could see it in the way his posture softened, in the way his eyes flickered with something like hope—something he had long buried, but was slowly beginning to resurface.

"I don't deserve you," he whispered, his voice breaking. "I've done so many things..."

"None of that matters now," I cut him off, the words tumbling out before I could stop them. "What matters is who you are now. And that's all I need."

For the first time that morning, Jonah looked at me—really looked at me—as if seeing me for the first time. As if, maybe, he was finally ready to let me in completely.

And in that moment, something shifted between us. Something unspoken, but undeniably real. Something that could weather any storm, even the one we were about to face.

The fog outside had begun to lift, but the storm within our hearts was only just beginning to gather.

The tension between us felt tangible, thick as the fog that clung to the streets outside. I could see Jonah trying to put up his walls again, though they were no longer as strong as they once were. The cracks had started to show, and every day I spent with him, I felt the armor he'd constructed around his heart grow weaker. He had been determined to carry his burdens alone for so long, but the weight of his past was proving to be far too much for even him to bear.

And now, just when we had begun to rebuild our lives, the very thing he feared most had returned to undo everything we had fought for. David's shadow loomed large, stretching across the life Jonah had so desperately tried to leave behind. I couldn't imagine the ache it must have caused him to face it all over again, the long-buried memories rushing back like a flood.

Jonah's eyes remained focused on the window, but I could tell he wasn't seeing the mist or the pale light anymore. He was lost in the past, trapped in a moment he wished he could erase.

"You don't have to do this," I said again, softer this time, my words a gentle pull on the fragile thread between us. "Whatever he's throwing at you, we'll deal with it together. You don't have to go through this alone."

Jonah's lips tightened, but there was no deflection this time. The tension in the room was palpable, a dance of unspoken words between us. After what seemed like an eternity, he spoke, the words heavy with the weight of everything he hadn't said before.

"David wants more than just revenge," Jonah confessed, his voice barely above a whisper. "He wants to destroy me. Not just my reputation, but my soul. He knows how to push my buttons, how to make me doubt everything. And I don't know if I can fight him anymore."

I stepped closer, my fingers grazing his arm, a silent reassurance that I was here, grounded, unshakable. Jonah had never been one to open up easily, but I could feel the dam inside him cracking. He had kept so much hidden, buried beneath years of pain and regret. He was an expert at wearing the mask of strength, but beneath it, I knew he was broken, a man who had fought too many battles and lost too much along the way.

"You're not fighting him alone," I reminded him, my voice steady despite the storm brewing within me. "And you're not broken. Not in the way you think."

He turned slowly, his eyes meeting mine, and for a moment, the world outside seemed to cease. There was something raw in his gaze, something stripped of pretense. I saw the truth of his fears, the vulnerability that he never allowed anyone to see. And yet, in that moment, I wasn't afraid. I wasn't afraid of the man he used to be or the darkness that threatened to overtake him. I saw the man standing before me now, the man who was willing to fight for us, even if he didn't fully believe he deserved it.

"I don't deserve you," he said again, his voice cracking, as though the words were a confession he couldn't take back.

"You never have to earn me," I replied firmly. "I'm not here because you deserve me. I'm here because I choose you. And that's all there is to it."

His gaze softened, just for a heartbeat, and in that small moment, I saw something flicker—hope, maybe. It was a fragile thing, but it was there. And I would hold onto it for both of us, if necessary.

But just as the silence stretched between us, the shrill ring of Jonah's phone shattered the fragile calm. He stiffened, his eyes narrowing as he glanced at the screen. I could see the hesitation, the unwillingness to face whatever news was about to come through. But there was no escaping it. Not anymore.

"Who is it?" I asked, already knowing the answer, dreading it all the same.

Jonah didn't answer immediately. His thumb hovered over the screen for a moment longer than necessary, his fingers tight with indecision. Then, with a resigned breath, he answered the call.

"Jonah," the voice on the other end crackled through the speaker, harsh and clipped. It was David's voice, unmistakable even after all these years. "You've had your time. Now, it's mine. You think you've escaped, but you've just been given a reprieve. I don't forget, Jonah. I never forget."

I could hear the smirk in David's voice, the venom wrapped around every syllable. I could see Jonah's grip tightening on the phone, his knuckles white, but he said nothing, letting the silence speak for itself.

"You know how this ends," David continued, his voice low and dangerous. "You've been living in a dream, thinking you've moved on. But you haven't. Not really. You're just as trapped now as you were then. And this time, I'll make sure you understand that."

I could feel the air in the room grow heavier, the weight of David's words settling like a fog. I reached out, my hand brushing against Jonah's. It was a simple touch, but I knew it was a lifeline. He squeezed my hand tightly, a wordless promise that he wouldn't back down, not this time.

But David's next words hit like a physical blow.

"If you want to protect her, Jonah, you'll have to come to me. Alone. You've got twenty-four hours."

The line went dead, leaving nothing but the harsh static of the empty connection. Jonah stood frozen for a long moment, his face pale, his jaw clenched in that way that told me he was preparing for war. His shoulders were squared, but I could see the tremble in his hands, the uncertainty flickering in his eyes.

"You don't have to go," I said softly, but there was no convincing him otherwise. Not now, not after that call.

He looked at me then, his eyes dark, stormy.

"Stay close," he murmured. "I'm going to need you."

And with that, the storm was no longer something we could watch from the safety of our windows. It was here, at our door.

Chapter 35: Redemption in Love

The city felt different under the heavy cloak of dusk. The skyline, usually sharp against the fading light, softened, its towering structures less imposing, like familiar faces fading into the background of my thoughts. The hum of the streets below—the clatter of late-night cabs, the distant thrum of traffic, the quiet buzz of the neon signs—was a soft lullaby I'd never realized I craved. I leaned into Jonah, my fingers tracing the outline of his jacket, the rough fabric grounding me, reminding me that this, this moment, was real.

His hand tightened around mine as he spoke, his breath warm against my hair. "I never thought I'd find a place like this," he murmured, his words a soft rumble. "A place where everything just... fits. Where it's easy to just... be."

I smiled, the corners of my lips curling up naturally, as if the weight of everything we'd been through had melted away, leaving only the warmth of us. "Funny," I said lightly, my tone more teasing than I'd meant. "I always thought I'd be the one who had to make everything fit. But somehow, I'm the one who's been given the gift of being free."

He chuckled, the sound low and warm, vibrating through me. "And I thought I was the one who was supposed to keep you grounded."

I turned to face him, my heart racing, a mix of emotions filling me. "You are keeping me grounded," I said softly. "But you've also given me the wings to fly."

He stared at me for a moment, his expression unreadable. It wasn't discomfort or doubt I saw in his eyes, but something deeper—something far more intricate than I could ever hope to decipher. There were layers in him that I had yet to peel back, though I could feel them all pressing against the edges of my consciousness, urging me to understand. Jonah was an open book, but only if you were brave enough to read the fine print.

"I've never been this sure of anything in my life," he whispered, his voice cracking slightly, as if even the thought of saying it out loud might make it unreal. "Not even when I thought I was."

I laughed, not in mockery, but in the kind of realization that felt so weighty, so pure, that it had to spill out. "I guess we were both wrong about a lot of things."

The tension between us shifted, and I could feel the warmth of our shared breath in the cool air as it flowed between us. Something about the way the city stretched out in front of us felt like it was holding its breath, as if waiting for us to make the next move, to write the next part of our story. There was no rush, not anymore. The storm, the battles, the heartache—they'd all led us here.

"I used to think I had all the time in the world," Jonah continued, his voice steady now, though there was a tension behind it. "But in the end, it's not the time that matters, is it? It's the people we choose to spend it with."

I nodded, squeezing his hand. "We've both done a lot of waiting, haven't we?"

He laughed softly, a sound that seemed to hold everything we'd been through. "I suppose. But no more waiting, okay? No more questions. Just this. Just us."

I wanted to believe that. I really did. But even as the words left his lips, I couldn't shake the shadow that lingered just out of sight. It wasn't doubt—no, not exactly. But something else, something lurking just beneath the surface. Something I wasn't sure I was ready to face, though I knew, deep down, it would demand to be reckoned with sooner or later.

For a moment, I let the silence between us stretch, breathing it in like the city's night air—heavy, full, and inevitable. I closed my eyes, letting the warmth of Jonah's hand in mine anchor me, grounding me in this reality. Because the truth was, no matter how perfect this moment was, there would always be pieces of the past that followed us, quietly, persistently. I couldn't pretend that they didn't matter, that they wouldn't eventually demand their place in this new life we were building together.

Jonah sensed the shift in my mood before I could even find the words to explain it. He tilted my chin up gently with his free hand, lifting my gaze to meet his. There was a softness in his eyes now, a tenderness that made my heart ache in the best possible way.

"We're not done, you know," he said quietly. "This... all of this, it's just the beginning."

My breath caught in my throat. "I know."

"But you're afraid," he added, a small smile tugging at his lips. It was a knowing smile, one that acknowledged the weight of unspoken fears.

I nodded slowly. "I'm afraid of all the things we still don't know. Of the past we haven't fully left behind."

His expression softened, and he brushed a stray strand of hair behind my ear. "We'll face them together. Whatever they are. And we'll come out the other side stronger. I promise you that."

There was a sincerity in his voice, the kind that made me want to believe every word, the kind that felt like home. And as I stood there, with him at my side and the city sprawling out before us, I realized that, despite all my fears, all my uncertainties, I was finally beginning to feel something I hadn't in a long time.

Hope.

It wasn't perfect, but it was real. And for the first time in ages, I believed that maybe—just maybe—it was enough.

The quiet rhythm of the city seemed to pulse in sync with my thoughts, a steady beat that I couldn't quite shake. It was as if, with each breath, I was beginning to see the world in a new light—brighter, sharper, and somehow more fragile than I remembered. My eyes traced the skyline once again, searching for something I couldn't name. It was beautiful, yes, but there was something in the way it loomed that made me uneasy. A quiet reminder of the past, maybe. Or perhaps, a warning.

Jonah's hand on my back pulled me back into the moment, his touch grounding me when I felt myself slipping into that old space of wondering what came next. His fingers, steady and warm, pressed against my skin, like a tether I could hold onto.

"I've been thinking," I said, my voice low, the words more vulnerable than I intended.

He raised an eyebrow, a mischievous glint flickering in his eyes. "I'm intrigued. You know that's a dangerous thing for you, right?"

I shot him a playful glare. "I'm always dangerous. You should've known that by now."

He laughed, a sound that always made my chest tighten, and leaned in closer, his face just inches from mine. "What is it, then? Spill it."

I hesitated, letting the words settle between us like a delicate dance. "I'm just... I'm not sure I know how to move forward. I mean, how do we leave everything behind? How do we really leave the past in the past?"

Jonah studied me for a moment, his eyes unreadable, as though he was measuring my soul with every glance. "You know, it's funny," he said finally, his voice quiet. "I thought I knew exactly how to put the past behind me. But it doesn't work that way, does it? It's not something you just forget about. It's something you learn to live with. And that's where the real work begins."

I wasn't sure I was ready for the weight of his words. But there it was, that truth sitting on my chest, heavy yet undeniable. I had spent so long running, holding onto the idea that I could erase the past, only to realize that it had been shaping me all along. Jonah was right, and in that moment, I knew he wasn't just talking about the two of us. He was talking about everything. The choices we made, the mistakes we couldn't undo, and the future we couldn't force into existence.

"Maybe we don't need to leave it behind," I whispered, my gaze still fixed on the city below. "Maybe we just need to stop letting it control us."

Jonah's hand found mine again, his fingers threading through mine like he was trying to pull the pieces of me back together. "I think that's the most honest thing you've ever said. The past doesn't define us, but it's part of who we are. And we can either embrace it or let it destroy us."

I couldn't argue with that. But there was still so much left unsaid between us, so many things we hadn't yet fully explored. And that made me uneasy, the fear of what could be buried beneath the surface, lurking in places we hadn't dared to touch.

"I wish things had been different," I said quietly, almost as if I were talking to myself. "I wish we didn't have to go through everything we did."

Jonah's grip on my hand tightened slightly, and he turned to face me fully, his expression unreadable but intense. "We can't change what's already happened. But we can decide what to do with what's left."

I met his gaze, feeling the weight of his words sink deep into my chest. "What if I'm not strong enough?"

"You are," he said simply, as though the question was already answered. "You've already proven that. And so have I."

I wanted to believe him. I really did. But there was still that nagging voice in the back of my mind, reminding me that things were never as simple as they seemed. Not for me, not for us.

"What happens now?" I asked, the question hanging in the air between us like a fragile thread, waiting to be severed or woven into something new.

Jonah's eyes softened, and for a brief moment, there was no one else but the two of us standing on that bridge, surrounded by the noise of the city but cocooned in our own world. "Now," he said, "we keep going. We keep showing up for each other, even when it's hard. Even when it feels like everything's falling apart."

"And if it does fall apart?" I asked, the words slipping out before I could stop them.

His smile was gentle, almost sad, as he reached up to tuck a strand of hair behind my ear. "Then we pick up the pieces. Together."

There was something in the way he said it that made me believe him, even if I wasn't sure I was ready for the weight of that commitment. There was no guarantee that we wouldn't stumble, that we wouldn't fall. But maybe that was the point. Maybe it wasn't about being perfect. Maybe it was about choosing to be imperfect, choosing to stand together in spite of everything we had gone through.

I took a deep breath, the cool air filling my lungs as I allowed myself to believe that for once, we might just make it. "Okay," I said finally, my voice steady despite the storm still swirling in my chest. "We'll figure it out. Together."

Jonah's smile grew, a slow, confident curve of his lips that made my heart flutter in my chest. "Together," he repeated, as if sealing the promise in the very air around us.

And maybe that was enough. Maybe, in that moment, it was all I needed to believe that despite the past, despite the fears that still clung to my every thought, there was something worth fighting for.

Even if the road ahead was uncertain, at least we would walk it side by side. And that thought was enough to carry me forward, one step at a time.

The city lights flickered like stars scattered across a black velvet sky, each one burning brightly in its own right but still a part of something much larger than itself. Below, the world continued to spin—people walking in a hurry, taxis honking, the distant rumble of an ambulance wailing somewhere down the street. Life went on, unbothered by our moment, unknowing of the storm we had weathered together, and yet, for all its chaos, there was a strange kind of peace in the air. Like the calm before something was about to shift, something big that none of us were prepared for.

Jonah stood beside me, his gaze not on the city below, but on me. He studied me like he could see every corner of my soul, every jagged edge I still couldn't bring myself to smooth out. I couldn't help but wonder if he ever grew tired of it—of all the weight I carried with me, all the things I still kept buried deep. If he ever longed for someone simpler. Someone whole. But then again, maybe we were both just as broken in our own ways.

"You're quiet," he said after a while, his voice cutting through the steady hum of the city. "What's going on in that head of yours?"

I shook my head, pushing the thoughts away before they could take root. "Nothing. Just thinking."

"About what?"

I was hesitant, unsure whether to say the words that had been hanging on my tongue for the past few minutes. Jonah had a way of making me feel like I was the only person in the world who mattered, but sometimes, that spotlight was too intense. It made me feel exposed, vulnerable, like he could see right through all my walls.

I took a breath, turning to face him. "About how... everything is different now. The way I feel, the way we feel. It's like we're both standing on the edge of something, and I'm not sure if it's going to be worth the leap."

Jonah's expression softened, his eyes searching mine as though looking for something—maybe an answer, or maybe reassurance. "You've never been one to hesitate before," he said with a crooked smile. "What's changed?"

I almost laughed at his question, though the sound came out more as a sigh. "What hasn't changed?" I wanted to say. But I held it back, because I wasn't ready for the answer that would come if I let myself go too far down that path.

"You know, there's no rule that says we have to have everything figured out," he said, his tone gentle but firm. "We just have to keep moving forward. One step at a time. That's enough."

"I don't know if that's enough for me," I replied, my words almost too quiet to hear. "I need more than just a step. I need to know that we're not... I don't know... just floating in this limbo, waiting for something to happen to us."

He reached for my hand, squeezing it gently as he stepped closer. "You've never been someone who waits for things to happen. You make things happen. Don't forget that."

I looked up at him, studying his face, the way his eyes softened when he spoke to me, how his presence filled the space between us like a kind of magnet pulling me closer. He was right, of course. I was a doer, not a sitter. But this time, I wasn't so sure. Maybe, just maybe, I didn't know how to act, didn't know what steps to take to get the life I wanted.

"I know," I whispered, almost to myself. "I've always been that way. But I'm not sure I can keep being that person for you. Not if it means I keep losing parts of myself in the process."

Jonah's fingers brushed against my cheek, tilting my face toward his. "Then don't lose yourself. Not for me. Not for anyone. You're enough, just as you are."

I opened my mouth to speak, but before I could form the words, a sound cut through the air—sharp, unexpected. A screech of tires, followed by a sickening crash.

My heart stopped. The world seemed to slow as I turned toward the noise, my breath caught in my throat.

Jonah's hand shot out, gripping mine with a force that startled me. "Stay here," he said, but I could see the panic in his eyes. He wasn't asking, he was commanding, though his voice was steady.

I didn't argue. I didn't have the words for it, even if I wanted to. My body moved on its own, following him as he rushed toward the intersection where the noise had come from.

The scene in front of us was chaos. A car had smashed into the side of a building, the metal twisted and crumpled in ways that made my stomach churn. People were already gathering, some running toward the wreckage, others pulling out their phones, probably to capture what they thought was an accident. But this wasn't just an accident. It was a tragedy, raw and unfiltered.

Jonah moved quickly, surveying the situation with an intensity that made my chest tighten. He was in his element—his calm, controlled demeanor cutting through the confusion like a knife. But even through the haze of panic, I could see the same tension in him that I felt in myself.

As Jonah neared the wreckage, I hesitated. I knew what he was capable of, what he had done before, and I wasn't sure if I was ready to watch him face whatever was coming. I wanted to stay behind, to keep myself distant from the mess of it all, but there was something in the way his back was set, in the way he gritted his teeth that told me I couldn't just stand by and do nothing.

I took a step forward, but before I could catch up, a figure emerged from the smoke and debris—a man stumbling out of the car, clutching his chest as if the weight of the world had collapsed on top of him.

My heart pounded in my ears, my pulse racing. Something told me this was no ordinary accident. This was something darker. Something Jonah wasn't prepared for.

"Jonah!" I called out, my voice thin against the chaos. "Jonah, wait!" But it was too late.

Chapter 36: Ever After in Paris

The warm cobblestones beneath my feet felt oddly alive, each step carrying the weight of something both thrilling and terrifying. The city around me hummed with its usual frenzy—taxi cabs honking, tourists milling about with half-filled maps, and the distant laughter of café patrons—but for Jonah and me, it was like the world had folded itself in on us. It was just us and the echo of our footsteps, weaving through the narrow streets of Paris, unspoken promises dancing between us. The air had a weight to it, a sweetness that clung to my skin, and for once, the urgency of time didn't seem to matter. We weren't rushing anywhere, not anymore.

Jonah's hand, warm and solid in mine, was the only certainty I had ever needed. His fingers twined with mine in a way that felt both intimate and defiant, as though he, too, knew we had just crossed some invisible threshold. The old bridges, the iconic landmarks—none of them mattered now. We'd left all the noise behind, the expectations of the world that had been piling up around us for months. Our life, stripped of all the things that had once defined us, now lay open, ready for us to claim.

It hadn't always felt this way, of course. We hadn't arrived here without the scars to prove it. There had been weeks, months, years even, when I couldn't have imagined a day like this one. The days when Jonah's smile felt like a luxury I could never afford. The nights when I wondered if we were just two people running in circles, always just out of reach of something we both wanted but never seemed to find. But now, with the soft Parisian sky turning to amber above us, I understood that what we had—what we were—was built from everything we'd been through together, the good and the bad. Maybe, just maybe, that was the secret to something lasting.

I caught Jonah's eye as we strolled past a café, the chatter of the customers inside spilling out onto the street, mixing with the clink of silverware. His lips were curved into a smile, the kind that had once made my heart stutter. I didn't need to ask, not when everything about him—his posture, the way his hand held mine with a certain tenderness—spoke volumes. "What are you thinking about?" he asked, his voice low but laced with amusement.

I gave him a sideways glance. "About how strange it is to be here." My voice came out softer than I expected, a note of disbelief hanging on the words. "How it almost feels like a dream."

Jonah chuckled, the sound rich and genuine, as though he could feel the surrealism of the moment too. "You mean, the way the sky turns pink, and the world seems to soften at the edges? Yeah, I'm feeling it too." He paused, and when he spoke again, there was something more serious in his tone, a hint of something deeper. "Or maybe it's just that we're finally here, right now, after everything."

"After everything," I repeated, my eyes catching the last light of the day as it streaked through the trees along the Seine. There were so many things I could say in response, so many tangled threads of memory I could untangle. But instead, I squeezed his hand, a silent acknowledgment of all we had survived to get to this place, and all we would have to face to stay here. No matter what came next, this moment—this beautiful, fleeting moment—was ours.

We turned a corner, and the city opened up before us like an old lover revealing the secrets she's kept hidden. I inhaled deeply, letting the scent of freshly baked croissants and the distant perfume of flowers from a nearby florist fill my senses. The city seemed to be holding its breath, waiting for us to take the next step. And so we did.

Jonah stopped in front of a narrow stone building, its façade aged but full of character, like the city itself. "I've been thinking," he said, looking down at me with a crooked grin. "We should get a place here. Not for now. Not for later. But for always."

I stared up at him, trying to make sense of the sudden, unexpected turn in our conversation. "Here? In Paris?" I laughed softly, trying to hide the way my heart skipped a beat. "What, are we going to live the rest of our lives in a café, sipping espresso and pretending we have it all figured out?"

"Why not?" His voice was playful, but his eyes told a different story. "Maybe it's not about figuring it all out. Maybe it's about living in the moment and taking it as it comes." His smile softened. "Together."

The simplicity of his words hit me harder than I expected. It wasn't about the house we'd live in or the city we'd settle down in; it was about the idea of sharing our lives, of finding a place where we could be, simply, us. "That sounds... perfect," I whispered, my voice catching in my throat. "Let's do it. Let's take the leap."

Jonah pulled me closer, wrapping an arm around my waist as we stood together on the edge of the city that had witnessed so much of our story. The wind shifted, cool and gentle, carrying with it the promise of new beginnings. For once, the past didn't matter. The mistakes, the fears, the heartbreak—none of it mattered now. All that mattered was the way we fit together, the way the world felt like it was ours, just for this moment.

"Paris," I murmured, testing the word on my tongue. "It feels like it's meant to be."

Jonah's laughter, deep and content, filled the space between us. "It is," he said. "It's been waiting for us."

We found ourselves drifting further into the heart of the city, as though its cobbled streets had a pull, a magnetism that was impossible to resist. Jonah's hand, still firmly in mine, led us down an alley lined with tiny boutiques and faded storefronts, their windows overflowing with flowers in shades of violet and pink. The scent of fresh bread and strong coffee wove through the air, inviting us to pause and sample the little pleasures that only Paris seemed to offer with such casual elegance.

I had always imagined that life would be grander when you finally reached a point of resolution—like the finale of a movie, all dramatic and sweeping with a soundtrack to match. But this was quieter. More intimate. The city wasn't offering us fireworks; it was giving us a slow, steady rhythm, a kind of pulse that felt more like breathing than celebrating. And I liked it. I liked the subtlety of it, the gentle feeling that something profound was happening without any of the fanfare we'd always expected from monumental moments.

Jonah paused in front of a little café, its tables arranged with neat precision under a wide awning. The chairs, painted in chipped shades of blue and white, beckoned us with the unspoken promise of a drink, a conversation, and a moment to breathe. He raised an eyebrow, a silent question in his eyes.

"Do you think we're ready for this?" he asked, his voice pitched low enough that it was more of a murmur than a question. I could hear the undercurrent of doubt, the edge of vulnerability that never seemed to leave him completely.

I met his gaze, willing him to see beyond the uncertainties we both carried. "I think," I said, my words coming more easily than I expected, "we were ready the moment we decided we could have this—whatever 'this' is. We've spent so much time worrying about the what-ifs that we forgot to just be in the moment." I shrugged, the weight of my own realizations settling a little more comfortably. "We're here now, Jonah. That's enough."

He smiled, but it wasn't the playful grin I was used to. It was softer, more sincere, like he was still processing the fact that this wasn't some fleeting moment but the beginning of something enduring. "Then I guess I'm okay with that," he said, pulling out a chair for me. I sat, watching as he slid into the chair opposite me, the space between us still charged with a kind of electricity I didn't quite understand.

The waiter, an older man with a neatly pressed apron and a suspiciously knowing smile, appeared at our table as though summoned by the very act of our quiet intimacy. He didn't ask for our order right away. Instead, he just studied us, his eyes darting from Jonah to me as though he could see the threads of history that bound us together. "A glass of wine, perhaps?" he suggested, his accent thick and melodic, as though he had been waiting for us to say something before serving us.

I nodded, suddenly aware of how dry my throat was. "A glass of your house red," I said, my voice just a touch hoarse. I felt Jonah's eyes on me, studying me the way I sometimes studied him, searching for the unspoken.

The waiter turned to Jonah, but instead of making a decision himself, Jonah's gaze flitted between the wine list and the man's expectant face. He frowned. "Do you have anything... a little lighter?" he asked, as though the mere mention of a full-bodied wine was a question he didn't want to entertain.

The waiter's lips twitched upward, the barest hint of amusement at the man across the table from me. "Of course. A glass of Chablis, then?" he suggested, nodding as though he had already anticipated the choice.

"Perfect," Jonah agreed, leaning back in his chair with a sigh of resignation, like he had just admitted to a personal failure. I found it charming, this quirk of his. How even after everything, he still hesitated, still doubted himself in the simplest of moments. It made him all the more real, all the more human.

As the waiter disappeared into the building, I took a deep breath and let the quiet hum of the city wash over me. The sky above us had turned a deeper shade of lavender, the first stars beginning to show through the thin veil of clouds. The streets felt alive, electric, and I realized that even after all these years, this city still had the power to surprise me.

Jonah leaned forward, his fingers drumming lightly on the edge of his glass. "You know," he began, his voice softer now, "I used to think Paris was just a place. A city, a dream, a postcard."

I looked at him, a small smile curving my lips. "And now?"

"Now?" He shook his head, as if the answer were both simple and profoundly complicated. "Now, I think it's where we started. The beginning. Everything before this..." He trailed off, as if he wasn't sure how to finish the sentence. But I knew what he meant. What we had was bigger than Paris, but Paris would always be where we first found each other. Where we first stumbled into a future neither of us had seen coming.

I leaned back in my chair, letting the cool breeze kiss my skin. "I used to think I wasn't ready for any of this. For him, for the life we've built, for any of it." I laughed softly, shaking my head. "Funny how life doesn't really ask if you're ready. It just... happens."

Jonah chuckled at that, and in the sound of his laughter, I heard the sound of my own release. It was a rare moment of honesty between us—no pretenses, no plans. Just us, in a city that had seen it all and still somehow managed to be fresh with possibility.

The waiter returned with our drinks, and the conversation turned to smaller things. Where we would go next, what we would eat, how we might one day look back at this exact moment as the first day of the rest of our lives. But all I could think about was how this—right here, right now—felt like the answer to all the questions we'd been asking. And for the first time, I wasn't afraid of what came next. I wasn't afraid of anything.

The night air wrapped around us like a soft blanket, its chill somehow welcoming after the warmth of the setting sun. Jonah and I wandered aimlessly through the city's winding streets, the clatter of our footsteps melding with the hum of distant conversation and the faint strains of music leaking from an open window. The Eiffel Tower loomed ahead, its iron lattice casting long shadows across the pavement, a reminder of the timelessness of this place. Yet, in the midst of all this grandeur, it was the quiet, unspoken intimacy between us that made the world feel alive.

We passed by a small bistro, its lights twinkling like scattered stars, and without a word, Jonah steered us toward the door. The moment we stepped inside, the smell of garlic, butter, and fresh herbs hit me with the kind of intensity that made my stomach growl in approval. It wasn't the kind of place where you needed reservations—just a couple of open chairs and a warm, welcoming atmosphere. The hostess, a woman with a friendly smile and an effortlessly chic bob, ushered us to a corner table by the window, where we could watch the last of the evening's light fade over the rooftops.

Jonah slid into his seat with a sigh, glancing over at me as I tucked my hair behind my ear. "I don't know if it's the wine or just the city, but everything feels... different. Like everything's starting over." His words hung between us like a delicate promise.

I smiled, leaning back in my chair as I surveyed the scene—couples tucked into cozy corners, laughing, talking, eating as though the weight of the world had momentarily slipped away. Paris had a way of making everything seem like it could last forever. "It's just the magic of Paris," I said, my voice playful. "I read once that the city has a way of making people fall in love with life again. You know, the art, the food, the wine—all of it's just designed to make you think there's something more out there waiting for you."

Jonah raised an eyebrow, his lips curling in that mischievous way I loved. "So, you're saying I'm just another victim of the Parisian charm?"

"Maybe," I teased. "But I wouldn't mind being a part of your downfall."

He chuckled, his eyes darkening as he leaned in closer. The playful banter between us had always been easy, but tonight, there was something heavier in the air, something that wasn't quite as light-hearted. He reached for my hand, brushing his thumb over my knuckles, and for a moment, everything else—the clinking glasses, the soft conversations, the distant murmur of the city—disappeared. "You know what?" he said, his voice quieter now, more serious. "I think this is it. This—this is the moment when I realized that everything we've gone through, every twist, every turn—it was all leading here. To this."

I wasn't sure what to say. Part of me wanted to nod, to agree, to let him have that belief, that certainty. But another part of me—the more cautious, the more guarded part—wanted to question it. To ask if we really could have this. If the world was truly as simple as it felt in this moment. Because what if it wasn't? What if the next corner we turned held something we weren't prepared for?

"Jonah..." I began, but before I could finish, the door to the bistro swung open, and a burst of cold air rushed in, cutting through the warmth of the room. I turned instinctively, expecting to see another couple seeking refuge from the night, but instead, a figure stepped inside—a man in a long coat, his face hidden beneath the brim of a wide hat.

He paused just inside the door, his gaze scanning the room like he was searching for something, or perhaps someone. My heart gave an odd, unsettling flutter. I couldn't place the feeling, but something about the way he stood there, motionless and observant, made the hairs on the back of my neck stand up.

Jonah's hand tightened around mine, his thumb stuttering over my skin as he, too, noticed the stranger. The man's eyes flicked over the room, landing briefly on us before shifting again, this time toward the back of the restaurant where the kitchen door swung open briefly. He took a slow step forward, and my pulse quickened, but before I could make sense of the sudden shift in the atmosphere, the stranger turned and disappeared out the door just as quickly as he had arrived.

Jonah and I sat in stunned silence for a moment, the weight of the stranger's presence lingering in the air between us. "Who the hell was that?" I asked, my voice low, the question hanging in the air.

Jonah didn't answer right away. He just stared at the door, his brows furrowed in concentration. Finally, after a long beat, he met my gaze. "I don't know. But that didn't feel like just a coincidence."

The waiter returned, his presence momentarily snapping us back into the warmth of the restaurant. He set down a bottle of wine between us, offering a smile that was more rehearsed than genuine. "Your wine, monsieur, madame."

But I couldn't stop thinking about the man. Who was he? And why did it feel like the moment he entered our little bubble of happiness, everything shifted? Jonah was talking again, his words distant and muffled, as though he were trying to pull me back into the moment. But I couldn't focus. Something about that man had unsettled me, and I wasn't sure why.

As I glanced over my shoulder one more time, my eyes landed on the empty doorway. But that wasn't what made my heart stop. It was the faint, barely noticeable shadow in the corner of my eye. Someone—or something—was watching us.

Milton Keynes UK
Ingram Content Group UK Ltd.
UKHW021838231124
451423UK00001B/122